D040174Ǝ

"ONE OF THE MASTERS OF PSYCHOLOGICAL FICTION."
—*San Francisco Chronicle*

"Wilhelm claims a leading place in the ranks of trial suspense writers. . . . As (she) spins her riveting tale, she not only makes the legal system comprehensible and compelling but also makes her readers care about her characters."
—*Publishers Weekly*

"Packs a wallop . . . Wilhelm's ability to wrap events up with a heightened sense of danger and drama is appealing."
—*West Coast Review of Books*

"An absorbing, well-paced story."
—*Portland Oregonian*

"Sensitive and provocative."
—*Ocala Star-Banner*

By Kate Wilhelm:

THE MILE-LONG
  SPACESHIP
MORE BITTER THAN
  DEATH
THE CLONE (with Theodore
  L. Thomas)
THE NEVERMORE AFFAIR
THE KILLER THING
THE DOWNSTAIRS ROOM
  AND OTHER
  SPECULATIVE FICTION
LET THE FIRE FALL
THE YEAR OF THE CLOUD
  (with Theodore L. Thomas)
ABYSS: Two Novels
MARGARET AND I*
CITY OF CAIN
THE INFINITY BOX: A
  Collection of Speculative
  Fiction
THE CLEWISTON TEST
WHERE LATE THE SWEET
  BIRDS SANG
FAULT LINES
SOMERSET DREAMS AND
  OTHER FICTIONS
JUNIPER TIME
BETTER THAN ONE (with
  Damon Knight)

A SENSE OF SHADOW
LISTEN, LISTEN
OH, SUSANNAH!
WELCOME, CHAOS
HUYSMAN'S PETS
THE HAMLET TRAP
CRAZY TIME
THE DARK DOOR
SMART HOUSE
CHILDREN OF THE WIND:
  Five Novellas
CAMBIO BAY
SWEET, SWEET POISON
STATE OF GRACE
DEATH QUALIFIED: A
  Mystery of Chaos*
AND THE ANGELS SING
SEVEN KINDS OF DEATH
NAMING THE FLOWERS
JUSTICE FOR SOME*
THE BEST DEFENSE*
A FLUSH OF SHADOWS:
  Five Short Novels Featuring
  Constance Leidl and Charlie
  Meiklejohn*
FOR THE DEFENSE
  (Formerly titled: MALICE
  PREPENSE)

* *Published by Fawcett Books*

FOR THE DEFENSE

Formerly titled MALICE PREPENSE

Kate Wilhelm

FAWCETT CREST • NEW YORK

A Fawcett Crest Book
Published by Ballantine Books
Copyright © 1996 by Kate Wilhelm

All rights reserved under International and Pan-American Copyright Conventions. Published in the United States by Ballantine Books, a division of Random House, Inc., New York, and distributed in Canada by Random House of Canada Limited, Toronto. Originally published as *Malice Prepense* by St. Martin's Press in 1996.

http://www.randomhouse.com

Library of Congress Catalog Card Number: 97-90213

ISBN 0-449-22556-9

This edition published by arrangement with St. Martin's Press Inc.

Manufactured in the United States of America

First Ballantine Books Edition: September 1997

10 9 8 7 6 5 4 3 2 1

SUMMER

PROLOGUE

IF HE ALMOST closes his eyes a certain way, the trees turn into black monsters that start to rush at him; then they go right by—*whoosh*—and the sun hits his eyes and he has to close them the rest of the way. *Whoosh.*

He wants to ask when they'll get there, but Gail told him grown-ups don't like it if you ask more than once, and it's best to wait until you have to go or something. He squinches his eyes again. *Whoosh.*

"Smell that?" Dad asks.

He sits up straight and sniffs. River, trees, the car, then he leans forward. *Skunk.* He can't see anything on the road, but the smell is all around, not bad, not like it was when the skunk got in their camp that time and they had to go away and camp somewhere else.

"Remember when we tangled with the skunk over at John Day?" Dad asks, turning to grin at him.

He nods happily. Maybe the skunk smell is really bad in Mr. Praeger's truck. He hopes it is. He hasn't seen the red truck for a long time. Maybe he had an accident and fell in the river. He hopes that, too.

"There's a shelter around here somewhere," Dad says. "Get your shoes on and we'll stretch our legs, have a look. That's where we'll camp tonight."

"Mr. Praeger won't stay with us, will he?"

"No way. Don't worry about him." He slows down and then pulls to the side of the road and stops. "See? Told you."

Teddy laughs and pulls on his sneakers. He doesn't bother to

3

tie them. Outside, with no more car noise, the only sound is the river, and the wind making whispers in the trees.

"Can I go look at the river?"

"Not now. Later, when we camp, there'll be plenty of time. If you have to go, now's your chance. Back around the shelter."

As soon as he steps around the little house without a door, it's just as if he's the only one here, a funny good and bad feeling at the same time. He spots a black-and-brown streaky rock and picks it up, examines it carefully, then puts it in his pocket.

"Teddy, you want a Coke?"

"Yeah," he calls. He aims at a flat rock sticking out of the ground and pisses. Reid said girls pee, boys piss. He grins at the rock turning shiny and black under his stream.

He was drowsy before, but when they start driving again, he's wide awake. "Dad, if you spit on a worm, you'll get a fish every time, won't you?"

Dad laughs. "Who told you that?"

"Mr. Versins."

"Well, maybe the worm gets more squirmy because it's trying to shake the spit off."

"I'll try it." Under his breath he says, "Wormy squirmy, squirmy worm, wormy squirm . . ."

Then they see the red truck in the road, with Mr. Praeger standing by the door. He looks mad. Teddy's stomach gets tight, and Dad reaches over and pats his leg. Mr. Praeger gets back in his truck and drives on a little dirt road. Dad follows.

"He's a grouch," Dad says. "Don't pay any attention to him."

"Like the Grinch?"

"Exactly like that."

Maybe this isn't the smallest road they've ever gone on, or the steepest, or the crookedest, but he can't remember another one like it. He strains forward against the seat belt, watching the red truck appear and vanish, appear and vanish. It looks too big to fit on the road, like it might fall off. He wishes he could see over the edge on Dad's side. If he put his hand out the window on his side, he could brush the mountain with it. Then they turn again, and there's nothing to see on either side, just trees. Maybe they're almost there, at last.

"Scared?" Dad asks.

Teddy looks at him, puzzled, and Dad grins.

"You'll have to put on socks and your boots when we get out," Dad says.

"Can I take my hammer and collection bag?"

"Sure."

After they stop, while Teddy is putting on his boots, Mr. Praeger and Dad start to argue. Teddy doesn't look at them; he pretends he can't hear them, because Mr. Praeger is mad at him again, because he's there.

"He'd better keep up. I don't intend to wait for him."

"He can keep up. I'll have to rein him in, in fact."

Then they start hiking, with Mr. Praeger way out in front. Teddy asks, "What does rain him in mean?"

"*Rein in* means 'hold back,' like you have to do with a horse that wants to run."

"*Rain,* like *raining*?"

"Nope. Different *rein.* Then there's another *reign,* like to be boss, to be a king. They just sound alike." Dad spells the three kinds of rain.

Teddy thinks Mr. Praeger wants to be a king, and Dad won't let him. Teddy likes the woods better than anything—the way it smells here, how it feels under his feet, the way the air is cold and hot at the same time. Where the trees don't make a roof, the sun makes slanty lines, like sliding boards. He can smell mushrooms. Big rocks are sticking up out of the ground, but no little ones he can pick up; they're all covered with needles and moss and stuff. But Dad said they'd go to a place where there are lots of rocks.

Mr. Praeger started off pretty fast, but he's going slower all the time; now Teddy is impatient. When the two men stop to rest, he darts off to one side of the trail, then the other, just looking at stuff. He likes to feel the cool moss on tree trunks.

They leave the trail to go up a steeper way, and Dad makes him stay in the middle, between him and Mr. Praeger. Teddy pretends he's Swift Foot, climbing the highest mountain in the world, leading Dad to a special place only he knows about.

At the top, Mr. Praeger stops to catch his breath and wait for

Dad. Teddy stops, too, staring; then he races ahead. "Wow!" he yells. There are piles and piles of rocks, hills of rocks, rows of rocks, rocks everywhere. He squats at one of the hills and begins picking up rocks, some as big as his hand, some bigger than his head, some with shiny little specks, like mirrors. He tosses most of them down again, puts a few in his collection bag. He darts to another pile, then another. He doesn't need his hammer here; someone else already broke them up.

Mr. Praeger and Dad look at a map and make lines on it while Teddy examines the piles of rocks. He pays no attention to them until he hears Dad say in his mean voice, "Jesus, Praeger, give it a rest. Who's he going to tell? I'm not leaving him out here. If I go in, so does he."

Mr. Praeger starts to talk too low for Teddy to hear; he walks toward the cliff behind the piles of rocks.

"Come on, Teddy," Dad says in his usual voice. "Now's your chance to see a mine."

Teddy watches Mr. Praeger bend over and go in a hole in the mountain; then Dad goes in the same way, bent over, and he ducks and follows them. It's a cave, he thinks in excitement, maybe a bear cave. But bears don't stay in caves in the summer, he remembers. They go through a little hall, and into a bigger room made out of stone, with a lot of rocks and stones all over the floor, everywhere. These stones and rocks are big, not already broken in little pieces like the ones outside.

Dad and Mr. Praeger go across the room; then Dad comes back and says, "We're going in a little farther. You stay in here until we get back, okay?"

"Can I break some rocks?"

"Sure. Help yourself." He goes out through another hole that looks black as night. He turns his flashlight on.

This room doesn't need a flashlight, even if the light is dim, like after the sun is down, but not really dark yet. Teddy begins to examine the rocks, and soon he starts to hammer on one to break off a chunk.

His collection bag is bulging when he hears Dad's and Mr. Praeger's voices again. He is turning a rock over and over, waiting to show it to Dad, but Mr. Praeger comes in first. Teddy drops the rock into his bag.

"Let's go," Dad says. "We'll go make camp, do a little fishing. You ready?"

They start down, this time with Teddy in the lead; Dad and Mr. Praeger follow, talking. Mr. Praeger wants Dad to drive out first, and Dad says, "No way. You'd be goosing us all the way down that miserable road." Teddy giggles when Dad says "goosing."

It's black dark now, no moon, although Dad says there will be later on. The wind is making whispers in the trees, and the river noise is loud. Teddy is in his sleeping bag in the little house without a door; Dad is sitting by the fire, drinking coffee.

"Dad," Teddy says, then stops. Reid said it's soupy to talk about feeling good and having a good time and this was the best day of his life and things like that. Mom said of course he could say it, but Reid said guys don't talk like that. Reid said, "Dad already knows; you don't have to tell him."

"What, Teddy?" Dad says when Teddy doesn't finish what he started to say.

"Will you tell me a story?"

"Sure." He drinks more coffee, then starts: "One time, the men of the tribe had gone to the coast to set up summer camp, and the women and children were following slowly when Swift Foot's mother came upon a deer with a broken leg."

Teddy smiles; he loves stories about Swift Foot, who is eight years old, just like him, and who does really neat things.

"Swift Foot's mother said, 'We'll butcher this deer and dry the meat. You'll have to cross the mountain and tell your father that we'll be with them when the moon is full, so they won't get worried about us.' She prepared his food, and gave him a rattle and a bunch of feathers. 'If you see a cougar,' she said, 'shake the rattle and feathers and jump up and down and yell as loud as you can, so that it will be frightened and run away. If you see a bear, become as still as a tree, because you can't frighten a bear, and you can't run faster or climb higher than a bear. If you don't move, it won't see you, and it will go away.' "

The wind whispers in the trees, the river noise becomes a song, and Dad's voice rises and falls, but Teddy's eyes are closed, and he is alone, trotting through the forest, where the bear waits.

FALL

ONE

FRANK HOLLOWAY HAD no intention of walking the few blocks to his office that Friday afternoon. It was October, the weather would change any day, and he had too much to do: some leaves to rake, a garden to put away for the season, tools to clean. . . .

When he entered his house from the back porch, he should have gone straight to the kitchen for the drink of water he needed, but instead, he found himself at his study door, where the telephone light was blinking. He scowled at the answering machine. It was too soon for Barbara to call, he reminded himself as he drew near and then pushed the message button.

"Hey, Dad, you can wrap up that Barton mess. I got the deposition this morning. You-know-who broke wide open, spilled everything. I'll fax it to the office and send the original by overnight mail. And last night, I ran into a couple of friends, and we're going to hike in Kings Canyon a few days. Expect me home Tuesday or Wednesday. I'll kiss a sequoia for you. Congratulations on the Barton deal."

He had to grin even as he hoped and prayed she would be careful, not fall into a canyon, not fall off a cliff, not get hit by an avalanche. His grin broadened. *"Cluck, cluck,"* he said softly.

He listened to the second message then. His secretary, Patsy Meares: "Mrs. Mary Sue McDonald says she must see you today. If she doesn't hear otherwise, she'll be in at four. I can call her back and put her off, I guess. If I don't hear by three, that's what I'll do. But from the way she sounded, I think you'd better see her."

Damn woman—Patsy, not Mary Sue. Patsy would check his

socks for holes if he let her. He listened to Barbara's message again, smiling at the laughter in her voice. Then he removed the tiny cassette, replaced it with a new one, and put the one with her message in a box with half a dozen other tapes that contained messages from his daughter.

That day, he had planted garlic, had thinned out winter kale and collards. It was one o'clock, time to knock off for a bite to eat; then maybe he would wander down to the office, see what was on the fax, see what was on Mary Sue's mind. Some damn do-good committee that wanted free legal advice, he told himself grumpily.

Later, in the office, his perusal of the fax was desultory, and he had to admit to himself that he couldn't care less if he saved Phil Barton a hundred thousand. And that was his problem, he knew: He was bored with it all. Working bored him; not working terrified him: his problem. Barbara had done a bang-up job, of course, just as he had known she would, although she was as bored with it as he was. Crooks skinning each other left and right. Let them.

But the real problem, he knew, was that if Barbara got too bored, she might take off. She preferred her ghetto clients, who paid in plucked chickens and zucchini, to his fat-cat clients. Give her an extra quarter and she was off climbing some damn mountain, hiking in some damn wilderness, tying beads or tie-dyeing T-shirts.

He studied the picture of his dead wife in a double silver frame, side by side with Barbara's photograph, so alike, so unalike. "We messed up somewhere," he said softly to the photograph. "Never taught her squat about valuing money."

Pam, the receptionist, buzzed him. Mrs. McDonald was there; should Shelley bring her back? Shelley? He recalled her then, a new girl, an intern. "Bring her on back," he said.

Shelley was pretty and still a baby, in her early twenties, with an awful lot of blond hair; she wanted to stay in the office when she delivered Mary Sue, but he thanked her and motioned her out. Poor Shelley, no one let her do anything interesting, he thought, and extended both hands to Mary Sue McDonald.

"Mary Sue, it's been ages. You look wonderful!"

She was five feet tall in her shoes with an inch of heel, and she couldn't have weighed more than ninety pounds after the biggest Thanksgiving dinner imaginable. She was seventy-four or so, well wrinkled and not trying to pretend otherwise, with startling green eyes and curly gray hair.

"I look like the incredible shrinking woman," she said with a dismissive wave. "I don't want money, or for you to join anything. What I would like is a glass of wine."

"You've got it," he said. "You want to sit over there or at the desk?" He pointed to several comfortable chairs and a couch grouped at a low table.

"Desk," she said. "This is business, not social." She walked to a client's chair by his desk—she was very erect—and he went to the bookshelf wall and opened the bar concealed there.

"Chardonnay, sherry, claret . . ."

She chose claret, and after he had handed her the glass and seated himself behind the desk, he thought again how diminutive she was, childlike from any distance. She had to perch on the edge of the chair or it would have swallowed her. She sipped her wine, then put the glass down.

"First," she said, "tell me something. Are you required to divulge what anyone says? I understand client/attorney relationship, but I just want advice. Does that make me a client? Do you have to tell what I say to you?"

"Tell whom?" Her mouth tightened. "But, yes, if you retain me to give you advice, you are a client. Horses wouldn't drag it out, Mary Sue."

"Do we sign something?"

"We have a verbal agreement as of this moment. Later, you can sign an agreement if you choose."

She considered this for a moment, then nodded. "Very well. You know about Harry Knecht's death, over at Stone Point? His murder?"

"Just what was in the news."

"I was there that day. I think I may have aided and abetted, or something like that, whatever the legal term is." She picked up her glass and took another sip, looking past him now, out the window.

Frank leaned back in his chair, acknowledging a soft, unvoiced *Ah* of satisfaction. "Just tell me about it," he said.

She looked at him with a sharp frown. "Well, that's why I'm here. But don't interrupt. Story first, questions after." She waited for his nod before continuing.

"Every summer for the past five or six years, one of the grandchildren comes around and we head out to the coast for a week or two. I hate driving the coast road anymore, and refuse the interstate—all those trucks—and you know what it's like eating in restaurants alone. . . ."

This year, it was James and Carla's daughter, Leigh, who had gone with her. They had arrived at their cottage at Stone Point about five-thirty, and Leigh had gone down to the beach for a walk or a run, whatever it was the young people did.

"I made the reservation months ago," she said, "the day I read that Harry would be speaking. I wanted to hear him, see how he turned out as a politician. Anyway, Leigh went down to the beach, and I sat on the front porch a bit; I got chilled and went inside for a sweater. We had cottage number one, on the point, almost directly across from the rear of the inn. And Harry apparently had the corner suite just opposite. I happened to glance that way when I walked back to the door, and I saw him in his room. No mistaking him," she said. "That big head. He was just inside the sliding door to the balcony on the second floor. Then he turned, and a second later he had a telephone in his hand, and he moved out of sight. I went on inside and got my sweater. It took a few minutes—I had to open a suitcase and rummage for it. You know those cottages?"

Frank shook his head. "I've been there, but I don't remember them particularly."

"There's a narrow covered walk from the carport to the door; it goes on to the front, where there's a nice covered deck. Wonderful for watching a storm at sea, more than a hundred feet up over the water, with a sheltered, unobstructed view. . . . Anyway, I was on the walk going back to the deck, when a movement caught my eye. I stopped at the same place as before and saw that it was a curtain blowing out the sliding door to Harry's room. The screen was open. Before I took even a step, another man came into view, a waiter. He had on black trousers and a white shirt with a black bow tie, and he was wearing white gloves, carrying a tray with a bottle. He walked into the room a few feet and then seemed to lose his balance or something; he nearly fell down and he dropped the tray, and next thing he bent down to the floor, out of sight. Then he straightened up again and looked back over his shoulder and ran out the sliding door to the balcony. Another man had entered the room, and he had a gun. He bent down out of sight, too, then straightened and started to run after the waiter, who had reached a post by then and was scrambling over the rail. The waiter dropped down to the ground and tore across the stretch between the cottages and the inn, straight toward me. And the one with the gun was running down the stairs."

She stopped and sipped her wine again, her gaze once more on the view out the window, past Frank's head. Her hand was trembling. He didn't move.

Her voice was steady when she went on. "At the time, I don't believe I thought through anything, I just acted. That young man was going to be shot, I felt certain, and something had happened to Harry. I was only a few feet from my cottage door. I simply opened it and pointed when the waiter dashed up, and he raced inside and shut the door. I went to the front deck and sat down, and not ten seconds later the one with the gun ran up. He yelled at me, had I seen anyone running, which way did he go, things like that, and he was waving the gun around in a demented way. Then a second man came up and pulled him back and they talked for a few seconds; the second one asked me, more civilly, the same things. I said I was locked out, waiting for my granddaughter to return from the beach, that I had seen no one."

She stopped speaking and drained her wineglass. Silently, Frank rose, went back to the bar, and brought out the bottle. He refilled her glass.

"You're not asking why," she said, taking the glass from him. "Later. For now, just what."

"I've asked myself why a million times," she murmured. She put the glass down without tasting it. "Anyway, what. They ordered me to stay still, and they were talking on walkie-talkie gadgets. There were four or five by then. I stood up and saw that someone was trying the cabin door, and someone else was looking through the car. You know, my Cadillac. I started down that way to tell them to leave it alone, and one of them nearly pushed me back into the chair and yelled at me to stay put."

She picked up her glass again. "I have to confess that made me a little angry."

Sipping her wine, she finished her story. The men had separated and run off in different directions. When Leigh came up from the beach and opened the cabin, Mary Sue had told her they were leaving instantly, to put the bags in the trunk; they would call the hotel from wherever they found rooms for the night. They were not going to go to the desk. They would not check out or make any explanations, but simply leave before someone got shot. Men with guns!

She had not seen the waiter then. Leigh went to the bathroom, and within five minutes they had everything in the trunk and were heading out the drive. One of the men—security men, she had learned later—started to wave Leigh down, but another one motioned for her to keep driving, and she did. They found a motel ten miles down the coast, in Florence, and when Leigh went inside to see if there were rooms available, the waiter had popped up in the backseat, opened the back door, and fled. He did say thanks, she added. She had not known he was back there.

"He must have gotten in while Leigh was in the bathroom and I was putting something in the trunk," she said. "I keep a throw in the back. I suppose he lay on the floor and pulled that over him."

"He could have murdered you both," Frank commented.

"I was more afraid of the idiot with the gun," she snapped. "Waving it around like a Fourth of July sparkler."

For several seconds, they were both silent while Frank considered all she had said.

"Now your questions?" she asked finally.

"A few."

She smiled a gentle, knowing smile. "I imagine our definitions of 'few' could be quite different. But I have to leave by five-thirty. I no longer drive after dark."

Frank nodded. "Why did you wait this long to come?"

"You mean today? I had to give them time to roust you off the golf course. If you mean so long after Harry's death . . . I played out so many scenarios. Elderly woman assists murderer's getaway. Implicated in the death? A conspiracy? Senile? I'm seventy-five years old; I don't believe many people pay a lot of attention to anyone my age. There's a lot of ridicule, a lot of finger-tapping impatience while they wait for you to move on, get out of the way. Or, perhaps, I was simply afraid. I'm not certain. Everyday I pondered it again. Everyday. I read the reports in the paper as they emerged. No mention of a missing waiter has been in the papers. Besides, he didn't do it. He found Harry, and ran. Just as I ran. I can understand that."

"Then why come forward at all?"

Slowly, she opened a large handbag and withdrew a folded newspaper clipping and handed it to him. "That was in yesterday's paper. That security man with the gun says he was chasing a young man in jeans and a white T-shirt, but he wasn't. There was no such man in sight. Frank, three people know that waiter didn't kill Harry. He knows, the killer knows, and I do. But if they catch the waiter, I doubt they'll look further."

"Why didn't you just go to the police?"

For the first time, she hesitated and looked embarrassed. "They came to the motel where we ended up, and . . . I told them the same story I told originally, that I was locked out, I hadn't seen anyone, and I was afraid of the men with the guns who were running around."

Frank frowned. "You signed a statement?"

She shook her head. "They just asked questions, first me, then Leigh, and they left again. I suppose they were satisfied. Brian—that's Brian Rowland, the owner of Stone Point—told them about me, gave me a good reference, I assume. He called me to apologize, make sure I wasn't suffering ill effects from being so frightened." She smiled slightly. "He offered me a gift certificate, one week free with a companion."

"Have you told anyone about this?"

"No." She was looking past him again, now more anxiously. "I really should go. I have to tell them, don't I? I need someone to go with me, advise me. It's a pickle, isn't it? I've put myself in the dilemma liars always face eventually. Will they charge me with a crime?"

"Let me give this a little thought. Okay? It's kept six weeks; a couple more days won't make much difference. Do you want someone to drive you home?"

"No, no. It's all right now. But later, all the headlights are hard to take. Getting old is a mixed blessing, isn't it, Frank. Should I come back Monday?"

They agreed on Monday at one, and he walked to the elevator with her. The office had emptied almost entirely. No one was at the reception desk; his secretary, Patsy Meares, gave him a hurt look when he said why didn't she go on home. One or two of the other attorneys were still in offices, but there was no longer the buzz of many people at computers, on the telephones, murmuring to one another. He saw Mary Sue into the elevator and returned to his own office and shut the door.

He thought about Harry Knecht, a local boy who had made good and gotten himself killed. Harry had been a teacher, dropped that to run for the state legislature, served a few years, and had been elected to the United States House of Representatives. And someone had bashed his head in in his hotel room at Stone Point on September ninth. So far, no suspects had been named, no evidence had surfaced to indicate an arrest was imminent, and there certainly had been no mention of a runaway waiter.

The one probable suspect had fled, vanished, and his client had helped him, Frank thought sourly. Would they dismiss her and her story, decide she was simply a dotty old lady who wanted a bit of attention? They might well do just that.

He walked home in no hurry, going over her story again, remembering her inflections, the pauses, her embarrassment.

Poor Mary Sue, he thought, she knew she was in for it. About all he could do would be to put her in the best light, go over it all again, make sure it was coherent, hold her hand a bit. . . . She took a grandchild off for a vacation because she didn't want to drive the coast road anymore, or eat meals alone in restaurants. He nodded. Exactly.

That night he made his own dinner in his own kitchen and read while he ate, as he usually did. Then he called Bailey Novell. "You know anything about the Harry Knecht case?"

Bailey knew little more than he did. "Funny thing," he said after telling Frank what the papers had already told him, "one of the security guys, guy I know, said there were rocks all over the floor. Beach pebbles. As if someone had dumped a bucketful of them. And he was done in with a rock about the size of your head."

"Rocks," Frank repeated.

"You want me to ask around?"

Frank said no. "Just curious. Be seeing you."

Rocks on the floor? He remembered what Mary Sue had said—that the waiter seemed to stumble, lose his balance. He shook his head. Rocks.

On Sunday, at eight in the evening, Mary Sue's daughter-in-law, Carla, let herself in the turn-of-the-century house in Bear Hollow, where Mary Sue had lived for fifty-two years, and Carla found her on her back on the kitchen floor. Both arms were spread straight out, palms up; in each hand there was a baseball-sized rock. Her head was turned to one side; the exposed side revealed bones and pale tissue. A pool of blood had dried and cracked like old leather; it looked like a pillow cradling her head. Next to her head was a piece of black obsidian streaked with orange, the kind found near Glass Butte in east Oregon. There was a lot of crusted blood on the piece of obsidian, which was bigger than Mary Sue's head.

Carla backed up, and screamed, and kept screaming until a neighbor came.

That night on the local news, the suspicion was voiced that a serial killer had claimed another victim.

TWO

BARBARA ARRIVED HOME late on Tuesday; she left a message on Frank's machine that she was back and too tired to do anything but soak in a hot bath and fall into bed. Exhilarated by three days of hiking among giant trees, and so sore that she felt each muscle throbbing, she drifted into a dreamless sleep.

She woke and stretched tentatively, then more luxuriously, to the point of muscular protest, and planned her day. Dad first thing, Martin's restaurant in the afternoon, a little grocery shopping . . . Her mood was buoyant through a shower and breakfast. The sun was shining and her little house was bright with golden light. Last year, her landlady had redecorated it inside and out. The day Barbara and Frank had come to inspect the changes, they had stood in open-mouthed wonder at the front door. The walls were off-white, and on the floor, on every floor, was white sheet vinyl streaked with gray, presumably intended to pass for marble. A few throw rugs, a couch and a chair, her CD player and rack, bookshelves . . . The hospital effect was muted now, but the house was bright, the woodwork glossy, and there was even a new stove—not a brand-new stove, but a new used stove that had four working burners.

She was humming when she drove to Frank's large house. It was only nine, early enough to catch him in, chat, fill in details about the architect she had deposed. . . . When Frank opened his door, she caught in her breath in fear. Heart attack was her only thought.

He was a big man, six feet tall, with broad shoulders, a deep chest, muscular and fit. But today he looked old and ill.

He gave her a welcome-home hug and kiss and drew her into the house, closed the door.

"What's wrong?" she asked. "Are you sick?"

"Come on, have coffee with me. Not sick. Just not sleeping enough maybe."

More than that, she knew, studying him at the kitchen table, where he had finished breakfast already and now sat down with a cup of coffee. He waved her toward the carafe and she helped herself.

"Tell me," she said when she sat opposite him. His eyes were sunken, with shadows under them, and he looked tired. And old. Sometimes he said he was too old for this or that foolishness, and it had always been a lie; she never had thought of him as old until now. But he was seventy-three. Old. The fear threatened to surge again and she lifted her coffee cup to her lips, as if to prove to herself that her hands were steady.

Almost apathetically, he told her about Mary Sue's visit and her murder on Saturday night.

Barbara breathed out. "My God! That poor woman!" She got up and went to the window. His entire backyard was a garden—vegetables, roses, flowers she didn't know, everything orderly—and even now in mid-October, it was full of blooms. She looked at him again and said, "You did the right thing, and you know it. She had been sitting on her story for weeks; there was nothing else you should have done then. You had to talk to her again, get a real statement, a description of the guy, some hard facts. And she had to leave. What more could you have done?"

"I didn't have to send her away without warning her," he said. "I'm going to hang it up, Bobby. I'm tired. My thinking's not what it was."

"Bullshit!" He didn't even look pained at her language. She went to refill her coffee cup and sat down again. "I would have done exactly what you did. Think it over, look into Harry Knecht's death a little, talk to her again, and then make a decision about the next step. Exactly what you did."

He didn't respond.

"You know she was right when she said she was caught in the liar's dilemma. Who knows how much her story would have changed after a few days?"

He remained silent.

Barbara reached across the table and took his hand. "Dad, you don't know enough to beat yourself like this. Maybe she was sick, Alzheimer's even. Maybe she fantasized the whole thing. The fact that she was at Stone Point that evening and left so fast might have sealed her death warrant six weeks ago. You just don't know enough."

Frank stood up. "I have some things to do," he said. "You'd better run along. Are you supposed to be at Martin's?" He picked up his plate and walked to the sink with it. "I'll call you in a few days."

"Have you talked to the police about Mary Sue?"

"Of course I did! Their reaction was just like yours. Crazy old woman talked to the wrong person, told her fantasy, and got zapped. They didn't believe a word of it. They'll check it out." He rinsed his plate and put it in the dishwasher.

"Dad," she said then, "is it okay if I come over and stay a few days, let my place air out?"

He turned almost savagely toward her. "I don't need a goddamn baby-sitter any more than Mary Sue did! Go on, do your thing at Martin's. I'll call you."

She might as well have stayed in bed, she thought later at Martin's restaurant, trying to pay attention to a Hispanic woman who was demanding to know who was going to pay for her couch, which had been ruined by water leaking from a roof that the landlord knew was leaking and wouldn't fix. What, he wanted her to climb up there and fix it herself?

There were two other drop-in clients, one she sent away when he proposed a scheme to make them both rich by suing either of two very wealthy people for anything that came to her mind. The other was a young woman in a custody fight for two children.

"All right," she said when she was done. She finished the

strong black coffee that Martin kept at her elbow the entire time she spent in his restaurant. She stood up and gathered her things, put her laptop in her briefcase, picked up her purse, and then sat down again. All right, but now what?

Martin came from the kitchen, where he had been doing prep for the dinner people. "You okay, Barbara?"

He was big and very black, a former football player, and the best cook she knew, better even than her father. "I'm okay," she said. "Thinking. See you Friday."

On Thursday, she went to the public library and looked up everything she could find about Harry Knecht's murder and the death of Mary Sue McDonald. The police were looking for the man the security officer said had been dressed in jeans and a white T-shirt. Mary Sue's man had been in a white shirt and black trousers. Obviously the same man. It appeared that Mary Sue had read the description in the newspaper and lifted it with minor changes to fit her story. Barbara felt restless and frustrated. Another few days, she decided. She would leave her father alone until the weekend, then try to talk sense into him. Hang it up indeed!

On Friday she read that Mary Sue's body had been released to her family, and the funeral would be on Saturday. "Shit!" she muttered. Frank would go to the funeral, and then be back in his fugue for the rest of the weekend. After tending to business at the restaurant that afternoon, she decided to drive to the coast early on Saturday, go up to Stone Point, just look around.

The valley had been sunny, but it was raining at the coast, with strong winds gusting fitfully. She knew exactly where the resort was, although she had never been there. She had read about it, had seen photographs when Harry Knecht's death had been the number-one news story. The resort included a golf course, a riding stable, tennis courts, an Olympic-size swimming pool outside, and another one inside, an elevator that went to the beach a hundred feet below, many cottages, and a four-star hotel and restaurant. A luxury resort. That Saturday as she drove on a narrow road from 101 to the entrance of the main building, she nodded at the gardenlike grounds—massive rhododendrons, fir trees, bonsailike pines. . . . Very beautiful, very expensive.

Driving slowly, she passed a parking lot off to her right, then an intersection where the road branched to go to the cottages. At the wide covered drive to the entrance were two jitneys complete with fringe on top to ferry guests to the golf course, the parking lot, maybe to their rooms. She parked near the entrance and entered the big building. The reception area with its long counter, leather-covered chairs, and potted plants looked like any deluxe hotel anywhere. She walked around for several minutes, located the elevators, telephone booths, a wide corridor to shops, a coffee shop, espresso cart. . . . No one paid any attention to her; a dozen or so other people were strolling, dressed in jeans, in high-fashion dresses, in business suits. She glimpsed several waiters in white shirts and black trousers; those carrying trays wore white gloves. On her way out, she picked up a hotel brochure, then returned to her car.

This time she drove the branch road to the cottages and stopped where it ended at the first carport. The hotel was screened by shrubs and trees; the cottage might have been alone in a wood. Frowning, she left the car and stepped up onto the narrow walkway that led to the front deck, which faced the ocean. She could not see the hotel through the trees and shrubs at any point during her stroll to the deck.

Abruptly, she retraced her steps just as the cottage door opened a few inches and a man called, "Is that you, Annie?"

"Sorry," she said, hurrying. "Wrong cottage."

THREE

A FEW DAYS later, on Halloween, a serious rain started to fall in the afternoon, and by eight she knew her bowl of candy would not be distributed. At eight-thirty she dumped it all into a paper bag and went out into the deluge to drive again to Frank's house.

"Trick or treat," she said when he opened the door. She showed him the bag of candy and he moved aside to admit her. He held the bag while she took off her poncho and shoes; then he held her.

"Ah, Bobby," he said.

They sat by a pleasant fire in his living room and ate candy. "You're not afraid a parent will come after you for rotting the kid's teeth?" he asked, rejecting a caramel for a soft chocolate.

"Did you worry about my teeth rotting at Halloween? All I remember are warnings about stomachaches."

He laughed. "And you got one every damn year."

"Worth it," she said, unwrapping another candy bar. They were hardly more than bite-size, not at all like the candy bars she used to put away.

They didn't talk much and said little of any consequence, but she was satisfied when she left. It had been a good visit. Neither had mentioned Mary Sue. But they would, she knew. Next visit, or the one after, they would have to talk about Mary Sue.

On Friday morning of that week, Frank had a call from an old friend, Clayton Worth, who did corporate law. Clayton did not waste words.

"I need a criminal lawyer," he said. "That is, my clients do. I told them I'd get them the best. Are you free?"

"I'm sort of winding down, Clayt," Frank said.

"Nonsense. Look, they are well-to-do, respected, honorable people and they're in deep trouble. What do I know about criminal law? They need you."

"What for?"

"Murder," Clayton Worth said in a hushed tone. "This is in confidence, of course." He didn't wait for reassurance. "They believe their son will be accused of the murder of Mary Sue McDonald."

Frank had been standing by his desk in his study at home. He sat down hard in the nearest chair. "Give me more than that," he said.

"Yes. They're Ted and Carolyn Wendover, and they live in Bear Hollow. They knew Mary Sue all their lives, as neighbors, friends, and the boy is . . . I don't know, retarded or something. The police have been around asking questions, taking some of his possessions for examination. I think they're right. The boy will be arrested." He cleared his throat quite audibly, then added, "Frank, I may have done something very stupid. I advised them to turn the boy over to his private physician, in a private hospital, not allow visitors. And instantly I realized that could look as if they believe him guilty. I can't handle this, Frank. So help me God, I can't."

You've got that right, Frank thought. "Where are they? Did they follow your advice?"

"They're here, in the conference room, on the phone to their doctor. I told them I would call you."

"Okay," Frank said. "Tell them to put everything on hold and get over to my office. I'll meet them there in half an hour."

Why? Frank asked himself, staring at the phone after he hung up. Even if he were still taking on such cases, he couldn't touch this one. He was too emotionally involved to get near it, but Clayt, damn him, had done those folks a disservice. Right, he told himself. He would give them a little advice, see that they got the right attorney, and get the hell away from it. He called his secretary to tell her to park them in his office if they got there first, give them coffee or tea. She sounded gratified that he was showing up at all.

He had to wash, change clothes; he smelled of linseed oil. He had been rubbing down the garden tools. . . . Half an hour later, he entered his office.

Carolyn and Ted Wendover were there. In their fifties, they made a handsome couple, well dressed, she in a nice slate-gray suit and he in sports coat and slacks, well-polished shoes. And both of them wound as tight as springs ready to go *sproing*. A coffee service was on the low round table but had not been touched. They shook hands, and he motioned toward the coffee.

"Let me," he said, taking one of the comfortable chairs, close to the coffee. Carolyn and Ted sat side by side on the couch, as stiff as mannequins.

"Clayt says you have a bit of trouble," Frank said, handing Carolyn a cup of coffee. She nodded. "Did you talk to the doctor?"

This time, Ted nodded. "I did. Then I called him back and said we'd talk again in an hour or so."

"Good." Frank finished fooling around with the coffee. They all had something to do with their hands now. That usually helped. "Why don't you just tell me about it and then we'll see what needs to be done."

Carolyn glanced at her husband. She was good-looking, in a quiet, almost serene, way. Her eyes were as gray as her suit; her hair was short and straight, dark brown, with a touch of gray at the temples. She looked athletic and fit, as if she ran, or played tennis regularly. Ted was tending toward overweight—not a problem yet, but something he would have to control or else fight obesity in a few years. His hair was light brown and wavy, his eyes pale blue.

"I'll do it this time," he said. "We told Clayt all of it pretty incoherently the first time around. This time, I'll start at the beginning. That's about fifteen years ago. . . ."

Frank listened without interrupting. For six years, Theodore Wendover, Jr.—Teddy—had been their only child. Then two more children had come along, a good family. Teddy had been very bright, keen in math and science, active in sports. In October fifteen years ago, Teddy's class had gone out to the Malheur Station Wildlife Refuge for a week of desert study—rocks, plants, volcanoes. . . . Teddy had had an accident, had tumbled down a hundred-foot cliff. Broken ribs, a broken arm, and a skull fracture had resulted. He had been in a coma for more than a week after the accident; when he woke up, he was different. There had been brain damage that was irreparable.

"He developed physically." Ted's voice was firm, his gaze on a vanishing point beyond Frank. "But emotionally, psychologically, and intellectually, he is a child." Carolyn put her hand on his leg; he covered it with his hand and no one spoke for several moments.

"Last week, after Mary Sue's murder," Carolyn said finally, "a detective came to the house. He said they were asking everyone in the valley for help. Had we seen anyone suspicious, heard anything? Were we home on Saturday night? Our house is about a quarter of a mile from Mary Sue's. . . ." Her voice faltered and she raised her coffee, which she had not yet touched. She took a sip and put the cup down again. "I knew they were asking questions; everyone knew. I didn't realize . . . they were asking specific questions about Teddy. Had he known Mary Sue? Did he ever go over to her house? Things like that. Everyone knew Mary Sue," she said softly. "Everyone in our valley had been to her house many times. Teddy used to go over and rake her yard, carry wood for her. He adored her."

Frank nodded. Everyone had known Mary Sue. Half the county had shown up for her funeral.

Ted got up and walked to the windows. Carolyn watched him with a look of deep pain, then continued. "This week, Tuesday, the detective came back with another one. They asked if they could see Teddy's collections. He collects a lot of things—pine cones, fir cones, sticks. Stones. That's what they wanted to look at." She drew in a deep breath. "And they started asking questions about other dates. I didn't know what they were driving at. September ninth, this year. January third, 1993. Where were we then? Where was Teddy?" She shook her head. "I simply didn't know what they were talking about. I couldn't tell them where we were on those dates, not like that. They asked if they could take some of his rocks, his collection bag, and I let them." Her face twisted in misery. "I just let them take what they asked for."

"Okay," Frank said. "Don't beat on yourself about it. Then what?"

"Last night, it dawned on me that one of the dates they asked about was the date that Harry Knecht was killed. We were at the coast that weekend. I was on a committee that arranged a speaking engagement for Harry, a luncheon fund-raising event for his reelection. Teddy was with me. We stayed in a friend's house. But they knew I was there. They already had checked Harry's schedule; they knew I had a meeting with him that afternoon. They already had asked me questions about it. They knew Teddy was with me. This time, they asked me who had stayed with Teddy when I met Harry. I told them he was alone on the beach from four to about five. I began to wonder about the other date, and Ted and I went through our calendar and checked. On or about January third, 1993, Lois Hedrick was killed at SkyView. We were over there skiing; the whole family was there. It's been in the newspapers—that the police suspect a serial killer, that all three murders were connected, committed by the same person. And we realized they suspected Teddy."

Frank made a soft grunting noise.

Still at the window, his back to them, Ted Wendover said harshly, "What connects them is the fact that Harry was one of the teachers on that field trip; Mary Sue was the principal of the school. Lois Hedrick was a classmate of Teddy's, along on that field trip."

"Christ on a mountain," Frank muttered. Now he went to his desk and sat in his big leather-covered chair and regarded Ted Wendover. "This is going to sound blunt and even cruel, but tell me the truth," he said, pulling out his legal pad from the desk drawer. "Does Teddy fly into rages? Has he ever had any kind of psychotic episode?"

Ted looked at him steadily. "No. He is a cheerful eight-year-old boy in a man's body. He doesn't even remember that accident. He's never recalled it. He regressed to a younger age and has been there ever since."

"Who's his doctor?"

"Herbert Ritter."

Frank wrote down the name. "What kind of doctor? Psychiatrist?"

Ted shook his head. "No. He doesn't need a psychiatrist. Herb is our family doctor. He's known Teddy all his life."

"Where's Teddy now?"

"Last night we called our other son, Reid, and our daughter, Gail. They're both going to the U of O. They picked him up this morning to take him on an all-day outing. I don't know where they decided to go."

Carolyn came to the desk, some snapshots in her hand. She placed them before Frank. "They treat him like a little brother," she said softly.

He looked at the snapshots: three good-looking kids goofing around, hamming it up, laughing. All three had Ted's light hair, his pale blue eyes. But gradually, the difference registered; one, the biggest one, was too sweet-faced and was not mugging for the camera the same way the other two were. He looked unselfconscious, making a face; the girl was trying to look provocative; the other boy was flexing his biceps. They both knew the effect they wanted; Teddy didn't. The second picture was of the three young people standing together, Teddy in the middle, his arms about their shoulders, again smiling broadly, not posing. He was taller than Reid by an inch or two. And he was better-looking in a disconcerting way.

"He doesn't have a mask," Carolyn said in a low voice. "Reid and Gail have both learned to put on a mask, the way we all learn. They have nothing to hide yet, but they have the masks. He doesn't."

"Right," Frank said. "Call the doctor back and tell him who I am and let me talk to him. Will you do that?"

Ted moved to the desk and made the call. When he finished, he handed the phone to Frank, who put his hand over the mouthpiece and said, "Now, if you don't mind, I'd like you both to go get some lunch, let me have some thinking time." He glanced at his watch: twelve thirty-five. "Come back at one-thirty. Okay?"

Carolyn started to protest, but her husband took her arm and said, "I understand. We'll be back." After a moment she nodded, and they left.

Frank talked to Dr. Herbert Ritter, who repeated what Ted had said: The boy had never had a psychotic episode; he had no indication of any mental illness, just retardation. "That boy's as harmless as a newborn child," he said bitterly. "It's ridiculous for anyone to suspect him in any way."

"I'll need his complete medical record," Frank said. "Neurology reports, psychiatrists' reports, tests, whatever you have. Do you have them all?"

He did. He had been the primary physician from the time Teddy was a toddler. He hesitated a second when Frank added that he needed it all that afternoon, but then he said, "I'll have everything copied and send it by messenger."

When Frank hung up, he hit the call button for his secretary. Patsy opened the door almost instantly, carrying a sheet of paper.

"I need whatever you can dig up in a hurry about Wendover, and find out if Simon Lange is around this afternoon, and then go to lunch."

She nodded, walked to his desk, and handed him the paper. She was short and thirty pounds overweight; her hair was black and would be black if she lived another fifty years. She was sixty. "I looked up Mr. Wendover while you were talking, just in case. And I ordered sandwiches for you. Should be here any minute now. Judge Lange, coming up." She beamed at him.

"You're a marvel, Patsy," he said sincerely. As he began to read the paper, she scurried from the office. Wendover was into land management and land sales; he owned bits of land here and there all over the state, leased out to others to develop—condos, a strip mall or two, a hotel. He brokered deals for other purchasers. Was on committees that did good things. Carolyn was active with the League of Women Voters, on committees that worked with the handicapped, on education committees.... Good, decent, substantial people.

He ate a sandwich, drank a glass of milk, and tried to think objectively about Teddy Wendover, and then about Mary Sue McDonald and the man she had helped escape from Stone

Point. He had made little progress with either of them when Carolyn and Ted Wendover returned.

This time, he sat at his desk and they took the clients' chairs across from it. "Tell me about the doctors who test your son."

Ted gave their names—a neurologist, a psychiatrist, a psychologist. "They are probably the best in the state," he said. "Recognized as such."

Frank nodded. "Let me lay it out for you. You can't hide him; it's the right and the duty of the police to find him and place him under arrest if they decide they have evidence to justify it. The next step is to go to the grand jury to seek an indictment, after which he'll be arraigned. The judge will remand him to Fairview for a mental evaluation, to see if he's capable of assisting in his own trial."

Ted was shaking his head vigorously. "Where would they take him? He can't be put in among a group of men anywhere." His face was pinched and pale. Carolyn was even paler. "And he can't be placed among children his mental age. What would they do with him?"

"Coming to that," Frank said, holding up a hand. "Let me finish. I'm waiting for his medical records right now. When was he examined last?"

"June," Carolyn said.

"Okay. What I'll do is file a motion for him to be placed in the custody of your psychiatrist the minute he is arrested or threatened with arrest. The state will demand that he be treated as an adult, even though he may be retarded; they'll offer a plea bargain, I have no doubt. You agree with their doctors that he had a psychotic episode, and they put him away in an institution. No trial that way."

Carolyn's pallor was taking on a greenish tinge. "For how long?"

Frank regarded her soberly. "As long as his sentence would have been if he had been found guilty and of sound mind, or until the state declares him cured. You say his doctors' prognosis is for no further change, and that means for life."

She swayed in her chair and gripped both arms. "He isn't crazy! No doctor can find him insane."

"I'm afraid they can," Frank said. "That's how it works. The law says that if he's ordered to a state institution for evaluation under the authority of the Mental Health and Developmental Disability Services Division, the Psychiatric Security Review Board will determine if he needs treatment and care. Under the law, the period of their jurisdiction is for as long as his sentence would have been if he had been found guilty by a jury, or if you had accepted a plea bargain that stipulated his guilt except for insanity."

He pretended not to notice that Carolyn looked as if she might faint. "Now, if he is held over for arraignment and trial, we'll have to try to keep him in the hospital for months. They aren't likely to grant bail in a multiple murder case. Does the hospital have security that would satisfy the court? Can you afford to do that?"

Ted nodded without hesitation. "We aren't wealthy by many standards, Mr. Holloway, but we have parcels of land we can unload fairly quickly if we have to. We'll manage. The hospital is Crag Manor, out of Newport. They can handle the security."

"With multiple murders . . . it isn't going to be inexpensive, Mr. Wendover. We're going to have to look into each death—"

"I don't care what it takes," he said harshly. "Teddy didn't kill anyone. If they take him, lock him up, they'll kill him. That's the bottom line."

FOUR

BARBARA GOT HOME at ten-thirty that night. Junk food for dinner, bad movie, good friends to share it all with, not a total waste. She switched on lights, glanced in her tiny office, and saw her answering machine blinking. She took the two steps to her desk and pushed the message button, heard her father's voice: "Honey, if you get in before midnight, give me a call. First thing in the morning otherwise."

She called him. "What's up?"

"Too tired for a little talk? Won't take more than three or four hours."

"You kidding? You know what time it is?"

"Well, before midnight. I'll turn the lights on for you."

She laughed as she hung up. If she did that to him, he'd hit the ceiling. On the other hand, she would be up reading for a couple of hours. A couple, she mocked herself. Three or four. It was harder all the time to force herself to go on to bed. Having this evening end at ten-thirty was indicative of the problem, she told herself; her friends had each other, a little lovemaking to do tonight. The movie had been bad, but erotic; they had made no pretense of not being turned on by it. She had been turned on by it.

She erased her father's message. Not too late, she mouthed at the telephone. Whatever was on his mind would be more interesting than staying home and feeling sorry for herself. She picked up her purse, slung it over her shoulder, and left the house again.

She listened to Frank in growing dismay, unable to suppress a shudder when he described the boy, Teddy Wendover. "No," she said when Frank came to a halt. "This is impossible. You can't be serious." She ignored his glower and started to pace his living room: fireplace, to doorway, windows, back to fireplace, detour to bookshelves. . . . "Look, first, he's a nutcase, something we both said many times we wouldn't touch. This case has no business in criminal court, for openers. Let the shrinks handle it."

"I talked to two doctors—three, actually. A psychiatrist and a psychologist, and his family physician. They all agree he's as sane as you are."

"If he killed three people, he's a nut," she said flatly. "Who else had a reason, and the opportunity? And the weapon! If I'd gone to school with him, I'd want him put away. You know as well as I do that the DA will have experts lined up from here to Detroit, all ready to swear he has spells of insanity, intermittent maybe, in remission, but murderous when they occur."

Frank's scowl deepened. "Are you finished yet?" he asked coldly. She sank back down into a chair. "Judge Lange will rule Monday on my motion to have Teddy put in the custody of the director of Crag Manor if the police decide to go through with an arrest. He ordered the DA to keep hands off until his decision. That's a start, and a damn good one." He got up to poke at the fire. "Besides," he added, "he didn't kill Harry Knecht, and if one killer got them all, that leaves him out of the other cases, too."

"Why not Harry Knecht? You don't know that."

He regarded her with a questioning look. "You didn't believe Mary Sue," he said after a moment. "I did . . . I do. If Teddy had gone through the hotel that day, he would have been seen, identified. He stands out," he added. "They would have come for him already. And if he'd gone in by the outside stairs and balcony, Mary Sue would have seen him, and she didn't." He gave the fire another poke, added a small log, and sat down, watching the sparks dance. "Mary Sue saw someone—not Teddy, and not the killer. But someone."

Helplessly, Barbara shook her head. "You're guessing and affirming your hunches, your wishes, as fact."

"Look," he said, "let's play with the time element, pretend we both believe what Mary Sue said, and go on from there. She and her granddaughter got to the cottage at five-thirty. Five or six minutes later, she saw Harry Knecht. A few minutes after that, she saw the waiter, saw him drop the tray, run. The time is exactly right—ten minutes after they entered the cottage, at five-forty, Harry was killed."

Barbara was shaking her head. In a low voice, she said, "Dad, I went out to Stone Point. I walked on the walkway from the door to the deck of the cottage Mary Sue and Leigh had. You can't see the hotel, the balcony, any of the rooms, or the windows. There are too many bushes and trees screening it. She couldn't have seen what she said she did."

His face went blank in a peculiar way; he looked absent,

asleep, maybe even dead, without expression, not breathing apparently, not blinking. Neither spoke again for a minute or two.

"When?" he asked.

"Saturday, a week ago tomorrow."

He nodded. "Security guy chased someone."

"He says it was the killer, wearing jeans and a T-shirt."

He thought about Mary Sue. What had she seen, how clearly? Finally, he said, "She saw someone, gave someone a ride out of there. I don't believe she'd lie to protect a neighbor's retarded son. What for? All she had to do was keep her mouth shut."

"Maybe she knew that if they picked him up, he'd tell. The story in the paper must have made it seem likely to her that they were getting near him."

"Maybe," Frank said. "Maybe." He narrowed his eyes, remembering how she had looked, how she had sounded.

"Dad," Barbara said, "something made her run away half an hour after she checked in. Would it have been likely for her to open her door to a stranger? Isn't it more likely that she saw the young man she had known all his life, believed him to be in danger, and sheltered him?"

He nodded unhappily. "Ah, well," he said. "We'll still try to keep Teddy out of court, keep him in the hospital. That's going to take some arguing; I'll be busy writing petitions to the court. The other thrust of our strategy will be to find out what we can about those three murders. That's your department for now. Okay?"

She bit back a protest. She wanted no part of this. She felt revolted by a nutcase, even when it was remote; to be intimately involved in one was unthinkable. But Frank would handle that part of it, she told herself; if anyone had to meet and talk to Teddy, it would be Frank. It wouldn't go to trial, since Teddy was incompetent. Reluctantly, she nodded.

"I'll have to get Bailey."

"Wendover can pay," Frank said.

How unfair, she thought suddenly. "If I brought in a case like this," she said then, "you and Sam would be after my head!" Sam Bixby was the other senior partner; beneath his name came

Frank's, and there followed a couple dozen more, but the firm was Frank and Sam's, and everyone knew it.

"So? Hang around and get some seniority."

The look she gave him was murderous.

For a moment, they were silent, and then Frank asked, "What is it, Bobby?"

"You, your part in this, my part. If Teddy did it, I really don't want to help get him off, wait for the next classmate to get her head bashed in. It scares me. If he's truly insane, that scares me."

He nodded. "Fair enough. What if he's exactly what his doctors and his parents claim, an innocent eight-year-old boy trapped forever in a man's body?"

She shook her head. "I don't know. But, Dad, what if he killed your friend Mary Sue? What if he loses control now and then, kills someone, and then becomes the smiling little boy again?"

It wasn't the money, Barbara told herself when she reentered her house at one-thirty. Frank had believed Mary Sue's story and had felt compassion for the Wendovers, believed them. Then, when she, Barbara, had pulled out the underpinnings and collapsed his belief in Mary Sue, he had been stuck with a commitment that had become meaningless. She knew how stubborn he could be, but this was not his standard case, with a standard suspect to be protected from the overwhelming weight of official accusation, trial, sentencing. . . . Either Teddy was what they claimed and as such was incompetent to stand trial as an adult or he was a cunning killer. A no-win situation.

Although it was late, she read the notes, the summaries of all the murders that her father had gathered so far.

Lois Hedrick, age twenty-six, had gone to the SkyView ski resort to stay in a cabin in order to write her dissertation. She had attended a New Year's Eve party at the hotel, and that was the last time anyone admitted to having seen her. Her parents had reported her missing on January eighth; a search had been started, but heavy snow intervened, and the search had to be put off until spring. In April her body had been found just off the trail between her cabin and the lodge; her head had been smashed in with a heavy object—probably a rock.

More than a year later, on September ninth, Harry Knecht had been killed. His head had been crushed by a rock, rocks strewn about the floor. And in October, Mary Sue had been hit in the head with a rock and killed.

Principal of Teddy's school, a teacher, a classmate. Barbara could imagine all too clearly the words a prosecutor might use: Walks like a duck, looks like a duck, quacks like a duck . . .

Was there a possibility that anyone but Teddy or his parents would have had a reason to kill those particular people? Was there even a remote possibility that a sane person had done the murders?

That night she dreamed of a woman with long white hair that swept the floor as she ran. She was naked, shrieking, running, her hair flowing behind her, and she was running toward Barbara, both hands outstretched, her nails like claws. . . . Barbara ran the nightmare gait that went nowhere and the madwoman drew closer and closer. Barbara screamed and woke up, shaking.

Their neighbor had gone mad, she remembered. Mrs. Rauschler. She had come to Barbara's mother, shrieking, wearing only a man's shirt. Her husband had followed her, crying. Barbara remembered her shock at seeing him cry, seeing her nearly naked and screaming. They had taken her away, put her in a hospital. Barbara's mother had said, "You mustn't be afraid of her; she won't hurt you. She's out of control; she doesn't know what she was doing."

She could think of nothing more terrifying than insanity, being out of control. Like Teddy Wendover, she heard in her mind, and she clamped her lips, but it was there, the thought, the fear, the suspicion. The dread.

FIVE

BAILEY WOULD MEET her and Frank in the office at ten, plenty of time for her to take a little run out to Bear Hollow, she decided. It was drizzling, not very cold. She drove south on Willamette, up the big hill, past Spencer Butte, and watched for Bear Hollow Road, where she braked and made the turn.

Little Bear Creek was gurgling right along; the trees were dark, dripping, and massive. No ax had ever invaded Bear Hollow, evidently; old-growth fir trees everywhere attested to that. The narrow blacktop road was gently crowned; not many houses were visible through the trees. It was a pretty, secluded area; the nearest city might have been hundreds of miles away, not the four or five of reality. A chain was across the driveway to Mary Sue's house. Farther down, the Wendover house came into sight, a large building with tall expanses of glass, decks here and there, one that apparently had been built around a holly tree. Little landscaping had been attempted along this road— deer country; they ate everything that was prized, cherished, valuable, professionally planted. No one was out and about that wet morning. She continued to the end of the road, where a small waterfall sang, tumbling down five feet from a rock ledge. The forest closed in there.

"So, anyone going to Mary Sue's house probably came from Willamette, or else from another house in the valley," she said later to Bailey Novell, pointing to a map spread across the low round table in Frank's office. Frank was in one of the comfortable chairs. "Her house is the third one. There's privacy they haven't even used yet; it would have been easy enough after dark. I don't know the layout of the property, only that you can't see the house from the road."

Bailey slouched down in one of the overstuffed chairs, holding a coffee mug as if his hands were frozen. He held a glass of bourbon on the rocks in exactly the same way, or a glass of wine, anything. He was a slight man who looked as if he shopped at Goodwill and took whatever he came to first on the rack. Nothing ever fitted him quite right, and usually his clothes looked ten years or more out-of-date. His face was deeply lined, creased, folded-looking. He was the best detective on the West Coast, Frank always maintained.

And Lois Hedrick, she continued, had grown up on the same road as Teddy, the same road as Mary Sue. . . . Ten years ago, the Hedrick family had moved to Corvallis.

Barbara folded the county map and put it aside, replaced it with the brochure she had picked up at Stone Point, and a chamber of commerce tourist map of the coast from Florence to Yachats.

"Here's where Carolyn Wendover says she stayed with her son. About half a mile from Stone Point, on the east side of the road. And here's the motel, Gull View, where Mary Sue and Leigh ended up that night, about ten miles south of Stone Point. Now, if a guy did run away from the hotel and go with Mary Sue, that's where he ended up, too. But where was his car? Where was he staying?"

Bailey put his mug down to make a note.

"And," Barbara said without looking at her father, "there's a good chance that if Mary Sue actually had someone in the back, it might have been Teddy Wendover, and if it was Teddy, it doesn't seem likely she'd take him ten miles down the coast to let him out. Leigh knows if they stopped anywhere before they reached the motel." She glanced at Bailey, who nodded, making notes again.

"Okay," Barbara said. "Next, Lois Hedrick." She filled him in with what little she knew. "That one's going to be really tough."

"Unlike the others," Bailey drawled. He made a few more notes and glanced at Frank. "You think the kid's crazy?"

"Not according to a bunch of doctors," Frank said.

Bailey looked from Barbara to Frank, then back at Barbara. "Uh-huh," he said. "Is this going to be one of those messy situations with infighting all the way?"

Frank said coldly, "You worry about your work and leave family matters to the family."

Bailey laughed. He asked a few questions, then left, ambling as if hurry had not yet been invented.

"He's getting above himself," Frank growled.

Barbara grinned. "Can't have it both ways. If he were dumb, you wouldn't hire him."

"Let's go meet Teddy."

The Wendover house was all up and down, up one flight, down two, up three. Windows had been installed in places where few people would have thought of them, eight inches wide, eight-feet-tall glass panels at a staircase, skylights here and there, a whole southern wall that seemed to be all glass. . . . Potted plants were thriving under so much light. The house was warm and comfortable—a sweater on a chair in the living room, books on the floor by a couch, a glass with juice on a side table. It all looked well used, well lived in, belying how very expensive it was.

Ted was out, Carolyn said; he would be sorry to have missed them. The children were in the den. She was serene, to all appearances. Dressed in chinos, a cotton shirt, with a sweater about her shoulders, she was youthful; but more, today she was the most self-possessed woman Frank had ever seen. She apparently had no poses, no image to project. It occurred to Frank that if she was as nervous as the situation deserved, and if she was bottling it up, hiding her true state of nerves, she was a consummate actress, or else headed for an ulcer at the very least, a breakdown at the worst.

"Does Teddy know anything about us? Why we're here?" Frank asked.

She shook her head. "Gail and Reid do, of course. Teddy wouldn't understand." She looked at Barbara, then Frank. "If the judge allows him to go to Crag Manor, we'll act as if it's just another series of tests, the sort he's had all his life. I'll go with him and stay also. I've done that in the past, always for just a few days, of course, but it will be the same to him, I think. Nothing frightening or threatening."

She started to walk toward an arched doorway, but Barbara said, "Mrs. Wendover, what happens if he becomes frightened, or feels threatened?"

Carolyn Wendover stopped moving and said in a low voice, "He might cry, or sulk, or even stamp up to his room and slam the door. He might try to hide in his closet, or in Reid's room, or Gail's. At least, that's how he used to behave. We try not to frighten him, and no one threatens him, of course."

"Has anyone questioned him? About Mrs. McDonald, or Harry Knecht, anything?" Barbara asked.

"No. I told him there was a terrible accident and Mary Sue is dead, and he is not to go to her house again. No more than that. He understands about death, in a sense. We've had pets die, of course. We never tried to pretend, to hide the fact." She said more sharply, "He knows nothing about Harry Knecht. He's never been in Stone Point in his life. When we go to the shore, I walk with him to landmarks and point out where he can go, where he has to stop. He always does. He wouldn't have gone near the stairs or the elevator to Stone Point."

"Could he cross the road by himself?"

"Yes. He can do anything an eight-year-old child can do. He can ride a bicycle, prowl up and down the valley here. . . . He can't go out to the highway, or climb the hills, but that gives him a lot of space that he can use and explore." She started to walk, then stopped to say, "In child-rearing books, they describe the various stages of development—the terrible twos, the cooperative threes, assertive sixes. Eight is a good period, independent in most ways, loving and trusting." She nodded. "Eight is a good age. Come along, this way."

She led them to the den, where Teddy was sitting on the floor at a long table covered with Lego pieces. He was making a village with the small plastic bricks. He looked up and smiled at Carolyn, ignored Frank and Barbara, and returned to his construction. It was hard to get an idea of his size because he was sitting cross-legged, but his shoulders were broad, his hands large; he looked like a big man, a man active in sports or outdoor work. He was deeply tanned; his brown hair was short and wavy; his face was as smooth as his mother's. He was barefoot.

Carolyn introduced the other two children: Reid, who was twenty, and Gail, twenty-two. Handsome children, healthy, complete in a way that Teddy was not, they were interested in Frank and Barbara because of an abstraction: their profession. Reid and Gail were curious and polite—civilized. Teddy was an eight-year-old; neither Frank nor Barbara had done anything to merit his attention. He ignored them.

"You want to ask Teddy questions?" Reid asked, casting a doubtful look at his mother. He was lanky, still adolescent in appearance, with the blue eyes and the same wavy short hair that Teddy had.

"Well—" Frank started.

Barbara interrupted. "What I thought we might do," she said, "is let me talk to you and your sister, maybe over there, while Dad and your mother and brother have a talk over here." She pointed to the far end of the room. The den was very large, with an oversized television, a pool table, and several other tables, one set up with a chessboard and pieces. There were tartan throws on a couch and a large chair, and many large colorful pillows on the floor. The area Barbara pointed to had a red leather-covered couch and a card table with an incomplete jigsaw puzzle on it.

She knew Frank's gaze was cool, disapproving; she didn't look at him, but moved to the other side of the room. Reid and Gail followed.

Gail was a slender young woman, with short brown hair, blue eyes, tall and self-possessed. Regular features, nothing outstanding, nothing remarkable about her. She was just a good-looking young woman with steady eyes and a calm manner.

Barbara sat on the couch; they pulled up straight chairs and sat opposite her. "They will claim that your brother is free to come and go, and that he was out the night Mrs. McDonald was murdered," Barbara said. "Can they prove that? Can you disprove it?"

Gail shook her head. "I was at the quad, where I'm living, near the university. But Teddy never goes out alone at night. He's afraid of the dark."

Reid said he was at his apartment, which he shared with another student.

"Why is Teddy afraid to go out alone at night?"

They exchanged glances, and Gail said matter-of-factly, "I think a lot of little kids are afraid of the dark. I was."

Her gaze held Barbara's until Barbara turned away. At the other end of the room, Frank was sitting in a low-slung chair across the table from Teddy, talking, putting Lego pieces together. He held up something and Teddy took it and turned it around and grinned. Barbara looked down at the puzzle pieces on the card table near her. A monochrome, the pieces all looked alike.

She asked if they had known Lois Hedrick. "Not really," Gail said. "They moved ten years ago, and she was six years older then me. That's a pretty big spread when you're kids. I never saw her, or recognized her if I did, up at SkyView."

Reid nodded. "Me, too. I wouldn't have known her if I saw her."

"What does Teddy do up there? Does he ski?"

"A little cross-country—he plays at it," Reid said. "We take turns skiing with him. That's cool. He likes to play in the snow, build snowmen, slide on a snowboard or a sled. Things like that."

She looked again at her father and Teddy across the room. Teddy was talking, pointing to the things he had made. She couldn't make out his words.

Barbara turned back to Reid and tried to imagine him almost two years ago, not yet nineteen, playing in the snow with his "little brother," who outweighed him by many pounds and tow- ered over him by many inches. One big happy family, she thought cynically.

Almost as if reading her thoughts, Gail said in a low voice, "We think of him as younger than us. I really can't remember him any other way. It's okay," she said, looking at Barbara calmly. "If anything, maybe we're all closer because of what happened. And we sort of had our futures laid out for us. Reid's going into physiology, brain physiology; I'm studying psychology. No one told us to. But we decided. What happened to Teddy could happen to any of us—you, me, anyone. Why? What happened? Why can't it be fixed? He's sweet and loving, and he'll never change! I think of all the books he'll never read, the movies he won't see, the music. . . . He'll never have sex." She picked up a puzzle piece and put it into place without hesitation. "He can't deal with anything abstract. He hasn't any real sense of logic," she said in an even lower voice. "You know some of the tests they give? The tall, skinny pint bottle and the squat quart jug? He'll say the pint holds more every time. He loves riddles—things like, What has wheels and flies? A garbage truck. But he has a conscience; that was left intact. He broke one of Mom's good glasses and cried over it. He cries over animals that get hurt, and when I smashed my finger with the car door. He has empathy. And, Ms. Holloway, he would not hurt anyone. Or anything. He's incapable of hurting anyone deliberately. He simply couldn't do it."

This was said in a tone of absolute certainty.

"What about hurting someone unintentionally? In a fit of anger? Shoving too hard? He's very large and strong-looking."

Reid shook his head. "Funny thing is, he doesn't know how big he is. Or how strong. It just isn't in his consciousness. And he's never shoved anyone that I know of, or hit anyone."

Barbara looked from Gail to Reid. "You both love him very much, don't you?"

They nodded, and Gail said, "Of course. He's our little brother."

Barbara stood up. "Thanks. There will be more questions, a lot more, I'm afraid, but we'll do our best for your brother."

She went to the table where Frank was attaching a wheeled thing to another wheeled thing. Making a train? A fantasy train.

"I was just telling Teddy that when you were his age, you had Lego, too. You built a castle, remember?"

She certainly had not played with Lego ten years ago, Barbara thought coldly, looking at Teddy's big fingers handling the small pieces of plastic.

"A castle?" Teddy said. "How big?"

His voice was high, childish. She thought of what Gail had said: He would never have sex with anyone. His hormonal system had never developed his sexual characteristics, the secondary characteristics—facial hair, deep voice, the things that signified an adult male. Reluctantly, she looked from his fingers to his face, as smooth as a girl's, eyes as bright and candid as a child's.

She reached out and held her hand a foot above the table. "About this high," she said. "I made a moat around it, and water leaked out all over the floor."

He grinned.

"He has a job," Frank said, driving home. "With a landscape contractor, yardman, whatever he is. Hank Versins. He lets Teddy help with stuff, carry things, rake, move stones. Pays him five bucks an hour, two, three hours, twice a week."

She made no comment.

"Carolyn says he called her, Versins did. Detectives got a signed statement. He isn't real sure what he signed, he said."

"We can't let them ask Teddy anything unless we're right there, too," she said. "Does Carolyn understand that?"

"She does now. They all do."

He had a job, he knew right from wrong, he had motive, opportunity, weapon. . . . Barbara scowled at the streaks left by the windshield wipers. "They'll be after him soon," she said.

Frank nodded. "I know."

SIX

On Monday Judge Lange called a meeting in his conference room for two in the afternoon.

It was a full house, Frank thought, surveying the other attendees. Barbara, in a nice blue suit, blue sweater, even stockings and real shoes, was there. All five Wendovers were there; Teddy was the tallest person in the room.

The state was represented by Assistant District Attorney Grace Heflin, who was in her early forties, thin and intense. There were two detectives in suits, and a doctor in a sports coat and slacks. He was Gregory Leander, psychiatrist, director of the Crag Manor Institution. The court recorder was at a separate table. Judge Lange introduced everyone and indicated chairs around a long table as polished as glass.

Judge Lange was known as a juvenile advocate, often taking the minor's part in contesting evidence not properly prepared or presented, or if it appeared an attorney had not done enough homework on his young client's behalf. He was fifty and very wealthy from forest products' money in his family for three generations. Today Judge Lange had on a gray business suit, and he looked like an accountant, with thinning gray hair, a deeply furrowed forehead, and a slight squint, as if normal light was painful to his eyes. He studied Teddy openly as they all seated themselves.

"Teddy," he said then, "do you know why we're here today?"

Teddy nodded. "It's a meeting, Mom said."

"Yes. Do you understand why we're meeting?"

Teddy looked at his mother, then his father, and back to the judge. He appeared worried, upset possibly; a frown crossed his face, left again, and finally he shook his head. "I don't know."

"All right," Judge Lange said in a kind voice. "I'm going to ask your brother and sister to go out into the other room for a while with you, Teddy. Will you do that?"

He stood up quickly. "Sure. I mean, yes, sir."

Gail and Reid got up from the table and the trio walked from the room; everyone watched them until the door closed. Carolyn drew in a breath then and raised her chin higher, almost defiantly.

Judge Lange opened a folder on the table and withdrew a sheet of paper. "Mr. and Mrs. Wendover, the police have issued an arrest warrant for your son, Theodore, known as Teddy. It is within my purview as a circuit judge to stay the execution of the warrant for a limited time, during which Teddy will be examined by one or more doctors chosen by this Court to ascertain his competence to stand trial."

Grace Heflin started to speak, and he frowned at her; she leaned back in her chair in silence.

"I must warn you, Mr. and Mrs. Wendover, that this step has its own perils." He outlined the differences between being found guilty of murder except for insanity and being found guilty as a competent person.

"A vital difference lies in the rules of evidence," he said. "A preponderance of evidence is all that is necessary for a verdict of guilty except for insanity, but evidence of guilt beyond a reasonable doubt is required for the conviction of a competent adult in a felony trial. Also, the sentencing guidelines are quite different. . . ."

Barbara watched Carolyn and Ted Wendover being told that their son might be sentenced to a lifetime in an institution, or be placed on death row if found guilty of murder. Carolyn was pasty-looking, Ted only slightly less so. They were holding hands tightly.

"The next alternative we must consider," Judge Lange was saying, "is the possibility that Teddy's mental development, if confirmed by examination, precludes his being tried for a felony. If such an examination determines that he is both psychologically incompetent and a menace to himself or society, he will be placed under the jurisdiction of the Psychiatric Security Review Board."

Barbara wanted to interrupt, to explain what a preponderance of evidence meant. Fifty-one percent is a preponderance, she wanted to say. But evidence didn't come with numbers attached; motive, opportunity, the weapon, physical ability, those were the aspects they would consider. And they didn't have to prove beyond reasonable doubt that any one or two were present; they could make the assumption, if only by exclusion. They could declare him guilty except for insanity today, without asking a question.

Finally, Judge Lange finished and turned politely to Grace Heflin, who wanted it on record that her office wished to serve the warrant and proceed with the indictment and trial. "It shall be so noted," he said, and turned to Frank.

"How long will you grant the board for its review?" Frank asked.

"Thirty days," Judge Lange said. "Dr. Leander is prepared to take custody of Teddy today. I am satisfied with the security of Crag Manor. Furthermore," he said, "no one is to breach the confidentiality of this meeting, and no one is to interrogate Teddy Wendover until after I have received the full evaluation report. . . ."

"We have a month to make a case," Frank said in his office an hour later. "I don't know what the DA has, and without an indictment, we can't find out. We will assume they think they already made a case."

Bailey was to bear down on the Stone Point murder of Harry Knecht and the man Mary Sue had transported to safety. Find people who would testify that Teddy had been on the beach and nowhere near the Stone Point entrances. Barbara had the Lois Hedrick murder. The meeting was very short.

That afternoon, she packed a bag and headed out the highway to a ski area of the Cascade Mountains in the vicinity of the town of Sisters, sixty miles east of Eugene.

Highway 126 was wet, with drizzle turning to rain, turning to drizzle again, with the temperature hovering around the freezing mark. Although at higher elevations there could be icy spots, she didn't run into any. Traffic was light—too early in the season for skiing, too late for most hikers and campers; the traffic was largely commercial—movers, container trucks, log trucks.

Just outside the town of Sisters, she heard the first radio news story linking Teddy with the three murders. "Damn, damn, damn," she muttered.

She passed the turnoff to the SkyView Resort and continued on four more miles to Sisters. Rain dripped from the fake fronts of tourist shops, now sad-looking and deserted, some of them with CLOSED signs. When the ski season started, they would reopen. Much of the original old western village had been razed in order to create a new, more authentic-looking western village with red-stained wood in place of the silvered fir and cedar. A few buildings that had not been leveled had been redecorated instead, with false fronts, hitching posts. . . . She spotted the motel where she had made a reservation and pulled into the covered area.

Everyone she met was friendly—gas station attendant, coffee shop manager, desk clerk—and not a one of them said anything useful. The woman who had checked her in said there were a lot of really good restaurants in town—Sizzler, Wendy's. Barbara had spotted two others not on the short list, and she headed for one of them, the Chanterelle.

There were two dining rooms, one of them closed, and four people besides her in the other, two separate couples. They all nodded to her when she entered, took off her dripping raincoat, and was escorted to a booth. The woman at the nearer table was watching her openly, and the couple in the booth farther down were eyeing her and speaking together in low voices, looking from each other to her again and again.

She ordered; then she returned the stare of the nearer woman, who blushed and ducked her head. Barbara turned her gaze to the other couple; this time, the woman stood up and left her companion in the booth, headed toward the front of the restaurant, presumably to the rest rooms. Barbara watched her a moment, then got up and followed. The woman was young, mid-twenties, tall and powerfully built, with broad shoulders and heavily muscled legs under a short, tight skirt.

Barbara entered the rest room and went to the sink to wash her hands. The young woman was brushing her hair, sleek, black, and very short, perfect. She looked embarrassed and moved toward the door, but Barbara said, "People have been talking about me, I suppose. Is that it? I'm asking questions; probably everyone in town knows that by now."

The young woman paused, then nodded. "They say you've been asking questions about Lois Hedrick's murder, and I'm one of the ones who found her. I didn't mean to be rude, staring at you like that. I thought you might have come in looking for me."

Barbara introduced herself. "Mr. and Mrs. Wendover retained my firm to represent their son. Do you suppose everyone is going to be watching my every move?"

"Sure."

Barbara laughed. "I'd like to talk to you, but not while you're having dinner. Later? Tomorrow? Is there someplace I can reach you?"

"SkyView," she said. "I'm a ski instructor up there. Vicky Tunney." She added, "I'll be there tomorrow all day."

"Around ten?"

"I'll be in the ski shop," Vicky said, and left the rest room.

Barbara returned to her booth; no one paid any more attention to her, except for the waiter, who stopped just short of being intrusive. The rain had eased by the time she left the restaurant. The town was very dark, although it was only nine or a little after. She opened her umbrella and walked to her motel and was thoroughly chilled by the time she got there.

A few minutes later, down as low as she could get in a tub of hot water, she tried to think what she would put on disk when she got her computer out later to make notes. With few exceptions, everyone had said pretty nearly the same things: The family was nice; Teddy was a good boy. She thought of the exceptions.

The woman behind the window in the post office had said,

"When she first disappeared, people were all over the place, organizing search parties, asking a million questions. It all died down until spring, when they found her. Accident, they say. That poor girl. And that's how it sat until three weeks ago, this man with a scar on his face, he comes around asking questions, and the sheriff came back and stirred it again, and now you."

Barbara sat up in the tub, thinking about the words: ". . . three weeks ago, this man with a scar on his face, he comes around asking questions and the sheriff came back. . . ." Not the same? She played it again in her head. Not the same. A man, then the sheriff, then Barbara. How early had the detectives in Eugene suspected a serial killer, suspected Teddy? Three weeks ago? That would have been before Mary Sue's death. She got out of the tub and dried herself, pulled on her robe, and plugged in her laptop to start making notes. Who had come around asking questions before Mary Sue's death?

The next morning she drove to SkyView. She had studied the resort map, had traced the path Lois Hedrick was assumed to have followed the day of her death, if only because that was the path she had followed every other day. The path led from her cabin, behind another one, onto the trail, and to the lodge, half a mile away. Her cabin was on a road called Lower Loop One in the section closest to the highway; actually, this whole development was like a subdivision in the middle of a forest, with curving streets, small yards, and large trees.

What the map had not prepared her for, Barbara thought, driving slowly through the lower section of the resort, was the feeling of isolation and solitude, the size of the trees, the density of the forest. She stopped in front of the Hedrick house, someone else's house now; the Hedricks had sold it a few months after the body of their daughter had been found. The house was a two-story one, with unpainted silvery wood siding and a wide deck on two sides; trees pressed in closely on all sides. It appeared to have three or four bedrooms, and this was one of the less expensive "cabins," she thought derisively.

She could not see the trail from the car; she would have to inspect it on foot. It was raining intermittently. She had no

doubt that if she left her car and took a hike, the rain would
increase to a torrent. She drove back to the main road and turned
toward the lodge.

At the drive to the hotel, she consulted her map, then continued up Ridge Road, which was growing steeper now, with
houses farther apart and bigger than the lower ones had been.
The road had been cleared, but at this higher elevation, snow
was a foot deep on both sides. Anyone walking on the road
would be clearly visible from several houses, and, of course, to
anyone else on the road. There didn't seem to be any way one
could have kept to the woods between the Wendover house and
the Hedrick house. Too many ravines, too many steep banks,
rocks, a little creek. And, no doubt, there had been deep snow
here in early January. She started back down; it was time to find
the ski shop and Vicky Tunney.

The outside of the lodge was not at all imposing—a lot of
wood, glass, stonework, lava-rock work. Inside, it seemed the
building expanded magically; the entrance foyer had reception
off to one side, with plenty of space for outdoor sports gear. On
the other side, the room opened up to a huge lounge with many
low couches, chairs, tables big enough for dining, others as
small as cocktail tables, and two fireplaces. They were on opposite walls, each on an outside wall with tall windows flanking it,
to catch the morning sun and then the evening sun in stained-
glass panels of green and gold.

Parts of the floor were carpeted with what looked like knee-
deep gold pile carpeting; the rest of the floor was highly polished wood planks in random widths.

Barbara walked past the lounge, to two intersecting corridors
with signs: ski shop, elevators, restaurant, coffee shop, laundry,
gift shop. . . . She turned toward the ski shop.

Vicky Tunney was seated on a high stool behind a counter.
Sitting opposite her was the same man she had been with the
night before.

"Hi," Vicky said, easing herself off the stool. "This is Cy
Rowland. He sort of owns the joint, along with a few others."
She was wearing an oversized white sweater, baby blue tights,
white boots. She could have posed for a fashion magazine.

Rowland was about thirty-five, and as lean and muscular as Vicky. He was also deeply tanned. His nose was crooked and one eyebrow was thinner than the other, scarred perhaps. His hair was dark brown, coarse and thick, and longer than Vicky's. He was in jeans and a faded sweatshirt.

Barbara shook hands with Vicky, then with Cy Rowland. "This is a gorgeous place."

"Thanks. We think so."

"I told him what you're doing here," Vicky said. "He'll buy us a cup of coffee, if you don't mind."

"Good," Barbara said. "Two birds, all that."

A few minutes later, seated at a glass-topped table in the coffee shop, where they were the only customers, Barbara said, "Your family owns this resort, and Stone Point?"

"And Columbia Falls," he said with a grin. "That one is up out of Portland. They have conventions and big conferences." He glanced toward the windows. "This is my favorite. It's pretty when it snows."

Outside the windows was a small open train, gaily decorated with red-and-gold fleurs-de-lis. Barbara laughed. "I suspect that's a bit of an understatement. You're a skier, too?"

"He could have been an Olympic skier if he'd wanted to," Vicky said. "I'm almost that good, but not quite."

Barbara was served a cappuccino, foamy, fragrant, and too hot. "You know the Wendovers, of course. Teddy, too?"

"Sure," Cy Rowland said, and Vicky nodded. "It's in today's newspaper," he went on. "A crock of shit."

"Why do you think so?"

"The kid's harmless. And he's never alone. You want to make his brother or sister an accessory, that's what it would take. They pegged it right the first time around—Lois had an accident. They should have left it at that."

The same useless story. "Was anyone else around asking questions a few weeks ago?"

"The sheriff," Vicky said. "He came around after they opened it all up again."

"Anyone else?"

Vicky shook her head. Cy Rowland spread his hands and said, "Not around me. Why?"

"Just checking," Barbara said. "What did Lois Hedrick do all day, during the evenings? Did she hang out around the lodge much?"

"Nope," Cy said without hesitation. "We all know one another, naturally. We're a little community here. She came up to finish her dissertation, get her doctorate, although why she wanted it is a mystery. What can you do with a history degree? Anyway, she put in time working, took a walk over here once a day, had coffee or hot chocolate, picked up her mail, interviewed a few people who were hanging out, and then walked home again. She never came over in the evenings that I know."

"It was easy walking, not deep snow?"

"Hardly any snow at all, especially at the lower elevations. We have snow machines for the slopes, of course. It was wet, but she was used to that."

When Barbara got around to asking about Lois's disappearance, Vicky did most of the talking. "We made up search teams right away," she said. "We knew snow was on the way, and we worked around the clock for days. No luck. There had been a lot of rain that week and the dogs were useless. The little ravine where we finally found her is steep, overgrown with ferns and huckleberries; we simply missed her down there. Then the snow started. It snowed ten days, five feet. After the snow starts, no one uses the trails, especially the ones with log bridges. We can't keep them cleared, and they get dangerous." They were all silent for a minute. Then she said, "Okay, spring. The creeks around here run like crazy in the spring. We do a lot of inspection—the bridges, the trails, the roads, everything's at risk. You can have a bridge washed out overnight. So I was on the crew that covered the trail from Lower Loop One to the lodge, and I found her. The trail is pretty level most of the way, but it follows the creek for several hundred yards, and there's a drop-off the whole length until you cross over on a log bridge. I was inspecting the bridge when I spotted a boot about fifteen feet upstream on the bank." She stopped and gazed out the window.

After a moment, Cy Rowland said, "The crew had enough

sense not to bother anything, not to dig her out. They went to the lodge and called the sheriff. At that time, they said it had been an accident. She slipped, hit her head, and rolled down the embankment. I still think that's exactly what happened."

"Will you give me the names of others in your group?" Barbara asked Vicky. "And point me in the right direction so I can see where it happened?"

"I'll walk you over," Cy said. "It's closer to the lodge than to the houses on Lower Loop One." He pulled a notebook from his pocket and tore out a page. "Two others from the group," he said, writing. "They're both in Bend, waiting for the season to start."

"Were you here the day Lois was killed?" she asked him, taking the notepaper, slipping it into her own notebook.

"I don't know what day that was," he pointed out. "Usually, on regular days, I'd be up at the shack—the ski shack. We run the train from the lodge here to the lifts, and there's a building on top. A restaurant, coffee, snacks, sandwiches, drinks, the lifts, the beginning of the downhill slopes—a lot of people hang out up there, even when there's no skiing."

Barbara looked at Vicky. "Anything else you can think of?"

Vicky shook her head. "I know the Wendover kids, all of them. Teddy . . . just forget it. If he'd been here, hanging out, someone would have seen him. You don't leave kids alone in the mountains. It takes two minutes for one to step behind a couple of trees, be out of sight, lost. Two minutes is too long. One minute. See, we have to go out there and find them, two, three every year. We notice if we see a kid not attached to an adult. If he'd been around alone, someone would have noticed."

"Will you make a statement to that effect?"

"Sure."

Just then a stooped man entered the coffee shop. Cy Rowland stood up, and Vicky got a strained expression on her face.

"What are you two doing in here all morning? Who's taking care of things in the shop? We had a delivery and no one to accept it." His voice was harsh and rasping. He glared at Vicky. "You think I'm paying you to sit around and drink my coffee? You got it wrong!" He waved his cane and grasped a chair back. His hand was gnarly, brown, with large spots. "Go on back to work!"

"Father, this is Barbara Holloway. She's an attorney for Mr. and Mrs. Wendover," Cy Rowland said. His voice was strained, higher-pitched than it had been. "My father, Arthur Rowland."

Cy had not moved after getting to his feet, but Vicky was edging away from the table.

"Lawyer? You?" He examined her with suspicion. "What for? They want to sell?"

"How do you do, Mr. Rowland," Barbara said, standing now. "I was just leaving. Thanks for the coffee," she said to Cy.

"I'll take you for that walk," he said. "You want to come, too, Vicky?"

A test of strength here? Barbara wondered, watching the scowl deepen on Mr. Rowland's face. His face had turned dark red; the color had flared all over his scalp. He was almost bald; a few white wispy hairs combed straight back did nothing to camouflage the brown liver spots the size of quarters all over his head. Dalmation head, she thought.

Vicky had hesitated at Cy's invitation, then nodded. "Yes. I'll get our ponchos." She hurried away.

"What's she think I hired her for? Can you tell me that?" Mr. Rowland demanded, watching her until she was out of sight.

"She knows exactly why. She's the best ski instructor you ever had."

"Hah! I hired her because I got the hots for her pussy!" He turned and walked away, leaning heavily on his cane.

Cy Rowland went pale with the words, a tic jumped in his cheek, and his hands were clenched hard. Barbara pulled on her coat, and wordlessly they walked from the coffee shop to the outside door that opened to a wide terrace. Vicky was out there already, her face flushed with anger. She had put on a long poncho, black with a red-and-gold fleur-de-lis on the breast. She handed another one to Cy without a word.

"I'm sorry," Cy Rowland said, though whether to Barbara or to Vicky was not readily apparent. He pulled on the poncho and strode away from both of them, heading toward the road and the woods beyond.

As soon as they crossed the road, the trees pressed in, dripping, heavy with moss, massive and black. The light beneath them was perpetual dusk, deepening to almost night-dark, lightening a bit, darkening again. The trail was slick, with icy spots here and there, but it was not steep or difficult. Within a dozen paces, the lodge was out of sight; they might have been miles away from another person. The trail curved, and ahead Barbara could see the log bridge. She approached it slowly, studying the layout of the logs, the density of the forest, hearing now the rush of water.

Lois had walked this trail in the afternoon, and someone had come after her. Someone she knew, or at least had no reason to fear, because she could have screamed, or run, or struggled enough to leave traces so that the searchers would have concentrated on this area. Across the creek, the trail was visible for more than a hundred yards; if anyone had come from that direction, she would have seen him. Barbara turned to look back the way they had just come. The woods closed in less than fifty feet away. She nodded, then stepped onto the bridge to gaze at the banks fifteen feet upstream. The creek was ten feet down and only two feet wide, but it was rushing over rocks, noisy. The water looked gray—snowmelt. The banks were thick with brambles and huckleberry bushes and ferns. She could have lain in there forever without being seen.

Barbara came to a stop, still on the logs that made up the bridge. Where had the rock come from? The trail was hard-packed shredded bark, with no loose rocks in sight. The only rocks she could see were in the creek. Would anyone have gone to the trouble of scrambling down through the brambles, finding a proper rock, climbing back up? No one sane, she thought then, and pulled her coat tighter, chilled, as the rain started to fall again. In her mind, the image formed of a large man with a child's smile; he was carrying a shoulder collecting bag that bulged with rocks.

SEVEN

BACK AT THE lodge, Vicky and Cy entered the main lobby, and Barbara returned to the coffee shop. This time she sat at the counter on a stool.

The woman behind the counter was fiftyish, with yellow hair and rings on all her fingers. Barbara knew it was pointless to pretend she was not on business here; therefore, she plunged right in. "I'm working for Mr. and Mrs. Wendover," she said. "You've heard about their son Teddy being accused of murder?"

The woman sniffed. "Idiots." Her name was Wanda Isleton, she said, and spelled it. "Sure, I'll make a statement, not that it's going to be worth much. I mean, I was in here all the time; about all I could say was the kid never came in here." Barbara made a note of her name and telephone number.

"Me and Bud Ashton—he's the bartender—we were talking about him just last night, when all this was coming out. Just didn't seem right to lay it on him like that—because of how he is, I mean." There was no one else in the coffee shop. Wanda pulled a stool from under the counter, sat down, and leaned her elbows on the countertop.

"Did you ever see him talking to Lois Hedrick? Or hear her mention him?"

"Naw. She was here off and on all that fall, you know, doing her school paper, history of Oregon. Beats me why anyone would want to do that again. Anyway, that's all she talked about, and to anyone who knew anything about the past, what it was like back as far as anyone could recall. She even got to old man Rowland, got him talking. She'd start on someone and pester and pester until they gave up and answered questions, and she took it all down on a tape recorder. She wouldn't have spent any time with Teddy, even if he'd been around, which he wasn't."

She stood up and pushed the stool out of the way, then began to wipe the counter. A man had paused in the doorway, and now he entered. He sat down at the far end of the counter.

"Hi, Mr. Praeger. What can I get you?" Wanda asked cheerfully.

Barbara rose and nodded to her. "Thanks," she said, and left the coffee shop.

Very few people were about—impossible to tell which ones were guests and which ones worked here; they all were wearing jeans and sweaters or sweatshirts. She ignored them and walked past the shops: expensive sportswear, boots, a magazine and newspaper shop. The corridors were wide, the shops large; in season, so much space probably was necessary, but now the scarcity of people gave the resort an eerie feeling, as if it were a movie set waiting for the cast. She continued slowly and then saw the sign for the gift shop; she headed toward it. Candy bars, toys, games, sweatshirts, puzzles . . . just what she was looking for. She nodded to a heavyset man on a ladder who was putting boxes on a shelf.

"Help you?" he asked.

She was as frank with him as she had been with everyone else, but he shook his head.

"No way," he said. "Knew of the kid, that's all. A loon. If he'd come in here, you bet I'd of known it, and would of watched him like a hawk."

"What do you mean, 'a loon'?" To her surprise she felt a rush of fury with this man.

"I mean a dope, a nut, a crazy, an off-the-wall whacko. You want it clearer than that?" He gave her a look of disgust and continued to put boxes on the shelf.

The urge to kick the small ladder out from under him was almost irresistible. She walked away and left the lodge. It was after one, she was hungry, and the drizzle was colder than it had been; it even smelled like snow. It was entirely possible, she knew, for heavy snow to occur at this time of the year, or, in fact, here in the high mountains, at almost any time of the year. And her chains were on the back porch of her house in Eugene, maybe.

She drove back the few miles to Sisters, then down the mountain toward Bend, a high-desert town twenty miles to the east. The rain stopped; the sun came out, and drought made itself known through the brown undergrowth, the dust on the sagebrush, a dust devil swirling in a field of dead grass.

Bend seemed to be having a building boom—new subdivisions, new strip malls, new banks; beyond the town, the high desert stretched away forever. She stopped at a curb and opened her notebook, found the two names and addresses Cy had provided—two members of the team that had found Lois. Then she set out to talk to them, get more statements.

But it was a waste of time, she admitted to herself later; she had learned nothing new. It was nearly time for Vicky Tunney to meet her at the motel, and she was aware suddenly that she had not stopped for lunch; her stomach was growling and complaining. With any luck, she thought, she would get back to the motel before Vicky showed up. Get her statement, eat, keystroke in the various worthless statements she had collected, tomorrow get signatures on printouts, see the sheriff, and beat it.

Barbara headed back to Bend by early afternoon the next day and went straight to the Justice Building, a pretty brick building with a nice lawn and trees out front, and the odor and ambience of bureaucracy inside. The walls were pale green, the floor brown vinyl, the furniture out of a government storehouse, where individuality was forbidden and all the desks were brown oak, or metal, and the chairs slightly wobbly.

Sheriff Harold Tourese was tall and thin, with smile lines at his eyes, and sun-bleached hair a touch too long. He was wearing cowboy boots, jeans, a wide leather belt with the biggest silver buckle Barbara could imagine. She doubted he could bend over with a buckle like that.

"Not much to tell," he said. "She was around on the thirty-first, picked up her mail on the third, her folks reported her missing on the eighth. We looked and didn't find her, and they found her a couple of months later. Hit in the head, left side of her skull crushed, probably died instantly. Not molested otherwise, far's we can tell."

"Do they know the weapon was a rock?"

He shrugged. "Rock could have done it."

"Was her cabin undisturbed?"

"Wasn't robbed, if that's what you mean."

"Did she have money there?"

"Two hundred, her folks said. It was there."

Feeling almost desperate, Barbara asked, "Could I have a look at the inventory of her place?"

After regarding her for several moments, he nodded. "Okay." He got up and strode to the door of his office; he had a long-legged, loose gait, a cowboy gait. He opened the door to speak to someone in the other room, then came back. "She had the key in her pocket," he said. "Cy Rowland sent Howie Frazier to check on her, and he used the house key to get in. Far's we know, no other keys were around. Her folks had two more, back in Corvallis. No sign anyone had broken in."

There was a tap on the door; it opened and a young man in uniform walked in and handed a folder to the sheriff, then left again. Tourese flipped through it, drew out a sheet of paper, and passed it across the desk to Barbara.

The list was of the expected belongings: house furnishings, food, clothes, books, both novels and poetry, history books and pamphlets . . . notebooks, pens, pencils . . . computer system, seven computer disks, dot matrix . . . computer paper . . .

She finished scanning the list, nothing out of the ordinary, nothing missing that she could spot; she started to pass it back to the sheriff, then paused. "Her dissertation isn't listed, is it?" She read over the list again quickly. "Printed papers," was on the list, but did that mean the dissertation? She looked at the sheriff, who was regarding her with interest.

"It's not there," he said, "unless it's part of a big stack of printouts, not labeled any particular way."

"You mean it was really missing?"

"She took a copy home with her for Christmas, worked on it

some at her folks' house. After that . . . Who knows? A laser printout turned up at her folks' house."

Barbara frowned at the list. "Did anyone look over the contents of the computer, or the disks?"

"Yep, we did," he said. "Mostly the disks are new, blank. One had addresses, personal letters, lists of books, stuff like that, nothing worth mentioning. Her hard drive was reformatted. It's blank."

Barbara was feeling frustrated and baffled by the stupid disks and the problems they presented. "Her active disks must have been in the cabin, or at her folks' house with the other copy of her dissertation. Where else would they be? Did she have a safe-deposit box?"

This time he shook his head no.

"So where are they? What's on them?"

He shrugged. "Don't know . . . don't know any way to find out."

"And there should have been hard copy at the cabin," Barbara said, thinking about it. "You make notes, write, do whatever she was doing, and you save it to hard disk, and back up on a floppy or tape, and you print out hard copy. And I heard that she taped conversations. Any tape recorder or tapes turn up?" She looked over the list again.

"Not in the cabin." He spread his hands and then stood up. "And that's about all I can tell you, Ms. Holloway."

"You've been very generous," she said, rising, wishing she knew the one question to ask that might start unraveling the mystery of the reformatted computer, the manuscript and the disks, the death of that unknown young woman. The question eluded her.

Disgruntled, unhappy with herself, she finished her tasks at Bend, then at Sisters, and was ready to leave by five that afternoon.

EIGHT

THE NEXT MORNING she drove to Corvallis to talk to Walter and Marta Hedrick. Marta had taught theater arts; Walter was head of the agronomy department at Oregon State University, and he had introduced many new varieties of vegetables over the years, enough to make him a national figure in agriculture. Lois had been their only child. Meeting them left her thoroughly depressed.

"Lois went home on December eighteenth," she told Frank in his living room as they sat before the fire that night. He had made popcorn. In an hour Bailey would drop in and they would listen to a tape Walter Hedrick had given her; she already had played a lot of it on the drive home from Corvallis. Now she was filling Frank in on her day.

"Lois stayed home until December thirtieth, and she worked on her dad's computer. She transcribed this tape, for instance. Dr. Hedrick was really helpful, numb but helpful. He made a copy of the tape and a copy of her manuscript for me, and all the papers the sheriff released to him a year ago. And I made floppies of everything she saved on his hard drive. He didn't even realize she was saving anything until we looked. Anyway, now we can print out what she had and check it against the papers they found in the cabin, see exactly what was taken, if anything. He thinks this is the only tape she had with her; it's filled and transcribed. And it's the only tape we have. She took the backup disks back to the cabin; they're gone. The manuscript he had is material she had put in order so far, but most of her material, he thinks, is still in note form—the papers from the cabin. Shelley work," she mumbled, thinking of the hours of tape, the hundreds of manuscript pages to read and compare with hundreds of other pages.

He nodded. Shelley work. Barbara was staring at the dancing flames, brooding. He waited, and when she didn't add anything else, he asked, "What did you make of them?"

"Devastated by the loss of their child," she said in a low voice. "He doesn't believe Teddy did it, but he can't suggest anyone else. Marta's headed for a collapse—maybe it's mental, maybe not, but she isn't really here. When I was ready to leave, he said they had a long talk with Lois when she was fourteen or fifteen. They convinced her that it was in her interest to remain a virgin until she married. Of course, they were thinking of a sexually transmitted disease, or pregnancy, but she agreed and followed through. Now . . . he regrets that. He regrets no grandchildren." She became quiet again, remembering what Gail Wendover had said about Teddy: He never would experience sex.

When Bailey arrived, they all gathered around the tape player: Barbara with a stopwatch in her hand, Bailey in a low chair very close to her, and Frank on the couch, his face in his hands, leaning forward. Barbara flicked the switch to turn on the tape player. Lois was speaking. She must have been talking to someone for a while, and only at this moment had turned on her recorder.

LOIS: Tell me again. You mean that from 1942 until now those mines have been just falling down, caving in?

MAN: Pretty much. The War Production Board Order in 1942 closed down the mines, and after the war, high wages, low gold prices, high cost of installation of equipment, it all added up to a lot of work and not much return. Not until recent times, anyways.

LOIS: But everyone knows where the mines are? They're on maps, in books?

MAN: Some are. Some not. What you do is you find placer gold and trace it back to the source. All's that is is lode gold that got the surrounding rocks and dirt washed away, eroded over thousands of years, and then the placer gold, generally just particles like sand, maybe even like dust, but sometimes in nuggets, it gets washed downstream, or down a mountainside, into cracks and crevices, sometimes clear down to bedrock, and it stays there. Anyways, you find yourself a good trail of placer and it'll lead you to the lode, if you can hear it calling you and follow it. Some of the lodes they found; most they didn't. Men get greedy, settle for what's at hand.

LOIS: And the lodes are really rich? Like the California gold rush, or the Alaska gold rush?

MAN: (Laughs) Make them look like warm-up, honey. Look, back when gold was only thirty-five bucks an ounce, they brought out millions of dollars from that district, and now . . . You know how much gold costs today?

LOIS: A lot. [Pause] It just doesn't seem likely that no one would have gone back after the war and started up the mines again.

MAN: New methods, new mining equipment, decent market prices—all make a difference, honey. Once they know it's there for the taking, they'll flock back.

LOIS: Guess I'd have to call this section Future History, or Predictions, something like that.

MAN: Honey, none of this stuff is for publication. Later, it'll be in every newspaper, but the lid's on for now.

LOIS: Just general predictions, something like one day they'll go back to the mines in southwest Oregon and new fortunes will—

The tape ran out there.

Bailey looked at Barbara in disbelief. "Gold," he said sourly. She nodded.

"You know how many times I've heard that story? Gold mines closed down, gold just waiting for the right time, the right guy . . . Barbara, come on."

Frank was leaning back on the couch, his gaze on the ceiling.

"Listen a minute, will you," she snapped at Bailey. "Lois took that tape home with her for Christmas. The only reason we have it is that she left it at her parents' house when she went back to the mountains. Now, if the transcribed pages are missing as well as her notes, it just might suggest that it was important. No paper record. Her hard drive was wiped clean; her floppies were taken. No computer record exists, as far as that guy knows. No backup record. She saved a lot of notes on her father's computer, but no one knew that. All right?"

Bailey shrugged. "What notes?"

"She probably made notes when she transcribed that audiotape," Barbara said. "That's the logical place for them, along with the actual taped words. Let's see what we've got before we howl old wives' tales. Okay?"

"Okay, Barbara, okay. Don't hit me again. What's the stopwatch for?"

"What I just did was use the stopwatch to note every time there was background noise that maybe is significant. Let's try it again."

She rewound the tape briefly and started it again at nearly the same place she had marked before. After a few seconds, she stopped the tape as Lois was saying, "But everyone knows where the mines are?"

"Listen," Barbara said. She rewound it and restarted it, and this time in the background there was the sound of an engine being revved, and music.

"Television," Bailey said.

Barbara nodded. "If we can find out when she made that tape, and then ask some questions, we might find out who she was talking to. Afternoon . . . night? Weekday . . . weekend?"

Bailey nodded and moved closer to the tape player, taking over. Willingly, she got out of his way, satisfied. His kind of work, not hers.

A moment later he held up his hand, then played a section over. In the background, behind the man's voice, was the sound of a fire snapping, as if someone had put on a log, and a few other voices, then a louder noise, as if something had dropped.

They listened again. Not anything that broke, like a glass or a cup. A piece of silverware, perhaps, on a bare floor, not carpeted, not tile. There were few echoes. . . .

"The big lounge," Barbara said, visualizing it: the dual fireplaces, the tables for drinks, coffee, light meals . . . part of the floor bare wood, part carpeted in deep pile. Voices would be muted in there, swallowed by the carpeting, deep upholstery, drapes. . . .

They played the tape over and over, until Bailey was satisfied he wasn't going to get anything else from it. "We could have a good studio have a crack at it," he said. "Anything on the rest of it?"

"It's a three-hour tape, and up to that part, it all seems to be concerned with homesteading during the Depression, the dust-bowl conditions in east Oregon. I did a lot of fast-forwarding. I don't think there was anything else like this. It looks to me as if Lois had been in the lounge talking to people and then began to talk to this guy, not thinking of an interview at the moment. I'd guess they had talked before; there's an ease there, not as if she had just met him. And he sounds a touch condescending."

"And at some point, he realized he was being taped," Frank said. He was still eyeing the ceiling.

Barbara scowled at him and said, "Okay, Dad, out with it. What's wrong?"

"Like Bailey said, we've all heard it before. Maybe not Lois—she was pretty young."

"And maybe he said something before she started taping that no one has heard before," Barbara said.

"Maybe," Frank said, not in agreement. "But I think we stay mum about that tape, and your theory, whatever it is. If it involves gold, anyway." Now he looked at her in a judicious way. "You can't prove when the tape was made, who the guy was, or if he said anything that has any importance. Nothing we heard proves anything. We can't use it."

"Or anything else," she muttered.

He shrugged. "But if she talked to him before, made a reference by name or something in her notes that are left, we might find him."

. No one voiced what Barbara was thinking: For all the good that will do us.

That night in bed, she lay wrestling with the problem of Teddy Wendover and the lack of any other connection among the three deaths. What else could Lois have had in common with the congressman? Or Mary Sue McDonald?

She was too tired to relax. All that gallivanting around, to the coast, to the mountains, the desert, Corvallis, just too bloody much running around. Too bloody, bloody much.

She twitched and tried to find a more comfortable place for her arm; then she heard the trains banging in the switchyards, three blocks away.

"Just how the hell do you expect to get any sleep with all that racket outside your windows?" Frank had growled months ago.

But it wasn't like that. The trains never caused insomnia; insomnia was the precursor to her hearing the trains. She groaned; she was too tired for insomnia.

Suddenly, she stiffened as a thought came to her. The connection—it was there after all. The rocks used as weapons on all three victims, the grotesque way rocks had been placed on or around two of them. If Teddy had not done that, someone was framing him. And the net they had cast now held only those who knew about Teddy and his obsession with rocks.

NINE

BARBARA WAS AT home catching up on the human-interest stories about Mary Sue that had appeared at the time of her death. It was difficult reading that she had put off as long as possible. She stopped scanning a newspaper story to study a photograph of Mary Sue, her son, and granddaughter, Leigh. Mary Sue looked almost childlike next to her granddaughter.

Something, she thought, there was something. Then she remembered: Mary Sue had been four feet eleven inches tall. She started to go to her office to call her father, realized it was after twelve, and stopped. It would keep until tomorrow, she decided. They were going to the coast; she would check it out first.

The weather was cold and clear in the morning, but as they crossed the Coast Range, they drove into clouds and then a light rain, and it turned warmer. Frank headed north on 101, to the house where Carolyn and Teddy had stayed the week Harry Knecht was killed.

Carolyn's friend was Ruby Crispin, her house was east of the coast highway, set back among wind-stunted fir and cedar trees. It was high enough to see over the highway, down to the water, and up and down the shore for a long distance, except that today visibility was less than a quarter of a mile because of rain, low clouds, and fog.

Ruby Crispin was fifty, a very tall woman with slender hips and no fat anywhere. She had been a model, and looked as if she could still model high fashion. Her black hair was in a tight chignon, emphasizing her high cheekbones and a lovely long neck.

She told them exactly what Carolyn had already told them: She had been gone the week Carolyn used her house; she knew Teddy could cross the road and go to the beach alone, and that he never went beyond where they told him he could. She would be happy to make a statement for the record to that effect.

"I've known Carolyn and Ted for thirty years," she said. "Teddy liked coming to the coast. Carolyn brought him over several times; they used my house, where they were comfortable, where Carolyn could even entertain a bit, if she chose. It's so . . . private." She didn't say it, but the words seemed in the air: *You know what I mean.*

"Teddy acts like a little boy," she said. "And he's very well behaved. He's no more crazy than you are," she added to Frank, and then smiled.

"Mind if we leave the car here and take a walk?" Frank asked in a gruff voice. He was very suspicious of women who smiled at him when he had not made a joke.

She shrugged, looking amused. "No problem."

The rain was little more than a settling mist when they walked from the driveway to a gravel road, across the coast highway, and down a rocky approach to the beach. They turned south. Carolyn had said two basalt boulders made up the southern boundary for Teddy. They spotted them easily and turned to go the other way, to where a creek flowed down to the ocean.

They walked in silence for a time until Frank said, "Wonder why Carolyn didn't go to a motel, or stay at the Stone Point hotel."

Barbara nodded. "She said she was not at the luncheon at the hotel. She was just on the organizing committee. Seeing to last-minute details."

He made a noise in his throat. Then, after a few more minutes of silence, he asked, "Did you get a look at Harry Knecht's schedule for the days he was over here?"

"No. Where did you see it?"

"It was in the newspaper. A couple of days of fund-raising stuff and speeches at the hotel, then a private dinner with friends on Sunday after the public duties were over."

She thought about this. "Carolyn?"

"Don't know," he said. "Suppose we can ask."

"And Crispin was gone all that week," Barbara said. "Do you suppose Carolyn was meeting Harry Knecht in Ruby Crispin's house?"

"That's a big jump," he muttered. "Too big. We'll ask."

She nodded. He supposed, exactly as she did. And that changed things, she found herself thinking then. Before, Teddy had seemed to be the only link between this resort and the mountain resort and Lois Hedrick's death. But maybe not. There were the Rowlands themselves, and now, possibly, Carolyn

Wendover, who had been at two places when murder was committed, and very close to the third one.

"Dad," she asked after a few minutes, "do we know where Ted Wendover was when Carolyn was here at the coast?"

"Nope. Another question we can ask," he said. He sounded disgusted. "I'm afraid it could become messy, Bobby."

Oh my, yes, she thought. Messy.

They reached the creek and debated staying on the beach and walking, or driving to the resort; she opted for the car. In the summer, or dressed in real beach clothes, walking would be okay, but now, November, neither of them wanted to wade the shallow stream that ran to the ocean. Nowhere was it very deep, but, as if trying to avoid its inevitable dissolution in the mother ocean, it had spread out more than fifty feet, tracing hieroglyphics in the sand. Barbara glanced ahead; the wet sand was like glass. It was impossible to tell where sea began and land ended. In the distance, the sand merged with the air to form a dome, with her in the center. The water splashed and sighed as the waves ran in and vanished, forming scallops that were erased by the next wave, over and over.

They retraced their steps in no hurry, each deep in thought.

"What made you suspicious of Ruby Crispin?" she asked when they were approaching the ascent to the road.

"Don't know. Her smile, maybe. Like a cat digesting the evidence."

Maybe, Barbara thought, but more than that. It was as if Ruby Crispin had been broadcasting: Read between the lines. Watch my body. Read the language of my body.

Ruby was nowhere in sight when they returned to her driveway and retrieved the car. Frank didn't suggest another visit, and Barbara was glad; the questions she had should be addressed to Carolyn and Ted Wendover.

"Let's go to the cottages first," she said when her father drove onto the grounds of the Stone Point Resort. He followed the narrow road around to the end, as she had done weeks earlier. It appeared that no one was using the cottage today. At least no one opened the door and called them when they parked and stepped onto the covered walkway to the door and the front deck.

The greenery appeared to be even thicker, denser than it had before, the cottage more isolated. Frank walked slowly to the deck; he looked disappointed. Barbara paused midway between the door and the deck and took a tape measure from her purse. She measured five feet and made a mark on the cedar siding of the cabin. Very slowly, she stooped until her eyes were several inches below the five-foot mark; keeping her gaze on the nearby bushes and trees that made an impenetrable screen, she edged sideways inch by inch. Then she let out a breath.

She looked up to see Frank watching her, and she motioned to him without standing up straight again yet. Through the lower branches of a fir tree, framed by rhododendrons on each side, was a clear view of the hotel, the second-floor windows with the drapes closed at the corner room, the balcony. . . .

She moved aside for Frank to look and the view became obscured by the bushes again. Only that one place was open, and only to someone as short as Mary Sue had been. Frank straightened up and nodded at her. He indicated the hotel, and they began to walk back to the car, to move it around front. He put his arm around her shoulders and gave her a little squeeze.

Inside the hotel, they wandered about the first floor, looking at everything, the espresso bar, the café, dining rooms, upscale clothing shops, golfing- and riding-gear shops. . . . Even now, in November, the hotel was busy; there was no mistaking the guests for the hired help here. The workers all wore black trousers or skirts and white shirts.

Finally, Frank approached the registration desk and asked for Mr. Rowland. The desk clerk was deferential and promptly vanished, to return several minutes later; Mr. Rowland would be along presently. It was only another minute until he strode forward to meet them.

Brian Rowland was a few years older than his brother, Cy; the family resemblance was strong, showing up in the same coarse brown hair, the same lean, muscular build, even the same way of walking, with one shoulder minutely higher than the other. He shook hands with them and said to Barbara, "I understand you've been over to the ski lodge, asking questions. Of course, we'll all do whatever we can to assist you. Let's sit over there and have a coffee." He pointed to a secluded space that looked as if it had been designed for tête-à-têtes, with red velvet-covered chairs, big potted plants screening them, and tiny marble-topped tables. He motioned to a waiter.

"Cappuccino," Barbara said, and Frank nodded. "The same." They walked with Brian Rowland to the little retreat.

"To clear the air," Brian said when they sat down, "first, I've known the Wendovers for many years. I don't believe Teddy ever hurt anyone. That's for openers. I think Harry had a lot of enemies, political enemies, who thought he had gone too far for environmental causes and wanted him out of their way. Some of them were registered here for that weekend, to heckle him, harass him, just be a presence—I don't know what for. But they were here. That's number two."

"You had known him a long time, too?" Frank asked.

"Yes. He came here several times a year to unwind. Never for long, a few days usually, but we talked. I got to know him."

"You know Ruby Crispin?"

His mouth tightened and he became more guarded. "I live up the road from her, about a mile."

"Ah," Frank said.

The waiter came with three cappuccinos on a tray. No one spoke again until he left.

"When Congressman Knecht came out here," Barbara asked then, "what did he do? Fish? Golf?"

"He didn't play golf. He liked to ride. We have a very fine stable, and miles of trails in the hills across the highway."

Frank asked him more questions, which he answered concisely without hesitation. He told them about the additional security he had hired for the weekend; he always did when a political figure came to speak. No one had been on duty to watch the beach elevator; that never had been necessary before. He had furnished the police with a list of the guests that weekend; he would give them a copy. No waiter or guest had turned up missing, except for Mrs. McDonald and her granddaughter. No unclaimed car had turned up in the parking lot.

After a brief pause, he agreed to supply them with Harry Knecht's complete schedule for that weekend.

"That'll do it, I suppose," Frank said. "I'd like to have a look at the room Harry Knecht had, just to complete the picture in my mind. And we'll need to talk to the security man who found him and chased someone."

"Of course," Brian said. They went back to the registration desk, where he spoke on the phone and got the computer key to the second-floor suite; then he led the way to the bank of elevators. The upper corridor was broad and brightly lighted, with potted plants at intervals, carved teak tables with magazines and books, mirrors. . . . The colors were dusty rose, grayed green, sand, with a bright floral carpet in pure pinks, greens, deep black. It was all very expensive-looking. He went to the end of a corridor, opened a door, and stepped aside for them to enter. The drapes were closed, and the air smelled musty. They entered a small foyer, with a bedroom to the right and a sitting room to the left. A bathroom door was open between the two rooms. Brian led them into the left room.

"The sitting room is where it happened," he said in a toneless voice. He crossed the room and opened the drapes, and then the sliding glass doors to the balcony. A cold breeze blew in. "It's been redecorated completely," he added. The same muted colors of the corridor walls were repeated here, the same brilliant carpet.

The view was spectacular in both directions: Due west was the Pacific Ocean, forever rolling ashore. South was a view of endless cliffs and surf, and, closer, many trees and shrubs screened off the cottages. From here, it was not apparent that there was a window through the trees.

"I asked Winston Brody to come up," Brian said, staying at the windows, looking out at the ocean. "He'll be along shortly."

Barbara wandered back to the bedroom and looked out the windows there. The balcony encircled the entire floor apparently. She walked to the small foyer and glanced into the bathroom with its large dressing area. From the foyer, she could see part of the bedroom but not much of the sitting room. She took a step, another, until she was in a position to see the room where Brian was still at the door to the balcony, gazing outward.

Mary Sue had seen someone there, she thought, trying to place the players of the deadly melodrama that had been enacted in this room. Harry had been on the phone near the glass doors; then he had moved. Chairs and a table were grouped by the glass door. The waiter had come into view, had knelt in Mary Sue's line of sight. . . . There was a tap on the door behind Barbara.

"Come in, Winston," Brian said, turning. He introduced the man who entered the room.

Winston Brody was forty-two, thick through the shoulders, with short legs and big strong hands. His hair was black, his eyes light brown and narrow. He had a five o'clock shadow that looked permanent. He appeared to be powerful, and he was wary as he studied them.

"Mr. Siletz said to give you this," he said, handing a folder to Brian Rowland.

Rowland glanced inside the folder and gave it to Frank. "The schedule and guest list."

"Thank you," Frank said, then turned to Brody. "Will you just tell us what happened that day?" he asked.

"Sure. I came in and Mr. Knecht was down and the kid was standing over him—"

Frank held up his hand. "Let's try it a different way," he said pleasantly. "You came to the door and entered. Why did you come in?"

"The door was open. Not much, but it was open. So when I saw the door open, I slipped in to see what was going on. If he'd been okay, I'd have said sorry or something and left. I heard something hit the floor in this room, and I came here."

"What did it sound like?"

"I guess it was the rocks he was throwing around. I didn't know then what it was."

"Okay. So then what? After you heard the noise?"

"I came in," he said. "And I saw this guy with his back to me, on one knee sort of, and the congressman on the floor. I yelled and the guy stood up and ran out to the balcony. I went to Mr.

Knecht to see if there was anything I could do, but there wasn't, and I ran out after the guy, but he was over the rail and running already. I got on the walkie-talkie and called for help and went after him. He must have gone down the cliff."

"Did you see him on the ground?"

"Yeah, running toward the cottages, but when I got there, he was out of sight."

"And Mrs. McDonald, did she see him?"

He shook his head. "No way. She was on the deck out front. She couldn't have seen anything from there. We figured he ran between the cabins and climbed down the cliff and hightailed it back up the beach."

"Did you get a good look at him? Can you describe him?"

"Sure. Young, brown hair, big build, six feet or more. He was in jeans and a white T-shirt, sneakers. And he had a bag, a canvas bag of some sort over his shoulder."

Brian Rowland was frowning at the floor, his hands behind his back. From time to time, Winston glanced at him, as if to gauge his reaction; there was none that Barbara could see.

After a few more questions, Frank thanked Brody, who turned a quick questioning look at Brian Rowland and then left. They thanked Brian Rowland, then went out by way of the sliding glass doors to the balcony. It didn't go all the way around the building, just the sides and back. The balcony was eight feet wide, with stairs on all three sides. They went down the stairs closest to the cottages, and at no point could they see the one Mary Sue had been in.

At the bottom, they turned to walk toward the cottages, passed between the first and second of them, then continued to the edge of the cliff top and considered the descent. It was almost perpendicular, with massive stones jutting out, and clumps of broom and dwarfed trees clinging to whatever purchase they had found. There were enough trees and broom to conceal a person.

She glanced at her father and shrugged. Neither of them believed anyone had gone down that way the evening Harry Knecht had been killed.

One more detail to check, she thought as they followed a trail along the cliff to the stairs to the beach and a small enclosure that housed the elevator. They rode the elevator down. It stopped at a platform about eight feet above the beach, with broad wooden steps going the rest of the way. From here, Barbara could see the creek that had made one of Teddy's boundaries. They didn't linger, but got back in the elevator, returned to the upper grounds, and walked to the car.

Neither spoke until they reached it and Frank unlocked her door. As she was getting in, he said, "Next Crag Manor, and then lunch." And he added, "All day we've been reading people pretty well, you and I. We got Ruby Crispin's message loud and clear, and Winston Brody's. I guess we agree he was lying."

She nodded. "And?"

"And I'm getting your message. And wish I knew why in God's name you're afraid of the folks up at Crag Manor." He shook his head, closed her door, and walked around the front of the car to get in behind the wheel. She stared straight ahead.

TEN

CRAG MANOR WAS on a hill overlooking Newport, up a steep road of hairpin curves, back a gravel road, then onto a smooth-as-satin concrete driveway bordered with low evergreen shrubs. They stopped at a gate across the drive; a discreet sign on a metal box on a post said: PUSH TO CONNECT WITH CRAG MANOR. Frank pushed the button, then, following directions, gave their names, and in a second the gate swung open.

The building they approached looked like a castle that would have been at home on the Rhine. "Ludwig," Barbara murmured as Frank parked. The manor was gray stone, with towers and turrets, massive double doors with the biggest brass hinges she had ever seen. The doors were fitted with rollers.

"Neat, isn't it?" a voice called as they neared the entrance. Here the stone underfoot was gray-and-green marble. An open door framed Dr. Leander, today dressed in jeans, a sweater, and running shoes. He did not look like Barbara's idea of a successful psychiatrist, but rather more like a failed art teacher. His face was clean-shaven, his hair pale and long, somewhat unruly, as if he had been out in the wind, and his teeth were not quite straight. Braces too late, or taken off too soon, or never installed to begin with. He came forward to greet them, both hands outstretched.

"My office? Or do you want to go straight on to Carolyn and Teddy?"

"Your office would be fine," Frank said, and he and Barbara followed Leander into the building. The foyer had green-and-gray marble flooring, oversized marble urns with plants, low couches covered with pale burlap, chandeliers of wrought iron. Narrow stained-glass windows completed the room, a mixture of medieval and modern that jangled.

"Claud Von Hausen built it back in 1920 for his bride," Leander said, making a sweeping gesture as they walked down a wide, bright corridor. Doors were painted in primary colors on both sides, contrasting with the marble floor in an unexpectedly pleasant way. "Frau Von Hausen took one look and fled back to Bavaria. It's changed hands a dozen times since then; but it's cursed, no one stayed. My group bought it thirteen years ago. We like it fine," he added with a broad grin.

Barbara found herself grinning with him. He sounded like a pirate, or a snake-oil salesman, but he knew it and wasn't pretending anything. They reached a dazzling yellow door, which he opened and waved them through. The room was bright, with chintz curtains, flowers in vases, and a vinyl floor of white and yellow stripes. A desk looked like a child's oversized red block. And the chairs might have fitted into a giant's kindergarten room. Barbara laughed out loud.

"Yes, exactly," Leander said. "I have a more prosaic room, of course, for lenders and inspectors, but I like this one."

They sat on blocky furniture that was comfortable, and he laced his fingers, crossed his legs, and said, "He isn't as crazy as ninety-nine percent of the people you meet every day going about their business."

"Have the state's doctors had a go at him yet?" Frank asked.

"No. No one's in a hurry, apparently; Teddy is happy. Carolyn finds it difficult, but she is a survivor in the deepest sense of the word. She's coping."

"You will be called to testify," Barbara said to Leander. "They'll ask you if he has a temper, if you ever saw him lose control."

"Of course," he said. "And he has a temper, but it is not a destructive temper. Male violence simply isn't part of his makeup. No testosterone development to speak of, a limited sense of injustice, and little memory of yesterday's injustices." He spoke like a teacher who had said the given lines so often, they required no thought. While it didn't make what he said less true, it sounded less than true. He continued: "You realize, Ms. Holloway, if they ask, and they will, I'll have to admit that emergent violence is possible. It's always possible in anyone."

She nodded, but before she could say anything else, he said, "I have an idea of the kinds of questions I'll be asked. I've been watching him, gathering information, doing a little research of my own to prepare my answers. Perhaps in a week or two, we can have another talk and discuss the possibilities?"

"Why?" she asked.

"Why am I getting involved?" At her nod, he continued. "I've seen the label applied too often, after which the institutions deal with the label, not the person any longer. Teddy doesn't need labeling. I'm afraid my own work might be held against me as an expert witness in this particular case."

"What do you mean?"

"I don't seem to believe in psychotherapy much," he said with a smile. "Or in the power structure that allows someone to label someone else mad and for all of society then to treat the labeled person as if he or she is mad. Here, in Crag Manor, we have a number of individuals, none of whom is insane, and none of whom can function in the real world at the present time, with the possible exception of Teddy. He functions just fine, but he isn't being allowed to do so right now. We have no therapy for him; he needs no therapy."

Frank glanced at his watch. "We'd better see Carolyn, if we're going to."

"Yes," Barbara said, but she was reluctant to leave this kinky office, and, she thought in some amazement, this kinky shrink. She grinned at him. "Next week? Would that be too soon for a longer talk?"

He laughed; it was an intimate low sound. His gaze was direct, an invitation. She did not avert her gaze, and he smiled. "I have Thursday from eleven on. Lunch?"

He walked out with them back to the reception foyer and then turned them over to a pretty young woman in a plaid skirt and sweater, Bea Wesley, who smiled at them and took Frank's hand. Barbara realized she was a patient.

"Carolyn is so lucky," Bea Wesley said. "She gets so much company. Can you stay for lunch? Today we're having sole with lemon and garlic. I love it."

Frank chatted with her just as if she were normal, and Barbara remained silent, feeling awkward and clumsy. They passed other people in the corridors, and glimpsed several in a room with a television and many chairs and couches. Crag Manor looked like a quiet, well-run hotel, comfortable and expensive.

Carolyn was in a room with a bright blue door that was open enough for them to see her in a chair, with an ivory-colored blanket in her lap. She put it down and stood up when they tapped on the door. "Come in," she said. "Thanks, Bea."

Her room had two chairs, a single bed, a dresser, and a nightstand. There was a desk with a computer system, and bookshelves that were filled. Good pictures hung on the walls: a Degas print, an Escher, a pair of Weston landscapes. . . . A picture crayoned on construction paper was there, too—a family group, the Wendover family. Barbara looked away from it. Carolyn sat on the side of the bed and motioned them to the chairs. "Not the Ritz, but not too bad," she said.

She had swept the blanket off the chair and Barbara could see that she had been crocheting it. Ah, she thought; how much of Carolyn's life had been spent waiting for Teddy. She had to do something with her hands. Needlework, the salvation of waiting women.

Frank had seated himself, but he got up again and closed the door. "Carolyn," he said then, "I need to know exactly when you left Ruby Crispin's house the day Harry was killed. Minute by minute, tell me about that day."

She clasped her hands tightly. "Yes," she said. "Of course. At ten that morning I drove over to the inn to make sure the guest list was on hand, that the speaker system was working. I stayed ten or fifteen minutes. Then—"

Barbara held up her hand. "Where was Teddy?"

"I left him at Ruby's. I knew I would only be a few minutes, and he was watching television. At three I told him he could go to the beach, and we walked the places he could play in, and I went on to Stone Point."

"How were you dressed?" Barbara asked, remembering the little creek.

"Slacks, sweater. I carried my shoes. I always do on the beach, unless it's freezing weather." At Barbara's nod, she went on. "I got to Stone Point at about four. The luncheon was over by then, and I had a few things to do with the hotel staff, arrange to have the flowers taken away, things like that. I had an appointment with Harry for four-thirty; I met him then."

"Where did you meet him?" Barbara asked.

"In his room. Why are you asking all these questions?"

"Look, we don't have much time before they call lunch around here. Where's Teddy?"

"Out with the gardener. Why are you questioning me like this?" she asked again, more sharply.

"We have to know where we stand. What time did you get back to Ruby's house?"

"About five-fifteen. I wasn't paying much attention."

"When did Teddy get back?"

"He was there when I got there."

Barbara shook her head. "Did you see anyone you know?

Anyone who can put you on the beach around five? Back in the house by five-fifteen?"

Carolyn shook her head. "A lot of people must have seen me. I don't know who they were."

"How about at the hotel? Did you go down on the elevator with anyone, talk to anyone in the hotel lobby, on the hotel beach, anywhere?"

"No," she said, staring at Barbara as if hypnotized now. "I left Harry's room and went down the outside stairs, then used the stairs down to the beach. What are you suggesting?" She nearly whispered the question.

"It's what the state is going to suggest," Barbara said. "They'll probably suggest that Teddy came looking for you and found you in Harry's room, in Harry's arms, and Teddy lost it and lashed out."

For several seconds no one moved or made a sound. All color drained from Carolyn's face. Then she picked up the blanket and her crochet hook and yarn and began to crochet.

"You know," she said, keeping her gaze on her needlework.

"Yes. And since we found out so easily, we have to assume the police either already know or they will."

Carolyn nodded. "When Teddy was hurt, it did something to Ted and me. I never could understand what happened; it was as if a curtain had fallen between us that neither of us could get through." She spoke in a low voice and didn't look up. Her hands seemed to have a life of their own now, drawing yarn from a ball, increasing the blanket stitch by stitch. Her fingers were long, beautifully tapered, her nails quite short, a soft pink. Her hands were very steady.

"Harry was devastated," she said. "He was more emotional than Ted, more demonstrative. He came to us and cried, and Ted ... Ted couldn't stand it, having Harry break down that way. He ran out and didn't come back that night. Harry stayed; he held me and we cried together. Ted couldn't let go like that, and he couldn't let me give in to grief. I needed Harry, someone like Harry, and he needed me."

She looked at Barbara and then Frank. "This must sound hypocritical or untrue, but I love Ted very much. And I loved

Harry, too. We were together one or two times a year for four-teen years. We never discussed having anything more than what we had."

"Did Ted know?"

"No. I'm sure not." She ducked her head lower. "He had an affair or two the year after the accident; we both pretend I know nothing about them."

"Were you planning to be together with Knecht on Sunday that week?"

"What difference does it make?" She was still calm, but there was an edge in her voice now. "That has nothing to do with Teddy. Why are you asking these questions?"

Barbara regarded her with mounting frustration. "Don't you realize what all this could mean? You've given Teddy a motive, not his faulty memory of an event from the past, not revenge for his condition, but a present-day motive that everyone under-stands: a boy trying to save his mother by killing her lover."

"But how can they tie that in with Lois Hedrick, over at the ski resort?" Carolyn demanded.

"They don't need to. If they accuse him of Harry's murder, and Mary Sue's, because she might have seen him, they won't need more."

"But you can point out how ludicrous it would be to try to make a case for all three."

Barbara glanced at her father, who was listening with con-centration, making no effort to join in. Her show, his attitude said distinctly. Suddenly, she wondered how it had come about that she was doing the questioning, making the explanations. She shook her head. "I won't be allowed to introduce anything the prosecution hasn't already brought up. If they don't want to talk about Lois, we won't talk about her."

Carolyn looked pinched and old as she took this in. From a distance, a chime sounded; she stood up quickly. "It's lunchtime," she said. "Would you like to join us, as my guests?"

Frank shook his head. "Thanks, but no. We'll have to come back, you know. There are a lot more questions that need answers."

"Yes, of course," she whispered. "I understand."

Frank and Barbara headed toward the blue door. Barbara paused and asked, "Do you and your husband own stock in the SkyView Resort?"

Carolyn looked startled. "Yes. We own our house up there, and we owned a bit of the land before they built the resort. We have a very complicated arrangement with the Rowlands."

Barbara nodded. "How about the other resorts, Stone Point, and the one up the Columbia River?"

"No. Just SkyView."

"Okay. Thanks, Mrs. Wendover. I have to come back this way next Thursday. Would that be a good day to see you again? In the morning?"

They made the date, and Barbara and Frank left her standing at her bedside, holding the blanket.

"Wonder what other little surprises they're likely to spring on us," Frank muttered, heading toward the car. The rain was harder now, colder, with more wind behind it.

Barbara lifted her face into the wind. "Next they'll mention casually that Ted was having an affair with Lois Hedrick," she said.

Frank made a snorting noise and unlocked his car door, got in, and opened the passenger door for her. "Speaking of affairs," he commented, "you and that shrink were all but making out right there in front of me."

She gave him a startled look and then looked out the passenger window quickly. That obvious? She doubted it. Frank was just a pretty astute old man—a nosy old man, she corrected—who knew her very well indeed.

ELEVEN

ON TUESDAY BARBARA was at the low table in Frank's office, reading reports that Bailey had been handing in over the last few days. Nothing, she thought impatiently.

Her father was at his desk across his office, frowning absently as he read. He had a stack of law books on his desk, half a dozen open and spread out like a fan before him. He picked up the phone when it rang; Patsy was putting through only necessary calls, and Patsy was hard to get around.

"Holloway," he said, putting a finger on the text he had been reading. He listened, nodding. "Can't they screen your callers, keep people out of there? What kind of security do they have?" He listened again. "Okay, take it easy. Barbara has to be out there tomorrow. She'll talk to you then; meanwhile, tell them to keep people away, no calls except family, or us. I think they can manage that." He listened and then said, "I know it's hard. Just take it easy, okay?"

When he hung up, he said to Barbara, "Sorry about that, but it's either tomorrow or Friday." At her look, he added, "Thanksgiving Thursday, remember?"

She had not given it a thought, and neither, apparently, had Gregory Leander. She would call him.

"Well," Frank said thoughtfully. "Something maybe. A guy called Carolyn Wendover and then paid her a visit. He insinuated he was from Harry Knecht's office, on his staff, cleaning up some details, so she let him in. And he came on like gangbusters, full of questions. She called Knecht's aide and *he* had never heard of this guy John Morrow. Carolyn will write down as much as she can remember and go over it all with you tomorrow. Is there a woman named Agnes on one of those lists?" He pointed to the papers she had been scanning.

She shrugged. "Good heavens, I don't know. Agnes who?"

"Don't know. Morrow asked if she knew Agnes, who she is, where she is."

"Morrow. Morrow," she muttered, and found the list of names Bailey had supplied from the motels around Stone Point. "Morrow . . ." She tossed the list down again. John Mureau was the name on the list that had rung a bell. After a second, she picked it up again and looked at the name, said it in her head, and finally nodded. Could be. John Mureau had stayed at a motel called Blue Harbor on September ninth. She circled the name. Tomorrow would be a busy day, she decided.

Carolyn was leaning against a post on a wide veranda when Barbara was escorted to her by Bea Wesley, who held her hand all the way. At first Barbara had resisted, but the girl's hand had found hers and grasped it; to escape, Barbara would have had to make a scene. Bea made it seem natural to walk holding hands. Carolyn was watching Teddy place big stepping-stones on a path. A gnarly old man was at Teddy's side. It was cool; the sun brought up drifts of steam from concrete walks that wound about the grounds.

"Thanks, Bea," Carolyn said.

Bea gave Barbara's hand a little squeeze, and Barbara said thanks and watched the girl leave.

"I wrote down everything I could remember that man saying, what he looked like, everything, just as your father asked," Carolyn said. She handed Barbara a sheet of paper. "It's frightening," she added, hugging her arms about herself. "He made a case that sounded legitimate, and he got in here. Some security," she said bitterly.

"Okay," Barbara said, tucking the paper into her purse. "Just tell me about him."

Carolyn nodded, keeping her gaze on her son as he lifted a great flat rock and carefully set it in place. He stood up; the gnarly man said something, and Teddy shifted the rock and looked up for approval or instructions. He made Barbara think of a well-trained dog waiting for a smile, or a Milk-Bone, or something. She turned away.

"He called, John Morrow, last Thursday," Carolyn said. "He said there were a few questions about the luncheon I helped organize, and could he drop in and discuss that. He came yesterday. He's about five ten, muscular but not heavy, like a runner. He has blue eyes and dark hair, almost black. About thirty-five or forty. No wedding ring. A scar on his cheek, about this long." She held her fingers two inches apart.

Barbara felt her heart speed up with the words. Scarface! Again!

"He . . . he looked tough somehow," Carolyn said. "I don't know how to explain what I mean, but he wasn't smooth and polished like a politician, or someone from a politician's office."

Barbara nodded. "That's good," she said. "That's the kind of detail that can be important. What else?"

"He was wearing gray slacks, a black sweater, running shoes." She stopped then. "I just couldn't think of anything else to say about him."

"Fine. Can you recall his words, anything he said?"

Carolyn nodded toward Teddy. "He asked about him, how he was getting along. He said it in a way that suggested he knew all about him. Then he began to ask me about that day at Stone Point—when had I seen Harry, how he had seemed, if he had acted upset or worried, when I left him. . . . He was like a policeman. I told him exactly what I told you and your father, that I saw Harry and left and returned to the house around five. And he asked, 'Who is Agnes? What's she to Harry?' " She shrugged helplessly. "I never even heard Harry mention anyone named Agnes."

"What made you suspicious of Morrow?"

"The way he kept asking questions, I suppose. Not the kind that I expected, if they just wanted to put things in order. Questions about my whereabouts, about Teddy, about Agnes."

"Did you see any ID?"

She shook her head. "I . . . He just sounded so reasonable at first; he knew about me, about Teddy, about the luncheon.

When I balked and asked for some ID, he pretended to search his pockets, and said he must have left everything in his hotel room. I told him to leave, and he did. But he was pleased with himself, I think. He was after something that he got. I have no idea what it could have been."

Barbara asked questions, but Carolyn had nothing to add. Barbara switched to the skiing party at the time Lois Hedrick had been killed. She was still asking questions when the chime announced lunch. She left Carolyn to go find Dr. Leander for her own lunch.

Dr. Gregory Leander was waiting for her at the front entrance. He took her hand in both of his and gazed at her a touch too long. "Hi," he said then, and she said hello, and he released her hand. "Lovely day," he said, opening the door. "It will rain by night, but for now, it's very fine."

She nodded. Parked outside was a white low-slung convertible with the top down. In November?

"We aren't going far," he said.

They got in and he started to drive, not very fast, but the air chilled her quickly. He glanced at her and laughed. "You'll be as red as a ripe berry."

The restaurant was set back in the hills above Newport, with a view of old Newport on the Bay. It was quite busy, and, she was grateful to notice, it was warm. A window table was set, waiting. A bottle of white wine was chilling in a bucket of ice. A waiter appeared instantly to pull out chairs, seat them, and start reciting the chef's special efforts for the day.

"A salad," she said when he paused. "A seafood salad, crab? Shrimp? Something like that."

Leander nodded and said to the waiter, "His special salad with the lobster. He'll know. For two."

When the waiter left, Leander said, "I looked you up. You're single, a personality, extremely smart, savvy, wise, compassionate, driven to succeed, and equally driven to avoid the accoutrements of success." He beckoned the waiter and pointed to the wine; there was a minor show of opening the bottle, the ritual tasting, and then the pouring of wine, all done without a word. The waiter vanished again.

"I looked you up, too," Barbara said after a sip of wine. It was very good. She imagined she could buy enough super-market wine to last her a month for what he had paid for this bottle. "Married three times, brilliant, six books published, either being sued or have just been, or will be tomorrow or the next day. You spend as much time in court as I do."

He laughed. "That's why I won't make a very good expert witness. They'll drag out the gory details one by one."

"Maybe not," she said thoughtfully. "Your lawsuits have nothing to do with your profession. Your ex-wives aren't a problem—"

He laughed harder, and after a second she did, too. "For me, us, our team, they're not a problem," she said. "Anyway, you said you'd be thinking of what approach to take with Teddy, how to describe him to lay people, I hope."

"First, my credentials," he said. "I know the drill. I looked that up, too. Chairman of the Department of Psychiatry at Northwestern; director of the world-famous Martin Memorial Institute in Chicago; past professor of psychiatry at the Denver Medical College; president of the American Psychiatric Association. Dates go with all the above. And then the list of books I've written and journals I've contributed to—"

He stopped when she began to laugh. He waited her out and then continued. "I'm forty-eight, and at present director of the world-famous Crag Manor Institution. It is famous, you know."

She nodded. "I know. I looked it up, too. How busy we've been, looking up each other. I wonder why I think you've given your credentials more to impress me than to demonstrate that you know the routine and you're prepared."

He drank his wine. "I knew you'd be fun," he said. "It's in your eyes."

"Would it bother you to be attacked in public?"

"Not really. They can't touch me professionally; the best in my business can't, and I'm the first to admit that my private life is chaotic and always has been. Unfortunately, the prognosis is not favorable."

They drank more wine and chatted and teased and flirted, and it was fun. Playing this game with an aware partner was entertaining; she had missed this more than she had known. They ate their salad and finished the bottle. She shook her head when he signaled the waiter for another one.

"Coffee," she said. "I have to ask a few questions, you know."

"Double espresso for two," he told the waiter, and leaned back. "Shoot."

"Okay. On the medical record it says that Teddy had seizures following his accident. Can they make a big deal of that?"

"They'll try," he said. "It always frightens people to know someone has seizures. He had edema, swelling of brain tissue, which was the immediate cause. When the swelling subsided, the seizures stopped. He doesn't have epileptic peaks in his EEGs."

"Good. Now, the amnesia. He doesn't remember the accident and his memory for five years before the accident seems to have been erased. Is it possible that he does things now, today, and then has amnesia about them?"

"Not really. Differential amnesia is common following trauma. In his case, the amnesia is strictly defined. He regressed to the age of eight, and nothing beyond that age was retained. His memory today is also strictly defined. His intellectual capability is that of an eight-year-old. You can tell him things beyond his ability to comprehend, or read to him, or explain things, and he will forget almost instantly. Exactly the way a two-year-old would forget analytical chemistry, or differential equations."

She continued to ask the questions she knew the prosecutor would ask, and he was prepared for them all. Finally, she closed her notebook.

"One more thing," he said. "If you ask my opinion for the best way, in fact the only way, to treat Teddy, my advice is to deal with him as a child of eight. He can respond to little else. Not a retarded eight, or dysfunctional eight, but a normal, healthy eight-year-old."

She had hardly noticed when the waiter brought the espressos and a small tray of sweets. Now she picked up a chocolate and closed her eyes as she savored it. "If there is sin," she said, "that's it."

"You're not going with me, are you?" he asked.

She opened her eyes and shook her head. "You're too perceptive."

"I know. That's why the three marriages. I knew hours ago, when we were having fun. Why not?"

"I'm not sure. I thought I was, but when you asked, I realized that I had decided no. Without any argument, or discussion with my hormonal system that's screaming yes, just no. I think you're dangerous for me."

He nodded. "Fair enough. I don't want marriage number four. It wouldn't work any more than one, two, and three did."

"I suspect you're right."

"I think *you'd* be dangerous. Being a lawyer, you'd want all kinds of agreements, signed, notarized, tucked away safely, before, during, and after. Wouldn't you?"

"Absolutely."

"Another hairbreadth escape."

They both laughed and it was easy again, as it had been two and a half hours earlier. "I'll call you sometime," he said when they were ready to leave. "You'll have to call me about the trial and Teddy, but I'll call you about life. Okay?"

"I'd like that."

The rain Gregory had predicted for that night came early, while Barbara was driving down the coast looking for the Blue Harbor Motel. It came in driving gusts from the sea, blowing across the road in curtains, easing, then slashing across the road again. It brought rain-shrouded darkness with it. She drove slowly, cursing the poor visibility in a low monotone, peering out the windshield in a shoulder-cramping hunched position.

The road curved treacherously, climbed a steep grade, slid down the other side, and there was only darkness everywhere. Finally, the road widened; lights began to appear, businesses, houses, civilization, and no sea cliff to fall from now. She stayed in the right lane, slowing even more until she saw the sign for the Blue Harbor Motel. She pulled as close to the entrance as possible; there was no overhang here. Considering her dash to the door, she knew she would be drenched. She clenched her teeth, got out, and dashed to the entrance, and was soaked.

A pretty plump girl was watching her from behind the front desk, smiling. "No way you weren't going to get wet," she said. "You want a room?"

Barbara ran her hands over her hair, shaking out water. " 'Fraid not," she said. "Information." She found tissues in her purse and wiped her face and hands, and then introduced herself. "I'm really looking for a man who was registered here in September. We think he might have witnessed an accident. We sure could use a witness."

The girl dimpled and her eyes widened. "Who is he?"

There was an algebra book open before her and a notebook with one page covered with equations. She put down a pencil and leaned forward.

"Well, we think his name is John Mureau, or maybe John Morrow. He was in the area September ninth."

The girl nodded and opened the guest register and began to thumb through it. "Morrow, Morrow. Here we go. Mureau. Yep, he was here. Oh," she said then in excitement. "I even remember him!"

Barbara eyed her warily. "You do? Why?"

"I wasn't here when he signed in," she said, "but I saw him later on getting stuff from his car, and I thought he'd be sort of good-looking, except he had a scar on his face. I wondered why he didn't go to a plastic surgeon or something and get it fixed." She said this in a breathless rush. "You remember stuff like that. And then later on when I saw him on a bike, I knew I'd probably never forget him. You don't," she added. "I mean, you just don't pay out sixty-five bucks and take off on a bike, do you?"

Barbara shook her head weakly and agreed. "What's your name?" she asked.

"Marion Hamilton, but soon's I'm out of school, I'm changing it. Deirdre. I love that name."

"Deirdre, let's start from the beginning," Barbara said. The girl flushed with pleasure. "He came here and registered. Was your mother at the desk?"

"Yes. I didn't get home until after four, you know. School and all that."

"Right. So he was here when you got home and you saw him. Do you know what time that was?"

"Right away. He was taking stuff out of his car, putting it in his room, and I saw the scar."

"Okay. Then what?"

"He left in the car after a minute, toward town."

"You mean Florence?"

"Yes, sure. And next thing, I was on the desk later, you know, so Mom could go eat and stuff. We sort of take turns. And I saw him go by on a bike. Straight past."

"What time was that?"

"Before seven, I guess. I finished eating and came on out here and Mom took off. She likes to watch the news at seven."

"Which way was he going when you saw him that time?"

She pointed up the road Barbara had just driven, toward Stone Point.

"When did you see him again?"

"I didn't. See, we filled up, and we put up the 'Closed' sign and turned the lights down and went back to our place. But he came back sometime and got his stuff and left. He didn't sleep here, but that was all right, because he paid cash in advance, and it just meant Mom didn't have to do his room the next day."

She let Barbara look at the registration book. He had listed a rental car, a Ford, and its license number, no home address. Just cash in advance. She copied the license number, thanked Marion, who wanted to be Deirdre, and gave her ten dollars.

The drive home was hellish, with the lashing, driving rain all the way, but she was in no hurry. John Mureau, or Morrow, she thought, had come to the motel the day Harry Knecht had been killed. He had been asking questions at Sisters. He had questioned Carolyn. Was he still hanging around? But they had a name: John Mureau, the way he had signed the register. And they had the rented car.

"We've got you, kiddo," she muttered, wishing she could see the markings on the winding mountain road, awash with water running like a river.

TWELVE

ON MONDAY FRANK called her. "Meeting tomorrow at nine in Judge Lange's conference room."

"Did anyone say more than that, just a meeting?"

"Nope."

"Right. See you there, Dad." She hung up but didn't move away from her desk yet. It could all come to a head tomorrow, she thought, and the idea filled her with uneasiness, dissatisfaction.

She called Martin and told him to hang her BARBARA'S IN sign in the window, she would be in around noon. She could almost hear his smile when he said, "Good job."

But it was a slow afternoon. Monday wasn't her usual day; Wednesdays and Fridays were. Old Mrs. Toman dropped in for advice on how to sue the city for a pothole in front of her house, and Tyler Bates wanted to know how to go about getting a permit to build a fence. He needed a fence, or else he would have to strangle his neighbor, he said gravely. A man and woman, Juan and Maria, came by to ask if the baby, expected momentarily, from all appearances, would be a citizen if Maria had a midwife.

If they had chosen to give a last name, it would have been Smith, Barbara knew. "A birth must be registered," she said. "Doctor, midwife, whoever delivers it is required to register it."

They exchanged glances, and Maria asked softly, "Do I have to say who the father is?"

Illegal aliens, Barbara thought. Or he was.

"You must give a name for the parents, but if you don't know where he is, you can't add that, can you?"

They exchanged glances again, dark eyes giving and taking information not accessible to Barbara. After a moment, Maria asked in an even softer voice, "If I return to my mother's house in Mexico, and if we register the birth there, will the baby still have citizenship?"

"You want your child to have citizenship in Mexico and in the United States? Why?"

This time, they did not shift their gaze from her; evidently, they knew their reasons and had no intention of revealing them. They waited.

"I don't know the laws of Mexico," she said slowly. "I don't know very much about immigration law, but I can try to find out something for you. Can you come back on Friday?"

She was a beautiful girl, seventeen, eighteen, with lustrous black hair, deep chocolate-colored eyes. And the thought occurred to Barbara suddenly that if she had had a child at Maria's age, that child could be this girl, ready to give birth.

She met Frank outside Judge Lange's conference room the next morning and they entered together. Already present were Grace Heflin, the assistant district attorney, and another woman, Sarah Ghormley, whom Barbara had met once or twice before. She was a heavyset woman with brick-red hair in tight curls, dark blue eyes, a wide, infectious smile, and was said to be very brilliant. She was chief investigator for district court, a misleading title, since she often made decisions about court matters that generally were made only by judges. She had been a psychologist, turned lawyer, turned investigator.

She greeted Frank and Barbara warmly; Grace Heflin nodded at them, decidedly cool. Judge Lange entered, and they all sat at the long conference table.

"Good morning," Judge Lange said. "And thank you for coming. I don't think this will take long." He glanced at Grace Heflin. "Yes?"

"Your Honor, the state is willing to stipulate at this time that the suspect, Theodore Wendover, Jr., has the mental age of an eight-year-old. We agree, he cannot be tried in court as a competent adult."

Barbara listened to her carefully. She talked a little too fast, clipped her words, a style that would not wear well during a long trial. On the other hand, no doubt she had another persona who played her role in court, just as Barbara did, part ham, part Shakespearean actor, part fraud. . . .

Grace Heflin continued. "However, since no one has yet questioned him concerning the several deaths, we also request that he remain in custody until such time that interrogation can take place."

Frank snorted and opened a thick file folder. Judge Lange eyed it gloomily and said, "Hold on a minute, Frank." He glanced at Sarah Ghormley. "Have you read the reports and statements?"

"Indeed I have," she said. "Teddy can't be held under the law unless he has been charged with a crime, and even then the state would be able to remove him from his parents and place him in a proper home only until the matter is resolved. Certainly not in jail, but in foster-home care. However, since he has been charged with nothing at this time, that is not an option." She looked at Grace Heflin and said, "Charge him or cut him loose."

Grace said, "Your Honor, his parents are affluent. There is nothing to prevent their packing him up and fleeing to Mexico or Brazil if he is released from custody. The state must have access to him in order to question him."

Frank closed his folder and leaned back in his chair, content to let the judge and the investigator win this battle for him. "We'll produce him for questioning under the proper circumstances," he said.

"You can't guarantee that," Grace snapped.

"Hold it," Judge Lange said. "Dr. Ghormley, what is your recommendation?"

"Obviously, he must be asked questions—the sooner the better. I would say today, if that is possible."

Grace Heflin shook her head. "We have to call in our psychologist, prepare questions. That's too soon."

"You recall the lectures you suffered through concerning habeas corpus?" Frank asked lazily.

She glared at him.

"Not today, then," Sarah Ghormley said. "Tomorrow. And if by four tomorrow afternoon the state is not prepared to charge him, he should be released."

"I suggest we all meet out there at Crag Manor to conduct the interrogation," Barbara said then.

Grace turned her glare to Barbara. "For heaven's sake! Why? That's just inconveniencing everyone."

"Well, someone has to be inconvenienced," Barbara said reasonably. "Why Teddy and his mother? Why Dr. Leander? You bring Teddy in here to a strange place, surrounded by strange people, who knows if he'll say a word? He's comfortable out there; his doctor is there. He's used to being tested out there."

Sarah Ghormley nodded. "I agree. Tomorrow at one. Now, we have to set the parameters—who can be present, how long the session will last."

Barbara didn't interrupt as the others wrangled about procedures. In her mind's eye, she was seeing again the crayon picture on Carolyn's wall: a nice white house with yellow windows, a tall father and mother, a tall girl and boy, and, centered in the group, a small child holding a red ball. The sky was blue and a bright yellow sun was shining. All the people were smiling.

There was a real gang present at Crag Manor the next day at one. Ted and Carolyn were there with Teddy. Sarah Ghormley was on hand, and Detective Wayne Noh, Gregory Leander, and the state's psychologist, Dr. Virginia Janec. She was very blond, with short, straight hair, oversized glasses, and beautiful pale skin.

They were in a pleasant room that was quite conventional, with comfortable chairs, several low tables, and a large round table with crayons, pencils, a stack of paper. Some blocks were in a box near a window; a wooden train and trucks were on the floor by it.

Teddy was nervous, staying close to his parents as the others arranged themselves in the easy chairs. He had smiled at Frank and Barbara when they entered, but he regarded the strangers warily. He had started to sit in a chair, then moved instead to sit cross-legged on the floor between Carolyn and Ted. Even seated on the floor, he looked very large.

"Before we start, for the record, Mr. Holloway, Ms. Holloway, has either of you questioned Teddy about the matter we're considering today?" Sarah Ghormley asked pleasantly. She had a tape recorder.

"No," they said together.

"Fine. Detective Noh, would you like to start?"

He was in his forties, as broad as a football player, with large hands, a big face, and not much hair.

"Teddy, we're trying to find out what happened to a man we knew. We think you might be able to help us. You remember one day if you went up the beach to a lot of stairs and went up to a really big building? A hotel?"

His manner was wrong, Barbara decided, too condescending. She was watching them all, but taking her cues from Gregory Leander, who was sprawled in a chair. He didn't react to the question.

Teddy shook his head.

"Maybe you got in an elevator and rode up. You ever do that on the beach?"

He shook his head again.

"What do you do when you go down to the beach alone?"

He shrugged. "Nothing."

Barbara suppressed a sigh. It was going to be a long hour. After another fruitless question or two, Dr. Janec tried.

"Teddy, if someone hit you, what would you do?"

He looked puzzled and shook his head. "Nobody hit me."

"When you're scared, what do you do?"

"Run away."

"What if you couldn't run away?"

He looked over his shoulders, first at his mother, then at his father, as if for help. "I don't know."

Looking at the big man-child fidgeting now, scratching his knee, eyeing the toys under the windows, Barbara realized she

was seeing him the way his parents did: a very large little boy.
She bit her lip.

"Teddy, what would you do if someone took something of
yours away from you?"

"Tell Dad. Somebody took my sled and he got me another
one."

"When someone took your sled, did you get mad?"

"I told Dad."

"But did you get mad first?"

He shook his head. "I told Dad."

They asked if he remembered his accident when he fell off a
cliff. He didn't. He didn't remember his teacher, Mr. Knecht,
and shook his head when they showed him a picture. He didn't
recognize Lois Hedrick. He nodded at last when Dr. Janec
showed him the picture of Mary Sue McDonald.

"I rake her yard, and she makes a fire and we toast marsh-
mallows. She gives me cookies. Or pears. She has a pear tree.
Sometimes I can climb the pear tree and get pears for her. But
they aren't good yet. You have to wait. She died. White Paws
died, too."

Dr. Janec's voice turned silky. "How did White Paws die,
Teddy?"

"I don't know."

"Feline leukemia," Carolyn said quietly.

"How did Mrs. McDonald die, Teddy?" Dr. Janec asked,
ignoring Carolyn.

"I don't know."

"What does it mean to die, Teddy?"

"Reid dug a hole and Gail put White Paws in a box and we
put her in the hole and put dirt on it. And stones. Me and Gail
cried."

Barbara felt a chill flash through her body. She was very
careful not to move.

"You put stones on White Paws?"

"Yes."

"Were they your stones?"

"Some of them. I have a lot of stones."

"Did you put stones on anything else?"

He looked puzzled again. "Me and Mr. Cressman put stones on the path. I put stones on my shelf, and in the basement. I put a lot of stones in the basement."

"Did you ever put stones on a person, Teddy?"

He looked as if he thought she was teasing. He examined her face for a moment, then shook his head.

"Did you?" she asked again, more insistently.

"No."

"If you thought a person was dead, would you put stones on that person?"

She had lost him, Barbara knew. He shook his head and eyed the toys again, then scratched his other knee. His big hands were as rough and calloused as a laborer's.

Dr. Janec asked a lot of questions about stones, and got nowhere. He was fidgeting more and more and Sarah Ghormley called a halt.

"Recess," she said. "Let's stretch our legs a bit. I wonder, Gregory, if there's any coffee around?"

When they resumed, Barbara said, "Dr. Ghormley, would it be appropriate to have Teddy show us what he did on the beach that day? He hasn't been back since then, has he?" she asked Carolyn, who shook her head.

Sarah Ghormley considered the idea. "I think we might get more from his acting out than by laborious questioning. Dr. Janec?"

She appeared more reluctant, but she nodded. "Perhaps it would reveal more."

They went in two cars; Detective Noh drove the Wendovers, and the rest of them rode with Frank. In Frank's car not a word was spoken until they pulled up to Ruby Crispin's house. She came out with a look of astonishment on her face.

"I'll explain later," Carolyn said. She turned to Teddy. "Remember when we were here? We walked down to the beach together."

He nodded. "You let me play by myself."

"Let's show them where you went that day. First, down the

drive." They started to walk; Teddy dwarfed his mother. He walked fast, obviously eager to get to the beach again. There was a cold drizzle in the air, not quite rain, and little wind. Fog drifted in and out of the firs along the drive and hid the higher treetops and the hills. At the road, the fog was a closed curtain in both directions beyond a hundred feet. Teddy hesitated, as if uncertain with such limited vision.

"I took you across the street," Carolyn said. "Let's go." She held his hand.

On the other side they started down, with Teddy leading. It was muddy today. Frank and Barbara had worn boots; all three Wendovers wore sneakers, and Leander had on what appeared to be his daily uniform of jeans and running shoes, but the others were in city clothes. Barbara felt a twinge of pity for them. It was short-lived.

When they reached the sand, Sarah Ghormley eyed the long stretch of deserted, fog-shrouded sand. "Maybe we don't have to retrace every step. I understand that you went to the southern boundary with him first, then back to the upper limit. Is that correct?"

"Yes," Carolyn said. "I always walk the boundaries with him first." She looked uncertain. "Maybe we can start with the creek." She turned right and Teddy began to run ahead. He stooped to examine something, ran again, waited for her, and ran again.

A very large little boy, Barbara kept thinking, watching him. He was happy here, glad to be outside, excited by the world of ocean and sand, the detritus all around. They reached the creek and Carolyn stopped.

"Remember what I told you, Teddy?"

He nodded. "Don't get your feet wet. Stay out of the water. Are you going across the water now?"

She smiled at him. "Not today. Show us what you did after I left you alone."

He looked at the people following, back at her.

"We just want to watch what you did," she said gently. "It's all right."

At first he was self-conscious, too aware of his audience, but soon he began to race the waves. He ran, stopped occasionally to dig here, there, then ran up to dry sand, picked up something, tossed it down again, ran back to the water.

The fog was a confining wall that encircled them, sheltered them, kept the world at bay for now. Barbara remembered herself at his age, racing the waves, trying to decipher the messages they left in foam that vanished too fast in the litter of shells and seaweed. If one could get the right distance, be in the right place, and know enough, the messages would be legible, she had believed.

Teddy stopped near the boundary of the two basalt monoliths that were like giant eggs. He squatted over a tide pool and examined it carefully, then looked at the cliff more than two hundred feet away.

"We made a castle," he said.

Instantly, Sarah Ghormley was at his side. "Who made the castle, Teddy?"

"Me and some kids. Over there."

He pointed to the cliff where a clutter of logs was scattered in a haphazard heap. He started to walk through the deep, resisting sand.

The logs were ten feet long, twenty feet. . . . The sea had played with them for months, years, and eventually discarded them, tossed them onto the shore, where they had crashed against the cliff and settled. Hundreds of logs, whitened now, some glittering with sand, others encrusted with dried bits of shells, no bark anywhere, but sea- and sand-smoothed trunks and limbs, some pieces weathered so much, they looked like artifacts. Many fires had burned here, meals had been eaten, structures built and destroyed by storm tides.

Teddy went unerringly to a group of logs and pointed, and there was the castle. Barbara remembered watching him play with Lego blocks, the sureness of his hands. Here, three logs had been shifted, maneuvered into place to form a roof over other logs that could have been walls, a structure large enough for children to enter, to call a castle. Teddy could not have gotten inside.

"Who built this?" Sarah Ghormley asked.

"The kids were trying to make a roof and I came and helped and we made a castle," he said. "There's the throne." He pointed to a flat-topped boulder near the castle. "I was king."

Patiently, Sarah Ghormley questioned him. He had seen two little kids playing here and had come to play with them. Little, he said, putting his hand on his chest, like this. Barbara remembered the picture he had drawn with himself so much smaller than his brother and father.

"Their mom came and said leave them alone, but then she said that's all right, you can play, and we made the castle, and she took our picture a lot. And then she said it was time to go home and they went away and I went away, too."

It was over, Barbara knew. She faced the sea, although both Sarah Ghormley and Dr. Janec were still asking questions about the boys he had played with, about their mother. Barbara watched the gentle waves washing the shore.

Then they headed back, again letting Teddy set the pace, keeping behind him, now in several clusters. Barbara and Frank trailed behind the others. "I'm taking it easy," he had announced. "I'll catch up later."

"Good job," he said after a few moments.

She bent down and picked up a handful of sand, let it trickle through her fingers. "I used to imagine what a grain of sand could tell me. How it used to be part of a mountain, how the bears and wolves and mammoths walked on it once, maybe even dinosaurs. Then a shifting of the earth, and a piece of the mountain rolled down to a river, then another river, breaking up from a boulder to a rock to a stone, out to the ocean and seeing the whole world, and finally coming home as a grain of sand." She released the last bit of sand and said in a whisper, "Welcome home."

Frank slowed his pace and she moved more slowly in step.

"I tell myself it's too soon," she said softly. "I mean, there hasn't been time for him to make that trip yet, but I can almost imagine Mike's out there. Not almost. I think he's out there, part of the ocean, seeing the world now. And one day he'll come home to our beach. Is that crazy, Dad?"

He put his arm around her shoulders and held her without a word. At last, he thought with a prayer of thanks. At last.

"We came down here one day," she said, "and we ran exactly the way Teddy is running, like two children. It was raining so hard. We looked like drowned—" Suddenly, she laughed. "He said we looked like two drowned dream-children, innocence restored, all sin washed away." She patted Frank's hand on her shoulder. "He was a good guy," she said.

"I know he was, honey. I know."

Ahead, Teddy had turned without hesitation at the boulder that marked the beginning of the trail to the road. The others trudged along, following. It was ending too soon, Frank thought with regret. He wished they had another half hour out here, another hour, the rest of the day. . . . But it would be all right, he thought then. Now she could talk about Mike, who had been lost in the river a hundred miles from this place, and who was out there in the ocean, seeing the world. At last she would be able to talk about him.

They paused at the boulder and looked at the sea, so calm today, so gray and white, like an old movie. His eyes felt hot and he didn't even try to pretend it was the sea air, the cold, or the fog. Thank you, he thought. Thank you.

At the cars in Ruby Crispin's driveway, Gregory Leander said cheerfully, "We're all frozen and wet. What I suggest is that we head back to the manor and have some good hot drinks and dry out."

Detective Noh frowned and closed a notebook he had been writing in. He looked at Carolyn and asked, "Mrs. Wendover, what time did you say you got back here to the house?"

They had been out on the beach an hour and fifteen minutes, Barbara realized, and they had not covered half the ground Teddy had covered that day; they had not stopped to build a castle. He couldn't have gotten back before five, and Carolyn had said she arrived after he did. It was over, she thought, but what *it* was was only Act One. Detective Noh had just said the opening line to Act Two.

THIRTEEN

WHEN THEY GOT to the Buick, Frank settled in the passenger side with a grunt. "You drive. Too old for such nonsense," he said. "Wading through sand up to my hips, climbing mountains. Just too damn old."

She laughed, but he was right—it had been a tough day. For a time, they were both silent. Before they reached Eugene, an icy fog was settling. It had started, she thought glumly, icy fogs that settled in and stayed for days on end. The cold penetrated any clothing no matter how heavy; it made lights tricky—too close, too far, too blurred, impossible to gauge; it even made it hard to hear anything properly.

"I'm too tired to cook," he said when they reached the outskirts of Eugene. "Thought I might talk you into going to that place you like so much, the Middle American restaurant in these parts."

They went to Hilda's, where Barbara was greeted almost like family, and where the fragrance of chilis and garlic was overwhelming. It was a noisy place, with a lot of laughter, a lot of talking on all sides. Everyone was dressed in jeans and sweaters, sweatshirts, boots, including the tall waiter who took their orders. The special was grilled snapper with spicy guacamole and red potatoes. It was heavenly.

As they ate, Barbara told Frank about Maria and Juan. "Obviously, they want dual citizenship to avoid a future draft, or to allow the child to buy property some day, or just to be able to travel back and forth."

He laughed, contented in the heat of the restaurant, with the heat of the food in him. "You're going to tell them it's okay," he said. "When they lock you up, don't say a thing until you make the call. I'll defend you, give you a cut rate even; we'll plead insanity."

"And speaking of defending," she said, "I guess we shouldn't really close the file yet on the Wendovers."

"I suppose," he agreed. "I'll call off Bailey and Shelley for now. No point in keeping them on full pay until there's a payer in the offing. Poor Shelley. She's scared to death I'll hand her over to Sam and she'll have to do wills and trusts."

He talked about his usual Christmas party, in the planning stage now, and asked if he should invite Bill Spassero. She made a face. But then she thought of Shelley with all that hair, and Bill, whose hair was like dandelion gone to seed, all fluffy and golden. She said, "I wouldn't think of leaving him out. And ask Shelley, too."

He threw back his head and laughed; his laughter filled the restaurant. He imagined the children they might produce: little golden-haired apes, hair all over them. He laughed again at the image.

When he took Barbara home, she kissed his cheek. "Thanks, Dad. Long day, good evening." She got out, knowing he would stay there until she was inside the house. She waved at the door when she let herself in.

He watched until her door closed. He had known very well that she would go home and open a can of soup. And he knew how much she hated the cold winter fogs. He drove slowly; there could be patches of black ice on the streets. He had mild regrets over Bill Spassero, but he had never thought Bill was the right one for her. She didn't need a worshiper. But maybe now that she was healing, maybe she would spot the right one soon. He remembered how sad and distant she had looked when she repeated Dr. Hedrick's regret that there were no grandchildren, that his daughter had died before she had really lived. He understood very well, he thought then, pulling into his driveway. He resolutely denied himself awareness of the time clock ticking away, and while denying it, he tried to remember if she was thirty-nine or forty. In his head, she was sometimes a very young girl, and then a woman older and wiser than he was; he no longer knew which image was more accurate. He suspected she was both, and then a few others, too.

It was hopeless, Barbara decided on Friday, studying her calendar. Christmas was edging in and she had not bought a single gift yet. Her clients had come and gone; at least she wasn't expecting anyone else, since it was nearly five. She started to pack up her things—laptop, paper, pencils, pen.

Martin came out and chatted a minute or two, invited her to stay and have dinner, as he usually did, and tried to tempt her with Binnie's filbert cream pie, baked in tiny tart pans, with crust made in heaven.

She shook her head. "You're an evil man, Martin. Evil. Another time."

He grinned and produced an envelope. "Guy came in this morning, handed this to me, and said I should wait until you're ready to leave to pass it on to you."

"A guy? Anyone we know?"

"Not me. Didn't leave a name. A guy with a scar on his cheek."

She felt a good dollop of excitement in the pit of her stomach, and she took the envelope carefully. Mureau! Her name was written on the envelope in bold black letters. It was perfectly flat, not a letter bomb, she decided, slipping it into her pocket. He wanted her to have it when she finished here, to be read at home, alone? Maybe.

She thanked Martin and walked out into the fog, and for the first time in a long time, she wished she had driven over, that she didn't have to walk home. The fog was thicker than it had been all week, and colder. Christmas lights here and there were lovely pastel glows; headlights were twin ghosts drawing closer eerily; taillights were like lines of fire seen through curtains, and traffic sounds were distant, muted. Footsteps would be swallowed by such fog, she thought, listening hard.

Inside her own little house, after making certain the doors were locked, the shades and drapes drawn, she sat down to read Mr. Mureau's letter.

It was short, written with the same bold black pen. "The kid didn't kill Knecht. Find out who was in the bedroom when Brody got there."

Well, well, she thought, studying the writing. Somewhere between cursive and block print, no flourishes. Very business-like, assertive. No shrinking violet, our Mr. Mureau, she thought. Of course, she had been easy enough to find in Martin's restaurant; there had been newspaper stories about her office there.

She got up to see if there was anything to eat in the house. Tomorrow she would show the letter to her father and see if Bailey had had time to run Mr. Mureau to ground before he had been called off. As she rummaged in her small freezer, she won-dered how Mureau had known to deliver his message to her and not to Frank.

"The boy's been doing his homework," she muttered, examining a frozen Salisbury steak dinner. She shrugged; it would do.

On Saturday, when Barbara took the letter to Frank's house, he told her Sarah Ghormley had called earlier. "They found the mother of those two kids Teddy played with on the beach. A Mrs. Musick. She gave a statement, checked out okay, and Teddy's home free. This is off the record until we get official notification first of the week, or sometime, if and when they recall we're waiting."

Barbara grinned at him. "I don't suppose you called Carolyn and Ted, off the record."

He scowled. Of course he had called them.

She handed him her letter. "See what you make of this."

Frank examined the letter with infinite care, the words, the writing, the paper, and then tossed it down on his dinette table. "He's hanging around," he said. "Why?"

"I thought I'd go over to the office and see how far Bailey got before you reined him in."

Almost offhandedly, Frank commented, "He, Mureau, is a consultant, out of Denver. Paid for the rental car with a credit card at the Portland airport."

She gave him a searching look. Of course, he still had Mary

Sue on his conscience; he'd be following up on anything already in hand.

"Consultant," she said with a sniff. "That can mean whatever you want it to. No more than that?"

"Nope."

She considered it for a moment, then let it go for now. "What we need to know is how much of the bedroom is visible from the entrance to the suite at Stone Point," she said. "And I wonder if Mary Sue could have seen the oceanside balcony as well as the south part of it. I didn't look particularly. Did you?"

"Nope."

"It will take two of us," she said, thinking. "One to get inside the rooms again, and someone else on the cabin walkway, watching. Bailey can do that part, and I'll have to get inside. I'd like to get on this as soon as possible, before the story breaks that Teddy's off the hook, so it will look as if we're still digging on his behalf."

Neither of them raised the point that they had no client, that Bailey's work would be on them. Bailey was not cheap. Frank crossed to the telephone stand in the kitchen and called him. "You might as well finish up with that Mureau fellow." He listened and said, "Yeah, all the way. And are you free tomorrow?" Then after a pause he said, "Talk to Barbara about it."

She and Bailey made arrangements to meet in Florence and make plans there. "Bring a camera," she said. "Telephoto lens."

Later, Frank invited Barbara to dinner, but she said no, she had a date. He looked hopeful.

"With friends of the female persuasion," she said. "We're going to a movie."

On Sunday morning on the front page of the newspaper there was a picture provided by Gloria Musick of Teddy and her two small sons building a castle of logs on the beach. Barbara stared a moment and then turned the paper over. "I didn't read it," she said, and left for the drive back across the Coast Range, back once more to Florence and Stone Point.

She didn't delay long at Stone Point. Brian Rowland was clearly irritated by her return, but he took her back to the suite, and as soon as she was certain Bailey had had enough time to get the pictures, she left. She drove to Florence, and this time pulled off onto the scenic drive to park and take a walk. The tide was rushing in.

Three times, she reflected, she had gone to the phone to call Gregory Leander, tell him she would be at the coast this afternoon, and each time she had left the phone untouched. He would have met her, and they would have gone to bed. He expected to take her to bed, if not today, then tomorrow or next month. He would wait for her call for a time, and then he would call her. She was not at all certain how many times she would walk away from him. She suspected that he exuded pheromones. Fun and games. It most surely would be that. And, she asked herself, was she ready for that, sex as fun and games?

She had to race a wave to dry ground; the tide was coming in fast now. She stopped in the soft sand and looked to the sea. Huge waves were crashing into offshore rocks and pillars, sending spray fifty feet into the air. Wave fronts raced, stretched upward, crashed, one piling on top another now in the mad dash to land. She tasted salt on her lips. Messages from the sea.

She watched the thunderous waves a long time before she turned to retrace her steps to the car, curiously satisfied, ready to drive over the mountains and home.

On Monday morning, after retrieving the newspaper from the front porch, she glanced into her office and saw her message light blinking. She stepped inside and pushed the message button. It was her father: "Bobby, they're closing in on Ted Wendover, maybe this afternoon. Ted and Carolyn are coming to the office any minute. Get here as soon as you can."

WINTER

FOURTEEN

THE WENDOVERS WERE in Frank's office when she arrived. They were both pale, but Carolyn looked ghastly. Even her lips were colorless; she had not put on makeup, and she looked older than her fifty-one years. She was as still as a carving. Ted was so tight, he looked clenched all over. A tic jumped in his cheek, jumped again. They both had hands of ice when she shook hands with them.

"We've done the drill," Frank said. "They know what to expect. We waited for you to go over his alibis for the time of death for both Harry Knecht and Mary Sue McDonald. Those are the two times they've been hitting him for. So far, it's just been questions, no signed statement. They want that today, and they're arranging a lineup," he added without expression.

That meant they had a witness, or thought they did. She nodded and sat in the third visitor's chair by the big desk. "Harry Knecht first," she said. "What have you told them about that?"

Ted swallowed first, then said, "I was in the Rogue River area near Illahe. I camped out and drove home the next day. I was alone," he added unhappily. "They wanted to know if I saw anyone, if anyone would recall seeing me. I saw a lot of people, but I didn't stop and talk. I had something else on my mind."

She realized he had lost weight since she first met him, only weeks ago. Not a drastic weight loss, but enough to be noticeable. "When did you go down there?" she asked.

"On Thursday, the eighth, I drove down to Brookings for a business meeting. I met with people early on Thursday, and again in the afternoon. Then I drove up to Gold Beach and got a room for the night. I gave them the name and time I got there, the name of the restaurant I ate in. Early the next morning, I left for Illahe. I was in the forest Friday night, most of Saturday. I have a Land Rover outfitted for camping—tent, refrigerator, little stove, like that. I'm often out in remote places and spend the night. That's part of my business."

"So you didn't stop anywhere," Barbara said impatiently. "You cooked out and slept in the woods."

He nodded. "That's exactly what I did." There was a flash of belligerence that faded as rapidly as it had appeared. "It stinks," he said hopelessly. "I know that."

"You said it," she agreed. "Later we'll come back to it, who the people were you met with, why you were in the wilderness. I'm afraid all of it will have to come out, but for now, let's move on. The night Mary Sue was killed, what did you tell them?"

"Wait a minute," Ted said, the tic in his cheek jumping. "Why are you phrasing it like that? What did I tell them, not what did I do?"

"Because you've answered their questions and they have your answers on reports. If there's any departure now from what you said earlier, any discrepancy at all, they'll pounce on it like a coyote after a jackrabbit," she said calmly. "What did you tell them about the night Mary Sue was killed?"

He took in a deep breath. "Exactly the truth, every time. That night was just like every other night we're home. Dinner around seven. We clear the table together. I play a game with Teddy for half an hour or so. He takes a bath and then Carolyn reads to him for a while. I read, or do some work in my office, or watch television while she's up with him. That night, I had some work to do for a couple of hours." He shook his head. "The police went over it step by step when they were concentrating on Teddy. Then, they wanted to know if he could have gone out. I couldn't give them a minute-by-minute account; I still can't."

Barbara nodded. "Okay, it's straightforward. Just stick to it."

"I looked in on him when I finished reading to Teddy," Carolyn said. "It wasn't ten yet, about ten minutes to ten."

Of course, you did, Barbara thought, but she said, "We'll get that in." She regarded Ted. "Did the police insinuate there had been anything between your wife and Harry Knecht?"

He looked down at the floor, glanced at Carolyn, and studied the carpet again. "They, one of them, said it's tough when a man knows his wife is running around, knows who the guy is. He said no one really blames a man for taking steps when he knows he has to. He said a guy in Michigan got eighteen months after killing his wife when he found her with someone. They know," he added in a very low voice.

Carolyn looked agonized. She reached out toward him, then drew back and folded her hands tightly.

"All right," Barbara said briskly. "Have you made any statement about that? Did you respond?"

He shook his head. "I didn't say a word."

Barbara thought for a moment. "When was the last time you were in Mary Sue's house before her death?"

"A few days earlier. Teddy had been over there and forgot his jacket. We walked over together and I chatted with her in her kitchen for a few minutes."

"And Stone Point?"

"Months ago, June. I had business with Brian Rowland. I wasn't up in any of the rooms, just in his office." He looked from her to Frank. "Why?"

"They've lifted prints everywhere," she said. "They'll print you and start comparing them. Nice if we know ahead of time what they're likely to find."

Carolyn made a soft sound and ducked her head. Tears were falling on her clasped hands. "It's all my fault," she whispered.

Ted rose from his chair and, after an awkward pause, knelt at her side, took her in his arms, and held her as she wept against his chest. "Shh," he murmured. "Shh. It's going to be okay."

Barbara wished she could guarantee that. She went to the door. "Why is there never any coffee around here?" she demanded as she yanked the door open and walked out. At the secretaries' offices, she said to Patsy Meares, "Where's Shelley? I want her. As soon as Dad leaves with Ted Wendover. And we need coffee now."

"Shelley's doing something for Mr. Bixby," Patsy said.

"Well, tough. I want her."

Patsy grinned and saluted. "You'll get her."

"And give Bailey a call, will you? I'll be here the rest of the day. I want him, too." She started to walk away, then turned. "Thanks, Patsy."

Back in the office, she said cheerfully, "Coffee's coming. Dad, what time do you have to leave?"

He raised his eyebrows. "They want him at ten-thirty."

Ted was in his chair again, but he had moved it very close to Carolyn's and he was holding her hand. She was calm now, red-eyed, but no longer weepy.

"We don't have much time, Ted." She used his name deliberately; until now, he had been Mr. Wendover. "Are you comfortable with me for your trial attorney?"

He looked surprised. "Of course," he said. "I assumed that from the start."

"Good. Now, Dad will go with you this morning. This is really just routine. Not for you, of course, but for us it is. Dad knows more about the ins and outs of law and constitutional rights than they know are on the books even. He'll take care of you, and I'll start on the million other things we'll have to do. When you're through over there, we'll know more than we do now about what they think they have."

Patsy brought coffee and while Frank poured, Barbara continued to ask questions. She talked about the need to have someone with Carolyn, just in case Ted was held, someone who could field the media, screen phone calls, stay with Teddy when Carolyn had to go out. "Teddy will have to be watched, or some idiot will get to him and ask questions, take pictures, have a real human-interest story. You don't need that. And no one should make statements to anyone." Then it was time for Ted and Frank to go. Barbara walked to the low round table and shuffled papers as Carolyn and Ted said good-bye.

Almost instantly after Ted and Frank left, Shelley tapped on the door. Barbara crossed the room to speak to her. "You're on again," she said in a low voice. "Back to comparing the manuscript Lois Hedrick left at her parents' home and the material found at the cabin at SkyView. You up for that?"

Shelley exhaled. "Oh yes! Right now!" She pivoted and nearly dashed away.

Barbara grinned faintly at her retreating back and pulled the door shut. She said to Carolyn then, "Let's sit over there and talk. It's going to be hard waiting; you might as well be doing something, and I'm going to have to ask a lot of questions."

Frank returned alone. He nodded to Barbara and went to sit by Carolyn on the couch. He took her hand in his and said, "They're charging him with the murder of Harry Knecht. You can go over to the county jail in a couple of hours and see him. I have a list of things you might want to take."

Barbara slipped out of the office while he was talking. Gregory Leander had said Carolyn was a survivor, meant in the old-fashioned sense, and she'd better prove him right. First her son, now her husband. She looked in on Shelley, got a drink of water, and wandered to the reception desk and back, killing time, she understood, but she believed that at this moment Carolyn would be better off with Frank coming on like an uncle than with their team coming on like attorneys.

When she rejoined them, Frank was saying, ". . . most of all, trust. Sometimes it might be hard to answer our questions; it will be for him, too. . . ."

Carolyn left soon afterward. She was composed and dry-eyed, but her look was despairing as she said good-bye.

"Well?" Barbara said when she was alone again with her father.

"They've got three witnesses, Anna Leiter, forty or so, who picked him out of the lineup. She claims she saw him going up the driveway to Stone Point at about five-thirty. The hotel manager saw him in the lobby about five minutes later. And, of course, Brody."

"How good was her identification?"

"Good enough. They booked him."

"Where was she?"

"Bobby, come on. They didn't fill me in with the details. I don't know where she was."

She looked at him sharply. "Do you believe Ted's story?"

He shook his head. "Christ, I don't know." Saying the words, he realized that he hadn't decided. He didn't want to think about it now, especially on an empty stomach. "I'm going to go get some lunch. You want to come?"

She shook her head. "Later. Bailey should be here soon, I hope. What color is Ted's Land Rover?"

He threw up his hands. "Ask him," he snapped, and walked out.

Half an hour later, when Pam buzzed her to say Bailey had arrived, she was at Frank's desk, scribbling as fast as she could write. Heading the list of questions she had jotted: "Where is Mureau?" And the next one was: "Who is Agnes?" It was underlined.

Bailey didn't seem surprised to see her at Frank's desk, but Bailey seldom looked surprised about anything. She filled him in on Ted's arrest.

"So, we have a client, and a million leads to follow up on. First: Mureau, what do you have?"

"Private mining consultant, works out of Denver, but he's everywhere there's a hole in the ground. Report's in here," he said, pulling a folder from his briefcase. "Just scratched the surface so far."

"Mining," she said softly, remembering Lois Hedrick's last interview, someone talking about gold mines. "Go on."

Noncommittally, Bailey said, "I don't know what he had to do with the congressman. Neither does his aide, Mal Zimmerman. He never heard of John Mureau. Anyways, he's got a good reputation, best-in-his-class kind of thing. Worked for BLM for a few years, then went freelance."

"Where is he *now*?"

"Damned if I know," Bailey said cheerfully. "Not in his office. Answering machine's all. Any coffee in that pot?"

"Help yourself. Okay. We need him. First thing. Did you get the hotel guest list? Are the pictures developed? Could you see me on the oceanside balcony?"

He took his time getting coffee and sat down with it before he answered. "Couldn't see you when you turned the corner of the balcony. Got the pictures. They're in there, too. And the list of room numbers and occupants. People next door, Benjamin and Tilly Rothman. She calls him Beanie. Nothing on Agnes." He grinned and sipped his coffee.

"You talked to Knecht's aide? Zimmerman? Where is he?"

"Yes. Yes. Salem. Something of a zealot. You know, glittery eyes, that kind of thing. Said Knecht wasn't interested in mining, just a bunch of other lost causes. Look for a logger. They sent him dead owls, the whole shtick. He's sorting Knecht's papers. Anything turns up about mines, he'll get in touch, but don't hold your breath. He gave me a lot of handouts; they're in the file, too. He's working for an environmentalist newspaper."

"Okay," she said. "I've got a list of things we need to get started on. But keep Mureau up front until we've got him in hand." She began to read from her notes, and Bailey got out his notebook. They were still at it when the door opened and Frank entered, carrying a deli bag.

"Brought you a sandwich," he said, placing it on the desk. "Knew you wouldn't get around to food." He nodded to Bailey and sat down in the other client chair.

She took out the sandwich but didn't unwrap it yet. "Carolyn said that Ted acts as broker, sets up an escrow account and then finds suitable land for whatever the client wants it for. A gas company wants to build a station at Burns, for example. He goes out and scopes the local ordinances, finds the ideal site, and puts down earnest money. All in the name of his company, Wendover Development. So it makes a certain amount of sense that he was in the wilderness, I guess, looking for land for someone."

Bailey nodded. He was eyeing her sandwich, she realized, and she opened it to take a bite. He could buy his own lunch.

"I know he has land or something that Arthur Rowland is after," she said next. "He asked me if Ted was ready to sell. And Ted said he had business with Brian Rowland last summer. Anyway, find out what you can about him and his business." She took another bite; Bailey looked aggrieved but resigned.

"Investigate your client," Bailey said noncommittally.

"Yes. Whatever he tells us might not be the same as what the state digs up. I'd like to know what they have as early as possible. After we begin talking to him, I'll have more for you, natch, but that's for openers. Can do?"

He shrugged. "I'll need help."

"Get it," she said.

After Bailey left, Frank moved to the couch by the low table. "You in a hurry?" he asked. "Want a glass of wine, booze, anything?"

She shook her head and crossed the spacious office to sit in one of the comfortable chairs. "What is it?"

"Nothing in particular, I suppose. The media circus has started. Who talks, you or me?"

"Would you mind?"

"Nope. You stonewall, I talk. Right." He was very good at it; she tended to get impatient, even snappish. "They put Mary Sue's death on the back burner," he said. "That means they'll go after Ted for Knecht, and if they get a conviction, do it all over again for her murder. And it means they don't have to tell us diddly about what they have concerning hers." His gaze was distant, troubled. "Thing is, I keep seeing Mary Sue laid out, her hands full of rocks. Someone made a mockery of her death. Wasn't enough to kill that old woman; he had to have a little fun, too." He sighed deeply, then muttered, "Those damn rocks. Those goddamn rocks!"

He heaved himself from the couch. "You want me to do the indictment appearance, the arraignment? Keep you in the background for the time being?"

She nodded. Just routine, she said to herself. And then, one guy's routine, another guy's journey through hell.

They decided that he would go out the main entrance of the building and meet the press. She could duck out the service door in the rear and beat it.

"I can't avoid them for very long," she said, pulling on her jacket, "but for now, that's good. When they do corner me," she added, "I'll tell them to go ask Daddy."

He grinned faintly, and they walked down the wide corridor together; most of the other lawyers and the secretaries, as well as the clerical staff, were all gone by then. It was very quiet. She kissed his cheek and watched him get in the elevator; then she started down the stairs, trying to ignore the disquiet his troubled little conversation had raised. She tried to banish the image he had put into her head: Mary Sue stretched out on her kitchen floor with her head beaten to a pulp, her arms outstretched, with each hand clutching a rock. The image persisted.

FIFTEEN

THE INDICTMENT HAD been handed down by the grand jury; arraignment had followed, the trial date set, bail denied. All routine, Barbara thought morosely in her kitchen a week before Christmas.

She checked off the list of things she had done, had yet to do. Bill Spassero's present was a beautifully illustrated book of antique cars. She had no real reason to suppose he would appreciate such a book. She shrugged. On Tuesday, she would pick up two Maine coon kittens for her father. Again, she was not at all certain he even wanted two kittens, although they always had had cats when she was growing up, but wanted or not, they were gorgeous, and they were for him. The image in her mind was one of him before the fire, reading a leather-tooled book, with both golden kittens curled up in his lap, purring. The reality might be that they would shred the furniture, eat his slippers, shit in his bed. . . .

And then, perversely, she was brooding again about John Mureau. Where the devil was he?

Bailey had dug up a lot about the man: He was forty-three,

divorced, father of two children, aged ten and eight. He and his ex were on good terms; he supported the kids generously; she was remarried to Milton Freeland, and they had a daughter, aged two.

She wondered if Mureau missed the kids at Christmas.... Ted's grief over being locked up this season was wrenching. Abruptly, she went to her office and called information for Mrs. Milton Freeland's number in Wheeling, West Virginia. She placed the call.

A child answered; she yelled for her mother to pick up the phone.

"Mrs. Freeland," Barbara said then, "I need to get in touch with Mr. Mureau. I wonder if you have a number where I can reach him."

"Why?" the woman asked. "Who is this?"

"I'm an attorney," Barbara said. "My office believes he might be a material witness for a case we're handling. If I could just talk with him, we probably could clear it up in a few minutes." Her every instinct was crying out that this was a mistake, she should have let Bailey do it his way. *Now* she was being warned. Where were her instincts before the fact? There was a long pause at the other end.

"If you have business with him, get in touch with his office in Denver. He's in the book." Mrs. Freeland hung up.

Did that mean he was in Denver? If so, why hadn't Bailey found him? At least, she thought gratefully, she had not given her name and number. Not a step forward, but neither was it a fall.

Bill Spassero picked her up at seven-thirty to go to Frank's party. He was carrying a small Christmas tree trimmed with gold and silver bells. Real gold and real silver, she realized, gazing at it. It was only eighteen inches tall, beautifully shaped, fragrant.

"It's perfect!" she said. "So beautiful. Thank you." It was an absolutely perfect present. She had set the rules a long time ago—no personal presents, no jewelry or clothes—and he followed them meticulously. On a table next to her good chair, the tree made everything else in the room look shabby.

She gave him the book and he said he loved it, putting enough enthusiasm in his voice to get past the awkward moment. He was tall and broad, but what people saw and remembered was his hair, there was so much of it, platinum-colored, as soft as down. Although he looked like a boy dressed for the senior prom, he was becoming a very good attorney, doing exceptionally good work in the public defender's office.

"Wonderful party," Barbara said to Frank at one in the morning. "Good ebb and flow."

He nodded. People had filled the living room, dining room, the kitchen and dinette. He had opened his study, and that space had filled, too. Most of them now were gone. "Good party house," he said. "Bill and Shelley seemed to hit it off."

She grinned. They had been inseparable. When she suggested that Bill might take Shelley home, since she, Barbara, was on cleanup detail, he had not objected.

A few guests still huddled by the fire in the living room, speaking softly, and a few more were in the study, arguing politics. Quietly, Barbara and Frank began to gather up the glasses, cups, plates, silverware. . . . The lingering guests came to realize the party had ended, and gradually the house cleared, until by two, none of them remained, and the cleanup was as done as it would get that night. The dishwasher was chuckling to itself. Barbara stood in front of the Christmas tree with its familiar ornaments. Some she had made thirty years ago, she realized with a start.

"Let's call it quits," she said. "I'll come in the morning and help finish up. You really know how to throw a party, Dad."

"You want to take my car, bring it back in the morning?"

She shook her head. "Unless you're too tired, it would be better if you run over with me. Not the greatest neighborhood to park a nice Buick in overnight."

His mouth tightened; then he said he'd get his coat on.

It was not very cold and it was not raining. She stood on the side of the porch to wait for him to get the car out of the garage.

Earlier, every fine old house on his street had glowed with Christmas lights on bushes, trees, lights from windows; now they were almost all dark. City light reflected from low clouds had turned the sky mauve. Some nights, like this one, with the air calm, the clouds as low as a ceiling that could be touched, she could smell the river from here. It smelled good, alive and mysterious, carrying messages to the sea.

He had backed out and stopped; she opened the door to his big luxurious Buick and got in. The drive was short, twelve blocks, but it took her from his world to a different one, meaner and sordid; she felt she belonged to neither.

It was nearly eleven the next morning when she was ready to leave for Frank's house. "Early enough," she muttered, pulling on a jacket. She had not gotten into bed until three, and she had not gone to sleep for a long time. She opened her door and stopped moving. *He,* Mureau, the man with the scar, stood on her porch.

"Don't you ever call my former wife again! Do you understand?"

"How did you know?" she asked.

"None of your business."

She shook her head in bewilderment. "How did you get here?"

He was dressed in a hip-length Gore-Tex jacket, boots, jeans. He was bareheaded; his scar was a livid thin line two inches long that started near the outside of the bottom of his right eye and slanted in toward his mouth. His face was twisted in a furious scowl.

"Look, Holloway, I have very little to say to you. And I don't owe you anything. You understand? I don't know why you've been trying to find me, and frankly, I couldn't care less, but when you start after my family, that's going too far. Just leave them alone. Butt out." He turned and started to walk away.

"I'll hand you over to the cops," she said. "See how much you have to say to them."

He stopped and faced her again. "Okay, spit it out. Let's see what you've got."

She shook her head. "I don't owe *you* anything, Mr. Mureau. I can put you at Stone Point when the congressman was killed. That's enough to give to the police."

He looked her up and down. "Then why haven't you?" he asked coldly.

Good question, she thought. She said, "I wanted to. I was outvoted." Then she said, "I'm going to my father's house. You know enough about what's happening to know he's my colleague, my partner. I suggest you tag along and talk with us."

He studied her for a moment, then nodded. "I'll follow you."

"I'm going to call him and tell him to expect us," she said. She reentered her house without watching to see if he would wait. She hurried to her office and pushed the automatic-dial button. "Be there," she muttered as she willed her father to pick up the phone. His machine came on instead. "Dad, pick up the phone," she said, and waited a second. "Okay, I'll hope you get this before I show up. Mureau is here. I'm bringing him over. I haven't seen any sign of a gun, but he's mad. If you don't want to talk to him now, just don't come to the door, and I'll try to get him to make a real appointment for the office. Five minutes."

When she went out again, Mureau was in a car parked behind her gray Honda. His car was an eye-hurting metallic green, probably another rental. Well, he fitted right in, she thought, getting behind her wheel; Eugene was green, from the towering conifers to other conifers that hugged the ground, and broad-leaved myrtle trees, hollies, photinias; everywhere she looked, it was green. And the ever-growing grass was as green as June lawns.

Think, she told herself, turning east on Fifth. What were they supposed to do now with a very angry John Mureau? There was little traffic to slow her down; she wished for more. Few people were out on that Sunday morning. She passed the jail, and said under her breath, "Maybe it's a break for you, Ted." She drove past the post office, to the corner of Yuppie Heaven, where she made her turn toward the old section of town and Frank's house. Everyone here had given the grass a final mowing, bushes a final trim; everything was picture-neat, clean, and very green.

Think! she reminded herself, and drew only a blank. Okay, she would play it by ear and hope Frank wouldn't ask too many questions about the sudden appearance of John Mureau. She pulled into his driveway. Mureau followed.

Frank opened the door instantly at her ring. He looked past her with interest. "Mr. Mureau. Frank Holloway. Come on in."

She saw with dismay that the cleanup job looked much less thorough this morning than it had last night. A wineglass was on the table in the foyer, and a pair of white kid gloves. When they stopped at the door to the living room, Frank glanced inside and shrugged. Another wineglass nestled in the greenery on the mantel; a crumpled napkin was at the end of the couch.

"It might be better in the study," Frank said. "Mr. Mureau, let me hang up your coat."

Barbara had shrugged out of her jacket already and was hanging it in the hall closet. Mureau shook his head. "I'll keep it. This won't take long."

"Suit yourself," Frank said, leading the way to his study. "I'm an old man, keep the house warm. Pretty soon, you'll be hot and sweaty, and you'll get irritable and blame us." He sounded agreeable, oblivious that Mureau was more than just a touch irritable already.

The study was better, with less evidence of a late party the night before. Frank moved a small plate from an end table and shifted the lamp, then motioned to the chair nearby. Mureau remained on his feet. "As you like," Frank said, settling down into his old leather-covered chair. Cracks were showing in the brown leather here and there, and he wouldn't have it repaired, or replaced. "But, you see, if you're standing, we'll be talking to your knees, more or less. Doesn't pay to have someone standing higher than you are in a conversation. They found out how harmful it is with Ollie North, remember? The committee members were all lower than he was; he got the good angles; they had to look up to him. Made for mighty good television, poor dialogue."

Barbara suppressed a smile. He had arranged the chairs purposely; when Mureau sat down, if he did, he would be facing the wide windows that overlooked the back garden. A third chair was for her, a straight chair with a padded seat and back, no arms. She sat down in it, and now Mureau had to turn his head to see her, turn back to see her father.

"Well," Frank said after a moment, "you want to tell us why you're here? What can I do for you?"

"You can leave my former wife alone," Mureau snapped. "And get off my back."

"All right," Frank said, not revealing with even a glimmer any surprise he might have felt.

"Mr. Mureau," Barbara said coolly, "we know you were heading for the Stone Point Resort ten minutes before Harry Knecht was killed. We know you were at the Blue Harbor Motel, when you checked in and when you left, without staying the night, after paying cash for the room. We know you intruded on Carolyn Wendover and questioned her. We know you were at Sisters asking questions that concerned the death of Lois Hedrick."

"Why haven't you taken what you think you know to the police?" he demanded, facing her.

"We were retained to protect Teddy Wendover," Frank said, forcing him to turn again. "No one hired us to solve the mystery of Harry Knecht's death, or the other two. But if going to the police is necessary to protect our present client, we will have to do so." His tone was conversational, friendly.

"Wendover did it," Mureau said.

"Why did you send me that note saying Teddy was innocent and that someone was in the bedroom when Knecht was killed?" Barbara asked.

"I don't know what you're talking about."

"Just how long do you think it will take us to get a sample of your handwriting?" she asked scathingly. "I was very careful handling the note. Did you wear gloves when you wrote it?"

Abruptly, Mureau yanked off his jacket and flung it over the back of the chair he had rejected. He walked past Barbara to stand at the window facing out; he was behind Frank's chair now. When he spoke, Frank did not turn to look at him. "I was hired by Harry Knecht to look into a matter," Mureau said. "I was to meet with him. When I got there, I learned he had been killed, and I left."

Now he turned to look at Barbara. "That's all I can tell you."

Frank got up then. "It's eleven-thirty—coffee, brunch, something time." He walked out. "Come with me if you want."

After a moment, Mureau followed, and Barbara came after him. The dinette was in good shape, the table cleared, a small bowl of red and white carnations on it.

"You two stay over there out of the way," Frank said, going around the counter to the working part of the kitchen. The counter was covered with glasses. He had emptied the dishwasher and filled it again; it was chugging away. "I have a party once a year," he said, measuring coffee. "Get rid of all my social obligations at the same time, but it surely does leave a mess."

Barbara sat down at the table and Mureau sat down gingerly opposite her. Equals at last, she thought sarcastically, at eye level, no shadows here. Mureau played a pretty good game himself.

"I'm afraid your story just won't do," Barbara said. "I wonder why you didn't go to the police, especially since you were working on something so secret that Knecht's aide didn't even know about it." At his shrug, she murmured, "Probably you just didn't want to get involved. No one ever does." To all appearances, he had become hypnotized by the bowl of carnations. He ignored her.

She understood what Carolyn had meant when she said he might be a runner, muscular but not heavy. He had moved like a runner, with a sense of pent-up energy and strength. His neck was muscular, at least, and that was really all that was visible except for his hands, which were not very large, not manicured, weathered, but with no visible calluses. His face was weathered, too, not so much sunburned as hardened by wind maybe. His eyes were more gray than blue and his hair was short and dark brown. She remembered what Marion, who wanted to be called Deirdre, had said: He would have been good-looking if not for the scar. That wasn't really right. It was rather that his features were so regular and well proportioned that it substituted

for handsomeness, which Barbara was convinced required unusual features, cragginess, or sharply chiseled bones, something
irregular.

Frank had finished fooling around making the coffee. From
the other side of the room, he said in his most reasonable tone,
"Mr. Mureau, I truly do not want to involve you in any way if it
is humanly possible to avoid that. I sympathize entirely with
your position. But you have information we feel is vital for the
interest of our client, who may be found guilty and put on death
row within the next four months. If what you know will help
our client, we would be negligent if we didn't try to use it, but if
it doesn't help him, then"—he spread his hands—"what's the
point of dragging you through the wringer? We won't."

"Can I retain you?" Mureau asked suddenly. He swung
around to look at Frank.

"To do what?" Frank asked with honest interest.

"To keep me out of this."

Frank shook his head. "That would constitute a conflict of
interest, I'm afraid. But, you understand, of course, that you will
have to tell your story eventually, and I really hope you can see
that it would be better to tell us than the police."

Good cop, bad cop, Barbara thought, and she knew which
was her role. Coldly, she said, "We'll subpoena you, Mr.
Mureau, if you don't cooperate. Believe me, if I have to do that,
I'll drag you through more mud than you knew there was."

"Now, Barbara," Frank murmured. He brought cups to the
table.

Suddenly, Mureau laughed. It was a harsh, almost brutal
sound. "Knock it off," he said. "What little I know won't help
your client. Believe me, it won't. Like I said, I was hired by
Knecht as a mining consultant. He was in Denver last summer at
a conference, and he called me, asked if we could meet, said
he wanted to pick my brain. We met in a coffee shop. He wanted
to know about the cyanide mining process, if there was new
technology that would make it possible in western Oregon. He
knew enough about it that we could discuss it at a fairly technical
level. I told him I didn't think it could be done in a rainy climate,
not today. Then he asked about a man, a geologist, what his

reputation was, and what his specialty was. He wanted to know if he was working, and if so who for. And he made it very clear that this was to be on the QT. I said he might need a detective, not me, but he said not. He wanted someone who knew mining."

While Mureau was talking, Frank had brought coffee and poured it, and then brought cream and sugar. Mureau helped himself to both.

"Okay," Mureau said, after tasting the coffee. "That was June. Two weeks later, I reported by phone. He didn't want a written report." He shrugged. "I never gave it another thought until August, when he called me again. He asked me to meet him in Portland. He named the place, the Rose Gardens, and the time. I got there at three in the afternoon and he was on the bench where he said he'd be, and we talked. He had another little job, he said. He told me the name of a company, a mining development company, a subsidiary of one of the big corporations. He wanted to know what they were up to now, if they were buying up patents, things like that. And he wanted to know if Ted Wendover had any connection with them."

Mureau glanced at Frank and made his shrugging motion again. "I told him I could find out about the mining stuff. But Wendover was out of my field. He said maybe Wendover was just a front, the guy who bought up the property and turned it over to the company later. Some arrangement like that." He scowled at his cup, as if the coffee had left a bitter taste. When he scowled, the scar drew his face up into a grimace, all regularity wiped out.

"When I said no again, he . . . it was like he was begging me to find out something for him. I asked him why his own staff wasn't doing this job, and he said they were to know nothing about any of it. Nothing." After a pause, Mureau said, "I told him I'd do what I could, and he said he'd be at Stone Point in September, he'd keep an hour free on the ninth, that I should come to his room and report. He told me to call as soon as I got a motel room, to let him know I was there. When I called, I told him I had most of what he wanted, and he was pleased, excited maybe. He told me to come over at five-thirty and to bring a bottle of Wild Turkey. He said if I wore black pants and a white shirt with a bow tie, and gloves, and carried a tray, no one would see me—purloined-letter effect, he said. And then he said I was going to love Agnes."

He stood up and walked to the hall door, looked out, then crossed to the windows and gazed out at the yard. "I decided then that I was through with him. I didn't like playing detective. But I got the bottle and the gloves and tie, and I went. I found out that he had been killed and I left again."

Time and again, Barbara had felt herself tense to pounce, and each time she restrained herself magnificently, she thought. He was talking to her father; his attitude, his posture, everything made that very clear. She held herself back yet again.

"But you stayed in the area," Frank said. "Why?"

His shoulders seemed to relax and he turned to look at Frank again. "I suspected that he had been trying to protect Carolyn Wendover, and that's why all the secrecy. I liked him, liked what he stood for. If he was protecting her, I'd go along with that."

"Ah," Frank said, nodding. "And the note about Teddy?"

"They would hang it on him if they could," Mureau muttered. "I felt sorry for the kid."

"And why were you over at Sisters asking questions?" Frank asked, not in a demanding tone at all, but as if his curiosity was driving him.

"One of my contacts said the geologist had been hanging out over there. I was curious. If I met him, two geologists getting together, I thought maybe he'd tell me something. I never found him."

Frank nodded. "You've certainly given us things to think about. Just one little thing is bothering me, though. In your note about Teddy, you also said to find out who was in the bedroom when Harry Knecht was killed. What did that mean?"

Mureau hesitated. He drank his coffee, which had to be very cold by then; then he said, "It figured. If the kid wasn't the one who did it, and no one else ran away, the guy had to be in the bedroom."

Frank glanced at Barbara then, the first time in many minutes;

her cue, she understood. "Mr. Mureau, how do you know no one else ran away?" she asked.

"I read the newspapers," he said angrily. "No one reported anyone else running away."

"But Brody chased someone. It wasn't Teddy, and it certainly wasn't his father. I suggest, Mr. Mureau, that the story the police eventually will put together will be that you walked into the hotel, went up the stairs, carrying the bottle on a tray, and Mr. Knecht opened the door and admitted you. That a few minutes later, you ran out by means of the balcony when the security man Brody entered, and it was you he chased. Did you hear someone in the bedroom?"

He jumped up. "I've told you what I have to say. Do with it whatever you damn well please." He walked to the doorway in a stiff-gaited way that suggested he was determined not to run.

Frank held up his hand. "Mr. Mureau, you asked if you could retain me, and I said no. However, we could retain you as a consultant, and it would be almost the same thing. I don't have to tell anyone my private business, and you'd have a reason to talk with us. What are your rates?"

Mureau stopped and turned to study Frank intently. "Why are you doing this instead of handing me over to the cops? What's in it for you?"

"It happens that I don't believe you killed them."

"But if we have to hand you over, buster," Barbara said, "believe me, you're gone."

"Yeah," he said softly. "I know exactly where I am." He stood undecided, and then returned to the table. "What more do you want?"

"Let's start at the very beginning," Frank said, "and go over it all a mite more thoroughly. The first job Knecht asked you to do for him. Who was the man, and what did you learn about him?"

Mureau looked resigned. "Owen Praeger. He's an expert at sniffing out gold. He can go into a mine and tell you almost to the ounce how much you'll extract, and at what cost. He's mostly unemployed because there's little unexplored territory, and the big companies have gone to open-pit mining with cyanide."

"And who was he working for?"

"Connie Mines. He's the president."

"What's the other company?"

"The Carlyle Company, a gold-mining company, a subsidiary of the Lockner Corporation."

Frank whistled softly. "Big-time," he muttered. Lockner was a multinational corporation into just about everything.

"I told Knecht there wasn't anything they could do with the patents even if they were buying them up. Most of those mines in the southwestern part of the state are in wilderness areas, roadless areas, or they're worked out, or they'd take a fortune to start up again, and for uncertain returns."

"But Knecht thought Ted Wendover was mixed up in it somehow?"

"He wanted to know if he was," Mureau said carefully. "He brokered a couple of the sales—that's all I found out."

"Nothing illegal?"

"I don't know."

Frank leaned back thoughtfully. "Doesn't make a lot of sense, does it?"

"That's what I tried to tell you an hour ago," Mureau said. He stood up. "I'm a mining consultant. I've consulted with government people, all kinds of people. That's what I do. I met Harry Knecht exactly two times on business. If you think the police will hold me for that, go at it. I'm leaving now."

"Mr. Mureau," Frank said calmly, "where can we reach you if we need to? Seems you don't answer your phone or return calls."

"You have my Denver number. If I decide to take you up on the consulting job, I'll be in touch."

They watched him stride into the hallway, back toward the study, and emerge a moment later pulling on his jacket. Barbara waited until he was heading for the front door to say, "And if the police get a tip that they should hold another lineup that includes you, I wonder if Brody will pick you as the guy he chased that day. I wonder if the other eyewitnesses will admit to a mistake and pick you."

He turned to look at her once more, a long, measuring

scrutiny. "I wonder how you'd like it if I say Knecht told me Wendover was mixed up in something crooked and at all costs I was to keep Mrs. Wendover's name out of everything." He nodded to Frank and walked out. Frank strolled after him to make sure the door was closed properly.

"Now where's he off to?" Barbara muttered when Frank returned to the dinette.

"Reckon we'll find out," he said. "I told Bailey to get over here and keep on him until he lights." He was moving toward the other part of the kitchen, then stopped. "Gold mines!" he said, with such absolute disgust, she had to laugh.

"Told you so," she said. He glared at her and then resumed walking. After a moment, she said, "Dad, suppose there is something going on with gold. Just suppose. And Mureau knows what it is and wants a piece of it. But Knecht, who was an environmentalist, idealist, all that good stuff, decided to block it. All we know, really, is that Mureau got into that room, and he ran out."

Frank nodded soberly. Worse, he thought, Mureau knew where Barbara lived, knew where he, Frank, lived, and he seemed to come and go as freely as an unattached sparrow, here, there, wherever he chose.

SIXTEEN

WHEN BARBARA STARTED to make notes, Frank produced a tape recorder. "Had another one set up in the study," he said without a trace of embarrassment. "Figured we'd talk there or here."

She told him about her call to Mrs. Freeland.

"Well, you flushed him out all right." He sat down at the

table and drummed his fingers for a second or two. "We can't keep him under wraps."

"I know." Obstruction of justice was not a pretty situation for any attorney to get mired in; neither was tampering with a witness. "I just want another stab at it first, before we hand him over."

After a pause, he said, "He didn't lie about anything that I could see."

She made a snorting sound. "Right, but boy can he dodge. He walked over and learned Knecht was dead and left."

"But that's how it was," Frank pointed out. "He doesn't even dodge very well. He'll take Ted's place, I'm afraid." He gazed past her out the window, troubled.

She thought how Mureau had gone to the windows and looked out when the questions involved his actions at Stone Point. The police wouldn't provide a convenient window.

"Dad," she said, "we don't owe John Mureau a thing, and we do have a client to think about. Remember?"

"I know. I know. But if neither of them killed Mary Sue, then someone else might get a free ride."

"Dad," she said softly, "you realize that what he told us is all really on record? Who is buying up land, things like that. Even the fact that Knecht loved Carolyn—hardly a secret. I think he told us exactly what it suited his purposes to say, no more than that."

Frank thought about it a second or two, then nodded. "I think we'd better not underestimate Mr. Mureau." He went to the refrigerator. "I have a lot of leftovers. You want some lunch?"

He glanced at her when she made no response. "Bobby?"

"I wonder, in fact, if Mr. Mureau came here to find out how much we've learned about him."

Bailey called while they were eating. Mureau had a room at a motel on Franklin Boulevard, a couple miles away.

"When can we have more information about him?" Barbara asked.

"Hey, it's Christmas," Bailey protested. "I'm expecting a fax tomorrow, but who knows? People aren't too hot to work right now."

"Well, shake a stick at your people," she said. "And Bailey, two more items. Where he was January third and the following week in 1993? And where he was October twenty-second? Like, I need it yesterday, okay?"

"Oh sure," Bailey said. "I'll just give him a call and ask."

After she hung up, she said, "Do USGS maps have abandoned mines on them, do you suppose?"

"Bobby, sit down and eat. They do, and I don't have any in the house."

"But they're in the office library," she murmured. "Maybe I'll go over and have a look."

"What I intend to do is finish lunch, make a fire and read until suppertime, and be in bed by nine. I advise you to do the same."

In the office library a few minutes later, Barbara found the maps she wanted and took them to Frank's office, where she could spread them out on his round table. She unrolled the first map and weighted the corners with books, then got on her knees at the low table to examine it. It not only showed mines; it showed water spigots, she quickly realized; it showed rock formations and trails, sand dunes and creeks, shacks and ranches. . . . "If you stopped on a trail," she muttered to herself, "you'd likely end up as a feature here."

She located the Kalmiopsis Wilderness area and blinked. Parts of it were unsurveyed. That pleased her in some way she couldn't identify. But there was more than just one mine in there, she realized, tracing her finger this way and that, studying the terrain. She located the Rogue River where it was designated a wild river, then traced it westward, until she found Illahe. She nodded. On the edge of wilderness. There seemed to be mines everywhere. It wasn't clear which ones, if any, were working mines. Her finger moved downward along the Rogue River, no longer a wild river now, and she sat back on her heels and let out a sharp, "Ah!" Agness! She had found Agness!

Of course, they had had the wrong mind-set. Searching for a woman, no one had thought about the small town of Agness on

the Rogue River, but it was there, twenty miles or so south of
Illahe. Agness appeared to be the jumping-off place to dozens,
maybe hundreds, of gold mines. She needed help, she realized.
Working mines—who would know? The Bureau of Land Man-
agement? A bureau of mines? Tomorrow, she told herself.
Tomorrow.

After she put the maps away, she called Bailey's number and
left a message on his machine: "Forget Agnes. I found her." She
thought, If you want it done right . . . But she didn't add that to
the message.

Ted Wendover's weight seemed to have stabilized at about
twenty pounds less than it had been a few months ago, but he
had aged ten years. He was haggard and jumpy. "Have you seen
Carolyn? The kids?" he asked as soon as he was brought to the
room where Barbara was waiting for him in the county jail.

The room was tiny, with only a table and two chairs and
space for little else. When they both sat down, moved their
chairs to accommodate their legs, the room was filled.

"Not over the weekend," Barbara said. "Weren't they over to
visit?" She began to unroll the map she had brought along.

He paid little attention. "Yes. I just thought at home they
probably were different. They put on a cheerful face for me."
He shook himself and saw the map then. "What's that for?"

"I want you to point out to me exactly where you were down
there, the roads you took, things like that. Okay?"

"You haven't found anyone who saw me," he muttered.

"Not yet, but we're working on it. Meanwhile, let's trace
your route." She handed him a Hi-Liter.

He began at the coast at Gold Beach and traced the road
along Rogue River to Agness, then north. He turned in away
from the river before Illahe.

"Is that a road?" Barbara asked, peering at the map.

"Dirt and rocks. You need a four-wheel drive up there." He
continued tracing the zigzag road and then stopped.

"Ted, you told us you own that piece of property. But why?
When did you acquire it? What for?"

"I wish I knew," he said bitterly. "For nothing."

Patiently, Barbara nodded. "You brokered other pieces of land around there, didn't you?"

He looked startled. "What's that got to do with anything?"

"I don't know. Maybe nothing, but we're grasping at any straw we can find. Just tell me about it, will you?"

"Sure, but there's nothing you can use. A couple of years ago, about this time of year, Brian Rowland called me to see if we planned to be up at the ski resort over the holidays. His father had business to discuss. He never comes across the mountains. Brian planned to be there, but there was a gale that did some damage on the coast and he couldn't get away. I talked to old Mr. Rowland up at the resort. He told me they wanted to buy some land down around the Rogue, wanted me to broker it for them. I did that before, the Columbia site, and even the ski resort. It got complicated, but I was able to buy the land."

"Complicated how?"

He pointed to the map. "See all this wilderness area? Well, there are private holdings here and there, and when they come on the market, the state or the feds grab them." He looked up from the map and added, "They'd rather keep the wilderness areas intact, not have pockets of private enterprise dotting it. Forest-fire protection, wildlife protection, reasons like that. Anyway, I got the land, but it took longer than I had hoped, and it cost more than they liked. I had to go down there half a dozen times before we were done. I used to take Teddy on trips like that," he said in a choked voice.

Frowning at the map, Barbara asked, "There wasn't anything illegal about that, was there?"

"No. Why would there be? It's just a land sale."

"Okay. Then what? They wanted you to buy more land for them?"

"No, it wasn't like that. Brian called me again and asked if he could bring a man out to the house. The man wanted to buy land in that area, and Brian told him I knew the country down there like the back of my hand." He shrugged. "Not true, but I got to know it pretty well. They came out. The man was Owen Praeger, representing a company called Connie Mines. I was surprised; I'd seen him around SkyView a couple of times. Anyway, he knew exactly what he wanted—old mines and the land surrounding them. He said his company speculated in abandoned gold mines."

"Did you investigate his company?"

He shook his head. "He put up a cashier's check for the escrow account. That's how a lot of people buy land. They don't want the sellers to know who's interested, or the price might get jacked up. It was more or less routine, except I couldn't see why they wanted it. That's when I bought that strip I own. I decided something was going to happen in the region and I might as well go along for the ride. Well, so far, nothing's happened."

"Was there another deal after that?" she asked after a moment.

"One more. This time, I happened to have heard of the company. The Carlyle Company. And I acquired more useless property for them. They came to me directly, not through Brian."

"When was that?"

"Last March. I think they must have learned about Connie Mines buying up mines and they decided to get in on it. Nothing else makes much sense. So, I was back there a few times, four or five actually, and I made the deals for them."

Barbara tried to puzzle it out and failed. "Can you show me on the map where the parcels were?"

He glanced at it and shook his head. "It gets complicated. I have it all outlined on maps at the house. Carolyn will show you if you think it's important. After Christmas," he added swiftly. "Don't bother them now."

"If you were out there so often, it seems people must have come to recognize you or your car."

"I'm sure they did, but I got into Agness a few minutes after the tourist jet boat pulled in, and the mail packet was arriving. People were milling about, taking pictures, heading up to the inn to have lunch, things like that. I just drove straight through."

"And you turned off the highway before you got to Illahe," she said unhappily. "Is that the land that Arthur Rowland wants you to sell to them?" she asked, remembering his words to her up at the ski resort.

"Yes. The old man got testy about it when he found out I'd bought it. I think Praeger told him. Then Brian asked me to come over to Stone Point last June to discuss it. He was sore, claimed I was trying to horn in where I wasn't wanted. It doesn't even touch anything of theirs," he said. "That's why I went out there when I got through with Brookings, to try again to make sense of those purchases, to look at the pieces on the spot one more time."

"And?"

"Nothing. I don't know what they're all up to."

She kept at it for another half hour, but he had said all he knew, apparently, until she asked who had represented the Carlyle Company. "Wilmar Juret," he said, "the president himself. He thought he knew a lot about that part of the state, but it was all book stuff. Not like Praeger; he really knows it. He even met us over there to show me one of the parcels he wanted."

Barbara asked quickly, "Us? Who was with you?"

"Teddy," he said. "He loves to go out with me. We camp and hike. He finds things. He's good company. I would have taken him along in September if I hadn't had meetings in Brookings."

She hoped her disappointment didn't show as she began to roll up the map again.

She was surprised then to hear him say in a gentle voice, "Barbara, you really are grasping at straws, aren't you? Is it looking that hopeless?"

"Not yet," she said with false cheer. "We've just started, remember. We'll do a lot of fishing before we have dinner. That's how it works."

He nodded, but it was apparent that he didn't believe a word of it.

SEVENTEEN

AFTER LEAVING TED, Barbara returned to the office to read some more of the many pages of Lois Hedrick's work that Shelley had arranged meticulously. Shelley had been thorough; she had arranged the pages chronologically, as far as possible, and she had made separate hard copies of everything from Dr. Hedrick's computer that was not among the pages the police had found.

Frank was at his desk, now and then grunting at a report he was reading. She put down a sheet of paper and started on a new one, and then whistled.

"Dad, listen to this," she said, and read aloud. " 'P says gold mountain is real, or will be. Says goldbugs are real, some people can hear gold calling them. Like music, he says. Like voices singing. Sometimes just one voice and sometimes a chorus, like a big concert or something. Says you find a little bit of gold dust and it's like a voice from far off and you just follow it. If it gets loud enough, you start digging. Says southwest corner is Tabernacle Choir.' "

She stopped reading. "That part's in brackets, and then it goes into the tape we heard. It's the note I suspected she would have made. I've found other notes bracketed like that."

"Bobby, don't get in a frenzy," Frank said. "Lois Hedrick's death is not on our plate. Ted hasn't been charged with it, remember."

She was paying no attention. "P. Praeger. Owen Praeger is the man she was talking to that day or night, whenever. The gold expert, a goldbug."

"And you're all set to go off on a tangent."

"I want to see Ted's maps. Boy, do I want to see those maps."

"Christ on a mountain," Frank muttered.

She leaned back on the couch. Tuesday, tomorrow, she had to pick up the kittens, get a litter box and litter for them. Wednesday was the office party. No one would do any more work until after the first of the year; a lot of people would take off, leave the city altogether.

Chains, she thought then. She had not found her chains on the porch, where she was almost certain she had placed them. "Where's a good place to buy car chains?" she asked.

Surprised, Frank looked at her over his glasses. "Any auto store, discount store, dealers . . . Why?"

"I guess auto stores won't be packed. No way would I go near a discount store just days before Christmas. I have to go back to SkyView, and I want to talk to the sheriff again. I want to see the medical examiner's report. If Lois talked to Praeger, someone must have seen them. I want to talk to him—" Suddenly, she stood up. "Oh my God! I saw him!"

"Who?"

"Praeger. At SkyView, I was in the coffee shop, talking to a waitress, and he came in and sat down. She clammed up and I left." She closed her eyes for a moment, visualizing the scene again. "The waitress said something like, What can I do for you, Mr. Praeger. Fiftyish, wiry build, gray hair. Damn! I didn't pay any attention to him. I just got up and walked out." She groaned. "If I'd stayed another minute, I would have heard his voice."

That afternoon she continued skimming Lois Hedrick's papers, but she found nothing more of any interest. She felt very sympathetic when she considered that Shelley had read everything, every word carefully. That was followed by the thought that she should get Shelley a present. She put everything away and stood indecisively for a moment. Shelley. But what?

She pulled on her jacket, turned off the lights, and walked out into the hall. Lounging against the reception desk at the far end was Bill Spassero. He straightened and, grinning, walked down the wide corridor toward her.

"Hi," he said. "I was passing by, thought maybe you could get off the roller coaster long enough for a drink."

From the corner of her eye, she caught a glimpse of Shelley hovering at the door to the little office she was using. "I'm sorry," she said to Bill, who had reached her by then. His grin vanished. "Appointment." She turned to test the door, then said, "Oh, Shelley. That was really good work on those papers. Thanks a bunch."

Shelley stepped out of the doorway, blushing.

Barbara glanced at Bill and said, "Maybe she's free. Why don't you ask?"

His grin came back and he looked past her to Shelley. "Are you free?"

"Oh yes!"

Barbara kissed Bill's cheek and left them in the corridor discussing where they would go. Barbie and Ken, she thought, suppressing a smile. But with a difference, she added to herself at the elevator. This pair of dolls had brains to spare.

On Tuesday she bought chains, then drove twenty miles up the Marcola valley, where the rains had turned summer fields into winter marshes. She had come prepared for the kittens, with a carrying case lined with a soft towel in the car; at her house, she had a litter pan ready. The kittens were as soft as clouds, as golden as sunshine, and as lively as lightning. At home, one scrambled up the side of the chair instantly, the other in pursuit, and she laughed. Thing One and Thing Two, she thought, and watched them tangle themselves into a gold cloud that growled.

The office party on Wednesday was boring, as she had expected it to be, and later that night a party at Martin's restaurant was as much fun as she had expected. Everyone danced, everyone sang.

During the night she heard a child crying in the distance, a soft, plaintive sound that was infinitely sad. She pulled the cover over her head. Later, she heard a strange low-pitched motor noise that went on and on in a monotone, and this time she roused, turned over, and only then became aware of fluff near her face, and more fluff at her neck. "What the hell," she muttered, and sat up. Both kittens tumbled out of sleep, protesting with wails. They had treated the wicker bed she had bought for them as a toy, scrambling up the sides, falling over the top, racing around to do it again and then again. "Lonesome?" she murmured, gathering them together. Her father would love this, she thought then, as the kittens settled down again in the hollow made by the curve of her arm. Thing One and Thing Two purred themselves to sleep, and for a long time she did not move for fear she would wake them up again. A clock, she thought drowsily; that's what she would get for them. She had read that a clock would comfort kittens with its steady *tick tock, tick. . . .*

There was a message from Frank on her answering machine when she got up the next morning. Bailey would be at the house at one; Frank wouldn't be around much before that. She nodded. Neither would she. A clock, and something for Shelley. The kittens chased the bottom of her robe as she made coffee and toast, then pounced on her slippers when she walked to the tiny table with her breakfast. Toys, she thought then. They needed something to play with.

She arrived at Frank's house a few minutes before one, frazzled and grumpy, but that was to be expected. Why did everyone wait until the last minute?

Frank eyed the pretty cloisonné bud vase she had found for Shelley. "Why?" he asked. "You two getting to be buddies?"

"She's done some really good work," Barbara said. "And it's Christmas."

"And she's taking Bill off your hands," he said knowingly as the doorbell rang. He left her to go to the door.

"Ho, ho, ho," Bailey said a second later, entering the living room. He had a thick envelope. "Mureau's a wash, Barbara. More stuff will be coming in next week, but probably there's no point to it."

"Coat?" Frank asked, waiting for Bailey to take it off.

"Can't. We're catching a flight in just about three hours. Down to Hannah's sister in San Diego. A little deep-sea fishing, a lot of sunshine. It's raining, and it's going to rain forever here. Think of me getting a sunburn."

"What do you mean, it's a wash?" Barbara demanded. "And when will you be back? I want you to dig into Owen Praeger."

"Thursday. A week," Bailey said cheerfully. "As for Mureau, it's all in there."

"You mean you're closing down the office for a whole week?" Barbara asked.

"Aren't you guys?" His grin broadened. "Look, Barbara, Monday's a holiday, right? And anyway, anyone who shows up to work will be drunk all next week. Go with it." He handed her the envelope. "You're lucky to get this much this time of year. See you next week. Ho, ho, ho." He gave a mock salute, turned, and walked out with a bit of a swagger. Frank went to the door with him.

It wasn't even really raining, Barbara thought, opening the envelope. A little drizzle and off he went to Southern California. Some detective! The envelope contained many sheets of fax paper, newspaper stories, from the looks of them, Bailey's report, and a thin booklet or pamphlet. It was titled *Summary of Hearings of the Natural Resources Committee Concerning the Collins Mine Disaster of June 3, 1990.* A note in the booklet informed her that the entire matter contained therein had been printed in the *Congressional Record.*

She put the booklet down on the coffee table and started to read Bailey's report. He did not waste words. "Subject: John Mureau," headed the sheet of paper. "Born June 21, 1952, in Pikeville, Kentucky. One brother, one sister."

She was on the couch reading the report when Frank returned.

"Mureau left a message on the machine," he said. "He's going to the DA tomorrow." He picked up one of the faxes.

She nodded, reading. John Mureau, she learned, had gone into the mines immediately after high school, in 1970. Married, 1972; divorced 1986. Injured in a disastrous mine accident in 1974, when he was twenty-two, which resulted in his receiving the governor's commendation and medal for bravery, as well as the prestigious Carnegie Hero Fund Commission of Pittsburgh

Award. Four and a half years of hospitalization and many surgeries followed. Bailey had added in brackets, "More to come
on this." Mureau had left Kentucky to attend the Arizona School
of Mining from 1979 to 1983, worked for the Bureau of Land
Management from 1983 until 1988, when he started his own
consulting business.

When she looked up, Frank was clipping together two faxes
he had finished. "Like the man said, it's a wash," he commented, taking Bailey's report.

She started another fax. This was a human-interest story from
a Pikeville newspaper. "Yesterday, twenty years after his own
catastrophic accident, John Mureau returned to lead a team of
investigators to find the cause of the accident at the Milrose
Mine on October 22, which claimed the lives of four men. Milrose Mine is seven miles from the Healy-Grant mine, where
John Mureau nearly died and his father lost his life."

As she read the story, images formed in her head, the men in
the tiny cars going down into the mine, turning on their lights
as they left the surface, with the black walls closing in on them
in the narrow passageway. Another low train rumbling past,
loaded with coal on its way out. She could see the heavy beams
supporting the ceiling of the black mine, feel the weight of the
earth above her. They left the train cars and made their way on
foot for a quarter of a mile, then started to work, with black dust
swirling about them, their lamps casting eerie shadows, the light
made hazy orange by the dust. And then a creaking that did not
belong, and another, and a crash of falling beams and rocks and
coal all around them.

No one moved. The thunder of falling rocks ceased, and now
cries sounded from men trapped deeper in the mine. How much
earth had caved in? How thick was the wall separating them
from safety? They began to dig carefully, fearful of starting
another cave-in, and from deeper down, they could hear sounds
of other men digging. More ominous, timbers were creaking,
and there were sharp cracking noises, and now and again, stones
rattled as they tumbled from the walls.

After nearly an hour of digging, John Mureau's group had a
passage big enough to squeeze through. One by one, they

escaped the first pocket, but Mureau did not go through. He
turned to help dig out the men trapped beyond this section. The
creaking and groaning of stressed timbers increased; more rocks
rattled down. Working from both sides, they cleared another
passage, smaller than the first one, and Mureau pulled out the
first man to emerge, another one, and a third one, who was
badly injured. He carried and dragged him to the next hole and
to safety. Then he went back, and this time the creaking and
groaning foretold another imminent cave-in, and he was trapped
under beams, rocks, coal, his pelvis broken, both arms broken,
his left leg crushed. He lay there for twenty-eight hours before
rescuers reached him. Out of thirty men, nine survived. John
Mureau's father was among the dead.

Barbara was trembling when she put the papers down. The
worst nightmare, trapped underground in pitch-black, listening
to the earth shift, knowing no one could ever find you in time.

"Why the devil didn't he just go tell what he knew about
Knecht?" Frank said. "He's got nothing to hide, out of it all the
way for the murder of Mary Sue. Damn the man. If he wasn't
going to tell them, why the hell was he hanging around?"

Barbara stood up, unable to shake the feeling of dread the
story had aroused. No more, she thought, not now. Later.

"Story about the investigation of the cave-in last October,"
Frank said, not looking up at her. "He's something of an expert
investigator and witness, it seems."

"I . . . I have to go out," Barbara said.

"You don't want to finish this?"

"Not now. I have to . . . I'll call you later." She fled.

EIGHTEEN

DRIVING AIMLESSLY, OVERWHELMED by the need to escape the images of crashing rocks and coal, darkness and terror, she found herself slowing down on Franklin Boulevard. Diagonally across the intersection was the Comfort Inn Motel. She made the turn. There was his bilious green rental car. She parked next to it.

She approached Room 18, unmindful of the quickening drizzle that now legitimately could be called rain. She knocked on the door.

Rain drummed on her back, on her head; the overhang was no protection at all. At first she thought he must have looked out and seen her and wouldn't come to the door. Then it opened.

"You!" he said, with a look of disgust twisting his face. He started to close the door again.

"Can we talk?"

"You want to tell me what to say to the DA? Find out what I intend to say, cover yourself? Give me some free advice? What do you want?"

"Just to talk."

His face became smooth and blank and he opened the door wider. "You're soaked. Go dry your hair," he said, pointing toward the open door to the bathroom.

She walked past him to the bathroom. Her hair was dripping. She used one of the fluffy towels and then ran her comb through her hair. Drowned rat, she thought, and returned to the other room.

"Your father told you?"

She nodded. "Is that why you keep coming back, trying to decide to go to them?"

He turned away abruptly. "You said you wanted to talk. Your idea of conversation? Ask questions?"

"We know you went into Harry Knecht's room, carrying a tray with the bottle of Wild Turkey on it," she said in a low voice. "We know you stumbled and nearly fell, and dropped the tray. Then you knelt down, and Brody came in. You ran. You left the resort hidden in the back of a Cadillac."

He had stopped moving as she spoke. Now he swung around and asked, "Who's 'we'?"

"Dad and I."

He asked softly, "Did you actually come here alone to tell me that? Don't you think that was stupid of you?"

She shook her head. "No."

"You're right, we have to talk," he said, regarding her steadily. "Not here. Let's go somewhere."

"I'll drive," she said.

He yanked on a jacket, ready. At the outside door, he glanced at her hair. "Don't you have an umbrella?"

"At home," she said.

They ran to the car and got in. The lounge at Valley River Inn, she decided, and headed for the bridge. Traffic was very heavy, with last-minute shoppers heading to the big mall across the river. Neither spoke during the stop-start drive. She was regretting this choice by the time she made the final turn to the plush, sprawling hotel.

Driving into the property, she said, "I can take you to the door and go park."

"Just park. You don't seem to care if you get wet. I have a hat." He pulled a rolled-up hat from his pocket.

She was envious. She parked and again they ran, this time to the covered entrance to the hotel. Inside, she excused herself to go to the ladies' room to dry her hair on paper towels. He waited for her at the large fireplace, where massive logs were burning. A giant Christmas tree perfumed the air. "This way," she said, approaching him. At the lounge she asked for a table by a window, and they were led to one at the far end. At three in the afternoon, it was not yet crowded. Within the hour any table would be impossible. Beyond the window, the river raced, silver and black, lined with greenery on the other side. He nodded at the view.

They ordered, bourbon on the rocks and a glass of water for him, chardonnay for her, and then sat silently, regarding each other. She spoke first. "Am I right in why you keep coming back here?"

"Who told you? Why haven't you taken it to the police?"

"We couldn't. Hearsay."

He became silent again, turning to gaze at the river. "The old woman," he said finally. "Why didn't she go to the police?"

"I don't know. Then she knew she had to and she talked to my father on Friday. He planned to go with her on Monday, but she was killed on Saturday night."

"Hard on him," he commented, facing her again.

"Yes. Harder on her."

"That's what made you go after me," he said.

"Yes. Dad believed her story. He never believed for a minute that Teddy did it."

"Neither did I," he said flatly.

The waiter came with their drinks. She watched Mureau pour water into his and swish it around, then barely taste it. "Why did you go question Carolyn Wendover?"

He shrugged. "I wanted to see her and the boy."

"You saw Teddy?" No one had mentioned that before.

"Yes. He was playing outside the window, looking under rocks, poking at bugs or something. Exactly the way my son does," he added. "And I saw a picture he drew, with him half his actual size. It was enough. I knew that any decent attorney would get him off." He lifted his glass in a mocking salute and took another sip.

Slowly she said, "That's why you came back that time, too. Debating with yourself if you would tell your story." Then she asked, "How did you know where she was?"

"It was clear enough that they were someplace where doctors could get at him. I followed Ted Wendover out one day." He held up his hand when she started to say something. "My turn. We're taking turns, aren't we?"

Mocking her again? She couldn't tell. She nodded.

"After I talk to the district attorney, will you or your father tell what you know?"

"No."

"Why not? Your client is in the clink. Isn't it your duty to do whatever it takes to get him out?"

"He already told them about Mary Sue McDonald. They didn't believe him. If we follow you, they'll accuse us of collusion. We have no proof whatever, just the story of a dead woman, a story that contradicts what she told the police. There's no point in it. It wouldn't help Ted, and it might hurt."

"I told you before, Ms. Holloway, I can't help your client, either," he said grimly. "I repeat it. I can't help him because they aren't going to believe me, either." He stopped her protest before she could even utter it. "I went to the hotel that day and called Knecht from the lobby, and he said to come on up, he was alone. I went up the stairs and didn't see anyone. His door was open a crack. I assumed he had left it open for me and went on in. I stumbled on some pebbles; they rolled under my foot. I dropped the tray and bottle and knelt down by him, thinking he might have been alive. Then Brody came in. You know how it goes from there." He was talking very fast, as if he had gone over this again and again.

"But let me add just a couple of details," he said, clipping his words, talking even faster. "The door was open. He had been killed within the last couple of minutes. I could see that door from way down the hall, where the stairs are, and no one came out. Brody couldn't have been more than thirty seconds behind me, and still no one came out, or he would have seen him. I say whoever did it was still inside the place, in the bedroom probably. The open door to the balcony was a plant. No one could have gone out that way and got out of sight so fast. They didn't find my prints on the bottle because I never handled it until I had the gloves on. According to a newspaper story, the aide, Zimmerman, said that Knecht usually traveled with a bottle of Wild Turkey; they think it was his bottle and that he dropped it when he was attacked." He lifted his glass and this time he took a real drink.

"Just wait a minute," he said harshly when she started to speak. "I'm not through. None of that's as important as the real reason they won't believe me, not after they begin to poke around in my past." His voice dropped lower, a hard voice, biting and bitter. His gaze held hers without wavering, with stark intensity. "I was crazy, Ms. Holloway, paranoid schizophrenia, says so in my medical record. I had hallucinations, delusions. I confessed to crimes that hadn't been committed, and to some that had been. I was afraid people were after me. The whole works. And they'll bring that up and suggest I see a shrink. I'll go in there a pretty free guy, good at my job, content, and I'll come out shrink bait. That's how it's going to be, and your client will be in as deep a pile of shit as he is right now." He finished his bourbon.

"That happened before?"

"It happened before."

She turned away first. "Look," she said, pointing. A great gray heron was sailing past, inches over the racing river. That's what freedom really is, she thought, watching until it was out of sight.

Then she said, "Do you mind if I ask questions? The kind the DA is likely to ask?"

He sighed, lifted his glass to get the attention of their waiter, then said, "Shoot."

"Where was the phone you used inside the hotel?"

"Near the stairs. I walked straight through the lobby, following a sign to the elevators. I figured stairs would be nearby, and a phone. There were four phones. I used one, walked to the staircase and went up. A minute, maybe. Two at the most to get to the top and round the corner, where his room was in view from then on out."

"Where did you get the tray?"

"On a table near the phones. I took a coffeepot and two cups off it and put the bottle on, and stuffed the paper bag in an ashtray, one of those big ones with sand in the top section."

The waiter brought his new drink; he ignored it.

She did the numbers silently. Knecht told Mureau to come up; two or three minutes later, he was dead. Would there have been time for someone to knock on his door, be admitted, go to the sitting room with Knecht, take in the rocks, hit him . . . ? She shook her head impatiently. The killer must have been there already when Mureau called. He went to the hall door and opened it. Then he saw or heard something, and he couldn't get out that way. Mureau coming down the hall? No, he said the door was open when he turned the corner at the far end. Could he have seen it from there? She asked him.

"Not until I got closer, but it didn't move in that time, I'm pretty sure."

"He might have seen you through the peephole," she said slowly, "and realized he couldn't close the door or you'd notice and know someone else was in there."

"There was time to get out after Brody began to chase me," he said. "It was several minutes before others showed up to join him, maybe even longer before anyone got up to the room."

She nodded. "Why didn't you close the door after you went in?"

"I shoved it with my foot, but it caught in the carpet. I was going to put the tray down and go back to close it."

He was covering every base, she thought; nothing yet contradicted what Mary Sue had told her father. "What about the bike?" she asked.

Suddenly he laughed. His face twisted in a new way; the right side drew up tighter than the left. His teeth were white and even, good teeth. "I wish I knew just how much you've found out," he said then. "It would save time. Okay, the bike. The old woman and the granddaughter didn't talk much on the way to the motel. I think the granddaughter was sore, being dragged away from the excitement. I know she drove too fast; the old woman told her to slow down, that she'd make it up to her. Anyway, I jumped out and ran when they stopped, and I had to get my car and get the hell out of there. I was tempted to steal a car, but I saw the bike, a ten-speed outside a Laundromat, and I took it. I left it leaning against a sign at a roadside park a little past Stone Point. The sign said the park wasn't for overnight camping—day use only, something like that. I thought maybe a cop would spot it before someone else helped himself. I got in my car, went back to my motel, packed my gear, and left after it was dark." He held up his hand; he wasn't finished. "Up the road, north, away from everything, on to Portland and a flight out the next day, back to Denver."

"Mr. Mureau, why are you talking to me now?" she asked after a moment.

He shrugged. "Why not? It's going to come out, and you and your father might as well know everything I tell the DA. I guess they'll want me to hang around while they investigate me, then they'll tell me to get lost. Will they lock me up?" he asked suddenly, as if he had not thought of this before. His whole face seemed to go rigid; the scar turned pink.

"I don't know," she said slowly. "Technically, they could charge you with obstruction of justice, or hold you as a material witness, or even a suspect, at least until they investigate you. I don't know what they'll do."

He faced the windows again. The river was all silver now as dusk was settling; the rain had slackened. Soon, lights would play on the surface of the water, moving, shifting, ever in flux.

"I can't be in the jug Christmas Eve," he said tightly, not looking at her.

Christmas Eve. What could he, a stranger in a strange town, have planned for Christmas Eve? She continued to watch the river.

"You're not going to say a word, are you? No advice, no warnings, nothing." He regarded her with the same kind of intensity he had shown before, as if he couldn't help signaling when it was important, when it was less so.

"I can't," she said. "Conflict of interest. I don't think you really need my advice, anyway."

"I have to make a phone call, six West Coast time, and it's going to be an hour or longer. They wouldn't let me do that from jail, would they?"

"No." His children—she understood then. He planned to call the children on Christmas Eve. She remembered his fury with her for calling his ex-wife. He must still care for her, and care deeply for the children. This was a planned call, expected by them, no doubt. She picked up her wine and drank it. Then she said, gazing at the river, "A hypothetical case, Mr. Mureau. We both understand that this is a hypothetical situation I'm talking about." She saw his nod from the corner of her eye. "Suppose someone came to Martin's restaurant to consult with me. A stranger. And he told me something like the story we've been talking about and asked my advice. I think I would tell him to protect himself, protect those he cares about as best he can. Anything he might tell the police could as well be told to them after Christmas as before. There would be little point in bringing still more people to grief." The waiter came to their table and she ordered coffee. She still had to drive Mureau back to his motel, drive herself home.

"They'll ask me if I talked to you and your father," Mureau said when they were alone again.

"Yes. They'll probably act as if they know that we put words in your mouth, arranged the timetable."

"Well, you didn't," he said, and he grinned a very crooked grin.

"After you finish with the police," she said, "will you come over to the office, or Dad's house, whichever you prefer, and let us know how it went?"

"Okay."

"You should take an attorney in with you. We are allowed to advise about that, if you want." He nodded. "And we really do want to hire you as a consultant. We're in over our heads with those land deals involving mines. We'd like to take you out to Carolyn Wendover's house and look at Ted's map, see if you can make sense of it all. Will you do that?"

His nod was slower in coming. "At least we can talk about it," he said.

"I found Agnes, by the way," she said, and told him about the town of Agness. He laughed.

"I never even looked at the real map," he said. "You go by mining districts, Galice, Bohemia . . . like that. I looked for land and mine transfers in the Galice district. I don't think I even noticed any town names. Agness!" He leaned forward slightly. "Is the food good here?"

"Sure. It's very good."

"Have dinner with me?"

This time she hesitated and glanced at her watch. Five o'clock! "Okay, but I have to make a phone call, check in. No one has a clue about where I am."

"You went over to the motel without telling anyone?"

She nodded.

"That was pretty dumb, Ms. Holloway."

"Barbara," she said.

"Not Bobby?"

"Only Dad calls me that."

"John. Not Johnny. Only Mom calls me that." They both laughed. Then he sobered and asked thoughtfully, "Your father keeps track of your whereabouts?"

She made the snorting sound that Frank called unladylike and a bit disgusting. "Fat chance," she said. "We were in the middle of a discussion when I left. He just might think I'll come back to continue it."

He grinned again. "Go on, make your call. If the waiter comes back, I'll ask about a reservation. Will I need a tie?"

"Ask the waiter."

Frank picked up the phone on the first ring; when she told him where she was and with whom, he exclaimed, "Christ on a mountain! Do you know what you're doing? They'll scream you've been tampering with a material witness!"

"I'm not tampering," she said calmly. "I'll explain later. Will you be up after I drop him in a couple of hours? Looks like our dinner is going to be early."

"I'll be up," he said. "Good God, Bobby, be pretty damn careful."

"Oh, I will," she said. "I think he'll tell me all about mining. See you later, Dad."

They did not get a table by a window, and he did not have to wear a tie. She wondered if he owned a tie. He told her about mining.

"When I was with BLM," he said, "we inspected mines and

issued warnings, handed out fines and citations, but nothing happened. They paid the fines and nothing got changed. A slap on the wrist, that's what it amounted to. Then the government began its cutback of regulatory agencies; I got canned. And I thought there had to be a way to get their attention. Sometimes I work for insurance companies, and they adjust their premiums sometimes. That gets their attention." He said this with quiet emphasis and a great deal of satisfaction.

"You go down into the mines to see if they're safe? What if they aren't? I mean, there you are again." Very quickly, she said, "It's no secret that we've been looking into your past. You snooped around us; we snooped about you. I'd think that's the last thing you'd want to do, go back into a risky mine."

He didn't respond, but took another bite of his salmon. After a moment, he said, "I figure that every mine that's ever been dug is going to cave in eventually. The question is when." He shrugged. "I take that into account."

She told him about some of the cases she had worked on.

He told her about the time he stole a bicycle when he was ten and his mother made him take it back. "When I stole the bike over on the coast, I kept expecting her to show up with a switch in her hand," he said gravely.

She found herself telling how terrified she had been at her first trial. And he talked about mines and mining until she realized the restaurant was nearly empty.

"We have to go," she said.

"I know. And you still don't have a hat or an umbrella. I can get the car." He signaled the waiter for the check.

"No way. We go out the way we came in, in a dead heat."

He paid the bill and they went to the door. It was raining hard. "Oregon lives up to its name. Oh well," he said, taking his hat from his pocket. He reached over and placed it on her head and then pulled his jacket over his own head. "Let's go." They ran to her car.

At his motel she said, "Dad and I have Christmas Eve dinner together. Would you like to come?"

He regarded her for what seemed a long time. "Yes," he said. "I'd like that. Use his phone?"

"As long as you want. See you. Around five on Saturday."

All the way to her father's house, she kept hearing bits of their conversation play in her head and seeing the way his face changed with each emotion. *Forget it!* she told herself sharply. He has an ex he still cares about. And he might be crazy.

An image of the crazy neighbor woman came to mind in brutal clarity: Spit had been running down her chin. Barbara was seized by a deep shudder.

NINETEEN

FRANK WAS ANGRY and worried when he opened his door. It was eleven-thirty, reason enough to worry. When he reached for her coat, she said, "Not yet. Wait until I warm up a little." She went into his living room to stand close to the fire.

He sat down, glaring at her. "I hope you realize how this is going to look. You haven't done him or yourself any good spending so much time with him. They'll—"

"Dad, wait. Let me tell you. I didn't advise him in any way. Not really. He'll tell them I didn't." When Frank started to speak again, she said, "Just wait a minute, will you? He had to come back again and again, exactly the way he had to go back in the mine when he could have gotten out whole. He knows what's at stake. My God, he knows!" She spoke rapidly as she told him about her evening, what all John Mureau had said. "He'll go in the day after Christmas, and he has to take a lawyer with him. We'll see to that part. They can't hold him, not with those clippings, a phone call or two."

"A hypothetical situation!" Frank exclaimed. "Christ, Bobby, are you out of your mind? The day after Christmas is Monday, a holiday. They'll believe we've had him under wraps for a week, two weeks, coaching him. And a history of mental illness! They not only won't believe a word he says, you've given them ammunition to smear him, discredit him even further." His voice was harsh with anger.

"Dad," she started, but he shook his head.

"Let's not talk about it tonight. It's late and I'm tired."

"Dad, I invited him to dinner Christmas Eve."

He jerked himself from his chair, his face a mask. "You've gone too far, Barbara. I never brought business home for any holiday! What are you turning into?" Abruptly, he turned away from her. "I'm going to bed." He was almost rigid when he walked from the room.

She was unable to move until she heard his door slam. Then, as stiffly as he had moved, she walked to the front door, hesitated, and went back to the living room to close the fire screen and turn off the Christmas tree lights. Reaching for the last lamp switch, she heard him enter, and she stopped, her hand out.

In a very neutral voice, he asked, "Why did you invite him?"

"I don't know. He's lonesome, misses his kids. Christmas Eve away from his family. I'll make some dinner at my place. . . ." She realized as she trailed off that her actions meant that Frank would spend the evening alone.

"Is that all? You felt sorry for him?"

"What else? Dad, I had no intention of bringing up any business what-so-goddamn-ever."

"I'm sorry," he said then. "Of course you can't cook dinner for the fellow. He hasn't done anything to deserve that."

Even as her guardedness was washed away in relief, she knew there was something still between them, still unspoken, something that would have to be voiced eventually.

Saturday, she had changed clothes three times, dissatisfied with the result each time, and settled at last for a black wool skirt and a white sweater. Her skirt was covered with golden hairs at four in the afternoon when she arrived at Frank's house. She brushed off as many as she could and went to his door, holding the pet carrier under a towel. The kittens were mewing piteously.

"Merry Christmas!" she cried when Frank opened the door. He ushered her inside and eyed the towel and carrier.

"What's that?"

There was no denying what it was; the kittens wanted out. She set the carrier on the floor, removed the towel, reached in with both hands and brought them out, and put them down.

"Kittens," Frank said in a disbelieving voice. "You brought me kittens?"

"Think of it as a lease," she said hurriedly. "A three-day trial. If you don't like them after three days, back they go, and I give you a backup present."

"Kittens," he said again. They had huddled only a second or two, and now they were racing down the hall toward the kitchen.

"Maine coon kittens, Dad."

He followed the kittens to the kitchen, where one was already leaping for the fringe of the holiday tablecloth in the dinette. Frank acted as if he couldn't yet believe his eyes.

"I'll go get their gear," Barbara said, hurrying to the door. "He'll like them," she muttered. "He will." She had a shopping bag with the litter, the pan, food and dishes, toys, clock, and their registration papers. She took it inside and showed him the items.

"You paid a fortune for kittens," Frank muttered.

She rolled a hollow ball with a bell in it and both kittens raced after it. "One more thing," she said, and went back for their bed and pillow, which they had not yet slept in. She put it in the living room near the fire, hoping the warmth would tempt them to use it as a bed and not just a jungle gym.

Frank gave her a Seiko watch that made her gasp. "I'll be afraid to wear it," she said, gazing at it in delight. "Or I'll be checking the time every minute or two."

They had a glass of wine together, but she noticed that he kept tracking the kittens. They had discovered the Christmas tree. She hadn't thought of that, how attractive the ornaments would be, how tempting the tree itself would be. Then they were distracted by the dark under the couch and they made up a new game of hide-and-seek that involved fierce growling.

"Dad," she said, "if they're too much, I'll take them home."

"You said a three-day trial. Maine coons," he said thoughtfully. "Get big, don't they?"

"Their father weighed in at nineteen pounds, the mother eighteen," she said.

He nodded. "Big."

At five John Mureau arrived carrying a bunch of flowers in one hand and a bottle of Grand Marnier in the other. In the foyer, when Barbara reached for the flowers, he said, "Actually, they're for Mr. Holloway; the bottle's for you. I noticed that he's a gardener."

He was wearing a dark gray suit and a red silk tie that looked suspiciously new. As soon as his hands were free and they both had thanked him for the gifts, he shook hands formally with Frank.

"Better get these in some water," Frank said. "Barbara, you want to give our guest some wine, a drink?"

"If you'd like, I could arrange the flowers," John said. "One of the skills they taught me in a hospital." He studied the bouquet a moment, then added, "Three vases."

For a moment neither Barbara nor Frank moved, then Frank said, "Well, come on. Dinette table." He led the way. "I have a few things to attend to in the kitchen. Barbara knows where everything is."

He busied himself in the kitchen and Barbara rounded up the things that John needed: newspapers, a pan of water, vases, scissors. . . . She sat and watched as he clipped stems, studied the flowers, clipped again, and began to separate them into groups, talking most of the time.

"They said you try to mimic nature, but that's just because they didn't know what else to say, and that was wrong. In nature, flowers grow every which way, crowd each other, some take over. What you really want is to position each one in whatever way it looks best. . . ." He had taken off his suit coat, rolled

up his shirtsleeves; his hands were very deft, slender and
sinewy.

Now and again she glanced up to catch her father's gaze on
John or her. She could not read his expression. The kittens
romped underfoot. Good smells were all around. Bach fugues
played from the living room.

Then Frank said, "Way I figure it, the circuits will be tied up
for your call. Might take half an hour to get through, or maybe
longer. We'll eat around eight, a bit later if we have to."

He brought a silver tray of snacks to the table and stood surveying the arrangements that were nearing completion. Barbara
had found a slender cut-glass vase that her mother had reserved
for very special occasions. It now held a red carnation, a white
rose tinted with pink so faint it hardly showed, a bit of holly,
and a spray of delicate fern. Frank gazed at it. His voice was
husky when he said, "They taught you well. Good arrangements. That one could go on my desk in the study." He returned
to the kitchen and got busy at the sink.

"And this one in the foyer," Barbara said after a moment.
"And that one ... living room, I guess. They are all very
beautiful."

Then it was time for John to try to place his call. Barbara
showed him to the study, carrying the cut-glass vase with her.
She could feel Frank's gaze as she walked from the dinette into
the hallway, out of his sight.

She cleaned up the mess on the table, offered to help with
dinner, was refused, and sat down with her wine to keep Frank
company, only to find that she had nothing to say. The bell in
the kittens' ball began to ring as they batted and chased it. She
could hear nothing from the study, and that was just as well. She
didn't want to hear his voice when he spoke to his ex-wife and
his children.

Dinner was served at eight-fifteen. Frank had marinated a duck
in lime juice and onions and Chartreuse and he flamed it with
burning sugar cubes at the table. There were bright vegetables,
and wild rice with pine nuts, dinner rolls he had made, salad

from his garden.... Everything was as delicious as it was beautiful.

"He does it to shame me," Barbara said to John. "I'm afraid I burn Jell-O."

John and Frank began talking about an elaborate cat box to be built in the yard, with a closed chute to the house, screened sides to keep neighborhood cats out.... The plans got more and more involved and complicated; they were sketching their ideas as they talked.

When Barbara got up to clear the table, they both stood up to help. They all stopped in the hallway to laugh at the kittens, one of them on the first step, batting the other away as it tried to climb up.

"King of the mountain," John said. "Do they have names?"

"I've been calling them Thing One and Thing Two," Barbara said, "but it's up to Dad to give them real names."

Frank and John both laughed at her names. "I can see myself going up and down the street yelling, 'Thing One, here, Thing One!' " Frank said. "Guess that's their names, though."

Over dessert, a steamed fig pudding and coffee, John began to talk about a volcano in Colombia that was spewing out gold along with lava. "It happens that way," he said. "A layer gets deposited, covered over with pumice, lava, whatever else is shooting out, and eventually it gets covered with soil and rocks. That's your mother lode. That's not the only way, but it's one people are watching right now. They'll be in there in asbestos boots trying to dig it out."

"Is it true that some people claim gold calls them, speaks to them, leads them to mother lodes?" Barbara asked.

John shrugged. "We've all heard that. 'Singing in the blood,' some call it. Everyone in mining knows someone who knows someone who's had gold singing in his blood. It drives some men crazy, hearing the blood song of gold. I seem to be deaf." He finished his coffee and said, "I volunteer for cleanup duty. It's the least I can do after one of the best meals of my life."

"We'll all do it," Frank said gruffly. "There isn't a lot."

There never was when he cooked, Barbara thought, tying on an apron in the kitchen a few minutes later. John put on another one and started washing the few pots and pans. Frank stowed away leftovers.

When John looked around for something else to wash, Frank said they were done.

"I should be going," John said. "Thanks for the evening, the dinner." He took off his apron.

Frank had become sober-faced. "They're going to believe in their hearts that we've advised you this way or that," he said. "I'm going to advise you and you can honestly tell them I did. Don't go in alone. I can give you the names of three attorneys, all good guys, and one of them should be around. Tell whoever it is that I sent you. Level with him."

John nodded. "I will. Thanks again."

Frank went to the table and wrote down the names on a grocery order pad, tore off the page, and handed it to him. They all walked to the door together. When they passed the stairs, both kittens were in a tangle on the first step.

"Sleep heap," John said.

He shook hands with them both at the door. "I'll give you a call when it's over."

"You tired?" Frank asked Barbara when they were alone again.

"Not much. You?"

"Nope. Want a bit of the Grand Marnier?"

"I'll watch you. I don't want a bite or a drink of anything. You really outdid yourself, Dad. It was a fantastic dinner."

She waited in the living room by the fire while he went to get his drink. She felt content, which she attributed to the wonderful food, her lovely watch, good company, and the awareness that the kittens were successful after all. At the same time, she felt vaguely sad and dissatisfied, which she attributed to perversity.

"Good evening," Frank said, reentering the room. He sat down and contemplated the Christmas tree. "Remember when we painted all those wooden ornaments? You were eight, I think. So careful, so diligent. It got way past your bedtime and you insisted they had to be finished that night."

She had no memory of that part of it. She remembered painting them, how beautiful she had thought they were. "I loved making the cookies," she said. "Decorating them all. Do they still make those silver sprinkle things?"

"Probably. I'm sure they're poisonous. Nothing natural comes in silver, except silver."

"I remember the year I stopped believing in Santa Claus. I tried and tried to find out if you and Mother still did, because I didn't want to spoil your Christmas."

"That's the year I knew you'd be either a Jesuit or a lawyer," he said.

They reminisced, fell silent, and reminisced again.

She brought up John Mureau. "I like him a lot. He could become a good friend if he didn't live so far away." Her father's expression changed back to the wary look he had worn earlier. "I said a friend, Dad. That's all."

The fire had burned itself down to glowing embers, but it was too late now to add another log. He gazed at the glow and said, "I like him, too. He's a decent man, comfortable to be with. I think they'll hold him for a time, out of annoyance, if nothing else. They'll check him out and turn him loose, probably without any publicity. But, Bobby, they will check him out from here to forever; they'll have whatever medical records there are, because they'll know if you can't find any other way to get Ted off the hook, you'll have to use John to try to discredit their eyewitnesses. You won't have any choice but to call him."

She felt a surge of ice, as if a lightning-fast glacier had flowed over her, through her. Suddenly she understood the cause of his anger earlier. He had assumed that she had looked ahead, exactly as he had done, into the next few months, the trial, but she had been stalled in time, living moment by moment. Unbidden, a memory flashed into her mind, a classified ad she had smiled over: "Wanted to trade, two lambs named Jennifer and Peter for two lambs without names." She knew his crooked smile, his deft, almost delicate hands, the comfort of his presence. She knew his name.

TWENTY

ON THURSDAY JOHN called. The police had held him forty-eight hours. Frank took the call in his office, and when he hung up, he said, "He's mad as hell. They told him to get lost. He wanted to know if we still want him as a consultant. He'll be around after he cleans up. An hour or so."

Barbara put down the notepad she had been writing on and shook her head. "He should just go home."

"I'll tell him that." He regarded her from across the office, then added, "I'll let you explain why."

She said, "Shit," and he told her that was not proper language for a business office. She repeated it several more times.

John was still angry when he arrived; his face was rigid, fixed in a twisted grimace. He glowered at Barbara. "It was just like I said it would be. At first they were all over me, asking questions for hours, and then Jeremy Cushman gave them some numbers to call, and they went away. When they came back, they were . . . patronizing," he said in a grating voice. "They said maybe I should sleep on it. They wanted to know if I had flashbacks very often, when was the last time I saw my doctor."

Jeremy Cushman was one of the attorneys Frank had recommended. Frank held up his hands. "At least they let you go," he commented. "No charges?"

"They're thinking about it. Jeremy said they couldn't hold me, but they want me to hang around a couple of days. I'm to keep in touch. They'll let me know when I can go." His hands clenched, opened, clenched again. "They're getting a bushel of faxes from Kentucky. It will take them a couple of days just to

168

read everything. I told Jeremy to get copies of everything for me, too."

"It'll take them more like a week or ten days," Frank said thoughtfully. "They'll want signed statements, and this time of year . . . You comfortable in that motel?"

"Is a gorilla comfortable in a cage?" he snapped.

"I thought we might be able to find you an apartment on a weekly basis, something like that."

John rubbed his hands over his face. "Sorry," he said then. "That would be better. I didn't think of it."

"Well," Frank said, "you want to start that consulting job?"

John shrugged. "Sure."

Barbara called Carolyn Wendover. They could come over anytime, she said. Half an hour later, Barbara, Frank, and John drove into the driveway of the Wendover house.

The house was gaily decorated with lights in every window, lights strung on the decks. Inside, the Christmas tree was trimmed entirely with homemade ornaments, among them a chain made with red and green construction paper. Barbara bit her lip. She had made chains like that when she was little.

Carolyn was wan and tired. Gail was nearly as pale and worn. Barbara introduced John, and they all shook hands. Gail pretended not to notice his scar, and Carolyn said, "You came out to Crag Manor."

"I'll explain," Barbara said.

Carolyn glanced at Gail and let it drop. "My parents were here," she said, taking coats. "They left yesterday. It was a bit of a strain." The boys, she said, were watching a movie, but even as she said it, Teddy came up the stairs from the lower level.

"Hi," he said, looking around them, obviously looking for Ted.

"Teddy, you remember Mr. Holloway, Ms. Holloway, don't you? And this is Mr. Mureau. My son Teddy."

John held out his hand and after a second Teddy took it, looking embarrassed. He stared openly at the scar. "What happened to your face?" he asked.

Carolyn made a soft sound and Gail said, "Teddy, is the movie over?"

"I had an accident," John said. The harshness was gone from his voice; it was almost tender now.

"Does it hurt?"

"No. Not at all."

Then Carolyn offered them coffee, wine, anything, and when they said no, she led them to the study, where the maps were. "Ted told me Monday that you wanted to see them. If I'd known last week, anytime, I would have said come right over. He should have known nothing else matters now. I got them out for you." The maps were rolled up on a desk that was clear of anything else. "He always used to put them on the corkboard when he was using them," she said. "The pins are over there."

John unrolled the maps; the first was Curry County, then Coos County and Josephine County. The Coos and Josephine County maps had been meticulously cut to fit the Curry County outlines. Only when all three were in place, lined up with longitude and latitude lines even, were the parcels of land clearly visible. Ted had outlined each one with a Hi-Liter: green for Rowlands, blue for Connie Mines, pink for Carlyle Mining Company. His small finger of land was outlined in yellow, minuscule at seven and a half acres, compared with the other three tracts, which were vast.

John whistled, then said, "Must be over a hundred thousand acres."

About a third of the land was south of the Rogue River; all of it adjoined national forests, wilderness, or state lands. Fingers of the private lands reached into wilderness, turning some public lands into peninsulas; in one area, a small island of national forest was totally surrounded by private lands. Some bits of the encircled lands extended to the river, but the piece on the south side, Carlyle's property, had no riverfront at all. The little strip Ted had bought fronted the Agness/Illahe Road; across the road the land was state forest, and then the Rogue River.

The tracts had long been privately held, but with the brilliantly outlined boundaries, the visual statement of encroachment was dramatic. Whether public into private, or private into public could be argued, but the long, narrow fingers going both ways were graphic: landgrab.

Barbara backed away, making more room for John and her father, who both seemed entranced by the maps. She noticed Carolyn in the doorway, holding a manila envelope. She handed it to Barbara, and together they stepped into the wide corridor outside the door.

"Ted told me to give you all of it, the previous owners' names, sales figures, whatever you want. He's afraid," she whispered, her arms wrapped tightly about herself. "I'm afraid."

She was leaning against the wall, near a large photograph of a violin and two hands. Barbara looked past that one to another; she had seen them all coming up, but briefly, without paying a great deal of attention. She saw now that they were all black-and-white studies of a violin, the violinist, hands, two bows, two violins, the silhouette of a slender woman playing. . . . There were a dozen photographs on the two walls, beautifully mounted and in narrow silver frames. "You?" she asked.

Carolyn looked at them indifferently. "Me. Nineteen, twenty, about that. My father did them. That's how he sees the world, in black and white. He thinks they wouldn't be holding Ted without good cause." Her voice was bitter.

"You offered coffee a while ago," Barbara said. "Okay if I change my mind?"

Carolyn pushed herself away from the wall. "Come with me," she said.

They walked through the bright, spacious house without speaking until they reached an enormous kitchen, with a cooking island in the center. "When Ted's here, we often cook together," Carolyn said. She paused as she measured coffee. "We cried together yesterday, after my parents left and I went to see him. I guess I looked pretty awful. We both cried. He said if he'd been able to do that fifteen years ago, none of this would be happening now."

"Until the boys in the lab coats come up with a time machine, we're stuck with what we've done," Barbara said. "You, me, Ted—all of us would fix our own lives a different way if we could."

For a moment neither spoke; Carolyn finished with the coffee-maker. Then Barbara said, "You told us you never leave Teddy alone in the woods because you're afraid he'll get lost. But he's so good with landmarks. He knew exactly where to start up the cliff at the beach."

Carolyn stiffened and lifted her chin; her expression had changed, with no trace of the defeat she had shown a moment before. "What do you mean? We never left him alone up at the resort. You can ask anyone."

"I know you didn't," Barbara said. "But not because you were afraid he'd get lost."

"No," Carolyn said after a moment. "Years ago Arthur accused him of harassing smaller children in the pool. He said if it happened again, he'd call for a board meeting, force us out. He hates Teddy." She became vehement as she continued. "Some people are like that with him; an irrational hatred possesses them. But we owned our house up there long before there was a resort. We like it and use it often. The agreement with the resort is complicated, access rights, things like that. We didn't want to sell and find something else, and I didn't want any more trouble from Arthur. We decided to take care of it by keeping Teddy with one of us when we're up there. We did most of the time anyway; it wasn't a hard decision." She took cups from a cabinet and poured coffee for them both. "We told Reid and Gail we were afraid he might get lost, and they accepted that."

They sat on high stools at a counter with their coffee.

"You're talking about the father, aren't you? Arthur Rowland?"

"Yes."

Barbara thought about this for a moment, then asked, "Does Brian Rowland feel the same way about Teddy? Is that why you didn't take him with you to Stone Point that day?"

"Like father like son," Carolyn said. "Brian backed up Arthur all the way ten years ago. I never stay at Stone Point, or enter the lodge at SkyView. I don't know what's the matter with them. They seem almost afraid of Teddy."

"What about the other son, Cy?"

"He's all right. He manages the shack, and I see him up there, or on the beginners' slopes, giving pointers. Something happened to him," she said, squinting as if trying to see into the past. "I never knew what it was. He was ready for the Olympic ski team; he was good enough. Then he gave it up."

"What's wrong with Arthur, besides age, I mean?"

"They say he hurt his back skiing. He's had a cane as long as I've known him. He can't ski any longer, and I think he's insanely jealous of anyone who can." She paused, then asked, "Who is that man? Morrow, Mureau?"

"He's a mining consultant Harry Knecht hired, and now we've hired him."

"Why did he come asking me those questions?"

There were voices in the hall; Teddy stepped into the kitchen and said, "They want to see my rocks." He ducked out again and the voices faded. Carolyn looked at her coffee cup.

Barbara reached across the counter and put her hand on Carolyn's arm. "It's been hard, hasn't it?" She felt the muscles stiffen, then relax.

"It's been hard," Carolyn said in a low voice. "From the start my own parents urged us to put him in an institution, so he would be with his own kind, they said. They still argue for it. My father . . . he's a lot like Arthur." She shrugged. "We have a trust for him, so he'll never be a financial burden to Gail or Reid. They swear he'll always have a home with one or the other of them. But they'll have careers, get married, have their own families. . . . Ted is going mad with worry. And Teddy misses him so." Evidently she had forgotten that she had been asking about John.

She talked about the couple who had come to stay with her and the children. "They're more like grandparents to the children than my parents ever were. Especially to Teddy." Then Teddy stepped into the kitchen.

"I told them the best rocks are in my room. They want to see them." He looked at Barbara shyly. "You want to see them?"

She slid off the stool. "I'd like to very much."

He led the way to his room on the top level of the house. Up here, the halls were decorated with circus-animal prints. And his room was a little boy's room in every way, except for the size of a desk, and a double bed. Adult furniture in a boy's room. A robot was by the bed; cars and trucks were lined up before a model of a filling station; comic books were scattered about, posters of action-adventure heroes covered much of the wall space. On the windowsills were many rocks, some no bigger than marbles, some as big as a man's fist. John went over to kneel before them, with Teddy at his side.

"You know what they are?" John asked.

"Some of them. Agates. You wet them and they get shiny." He put one in his mouth, then held it up, a translucent ovoid.

"Another way," John said, "is to put a coat of oil on them. You get a little cooking oil and a paintbrush and just paint it on. They'll stay shiny a long time." He picked up a rock. "This is picture jasper, a very fine piece. And that's blue agate." He picked them up, named them, put them down again.

"This is gold," Teddy said, handing him a rock.

"I'm afraid not," John said. "It fools a lot of people, though. They call it fool's gold, pyrite. Look, I'll show you how you can tell. I need a penny for this." He pulled some coins from his pocket, selected one. "Good. Let's see if it'll scratch the pyrite." He scraped the edge of the penny against the rock, wet his finger in his mouth, and rubbed the mark. He showed the result to Teddy. "If that was gold, you'd see a scratch."

"Try it again," Teddy said, handing him another rock.

"Ah," John said. "You do it this time."

Carefully Teddy drew the penny across the other rock he was holding; he wet his finger exactly as John had done, cleaned the mark, and then examined it. "It's gold!" he cried. "I told you so! See, it made a mark."

"It's gold all right," John said. "Where'd you find that one? Do you remember?"

"Sure. Dad and me and this guy went to a cave and Dad said you stay up here but don't go outside and we'll be right back, and I said can I break open some rocks, and he said I could. I broke some open and that piece came out." He put the rock back on the windowsill. "I have a hammer to break rocks with."

"Your father and the other guy went back farther in the cave?" John asked. He picked up another rock and turned it over. Barbara edged in closer to see the rock with gold. It looked lumpy, dark gray; she could see a thin streak of gleaming yellow.

"Yeah, they had flashlights."

"They call this snowflake obsidian," John said. He pointed to the rock. "See that white stuff? It sort of looks like snow."

"I made a snowman," Teddy said. "I put rocks in for eyes."

"Did you show the other guy or your dad the gold you found?" John asked, turning another rock over and over.

"I forgot. I put it in my bag."

"This one's Oregon opal. It looks good if you keep it in a jar of water." He glanced at Teddy. "Who was the man in the cave with you and your dad?"

"Mr. Praeger," Teddy said. "He said does he have to come with us and Dad said yes and he said he didn't want to be responsible, or something."

"Some people are like that," John said; he moved on down the line of rocks.

Neither Barbara nor Frank had stirred after their simultaneous motion to get a glimpse of the gold; neither spoke while John continued to tell Teddy what rocks he had in his collection, how to care for some of them, how fine some of them were.

Finally John drew back. "That's a great collection, Teddy. You picked out exactly the right ones to keep in your room."

Teddy was smiling broadly. "You want to see my robot?"

"Not this time," John said. "It's getting late. Your mother probably wants to start dinner. We'll come back, if that's okay with you."

Teddy nodded. Barbara wanted to hug and kiss him, but she thought that boys his age didn't go in for that sort of thing; instead, she held out her hand. His handshake was very soft and gentle.

"Thank you, Teddy. It was awfully nice of you to let us see your collection. I'll come back, too, if that's okay."

"Yeah. And I'll show you my other stuff."

"I'd like that," she said, and turned to leave the room.

Carolyn was still in the doorway. She ducked her head and walked down the hall, speaking fast. "Well, if you have to go, coat time. They say it might snow in the next day or two. I hope it does. We all love the snow." She was nearly running.

The others followed slowly, with Teddy tagging along. When they reached the hall to the front door, Carolyn was serene again.

"Mrs. Wendover," John started, but she shook her head.

"Carolyn."

"Carolyn, would it be possible to borrow Ted's maps for a few days? It's pretty complicated."

"For as long as you like," she said without hesitation. "I'll just go get them."

They put on their coats, and by the time they were ready to leave, she was back with the maps. She handed them to John. Then she leaned over and kissed his cheek. "Thank you," she said.

In the car, Barbara waited until Frank pulled out of the drive onto Bear Hollow Road. Then she said demurely, "Dad, I think we've struck gold."

He cursed.

TWENTY-ONE

"THERE ARE SEVERAL ways to get at the gold," John said in Frank's house later that evening. They had taped the maps to the wall of the second-floor room that Frank had outfitted as an office for Barbara.

"Here, for instance," John said, pointing to a spot marked with crossed picks. "Heartbreak Mine. Tells you something, doesn't it? We're talking hard-rock mining here. Someone worked that mine with a pick, shovel, and basket. You dig out the ore, crush it, and then use a sluice of some kind. Pure gold's

specific gravity is nineteen point three, heavy. Say you have a
ton of ore. In theory, you wash away the lighter stuff and what's
left is gold, but it's never that neat. It's still mixed with whatever it's found in in small pieces, or sands, maybe greatly
reduced in volume now, say down to a yard. You can pick out
the gold grain by grain, or you can use chemicals to extract it.
The principle's the same if you're an individual working alone
or a big company with heavy-duty machinery. Some sluices
were half a mile long. Some are the gold pans you can buy for a
few bucks. They all work alike. The light stuff is floated away;
the heavy stuff sinks and is recovered for further processing."

"They all need running water," Barbara commented.

"Yeah. They could set up a series of conduits, or maybe a
waterwheel, whatever they could rig to bring in enough water to
wash the junk away. A bucket would work. A big problem is in
the crushing equipment. Gold comes in quartz ores, tellurides,
sulfides of various kinds, including pyrites; some of it lets off
pretty foul dust when it gets crushed, or toxic gases when it's
treated chemically or with heat. On a big scale, it takes heavy-
duty machines to do the crushing. It's all a mess." He put his
finger once more on Heartbreak Mine. "That guy probably used
a sledgehammer, some mercury to separate out the gold from
the sands—mercury bonds to gold. Then he heated it in a long-
handled skillet to melt the gold and vaporize the mercury, and
probably he ended up with a lump of pure gold and mercury
poisoning."

"Could you tell anything from that piece Teddy found?"

"Not much. Not without seeing what it came from. The fractures were new on the side that showed the gold streak; it didn't
go all the way through. From the outside, the weathered side,
nothing would have showed up. How deep it went into the
bigger hunk, who knows?"

"How valuable would that piece be?" Barbara asked,
thinking of it out in the open on the windowsill.

"As gold, a few dollars, maybe. Ten, twenty. You can't tell if
it thickens as it goes into the rock, or if that's all there is, what
you can see. As a specimen, whatever you can get. A collector
might go up to a hundred or more."

Frank was scowling fiercely at the maps. "I'm going to make us all something to eat," he said. "Tell you this, Bobby. There's gold all right, and it's going to stay exactly where it is."

"He's got a point," John said absently, still engrossed in the maps. "Wish I knew where that hunk Teddy found came from."

"I'll ask Ted," she said, and presently she wandered out after her father, remembering the phrase from Lois Hedrick's manuscript: ". . . gold mountain is real, or will be."

At dinner she said she would take the maps when she visited Ted the next day, let him pinpoint the mine Praeger had taken him and Teddy to see, the mine where Teddy had found the gold.

"Can I come, too?" John asked.

"Sure. You're working on his case as a consultant; it won't even count as a visitor."

They would meet at Frank's house at nine, they decided, and go over to the jail together. Frank said he hoped to find an apartment for John the next day; he had people working on it. "You want to bring books or anything and work upstairs until we get you a place, that's fine," he said.

Matter-of-factly John said he would do that. "Where's a good place to rent a computer and modem?" he asked. "There are a few things I have to catch up on, a little work to take care of."

"You can use mine," Barbara said.

"Now?"

"Sure. As soon as I help clean up."

Frank said that wasn't necessary, but both John and Barbara insisted, and in fifteen minutes they were done. Just then, a gold ball rolled across the floor, followed by Thing One and Thing Two. With a sigh Barbara retrieved the ornament.

"I'll help take down the tree Sunday," she said.

"What's left of it," Frank said, taking the ornament. "Those cats are already spoiled rotten. They came that way. Did you teach them to sleep in a bed, a people bed?"

"You can close your door."

"They sit outside it and howl."

She laughed. "Earplugs?" She turned to John. "See you at the house."

* * *

He was already parked when she got home. She waved and went to open the door and turn on lights. He followed her inside, then stood looking about the room as she took off her jacket. His gaze lingered on the lovely little Christmas tree Bill Spassero had given her.

"Office this way," she said hurriedly, and stepped inside the tiny room to switch on the desk lamp and turn on her system, then had to leave the office before he could get to the desk. He was carrying his jacket over his arm. She took it on her way out, realizing belatedly that she couldn't close the door without moving a box of computer paper. She never closed the door; the room was too claustrophobic. She left it open now.

She carried the jacket to the kitchen and draped it over a chair back, reluctant to take it to her only closet, in the bedroom. The jacket was still warm from his body. Then, briskly, she gathered up newspapers and put them in the recycle bag by the back door. She picked up her shoes in the living room, and put them away, then washed the few dishes in her sink. Each time she had to pass the open door to her office, she was very aware of him sitting at her desk, intent on the monitor, his hands on her keyboard.

In the living room, she opened her notebook and tried to concentrate on the tasks she knew she had to get to in the coming week or two. John stepped into the room and asked permission to use her printer. She nodded. "It's on. Paper's loaded."

In a moment she could hear the printer working. She stared at her open notebook and saw doodles, random lines, spirals. . . . She snapped it shut.

He finished a few minutes later, and she stood up. "Your jacket's in the kitchen. Do you want coffee, or wine?"

"Thanks, no. I'd better be on my way." He retrieved his jacket and came back, pulling it on. "And thanks for the use of your computer." He looked at the tree again. "That's very pretty. Gold and silver. It's in the air."

Then she saw the tag: "Love, Bill."

"It's from a friend," she said. "He's out of town."

"Ah. Well, good night." He crossed the room and reached for the doorknob.

Almost desperately, she said, "I'm sorry I bothered your former wife. You still care very much for her, don't you?"

He stopped moving, regarded her for a moment, then nodded. "I'll always love her." He opened the door and left.

In the county jail the next morning, the three of them crowded the small conference room almost too much to move. Ted was haggard and despondent, clearly not interested in the maps Barbara had brought along. John was watchful, uneasy to be back in jail for any reason.

"They haven't found anyone who saw me that day, have they?" Ted demanded. "There must be someone!"

"And they'll find him," Barbara said, trying to sound reassuring. "Meanwhile, we're trying to run down every other lead we possibly can. And that includes all those parcels of land you brokered in the southwestern part of the state. You said Praeger took you and Teddy to a mine. Can you locate it again on the map?"

"What for?" Then he said, "Sure. Curry County." He unrolled the map on the table. Barbara had brought along Scotch tape to fasten it down. When it was smooth, Ted pointed and said, "We went down the coast road to here, 5325 Elk River Road, and followed it along the river to the South Fork, here. That's the same road I drove out on in September. Rough road, not too bad. The next one, here, was worse." He peered at the map. "I don't know the number, an even narrower dirt road for five or six miles. Then we parked and walked the rest of the way, this trail at first for half a mile, then off trail through the forest about a mile."

Barbara handed him a Hi-Liter, and asked him to trace the route as best he could. When he finished, she asked, "Ted, what was the point in taking you up there? Why did Praeger want you to see that place, that mine?"

He rubbed his eyes. "God, I don't know. He said Connie Mines wanted mines that hadn't worked out to their potential, the lesser-known mines. He said that area between Ophir

Mountain and Iron Mountain was so rough that no one had stayed long enough to know what they had found. He wanted to show me the area they insisted on including in the tracts they bought."

There were trails into and out of the Connie property; some of them went on into the wilderness, others led to logging roads, BLM roads, Forest Service roads, or other county roads.

John was studying the map; he asked, "Did you know Teddy found a chunk of rock with gold in it in that mine?"

Ted looked disbelieving. "In that mine?"

"Was he in another one with you and Praeger?"

"No, just that one." He stared at the map a second, then said, "Maybe he was salting the mine. All I saw was a hole that went back a hundred feet, angled off another hundred feet, with a lot of rocks on the floor."

John drew back from the map, frowning.

"Would Teddy be able to find that mine again?" Barbara asked then.

"Keep him out of all this! He's a kid!"

"He's involved, like it or not," Barbara said calmly. "Has it occurred to you that someone tried to frame him?"

Ted sank down into one of the chairs and pressed his hands against his face.

"Whoever that was knows about Teddy's interest in rocks. I keep adding more names to the people who know that. Praeger's one. We have to find out what he was up to, and if that means locating that mine and looking it over, we'll have to do it. Is there any chance of finding it without a guide?"

"You'd never find it."

"Can we take Teddy and let him find it for us?" she asked softly. "He can do that, can't he? Go back to a place he's been?"

"He can find it." He looked again at the map and shook his head miserably. "My God, dragging him into this! Carolyn should go, too, stay with him."

John began asking questions about the roads. Ted pointed out the places he remembered being worse than others. "Here," he said, "on the last section, you want to be careful. The road's narrow; it will be muddy now . . . slippery. Just take it easy.

Take the Land Rover. And the trail gets pretty steep just before you reach the mine."

John made notes as Ted talked, and he put little violet circles on the map at the bad places; to Barbara's eye, there seemed to be altogether too many of the circles.

"Teddy and I camped out down here that night at Elk River, and fished the next day. Two hours in, two out, and however long it takes to hike one and a half miles in and then out again. An all-day trek. That was in good weather, and I was familiar with the area." He looked at John anxiously. "You drive back-country a lot? You know dirt roads, mountain roads?"

"I'm a mining consultant," John said. "And we all know mines are in the most god-awful places on earth to reach."

Ted grinned fleetingly. "Yeah. That's it. You'd better all bed down around Port Orford, somewhere close, so you can get started at dawn. This time of year, you'll be cutting it pretty close to make it in and back out in daylight. Unless you want to camp out in the wet forest. Teddy wouldn't mind."

"We'll get in and out in a day," Barbara said. Her gaze had landed on the map at Panther Ridge. Panthers? At least bears would be hibernating, she thought then. "And we'll wait until we have a few days of clear weather in the forecast."

John asked a few more questions, and they left soon afterward. She and John had walked to the jail from Frank's house. At the sidewalk, she said, "I'm going on to the office for a while. You want to keep the maps?"

He did. They walked to the corner of Pearl, where she turned south and he turned north with a wave of his hand. Her wave was just as casual. Yuppie Heaven had drawn as many bargain hunters as it had Christmas shoppers; cars were edging along the street as drivers searched for parking places. People crowded the sidewalk. Two teenagers passed her, holding hands. She thought of the casual wave of John's hand, like a pal, a brother. And that was the way to deal with him, she told herself. Exactly the way she treated Bill. But God, she was tired of brothers.

*   *   *

It was nearly four when Barbara returned to Frank's house to pick up her car and go home.

"I rounded up an apartment for John," Frank said when she looked in. "Mrs. Waverly's place. Over on Eighth."

She remembered Mrs. Waverly, who had provided the apartment many times over the years. Mrs. Waverly would talk him to death, if he let her.

"I moved in, and first thing in the morning, I'm taking off for the coast," John said. "Beachcombing, books to read. Can't think of a better way to spend New Year's Eve and Day."

Neither could she. "Things will be back more or less to normal on Tuesday. What a long holiday this has been! Do you have a poncho or something?"

"Yes, Mom," he said gravely. "And boots and everything."

Frank chuckled, then offered her a drink, coffee, some dinner in a little while; she turned him down, pleading things to do. It seemed obvious that John had been invited and had not turned him down, but it was too much. Brother, son, what next?

The weekend was interminable. John took off for the coast for New Year's Eve. The party she went to was boring, and dismantling the tree on New Year's Day was a dismal chore. After they were through, she went up to the office and stood before the maps, reading some of the names: Iron Mountain, Bonanza Basin, Independence Mine—she wondered if it had been—Smith Mine, Ash Swamp, Devil's Half Acre. . . . Few roads, many trails, the most rugged country she could imagine. What did they want with it?

TWENTY-TWO

BARBARA DROVE THE sixty-five miles to Salem in intermittent rain to talk to Mal Zimmerman; she drove the same sixty-five miles back in hard rain, and she had spent an hour and a half with the man. All for nothing, she thought darkly, another wasted day. Zimmerman would never back up John's story; he knew nothing about mines, and he doubted Knecht had been interested in mining. She didn't learn a thing Bailey had not already found out.

It was too late to go to the office by the time she arrived home. Instead, she went to Frank's house.

"We've got some more faxes," he said. His voice was almost toneless.

As soon as she had her jacket off, he handed her a sheaf of faxes. "Sit down and go through them. I'll bring you a glass of wine." She followed him to the dinette and sat at the table there.

"That bad?"

"Bad enough."

It was more on John Mureau, a brief bio, from the looks of it. She skimmed through the pages: parents, siblings, education, and then she read more slowly. Seven hospitalizations were listed with dates of admission and discharge. Four of them were in Lexington, Kentucky, a general hospital, and three of them were a mental-health institution in Pikeville. No details had been included, just the names and dates. Well, he had told her as much, she reminded herself, but it was different seeing it in black and white.

She put that piece of paper down and picked up another. This was a copy of police reports that listed the various false confessions John had made. There were six of them.

When she finished all the faxes, Frank put a glass of wine in her hand and sat down at the table opposite her. "They'll fry him if he gets called," he said.

"We knew all this," she said. Her mouth was dry. She drank the wine, too much, too fast.

"We knew and didn't know. Now we really know," Frank said slowly.

She began to put the papers back together, meticulously lining up the edges. He had confessed to the murders of John F. Kennedy and Martin Luther King, Jr. "Where is he?"

"His place, I guess. He'll check in at the office around ten in the morning. Bailey's coming around nine." Impatiently, he took the papers away from her. "This settles it. You can't call John Mureau. And if you can't call him, you can't use his story."

"I know," she said in a low voice.

She also knew that left her with three eyewitnesses who would put Ted Wendover in that resort hotel when Harry Knecht was killed.

That night in bed, listening to trains banging and clanking a few blocks away, she confronted the problem of both knowing and not knowing. How could that be? She had seen parents who knew their child had become a delinquent deny it, know it and not know it simultaneously, as if the brain had little compartments that allowed people to store both knowing and not knowing and never see the contradiction. Denial, she told herself. Simple denial. But she had not denied anything. John had been up front, had told her all about it; she had known from the first. Not denial, not this time. Amnesia? A basic flaw that made her forget he had been insane until evidence was before her eyes and memory surged back in? Had poor Mr. Rauschler known and not known about his wife right up to the final excruciating breakdown? The trains banged and clanked. In her head she heard her father's words: *Now we really know.*

* * *

When John arrived the next morning, it was to say he had found absolutely no reason yet for anyone to buy all that property with the useless mines. "They're great for hobbyists and collectors," he said. "A weekend camp-out, find a few dollars' worth of gold ore, have yourself a ball. For serious, commercial mining, I just don't see how they plan to extract and transport it. Some of those mines made a fortune back around the turn of the century, right up until the thirties, even into the forties. Now they're worthless."

Another dead end, she thought wearily. "How was the coast?" she asked then.

"Wet and windy. Pretty neat, actually. Big waves."

He was settled in okay, he said, and if they wanted to know anything about the Waverly family, just ask. He didn't stay long. He had a pal to talk to at the BLM office, and then back to the books he had borrowed from the library.

"If it isn't snowing tomorrow, I'm taking off for the mountains," Barbara said a few minutes later. "I suppose Bailey will start having stuff any month now, might as well get this out of the way while I can."

"Well, that car of yours is too light for mountain driving if there's snow or ice. Take the Buick."

She would never have admitted it to Frank, but she liked driving his boat of a car. It was warm, it handled beautifully, and the tape deck sounded better than hers. All in all, not a bad way to cross the mountains, she decided, until she hit the snow at fifteen hundred feet, after driving for an hour. From that point on, the drive was miserable, like slow-motion torture. There was more traffic at this time of year then there had been in the fall: Ski season had started. The cars and trucks all moved slowly to a wide area where the road was posted: TRACTION DEVICES REQUIRED. RV TRAVEL PROHIBITED. She pulled over along with a dozen other cars and got out to put on chains. A group of teenaged boys was hustling business. One of them approached her.

"Put on your chains for ten dollars."

"Deal," she said, and let them. They made it look very easy. The line of cars and trucks crept up the winding mountain road and over the pass, down the other side, where some dropped out at the Hoodoo ski slopes, some at SkyView, then Sisters; the rest of them stopped again, this time to take the chains off a few miles out of Bend. She waited for two boys to finish another car, and nodded when they drew near. The chains were off in a minute.

It was sunny and very cold in Bend; her motel room was overheated, the air stale. She turned down the heat and called the sheriff.

He met her at the door to his office. The outer office was deserted. Sheriff Tourese's face was red and raw; he looked exhausted. "We've been out looking for that fellow hunting mushrooms," he said, motioning her inside, then toward a chair. "Found him a while ago. Looks like he sat down to rest and never got up again."

"I read about him," Barbara said. "That was tough."

"Yeah, tough. Ms. Holloway, why are you back in these parts? Way I heard it, Wendover isn't being charged with Hedrick's death. They're separate cases."

"I don't believe it," she said. "They also say Hedrick's death was probably an accident. Do you believe that?"

"No. What do you want?"

"I want to see the final reports, the photographs of Lois Hedrick's body, the autopsy report, everything."

He shoved his chair back. "I can't do that."

"When I was here before, it was because the police were ready to arrest Teddy Wendover for three murders. If that had happened, I would have had access to your reports, the autopsy, all of it as part of discovery. That's what I'm asking for now, the same material I would have seen then. And, Sheriff," she added, "if they convict Ted Wendover, your case will be open in the books forever."

He leaned back in his chair again, listening, his eyes narrowed. When she stopped, he pushed himself away from the desk and stood up. "Wait here," he said, then walked out of the office. He came back in a few minutes with a thick file, which he placed on his desk, on her side. "It's all in there."

"Thanks," she said. She drew her chair in closer and opened

the file. Almost absently, she took a notebook from her briefcase and started to make notes.

The sheriff left, returned with two mugs of coffee. She murmured her thanks and lifted the mug. The coffee was terrible.
She resumed her note taking. At the autopsy report, she
skimmed first, then started over, reading very slowly now.
Finally she looked up, to find the sheriff regarding her fixedly.

"Am I reading this right? It seems to suggest the possibility
of two blows, the first one fatal, and a second one that did most
of the actual physical damage. Is that right?"

"The medical examiner said he couldn't be sure, but it looked
like a second blow had been struck, that one definitely a rock
that left fragments. He thought there were two centers of frac-
turing of the skull, not separated by much, half an inch maybe,
but that would explain the fractures. Since either blow would
have been fatal, the second one had to have been after death."

"That's why you said the murder weapon could have been a
rock, not that it was definitely. I didn't pick up on that. I should
have."

"Not much you can do with it, unless you have a lot better
luck than I've had."

"It doesn't make sense," she said.

"What doesn't?"

"She had eaten bread and milk hours before her death; that's
okay, I guess. She might have been on her way to the inn for
lunch. But her body was frozen within hours of her death. In
daytime? It had been raining most of that week, not cold enough
to freeze a person, surely."

"First couple of days after the New Year, daytime temperature up to forty, down to twenty-five at night. After the fourth
day, it was in the thirties, down to twenty at night." He had not
consulted notes. "That was at the inn, about the same elevation
she was at. Higher up, it was colder, and with windchill. . . ." He
shrugged. "Ranged from below zero to fifteen maybe. Seventeenth, snow came, over an inch an hour for twenty-six hours."

Softly Barbara said, "She was killed somewhere else and
moved after the snow started. Is that what you're saying?"

"That's what you said," the sheriff commented. He tasted his coffee and grimaced. "I'll put on some fresh. That's been around awhile."

"But why move her? And someone must have hidden her body for over a week, waiting for snow. That's why there wasn't any sign of a scuffle, why no one saw her on the bank of the creek."

The sheriff picked up his cup, still full, and left the office.

Barbara got up and paced the length of the office, back, and then again. Finally, she sat down and searched through the papers until she came to the photographs of Lois Hedrick's body. There was a sequence that started with a shot of the snow-covered bank, the stream no more than a black line at the bottom of the print. She could see the boot. Next, they had removed much of the snow from the body. Barbara paused over that one for several minutes. The body was aligned almost straight up and down against the steep bank. Her boot was wedged between two big rocks; they had stopped her slide into the creek. Right, she thought then. She had been lowered down the slope to the place they found her, lowered feet first, a frozen body, stiff, unmanageable. The last photograph showed the entire body, both arms at her sides, legs straight, facedown.

"How could anyone pretend to think that was an accident?" she asked angrily when the sheriff returned with two steaming mugs.

"I never did," he said. "Newspapers said it, not my office."

She sipped the coffee, still bad, but better than before. "Where do you think they hid her body? Not out in the open anywhere."

"Nope. Probably not."

"Is there a list of people who were there between the first and the eighth? And again on the seventeenth?"

He answered readily. "Yes. It's in there. I talked to every one of them. Got nothing."

She shuffled through the papers and found the list; it was long, over thirty names. Owen Praeger's name seemed to leap off the paper at her. The workers at the resort had their names underlined; Arthur's and Cy's names had underlines. Brian had been there from the sixteenth to the twenty-first. None of the other names was familiar.

"You want a copy, I suppose," the sheriff said. "Ms. Holloway, I have a feeling that you know something that I should know. Is this going to be a one-way street?"

"No. I found out something, I just don't know what it means." She told him about the audiotape Lois had made, with the voice she was certain was Praeger's talking about gold.

"Gold," he said flatly. "Great."

"That's what my dad said. But she did talk to him and that part of her manuscript was missing from the cabin, and he was up there all that time."

The sheriff looked disgusted. "Ms. Holloway, they've separated our case here out of the package altogether. I don't see how you intend to join them together again, frankly."

"I don't either, frankly," she admitted. "That's one reason for coming back here. And you've been extremely helpful. I really appreciate it. My next move, I think, is to see if Praeger is still around."

"Hang on a minute," he said, and lifted his telephone, punched in numbers, and waited. Then he said, "Hi, Milly. How're you doing? Sheriff Tourese here." He paused. "Yeah, I was with the bunch that found him. Look, is a guy named Owen Praeger still up there? Just between you and me." He listened, then said, "No, not serious. Traffic violation. We need the money. See you around. Thanks." He hung up. "He's gone. Left back in November, about the middle of the month. No forwarding address."

If she had been home with her father, she would have said *shit*, but she didn't say anything. The sheriff shrugged. "If you're done here, we can make you copies of what you need, and I'll go home and go to bed for a week."

They made the copies, and she thanked him profusely. "If you're ever over my way, please give me a call. I owe you a dinner or something."

"Bribery won't get you anywhere," he said with a faint grin. "What you might do is let me know if you make any headway.

And send me a copy of that audiotape and her pages from her folks' place."

She assured him that she would do that, then walked back out into the frigid air. The sky was still bright, not threatening snow, but it felt as if the temperature had plunged to zero. Not her kind of weather, she decided, hurrying to the Buick. It was too late to drive up to SkyView, wrestle with the chains, or pay someone to put them on, and then take them off again to return to her room. Tomorrow. Now she wanted to be warm and to think. There was a connection, and she felt closer to it than ever. Praeger was the link. And he couldn't hide, she told herself.

TWENTY-THREE

THE NEXT DAY, SkyView was crowded—the coffee shop was jammed and the lounge was filled, with massive logs burning in both fireplaces. Most of the guests apparently were between twenty and fifty. Most of them appeared extremely healthy, with the fresh appearance of people who had been outdoors in the cold a lot. There was a great deal of noise, people talking, laughing, calling out to one another, and music everywhere.

Barbara strolled through the resort lodge slowly; her guess had been right about the need for so much space in season. The corridors no longer seemed too wide, and the shops were so busy, they looked too small. The night before, she had called Vicky Tunney, who was reluctant to see her again. They were too busy, she had said, but then agreed to let Barbara join her and Cy for lunch. Barbara had come early in order to look around and ask a few questions, if she could find anyone to talk to her. It appeared that no one could do that; Vicky had spoken truly: They were all too busy. Hard rock came from the lounge, other music from shops, and the noise of video games from a room she hadn't seen before. A dozen kids were in that room, raising the noise level a few more decibels. She walked down the corridor toward the offices, noting signs on the doors: MAN-AGER, BOOKKEEPING, MR. ROWLAND. . . . Two unlabeled doors came next; Rowland's private quarters, she suspected. Then she headed back toward the reception area, filled today with arriving guests, others departing, people collecting mail at the wall of boxes. . . . Snow gear was everywhere: skis, sleds, snowboards, even snowshoes.

Before she headed for the little train that carried guests to the lifts, she walked around the lodge on the wide veranda, more cluttered with snow gear than the reception area had been. Some teenagers were having a snowball fight on the side of the road. Three sides of the veranda were wide, and evidently well used; the fourth side was narrow. She could see the windows of the offices. No one was in sight. Some windows had drapes closed—Rowland's apartment probably. There were no outside doors on that side.

Finally she returned to the front of the lodge and the area where people were waiting for the train. It pulled into sight, three cars with pneumatic tires, pulled by a fake steam engine, all gaily decorated with the red-and-gold fleurs-de-lis on shiny black. People tumbled out, some with skis, most empty-handed. She crowded aboard with the others; there were no seats, and no roof. The skis and poles made roofing impossible. In the car ahead of hers, a group of college-aged people started to sing "Ninety-nine Bottles of Beer on the Wall." She grinned. She hadn't heard that in twenty years.

The road they traveled was hardly wider than the train, with mountainous piles of snow on each side, making it a canyon. They turned around at a small building where there was a long line of people waiting for the lifts. Barbara walked past them to the young woman who seemed to be in charge, handing out tickets, checking the stamps on hands.

"I have an appointment with Cy Rowland," she said to the woman. "Are you Erica?"

Vicky had told her to go straight to Erica, who would put her on the high-speed lift without the wait. "Yes," the woman said. "Ms. Holliday? It'll be just a minute."

"Hey, I've got an appointment with Cy, too," a man called out, and a woman said, "Me, too." They both laughed, and Erica pointed Barbara toward a lift with four seats. There were several other lifts, and even some rope tows. She took a seat along with two other women and a man. "Trouble with downhill," he said, "you wait an hour for a lift for every minute you fly." They were whisked up the mountain. Off to the side, skiers flew past. Halfway to the top, it started to snow.

All morning the sky had been leaden; the weather report had said snow at 6,500 feet, rain in the Willamette Valley. On the whole, she decided when her ears began to pop, she preferred the rain and lower levels.

When she got off the lift, she blinked in surprise at what they had called "the shack," another large building, gray stone, with wide windows and another veranda. She was at the rear of the building, where she saw a sign for ski rentals. She entered and walked past the rental shop, where more people were in line, past a sales shop, past a young woman instructing a group of youngsters, twelve-year-olds maybe. There was a restaurant, Vicky had said; they would have a table reserved if Barbara got there first. Before she went to the restaurant, she looked over the rest of the building: coffee shop, a fast-food counter, another lounge with a central fireplace. People milled about everywhere, eating, crowded together at tables, talking, laughing. . . . Elevator? Of course, she thought, to the lower level. The building was high, two stories, but only the upper floor was above the snow level. She turned to the restaurant then.

In less than five minutes she saw Vicky enter. At a distance it seemed that Vicky was wearing a black satin cap, but it was her hair. She was as sleekly beautiful as Barbara remembered; today she was wearing black ski pants, white boots, and a white sweater. Her face was flushed and her eyes sparkling. She waved to Barbara and came to her table.

"I have until one," she said. "Starved. Cy will be along in a few minutes."

A waitress took their order: salad for Barbara, turkey and

Swiss cheese sandwich, minestrone, and milk for Vicky. She ordered the same for Cy.

"You must burn a zillion calories a day," Barbara commented.

"Cold does it, and, of course, skiing." She waved her hand in a dismissive gesture. "Anyway, you made us curious. Why did you come back?"

"Teddy's off the hook and his father is in jail awaiting trial. I need more background. You said 'us.' You and Cy?"

"We live together, in his cabin."

"I saw the way his father treated him," Barbara said slowly. "Why does he stay?"

Vicky hesitated. "This was before my time, but Cy told me about it. He was going to train for the Olympics, and Arthur pulled a real fit, a fake heart attack, the whole scene. Brian backed him up. A family knock-down-drag-out, I gather. When it became clear that Arthur wasn't sick, Cy demanded a deal, or he'd walk. They made a deal. When Arthur dies, Cy gets this resort. Brian gets everything else, the Columbia River place, Stone Point, the land down at Gold Beach, all of it. What Cy wants—all he wants—is SkyView. They can have all the rest of it as long as he can have this." She looked out the window. The snow was falling straight down. The trees were black on white, unreal. The whole landscape was surreal, black and white and gray.

"What about the land down at the Rogue River? Do they keep updating the agreement?"

"I don't know anything about land down there," Vicky said. "But they did rewrite the agreement a few years ago, change the wording to mean that anything listed and anything acquired in the future was to go to Brian."

"I didn't know they had another resort at Gold Beach," Barbara said.

"Not a resort, just land. Several hundred acres. They haven't done anything with it."

After a moment, Barbara said, "I don't understand why Cy made such a deal. As son, he would naturally expect to share an estate. Especially since he didn't leave to go into training."

Vicky hesitated again, as if considering whether she was talking too much; then she shrugged and said, "He made them give him the ski operation to run without interference. That's what he really wanted. He trains Olympic wannabes," she added. "Arthur threw a fit when he began the program, but the deal held. Before that they wouldn't let him buy wax without written permission."

Barbara thought about it for several seconds, then asked, "Did Arthur have a fit about you and Cy being together?"

Vicky laughed. "You bet. The day after he dies, we'll get married."

"Is his relationship with Brian that stormy?"

"No way. Arthur figures he had a good boy and a bad boy. We know who the bad one is. Brian's back and forth a lot, once a month at least; he oversees the hotel operation here. Arthur's happy as a kid when Brian comes calling." She looked past Barbara and waved.

Cy Rowland hurried through the dining room. He shook his head at a group of young people who called to him. "Later," he said, and came to the table. He kissed the top of Vicky's head before he sat down. "Turned them over to Boris," he said. "Let him wrestle with them an hour or two." He grinned at Barbara then. "Sorry. Hi."

She grinned back at him. His hair was shaggier than before, and he had the same kind of high color that Vicky did, the same kind of sparkle in his eyes. He looked younger than she remembered, boyish even. He looked happy, she thought then. Down at the lodge he had been on his father's turf; now he was on his own, and it made a difference.

"The team is a bunch of high school kids from Portland. They don't know which end of the pole goes down," he said. "Did you order for me?" he asked Vicky.

She nodded, and at that moment the waitress brought their food. They both ate ravenously. After a few minutes, Cy paused to ask Barbara, "Why are you here?"

"I'm trying to find out something about Lois Hedrick's death," she said. "And about Owen Praeger. You know him?"

"Sure," Cy said.

"A creep," Vicky said almost simultaneously.

"Creep how?"

Vicky shrugged and said, "For instance, he just will play cards, any cards, and he loses his temper and yells a lot when he loses, which he does most of the time. He has a hard time finding anyone to play with him."

"Ah," Barbara said. "Did you ever talk with him?"

"Not me," Vicky said. "Cy knows him better than I do."

"A little better," Cy said. "I don't think anyone knows much about him. He stays here awhile, then takes off and is gone for months, looking for gold. He talks about the Lost Dutchman Mine, the Blue Bucket Mine, mythical bonanzas, as if he was getting closer to them all the time. If only he had backing, he'll say, he'd lead the world to the richest deposits ever dreamed of. It's out there calling him. Most people begin backing away pretty fast."

"You mean he's a permanent resident, when he isn't off prospecting?"

"He showed up a few years ago. He stays in one of the small cabins at the end of Lower Loop One. There are four back there—okay for one person, or even a couple for a short stay. You know, an A-frame, with a sleeping loft, kitchen screened off from the rest, that kind of thing. Dad puts up with him; he even likes to talk to him, I guess."

"Do you know if Praeger spent much time talking to Lois Hedrick?"

"He'll talk to anyone who'll listen. If she'd listen, then sure, but I never saw them together."

"Do you recall anything about the day it started to snow so hard two years ago, when Lois Hedrick was missing?"

Vicky finished her sandwich and drank her milk, apparently trying to remember. "It started around noon," she said. "I was up on the ridge with Cy's group, searching." She looked at him. "Remember? It started coming down so hard, we had to pack it in and get back. We went to our cabin and stayed the rest of the day."

"Right," Cy said, nodding. "We kept going to the door to check, make sure it was still coming down. It was, so hard you couldn't see the next cabin. We were like kids, couldn't wait for morning so we could go out and play." He grinned. "In fact, we didn't wait. We went out to play around midnight. Not much in the way of help, I'm afraid."

Barbara agreed silently. "Was Praeger among the searchers? Did he seem concerned?"

Cy finished his milk, his gaze out the window at the falling snow. His voice was almost flat when he said, "I think Owen Praeger is crazy, literally crazy. He was sore because no one was around to keep him company. He couldn't have cared less about Lois. You know what a wilderness search is like? It's pretty tough. He could have been some help—he's a mountain man—but he never stirred a finger. Everyone was dragging in day after day, and he was griping about poker."

Barbara remembered Sheriff Tourese's exhaustion and nodded. "Do you know where he hangs out when he isn't here?"

They both shook their heads. Then Cy looked at his watch. "Time's up. You've got that class in five minutes," he said to Vicky. "And I'll go see if Boris has kept that gang from Portland intact. Take you to the lift," he said to Barbara.

Vicky dashed off as Barbara was putting on her coat and hat. Cy walked with her through the shack, to the rear entrance. He stopped to point out a window. Beyond it was a long, shallow slope with a group of youngsters awkwardly trying to stay upright on skis. He laughed, and they continued.

At the lifts, he gazed out over the long expanse of the closest downhill slope. Two people were going down. He watched them for a moment, then lifted his face to look past them, to look at the forest all black and white, with snow heavy on gracefully sweeping limbs. To Barbara's eye, it was a perfect Christmas card scene, beautiful and strangely alien.

Someone called Cy, and he seemed to come back from somewhere else, almost surprised, as if the spell had been deep and wonderful. "Back to work," he said. He saw her into the lift, then waved to the operator. She started down, alone this time.

The snow was supposed to stop, she thought, but it was getting heavier as she descended, and by the time the lift swayed and came to rest at the bottom, there was no doubt that she would be driving in snow at least part of the way home. She was checked out of the motel; the chains were on the car. Once she was over the pass, it would be rain, she told herself, boarding the gaudy little train. Back at the lodge, she didn't linger, but hurried to the Buick, and then, denying to herself that it was snowing too hard for safe driving, she started.

It was bad. Traffic crawled. She passed a car rammed up against a cliff, with a police car already at the scene. But it was too late to turn and go back; there wasn't anywhere to make a U-turn. Thankful for Frank's heavy car and chains, she followed a dairy truck painted white and black, like the markings of a cow. It faded in and out of sight, a ghostly presence beckoning on an invisible road that twisted and turned and twisted again, climbing, leveling out, then going down with even sharper twists and turns.

A long time later she realized she was out of the mountains. The road had flattened; she had reached the valley. It had grown dark, and the snow was still falling steadily. Cars began to pass her; she cursed them. Visibility was no better for those drivers than for her, and she couldn't see more than a few feet in any direction. The two-hour drive took six hours. She had awakened that morning with a headache from her stuffy room; fresh air had banished it, but now it was back, throbbing behind her eyes. When she made the turn off the Jefferson Street Bridge finally, heading for Frank's house, there were four other moving automobiles in sight. Snow was several inches deep, falling steadily, straight down.

Frank opened the door when she rang the bell. His expression was of furious amazement. "Goddamn it, Bobby! You don't have the sense God gave those kittens!"

She stepped inside. "I've had a pretty hard day," she said, not quite a whimper, but close.

He turned and stalked through the hall toward the kitchen.

Then she became aware of John Mureau standing in the doorway to the living room. "What makes you so tough?" he asked softly. His forehead was furrowed, as if she presented a problem he couldn't solve.

"Goes with the territory," she said. But she felt as tough as a dunked doughnut.

Frank reappeared at the end of the hall. "Bobby, so help me God, if you decide to go down to the beach and watch a tsunami roll in, I'm not going to worry about it. Come and eat something."

He had made spicy Louisiana red beans and rice and had reheated them in the microwave. She was ravenous.

As she ate, she told them what little she had learned about Praeger, and about Lois Hedrick. "She was seen on New Year's Eve; she, or someone else, picked up her mail on the third, and she was reported missing on the eighth. Her frozen body was hidden someplace until the seventeenth, when the snow began."

John looked sick, but Frank was nodding thoughtfully, at the moment seeing that death as she did, another piece of a puzzle. She wanted to explain how they alternated between the very human emotional reaction, the gray-faced reaction Frank had shown at Mary Sue's death, and the coldly distant professional one, but she found she had no words to use. He would either learn that by himself or he would think them monsters.

"I guess that means Wendover gets off, after all," John said after a moment.

"Not that simple," Frank muttered. "Hedrick's murder is a separate case. I wish to God I could see how you're going to link them," he added to Barbara.

So did she.

She and John both spent the night at Frank's house, she in the upstairs bedroom and he on the couch in the living room. She lay awake a long time, too tired and twitchy to fall asleep, until finally she got up to sit by her window and look at the falling snow. She thought then of Vicky and Cy, playing in snow like children. Exhaustion drove her back to bed.

She dreamed that she and John were playing in the snow; they laughed when their snowmen began to throw snowballs at them. Then, she was alone and the snowmen became monstrous, pelting her with snowballs, then with rocks, then boulders.

TWENTY-FOUR

WHEN SHE WENT downstairs the next morning, John was out shoveling the walk. Six inches of snow had fallen, Frank announced. He was nearly gloating as he said, "That cloche is in great shape, good insulation—"

"When did John come over?" She went to the counter to pour coffee and put bread in the toaster.

"Yesterday afternoon. He used the computer awhile, then we got busy putting together that cat box, and before we knew it, the streets were impassable."

She stood waiting for her toast. "Dad, let's keep him on a business level. Okay? I mean, we hired him to do a job. As soon as it's done and the police give him the nod, I want him out of here."

"And come back when the weather clears enough to go find that mine?"

"Exactly. Then he gets a check and he's gone. It would be a mistake to get attached to him in any way."

"I agree about that. I surely do." Then very slowly he asked, "Bobby, is it a mite too late?"

"No! I just want him gone. Away."

At eleven Bailey called. Barbara took the call on the kitchen phone. He wouldn't make it to town until they cleared his road, he said cheerfully, two or three days at least. "Meanwhile," he said, "I've got a couple of things for you to mull over. First, Connie Mines is a front. They formed it to buy that land down by the Rogue River. Praeger's the president; his only assets are that land and a truck. No known address except at SkyView."

Barbara interrupted to tell him Praeger had left there in mid-November.

"One more thing," he said then. "You know the old one, save the best for last. You know that security guy, Brody? Guess what? He's vice president of Connie Mines."

She drew in a sharp breath. "You're sure about that?"

"For what it means. After all, the company's a front, so what's he vice president of? Anyway, he is." He chuckled. "You haven't asked the most important question, Barbara. You're losing your grip. You were supposed to ask when he got promoted to vice president. And I'd answer, 'Last November.' "

"That's incredible," she said. "It's so blatant! Bailey, are you positive?"

"Sure as sin."

"Bailey, I love you. Anything else?"

"Nope. And I won't tell Hannah. See you at spring thaw."

When she hung up, she saw John standing in the doorway, his brow furrowed again, as if he kept trying to solve the same problem and kept failing.

"I have to move," she said. "I'm going out to make a snowman."

"Can I help?"

"You betcha!"

They made the snowman and threw snowballs; his aim was better than hers, but she was better at dodging, and all in all, it came out just about even. By the time they went inside again, she was sweaty and her feet were freezing.

That afternoon John said he would hand over his report the following day. "It's as complete as I can make it without inspecting some of the mines," he said. "Probably Knecht was going to have me take a look, that's why he mentioned Agness."

"We'll settle for the one Praeger was so insistent on getting," Barbara said. "Next month the snow should be gone in the Klamath Mountains. Maybe early February."

"Spring comes in February?" John asked in a disbelieving way.

"If it's still snowy up there—well, snowshoes, Eskimo garb,

sled team, the works." Her father gave her a murderous look and she laughed. "Kidding. Honest, just kidding."

They both spent the night again, and the next day the rains returned and the snow melted into slush that was getting washed away fast. Barbara walked to the office early in the day; at four John came in.

"Your report," he said. In his hand was a thick sheaf of papers in a folder. "The cops say I'm free to go." His face was masklike, his voice flat.

"I'll call you when we can make the trek to the mine," she said. She was at Frank's desk.

He came to the desk and laid the report on it. For a moment, neither spoke. Then he drew more papers from his pocket. It was another thick stack, folded lengthwise. "Jeremy received this. I had him make me a copy. You'll want it, too." He put the papers down. "See you next month," he said, and turned to leave.

"John, wait." He faced her again, his expression still almost blank. When he laughed, his face twisted, became lopsided; now, straight-faced, the scar was nearly invisible. "Your bill," she said after a moment.

"I'll mail it. Don't go driving in any blizzard." He walked out.

His absence left a hole, she thought irrationally; it was as if a void had opened in front of her.

Without a glance at the reports she had been reading, she stood up and took the folded papers to the couch across the room. She started to read the medical reports.

Multiple abrasions; pelvis broken in two places, crushed hand, left leg broken in two places, right leg broken, and a fracture. Four ribs . . . Gently, she put that part of the report face-down; then she found herself wandering in the wide corridor toward the reception desk, without any memory of walking there.

"Barbara," someone called. She turned, surprised to see Shelley there on a Saturday. Shelley had on a pink raincoat with a white fur collar. Her white boots had two-inch heels. "Barbara, can I ask you . . . Are you all right? You're pale as a ghost."

"Okay. I'm fine. What was it you wanted to ask?" Her voice sounded almost normal to her own ears. She started to walk back to Frank's office. Shelley came along. "Just ask whatever it is," Barbara said.

"Okay. Bill . . . you know, Bill Spassero? He asked me to go out with him. And I wondered . . ."

Barbara laughed and then had to bite her cheek to force herself to stop laughing. "Shelley, Bill is my overgrown kid brother. Honest." At the look of indecision on Shelley's face, she added, "Honey, nothing would make me happier than to see you guys get together." She entered Frank's office. "Good night," she said, and closed the door.

Across the room, the medical reports waited. She went to the bookshelves and opened the bar, got out a bottle of bourbon, mineral water, and a glass, then returned to the low round table. After drinking a lot of bourbon and a little water, she sifted through the papers to find the hospital admission and discharge dates, the procedures they had done. The surgeon's reports were typed, concise and thorough. His physician had scribbled his notes. It was in his execrable handwriting that the first episode of schizophrenia was recorded. "June 1, patient hallucinating, irrational." There followed scrawled words that appeared to be medications and dosages. She could not decipher most of them.

The next operation was a year later, April 20, 1975. Discharge date, May first.

The handwritten notes said on May twentieth, patient was irrational, hallucinating, admitted to Mt. Sterling Mental Health Services Clinic that day, discharged June fifteenth. Readmitted June twenty-seventh, discharged September tenth.

She read through the rest of the reports, but the pattern was set. The surgeon had done his work and sent John back to Pikeville, where after a few weeks, John had become hallucinatory, confused, irrational: schizophrenic.

Too much time had elapsed for a reaction to his medications in each instance, she thought then. You react or you don't, but you don't wait a month or more. She drank more bourbon and looked at that group of papers with hatred. Instead of reading further, she found the police reports of John's confessions and added them to his file, then closed it sharply. No more!

She finally left the office, retrieved her car at Frank's house, and drove home. The streets were wet and sloppy but not bad until she turned off Fifth into her own neighborhood, and here the slush was thick and slippery. She slid around a corner, nearly sideswiped a parked car, and eased away from it, holding her breath. When she applied the brakes at her own house, she slid several feet, then stopped by turning the wheel sharply to head into the curb.

"Good job," she muttered.

Inside her house, she picked up a few pieces of mail from under the slot in the door, tossed them onto the kitchen table, and started to peel off layers of clothes. She had left a trail of filthy wet prints, which she studied morosely.

Like a tape loop, his voice played over and over in her head: *Don't go driving in any blizzard. What makes you so tough? I can't help your client. Paranoid schizophrenia, says so right in my medical record. I'll always love her.* She saw in her mind his twisted grin.

Why hadn't they finished repairing his face? They must have offered plastic surgery as an option. Company insurance had paid his bills; would they have balked at that final one? Or had he balked?

Slowly she got to her feet and walked to her office to sit behind the desk and look up Gregory Leander's number. She didn't stop to question why she was doing this, but simply called him.

"Hello, Barbara. I hoped you'd be the one to call first. I almost did half a dozen times, but I waited." He sounded as if he was laughing. "I have a present for you," he went on. "It's a toy and it's on my desk. I love it so much, I couldn't bear to send it, but the day you pay a visit, I promise to hand it over."

She laughed. "My God, you have no shame!"

"Of course not. When can I expect you?"

"Gregory, believe it or not, this is really a business call."

"Oh darn," he said. "Okay, give. What business? You feel a little madness coming on?"

"Knock it off, will you. If I send you a bunch of medical reports, can you decipher them for me? Break it down into English?"

"Probably. Tell me more."

"It's a man, a potential witness. . . ." She described John's accident and as much as she had been able to get from the reports.

His voice became brisk and serious. "You want a second opinion about him, right? Let me see the material you have."

"I'll copy everything and get it in the mail Monday. Thanks, Gregory."

"See if you say that when you see my bill," he said. Then he was bantering again. "You want to come over and discuss the bill? Maybe compromise?"

"You're a nut, you know that?"

"Of course I know that. Send me the material, darling. Talk to you later."

She sat at her desk, her hand on the phone for several minutes after hanging up. The problem, she thought then, was not in simultaneously knowing and not knowing; the problem was in knowing and believing. "Okay, Johnny," she muttered, "you may love her forever, but I'm going to straighten you out."

And what if Gregory simply confirmed what she already knew? she asked herself mockingly. "Nothing," she said under her breath. John Mureau had walked into her life; when the case was over, he would walk out of it.

TWENTY-FIVE

DAY BY DAY, Barbara read Bailey's reports as they came in. She studied Ted's maps until she felt she had memorized every detail. She talked to his neighbors and friends, associates, service people, salespeople. Gregory Leander called to tell her that John Mureau's medical reports were incomplete; he needed more information. She called Jeremy Cushman and browbeat him into giving Gregory a call, fuming over one more hitch, one more delay, one more dead end. She read and reread all the statements the district attorney's office had provided concerning Knecht's death.

She studied Knecht's autopsy report, the photograph of his body, the left side of his head crushed. She narrowed her eyes and reread the autopsy report. The right side of Knecht's face had been bruised in his fall. She tried to remember what else she had read, something this reminded her of. Then she had it: the newspaper accounts of Mary Sue McDonald's death. She had been found on her back, the right side of her head against the floor in a pool of blood, the bloody left side of her head exposed. She had broken her right jaw when she fell. She buzzed Shelley and asked her to bring in the McDonald file.

Half an hour later, when Frank returned, she was pacing the office. He had been to the district attorney's office to inspect the rocks found in Knecht's room; he had taken along a geologist from the university.

"He'll do," Frank said. "He told me a hell of a lot more than I wanted to know about those rocks." He eyed her narrowly. "What's wrong?"

She sank down into a chair. "Lois Hedrick was hit twice,

remember? Knecht's face was bruised on the right side. He fell when he was still alive. Mary Sue's face was bruised; her right jawbone was broken. She was alive when she was knocked down."

For a moment they remained silent, then Frank muttered, "Christ. He must have picked up the rock and finished her off as she lay there."

"Knecht, too."

"Christ Almighty." He looked sick.

"Framing Teddy," she said bitterly. "What else was it for?"

On the twenty-seventh she called John's Denver number from the office. His phone rang twice, then he said, "Mureau."

"Barbara Holloway," she said. Her mouth had gone dry; her voice sounded hoarse. "Can you make it next week, anytime after Sunday?"

"Springtime in the Klamaths," he said. "I'll fly over Sunday. Mrs. Waverly said she'd have the apartment for me. I'll call when I get in."

She said faintly, "Good." They hung up. She looked up to see her father regarding her, and she said hurriedly, "Maybe we can give him some dinner Sunday night, plan our little jaunt."

He nodded.

"I have to get some fresh air," she said as she snatched up her jacket and nearly ran from the office. She should get her legs in shape for a mountain hike, she told herself, heading for the river at a fast walk.

That week Mal Zimmerman had sent her a copy of the environmental newspaper he was now working on. His lead article was a blast at the new congressman, Brownley, who, Zimmerman claimed, was intent on undoing everything Harry Knecht had stood for. Zimmerman had been so intense and bitter, she had expected his article to be a simple rant, but it was reasoned and thoughtful. She took the paper and the list of bills Knecht had been interested in to Frank's house on Sunday to finish reading.

John arrived twenty minutes after four. He greeted Frank as an old friend, and Barbara with cool politeness. She was equally

cool and polite. He admired the cat house and said the kittens
were really growing. His flight had been good. The apartment
was fine. Barbara wanted to scream. At dinner when he compli-
mented the food, she realized she hadn't noticed what she was
eating.

Very briskly she said, "I made reservations down at Port
Orford. I think we should be on the road by two. That means we
leave here at one-thirty. We can have dinner down there and let
Carolyn get Teddy settled in early. On Tuesday we should get
started by daylight."

John nodded. "Okay."

More briskly, she added, "That way we can be finished
before dark. We'll be home before ten. And you can catch a
flight out on Wednesday."

Frank took off his glasses and looked through them at arm's
length. "Excuse me," he said. "Thought I was going blind." He
left the dinette.

Barbara glared at his back. Almost desperately, she plunged
on. "Carolyn will pack food for us."

Gravely John nodded again. Then he said, "Is it permissible
to ask how your case is going?"

"Ask. The answer is, terribly. You haven't sent in your bill yet."

"I'm not done yet." He stood up. "I'll just help your dad clear
the table." He picked up his plate and a platter and walked out.

When she stood up to go help, they were talking about
fishing; they continued without pause as they all rinsed their
dishes and put them in the dishwasher, and then Frank poured
coffee. In the living room, they started to talk about hunting,
and Barbara said she had to go, she had all that reading to do,
and things to get ready for tomorrow. Neither objected.

At first, she had trouble tracking from one word to another, but
she became interested in Mal Zimmerman's newspaper and
read it closely. She had not realized how effective an environmentalist Knecht had been. Chairman of the Natural Resources
Committee, he had wielded great power, more than a single
person usually commanded, because he had won the confidence
and respect of his natural adversaries.

She read again the concluding paragraph of Mal Zimmerman's editorial: "His vision was of the whole. He molded disparate pieces into a single crystal without seams, without flaws. With one blow that crystal was shattered into myriad glittering fragments: Habitat preservation, river restoration, land-use restrictions, drilling regulations, mining controls—all of it is up for grabs, and the quick and the greedy are snatching up the pieces. God help us."

At one the next day she arrived at Frank's house. John was already there, perhaps as eager as she was to be on the way. He had a backpack, bigger than her own day pack, and he had Frank's thermos filled with coffee. They didn't linger. Barbara drove them to the Wendover house. Both Carolyn and Teddy were also ready to start; Teddy acted as if he had been ready for hours. He was excited and impatient to get going. Their stuff was in the car, he said, opening the back door of the Land Rover. Carolyn shrugged helplessly and followed him. And they were off.

John drove; Barbara directed him to the interstate, and again when it was time to turn onto U.S. 38. It was a lovely drive along the dark green Umpqua River, her favorite route to the coast, but today no one seemed to appreciate scenery.

In the backseat Carolyn played games with Teddy. After awhile, she gave him some new comic books, and he was quiet. Now and then, Carolyn pointed out something of interest: Golden and Silver Falls State Park was up that road, a wonderful place to hike. On the coast she said, "On down through Coos Bay, there's Shore Acres. It's such a beautiful garden in every season. . . ." But for the most part, they were all silent.

Later, Barbara realized John was watching the rearview mirror. She started to turn to see why, and he said, "There's a lookout just ahead. Maybe I'll pull over and have a look at the ocean, make sure it's there." They had not had a glimpse of it for nearly an hour.

She glanced at him; he shook his head slightly, and she felt herself tense. They pulled over and stopped at a railed turnout, but he was watching the road. A black car passed them. Barbara groped in her purse for a notebook and pen and then jotted down the license number.

From the back, Carolyn said, "It isn't far now. There's a lovely beach at Port Orford."

"Right," John said, and pulled back onto the road.

Soon they crossed a bridge over the Elk River. On the other side was the road they would take in the morning. It was a blacktop road close to the river, lost to sight among trees very quickly. Along this section of Highway 101, the forested mountains came down to crowd the road, hemmed it in on both sides. The Elk River valley appeared to be a very narrow, crooked slice through the trees.

A few minutes later they drove into Port Orford, perched on a rocky cliff above the ocean. Like most coastal towns, this one was bisected by the highway, which was lined with shops, filling stations, motels, restaurants.... Barbara spotted the black car, a Ford, at a filling station, its hood raised. She glanced at John; he had seen it. Then they saw the sign for their motel, Sea View. It was on a side street overlooking a bay; stacks rising from the water were swathed in mist; the beach curved invitingly, its far end lost in mist. It had tide pools.

"Can we go on the beach?" Teddy asked.

"As soon as we check in," Carolyn said.

They checked in and were given keys for three adjacent rooms.

"Let's meet at six and have dinner," Barbara said at the door to her room. It was five then. Teddy had flung his pack into the end room and was tugging at Carolyn's hand. She put her pack inside the door and let herself be dragged away to the beach. When they were out of hearing range, Barbara asked John in a low voice, "Was that car following us?"

"Hard to tell, since this is the only road to the south coast. I spotted it back near Reedsport, and then off and on the rest of the way." He shrugged. "If it was, and if it stays around here overnight, I want to call off this little expedition."

Slowly she nodded. Maybe it was a coincidence. Maybe the car was disabled, or maybe that was a ploy to let the driver stop

long enough for them to catch up and pass him, lead the way
again. She opened her door and pushed her pack inside, then
pulled the door closed, exactly as John had done.

"What are you going to do now?" she asked.

"Take a little walk, scope out a restaurant, see if that guy's
car is gone. Want to walk?"

They walked the block to the highway; the black Ford was
not at the filling station.

"Let's go up that way," John said, nodding toward several
motel signs. They walked faster now; the stiff wind coming in
from the sea was cold. They passed souvenir shops, most of
them closed, a hardware store with an open sign, a bank, a
motel. . . . Few other people were out walking. Traffic was light
on the highway. The Ford was parked at the third motel, in the
back of the parking area. They continued to the end of the
block, very close to the end of the town, crossed the highway,
and started back on that side.

"Okay," John said. "Did you see a restaurant you like?"

She gave him a hard look. "Are you kidding? That was the
last thing I was thinking of." Walking back, three blocks from
their motel they found a restaurant that offered more than
burgers and fish sandwiches.

"We still don't know if he was following us," Barbara said as
they drew near their motel. She saw Teddy and Carolyn climbing up from the beach. It was getting dark fast now, and the
wind was stronger.

"Let's talk about it after dinner," John said. He waved to
Teddy, who started to run toward them, carrying his collecting
bag in both hands.

"Look what I found," Teddy called. "Agates."

"Great," John said. "I have something for you in my room."
By the time he had his door open, Teddy had reached the room,
and crowded in after him.

Barbara waited at the open door for Carolyn to join her. They
stood together watching as John opened his backpack and drew
out a canvas bag with many flaps.

"See," he said to Teddy. "This is the kind I use when I col-
lect. These little drawstring bags are good to put rocks in if you

don't want them to get scratched up. Some of them have plastic linings for wet rocks." He was pulling out many smaller bags in various sizes. "These loops are where you hang your tools, your hammer, things like that."

"I don't have any more tools."

"I'll show you mine." John pulled out a second bag like the first one, but weathered and stained. He took from it a rolled chamois and opened it on the bed. "My tools," he said. "I keep them wrapped like this so they don't clatter and the edges stay sharp. This is a wedge. You put it where you want the rock to break and tap it with your hammer. That's a rock chisel. . . ." He described each tool, what it was used for. "A hand drill," he said. "Sometimes, if a rock is brittle, it breaks to pieces if you hit it with your hammer. So you drill a few holes up and down it, and then use the wedge. You'll get a nice cut, slick as a whistle."

"Can we go out and try it?" Teddy asked, almost breathless with excitement.

John laughed. "Too dark. Maybe there will be time tomorrow. Tell you what, when we get back to town, I'll take you shopping and help you pick out your own tools and show you how to use them. Okay?"

"Promise?"

"I promise."

There was little conversation as they ate; they were all too hungry. As soon as Teddy was finished, Carolyn said they would leave. "You two take your time, but we have to go. I have a chapter of *The Wind in the Willows* to read before bedtime. When should we be ready in the morning?"

"Six," John said. "Do you have anything we can eat along the way for breakfast? If not, we can do a little shopping tonight. I doubt we'll find anything open that early."

"I have plenty," she said with a smile. She and Teddy left.

"You still want to go up there?" Barbara asked when they were alone at the table.

"I'm going to disable the creep's car. He won't follow us."

"You don't know that he was," she said, alarmed.

He shrugged. "Paranoid, maybe, but there it is. I'm going to make sure he doesn't follow us tomorrow."

"How? What will you do?"

"Drill a hole in his radiator," he said.

She stared at him. He was as matter-of-fact as if he had commented on an old movie. "When?"

"About three-thirty. Not too many pedestrians about at that hour."

"I'll go with you," she said in a very low voice.

He shook his head. "No way. If they catch me, I'm just a nutcase. If they catch you, you could be disbarred."

"You'll need someone at the street to warn you if a police car is coming. That's what they do on the coast—drive up and down and shine lights here and there."

Now he stared at her.

At three-thirty she slipped from her room. She had put a scarf on, and her down jacket. The wind was fierce. He was already outside his door. Without speaking, they hurried away from the dim lights of the motel entrance and crossed the street, to keep to side streets. When they had to go to the highway, they moved cautiously, staying in shadows, behind trees and bushes as much as possible; they trotted the half block along 101 to the motel. The business buildings and storefronts were dimly lighted; in houses a faint light showed here and there. At the motel the light in the office was dim; a single light was at the front of the parking area. The black Ford, parked in the rear, was not visible. Half a dozen other cars were parked outside room doors. The wind blew without letup, a keening in her ears.

She stopped at a row of stunted evergreens that bordered the entrance driveway and watched him run in a crouch past the parked cars toward the end; he vanished very quickly. Then she watched the road. Headlights appeared in the distance, disappeared again as the car apparently turned in somewhere. In her hand she carried gravel. If anything threatening came, she would throw it. No whistling, no whispered warning, just the fall of gravel on the concrete parking lot. It had seemed a good idea before, but now she wondered if he would even hear it. All she could hear were the wind and the surf; the ocean sounded very far away.

She started to shiver and pulled the scarf up around her face, leaving only her eyes uncovered. Another set of headlights appeared, this time from the south. She waited tensely; a pickup truck came up fast, and continued fast through the town, out of sight. She let out her breath. A light in one of the motel rooms came on. She watched, her shivering forgotten, as her muscles tensed again. After a few minutes, the light went off; she felt weak with relief.

Then John touched her arm, and they ran back to the corner, turned down the side street, and ran to the shadow of a misshapen tree. His hand on her arm drew her to a stop. "Okay?"

"Yes," she whispered. "Did you do it?"

His face was a pale blur in the dark; he nodded. "Done. Let's beat it," he said.

It was four twenty-five when they made the final dash across the parking lot of their motel. "See you at six," he whispered at her door.

Inside her room, nearly frozen, she realized she was still clutching a handful of gravel. She began to laugh.

TWENTY-SIX

THE NEXT MORNING they left Port Orford at six-fifteen; it was still dark, but the wind had died down and the air was degrees warmer than it had been the day before. Barbara was aware that John was keeping an eye out for a follower, and now she understood his reason for leaving in the dark. If there were headlights following, he planned to drive straight back to Eugene. He had not said so, but she was certain he had decided to do that. Not by so much as a smile or a nod had either acknowledged their criminal act of last night.

They turned onto Elk River Road, as sinuous as the river it paralleled. John slowed down, still watchful, but more relaxed as the miles drifted by. Gradually the sky brightened, and the forest became a real presence, hiding the mountains, hiding the road beyond the next curve, hiding the world. There was only the river, the forest, and the sky above, turning gray-blue.

The river was high, frantic in this last dash to the sea, tumbling over rocks with great splashes, turning into white-water riffles, stumbling over itself in its rush.

Teddy asked when they were going to eat. He had left the motel carrying his new collecting bag, with the hammer securely in a loop. He held it in his lap now.

"As soon as it gets a little lighter," John said. "I'm starved, too. I remember seeing a camping area up ahead a bit."

He had studied the map as much as she had, Barbara knew, but he had noticed the distances, and she hadn't. By the time they reached the camping area, daylight had arrived. The sun had not cleared the mountains yet, but the sky was bright. The camping area was a marginal widening in the space between the river and the mountain.

Carolyn opened the back of the Land Rover and began to bring out camping gear. Almost absently, she called, "Teddy, don't you get wet."

"Okay," he said, already at the riverbank, his collecting bag over his shoulder.

John and Barbara walked that way. At the riverbank he stopped to look around in a complete circle. He grinned. "At this spot the world is an irregular circle with a diameter of less than a hundred feet." He nodded and added, "It's world enough. Listen."

She could hear only the rushing water. "I don't hear anything," she said after a moment.

"I know."

They stood in silence then until Carolyn called. The smell of bacon and coffee was overwhelming. They ate bacon and scrambled eggs with cheese and drank coffee and juice, and

very soon they were back on the road. The sun cleared the
mountains, and the temperature climbed.

John grinned at her. "Springtime in the Klamaths."

"It could change any second," she warned. It was an empty
warning; the sky was cloudless.

Now it seemed the road couldn't make up its mind if it was a
blacktop or a gravel road, alternating with no warning, and for
no reason that Barbara could see. It went up and down, back and
forth in sharp curves, always with the river on their left, the
mountain on their right. Their speed went from twenty miles an
hour to forty, to thirty, twenty. . . . They passed a second camp-
ground, almost identical to the first one, and shortly after that
they saw a crude shelter on the side of the road.

"Me and Dad camped here," Teddy exclaimed. "I caught two
fish and a bunch of crawfish. We ate them all."

John slowed down even more, watching for the dirt road on
the right. At a sharp curve, he braked. Ahead was a one-way
bridge at grade level; they had crossed many others like it. A
small white marker with illegible numbers indicated a road.

"That's it!" Teddy cried. "That's where we go up the
mountain."

John made the turn. This was more like a track than a road,
deeply rutted and very steep, wide enough for only one car. At
places, water stood in the holes gouged out by other vehicles; at
other places, their car had to work to find traction in oozy mud.
The road curved around the flank of a mountain, with the gorge
dropping farther and farther below them rapidly. On the other
side, tree roots had been exposed when the road was cut; the
roots wrapped themselves tightly around rocks and boulders,
some larger than the Land Rover, as if the roots were responsible for holding the mountain in place. Where some roots had
been cut off, the tree leaned precariously over the road; other
roots jutted straight out, as if seeking earth.

Then all at once, there was a sharper curve than ever, nearly a
U-turn, and afterward there was land on both sides. The mountain loomed over them on the right side, the forest on the left.

From the backseat, Carolyn said, "Whew."

"Me, too," Barbara said, and John laughed and said, "And me."

The road ended in a small turnaround where, it was obvious, other vehicles had turned to head back out. Barbara shuddered to think of meeting another car on the road they had just driven. At John's matter-of-fact suggestion, they separated to relieve themselves among the massive trees in the forest.

Then, back at the Land Rover, they hooked their water bottles on their belts; Carolyn handed out sandwiches, apples, and candy bars to be stowed away in their various packs, and they drank the coffee she had put in the thermos. They were ready for the hike. It was nine-thirty. By three they planned to be back here, to start the tortuous journey out.

Although the trail was not well marked, Teddy led the way unerringly, as nimble and quick as a goat. Looking at him from behind, Barbara realized that she never thought of him as a man any longer. He was a boy. But when she was with him, actually seeing him, her brain became confused, and he morphed from boy to man to boy again. Today he looked like a woods-smart man. He finally stopped and waited impatiently for the others to catch up.

"Come on," he called. "We gotta turn here."

How he had known was a mystery to Barbara; they were surrounded by noble firs, cedars, and rocks. The sky was hidden by the thick canopy and no shadows indicated east or west; it was all shadowed. Yet, once the new direction was pointed out, she could see that this way had been used, too. Others had walked here, left their traces: a sapling broken off, a bit of lichen scraped from a rock, even a deep footprint in muddy forest duff. Their progress became markedly slower as the new path zigzagged up the mountain. Twice they halted to rest. The air smelled so good, Barbara thought, breathing it in deeply. Incense cedar and forest mold. The ground felt spongy underfoot.

At last, after the steepest climb, one that had seemed almost vertical, they came to a level spot again. Teddy started to run. "There it is," he yelled.

A cliff rose straight up thirty feet away; mounds of dirt and rocks were like sand dunes here and there. Barbara could not see the mine entrance, but as she walked toward the cliff, it appeared, an irregular opening, five feet high, about that wide.

John had caught up with Teddy; they both ducked and entered the passage. Barbara waited for Carolyn, and they walked together toward the mine.

"Are you okay?" Barbara asked.

"Out of shape," Carolyn said. "I'm okay."

Outside the mine, piles of dirt and rocks made a nearly continuous wall on one side, as if at one time someone had tried to use care in the excavation, then had abandoned that concern and piled up the tailings more haphazardly.

She ducked and entered the mine, with Carolyn coming after her. They had to walk in a stooped position only a dozen feet or so; then the passage opened up to eight or ten feet wide and that high, dimly lighted from outside. It grew darker as they continued; the passage widened again, became a room twenty feet wide. A heap of rocks lay at the bottom of the left wall.

"Rockfall," John murmured as Teddy crossed to the pile.

"Here it is," Teddy said. "Here's the gold."

They all went to see the rock he was pointing to. It was four feet high, irregular and jagged along break lines. John played his flashlight beam over it.

"Greenstone, some serpentinite, a little pyrite, and look, a fleck or two of gold." Two very small spots gleamed even before he turned the light on them. He began to examine the wall behind the fallen rocks.

"Can I get some more?" Teddy cried. He had his hammer out.

"Sure," John said. "All you want." He continued to move his light up and down the wall very slowly. Teddy began to chip at the big rock.

The floor was uneven and dusty, difficult to walk on because of the rocks that jutted up, other rocks that apparently had been dropped or dumped. At the back, a narrow black opening gaped, as irregular as everything else in here, wider at the top than the bottom.

"You can see where it faulted," John said, running his light along a diagonal line from about two feet high on the wall to the far end, where it was about five feet high. "They had to dig out room to stand, but that's what they were after, a vein that ran along the fracture line there. Let's have a look."

"Me, too," Teddy said, abandoning his rock.

"Single file," John said. "I'll go first with the light, then Barbara, Teddy, and Carolyn."

"Wait a second," Barbara said. She opened her day pack and withdrew a flashlight the size and shape of a cigarette package. She handed it to Carolyn, who looked relieved.

John led the way slowly, moving with caution now; the floor was more uneven, at places without any horizontal surface at all, merely a depression where the two sides came together. The passage curved and the light from the mine opening was swallowed by the dark rocks pressing in on all sides. Then the passage opened again.

They had entered a space about ten by fifty feet, with the top angling down sharply in the rear. Piles of broken rocks littered the floor.

"Hold it," John said when they had all stepped into the room. He shone his light on the ceiling, where rocks made the surface chaotic, with jagged edges thrusting out, broken rocks that looked as if they might fall, others, smoother, jammed together. He examined the walls of the room, which were just as uneven and irregular as everything else. The whole mine looked as if children had gouged it out of bedrock. There was no other opening. This was the end of the mine.

"There's no gold in here, is there?" Carolyn said. She sounded hoarse. "I don't think the air's good."

John swung his light around, not in her face, but against a wall near her; she was illuminated. Her face was pinched, as if she was struggling against fear. "The air's okay. Maybe you'd better head back out." Then he said, "Teddy, you want to do a little mining with me?"

"Sure! I see gold up there." He pointed to the ceiling.

"We'll leave it up there. What I thought was that we might try that pile of junk, see what's behind it." He aimed his light at the back of the room, where the ceiling was no more than three feet high and the floor was littered with rocks.

Carolyn did not move away from the entrance as Teddy and John picked their way through the jumble of rocks to the other end. Barbara watched as John pointed to a big jagged rock.

"See, what I want to do is break off a piece here and there. I'll show you how to use the wedge."

While John was explaining to Teddy what they were going to do, Barbara became aware of Carolyn's labored breathing. "What's wrong?"

"I don't think the air's very good."

Barbara raised her head, conscious of taking a breath, as if sampling it. There was the smell of dust and rocks; the air seemed very dry, not very cold. The mine smelled the way a grave must smell. She became aware of the weight of the mountain above them, the pressure of rocks and dirt all around.

"Let's get back to the sunshine," she said briskly. "They'll be occupied a while, I bet." Teddy was tapping his hammer against the wedge, making a melodious rhythmic sound that echoed from all directions.

Carolyn looked hesitant.

"John will take good care of him," Barbara said, and Carolyn nodded. She turned to start out, using the flashlight Barbara had given her. Barbara stooped to pick up a rock the size of her fist, a souvenir, then followed. The sound of a second hammer on rock began before they had taken half a dozen steps.

The echoes died out, but the sound of hammers on rocks and on metal continued and was still audible when Barbara and Carolyn reached the first room. The light that had seemed dim when they first entered now seemed bright. Carolyn didn't pause, however; she went on through to the passage to the outside, and after a moment Barbara trailed after her.

It had grown very warm here on the south side of the mountain; the air was fresh and fragrant, without a trace of dust. Carolyn stood breathing deeply; when she glanced at Barbara, she seemed almost embarrassed. "I didn't know it would affect me like that," she said.

"I've heard that some people get the screaming meemies," Barbara said. "I'm going to eat. They can hammer all they want; my priorities are straight."

They ate their sandwiches, and Barbara stretched out with her pack under her head. The sun felt good. She was roused by the sound of hammering close by and sat upright. Carolyn was walking toward the mine. Barbara got up and stretched, then glanced at her watch. After two! She picked up her pack and dusted it off, then hurried back to the mine.

John was eating a sandwich while Teddy hammered at the rock he had originally found with gold in it. Teddy looked up happily; his face was smeared with dirt, his clothes limned with dust.

"I told him he could take as long as it takes me to eat," John said, grinning, also happy. "Then we're out of here. Right, kid?"

Teddy nodded and kept hammering.

"He'll eat in the car," John said. "That's how it is with collectors. Everything is secondary to getting that one last rock, that one last match folder, or trading card, or whatever."

The two collection bags, one old and stained, one brand-new, were side by side, both bulging.

John took his time eating the sandwich, then started in a leisurely manner on the apple. But at last it was time to go, and reluctantly Teddy put his hammer in the loop, hoisted his bag on his shoulder, and was ready.

Carolyn started out first. She had taken a step out into sunshine when the quiet was shattered by what sounded like an explosion that reverberated through the mountains. Carolyn wheeled about and dashed back into the mine passage, her face completely colorless.

They crowded one another getting back into the first room of the mine. Teddy wanted to know what was happening, what that noise was.

"Could you tell anything about where it came from?" John asked. His face was twisted in the way it became when he was angry.

Carolyn was shaking too hard to speak. John patted her arm, and Barbara put her arm about her shoulders and held her, watching John, who had gone to the beginning of the passage.

"What's the matter?" Teddy demanded. "What happened?"

"Shh," Barbara said. "It's okay. Shh."

"Wait here," John said, and, ducking low, he inched his way into the passage toward the entrance. There he stopped and yelled, "Hey, you with the gun! Knock it off! We aren't hurting anything. Come on down and talk." Two closely spaced shots exploded. John returned to the group. "He's over there, I think," he said, pointing toward the right of the entrance. "I couldn't see him, but I think the shots are coming from that way."

"Is somebody shooting at you?" Teddy asked, his face alive with excitement now.

"Why don't you go over and finish that rock you've been working on," John said.

"We aren't going now?"

"I'll tell you when you have to stop," John said quietly. He waited until Teddy crossed the room and began hammering again, then said, "I didn't see him, but he can't see us, either. I don't think he wants to negotiate." He became silent, frowning.

Carolyn was looking about the mine wildly, but Barbara knew that was meaningless. There was no place to hide if he decided to come in with a gun. Of course, they could throw rocks at him. She shook her head impatiently. If he came in with a gun, someone, maybe all of them, would be killed. They couldn't stay here until dark or they would not be able to find their way back down the mountain to the car.

"Why was he staying off to the right?" she asked in a low voice.

"There's no place to stand the way we came up," John said. "That was a steep ascent at the last. He'd have to be out in the open. Did you notice how far this ledge continues off to the right?"

She hadn't; she hadn't thought of this as a ledge. But it was, a rocky ledge with little vegetation until the trees started again perhaps a hundred feet away. That's where the gunman was, among the trees over there. She closed her eyes, visualizing the mine the first time she had glimpsed it, with all those piles of tailings scattered about. Trees started on the left much closer than on the right, she was certain.

"We'll have to try to get out and circle around to the trail," she said, still speaking as if she was afraid the gunman might hear.

John nodded; evidently his thoughts had led him to the same conclusion. He opened his pack and drew out a notebook. "Look, we're here, and the way we came up is here." He sketched rapidly as he spoke. "We don't know how steep it is over this way, but there are trees to break any slide. We'll have to risk it. Remember, if you go too far over, you'll come to the cliff overlooking the road. On the other hand, you may come across the trail, and in that case, just follow it on to the car. Be careful there; someone may be waiting. If I don't show up in fifteen minutes after you reach the car, take off. I'll walk out."

"What do you mean, we're to split up?" Barbara asked harshly. "Why?"

"I intend to keep him occupied as long as possible. You'll go out on your bellies, stay behind the tailings as much as possible until you get to the trees. Barbara first, then in a minute or two, Teddy. Carolyn last. Barbara, be on the lookout, make sure they end up where you do, and then stay together." He handed the notebook page to Barbara. "Got it?"

Silently she nodded.

"Leave your packs here. They'll slow you down."

Barbara and Carolyn began going through their packs to take out drivers' licenses, money, keys, credit cards. Barbara picked up her souvenir rock then put it down regretfully; it was too big for her pocket.

"I'll take my collecting bag," Teddy said, continuing to hammer.

"I'll bring it out," John said. "Promise." He looked at Barbara. "Don't pay any attention to whatever you hear from up here. Let's do it. Come on, Bobby, you first."

She started at his use of her nickname, but he already was hunched over, on his way out the passage. She followed. At the entrance, he crouched and squeezed himself against the wall so she could pass. For a moment she hesitated, then she was out. She flattened herself as much as she could behind the first of the tailings. She raised her head only enough to see where she should go to reach the safety of the trees. It was maybe thirty feet to the first tree trunk in sight. She began to inch her way along the ground, no longer in the shadow of the tailings, but in the open. If he could see her, he could get her, she knew; she would make an easy target, sprawled out on the ground. She moved behind a rock and took in a deep breath. Twenty feet to go. Behind her she could hear the *tap*, *tap*, *tap* of a hammer. She inched forward slowly until she felt the forest duff, and she rolled behind a tree trunk.

She was startled to hear Carolyn's voice in a piercing scream, "Teddy, stop that! You're driving me crazy!"

The tapping stopped. Barbara looked out from behind the tree. Teddy was at the tailings, flat on the ground, his face raised as he searched for her. She motioned, and he began to come her way. God, she thought, he was so big. Surely the gunman would spot him worming his way toward the trees. He paused at the same rock she had used as a screen and then continued toward her. The tapping started again.

Teddy joined her, grinning. "Careful," she warned. "It's really steep here. Stay behind that tree until your mother makes it." He sat down behind the tree she pointed to, and she took up her watch again.

Carolyn had almost reached the rock when John yelled, "Goddamn it, Teddy! Your mother told you to stop that!" The tapping stopped again. Teddy giggled. Then Carolyn reached the safety of the trees and stood leaning against one, breathing hard. She pushed herself away from it and said, "Okay. Down it is."

It was very steep here, but holding on to the trees, slipping and sliding, they worked their way downward. Muffled by the trees and distance, John's voice rang out once more, not the words this time, just the sound, punctuated by three quick shots. Barbara stopped to listen; there was nothing else. They continued.

They came to a ledge with a fifteen-foot drop. "We can jump down," Teddy said.

Carolyn held his arm. "We'd break a leg, or kill ourselves."

"Let's see if we can get around it," Barbara said, leading the way along the edge. The drop was deeper after a few minutes; they retraced their steps to try the other direction. They came to a spot where it was about ten feet down and considered it. The forest seemed to drop away again beyond this spot.

"If we hold Teddy's wrists, we can lower him most of the

way. Then I can hold you and he can help from below," Barbara said. Carolyn nodded.

Lowering Teddy was the hardest part, Barbara realized after a moment, feeling as if her arms were being pulled off. She and Carolyn were flat on the ground when he called to let him go. When she looked over the ledge, he was smiling up at them.

Carolyn rolled over on her stomach and eased herself to the ledge, with her legs over the lip. Barbara held her wrists as she went down slowly. Then Carolyn said, "He's got my legs." Barbara inched forward as Carolyn had to straighten up, move her shoulders over the edge. "He's got me," she gasped, and the strain was off Barbara's arms. She looked down to see Carolyn standing by Teddy.

"Take off your boots," Carolyn said. "If you can lower your feet enough to reach his shoulders, you'll make it."

Swiftly, Barbara unlaced her boots and dropped them over the ledge. Then she rolled to her stomach as Carolyn had done and began to work her body over the ledge. Her legs were over, but at an angle; she had to get her hips over the edge. There was nothing to hold on to; her fingers kept slipping. Gravity wins, she thought as she began to slip more. Then she felt hands on her legs, a hand on one foot guiding it to Teddy's shoulder, then on her other foot, while he held her hips firmly, and she was over the edge, leaning in toward the cliff, her feet planted on his shoulders. He held her thighs and began to lower himself, and Carolyn's hands reached her waist; she was down.

"Teddy, you're wonderful," she said in a strangled voice. She drew in a deep breath, another.

Teddy was grinning widely. "I saw them do that in the circus. They were clowns."

She sat down to put her boots on again. "You're no clown, Teddy. You're a hero."

He laughed.

After that the going was much easier, still downhill and still steep, but with no more real hazards. They found the trail and followed it to the clearing where the Land Rover was parked. They stopped short of it, to make sure no one was waiting for them. It was four-fifteen.

"Someone's been there," Carolyn whispered.

The windows of the Land Rover had been smashed; glass sparkled all around it.

"Let's wait here," Barbara whispered, and they settled down in the trees. As the minutes crept, she considered their next move. If the car was totally disabled, they would have to spend the night in the forest. They wouldn't dare start a fire, or even seek the shelter of the car. Hypothermia, exposure, a man with a gun; it would be better to walk to the shelter they had seen on the way in. Then she heard a soft whistle.

John was hurrying toward them; he was carrying both collecting bags, and he was limping.

TWENTY-SEVEN

"GIVE ME THE KEYS," Barbara said. Carolyn handed them to her.

"Wait to see if it'll start," Barbara said. After a swift look around the clearing, she dashed to the Land Rover. The taillights were smashed, but the tires seemed all right. She opened the driver's side door, brushed some of the glass off the seat, and climbed in. Then, holding her breath, she put the key in the ignition, turned it. The engine started instantly.

The others hurried to join her. When Carolyn and Teddy hesitated at the sight of the glass on the seats, Barbara said impatiently, "We'll stop and houseclean when we're in the woods. Let's get out of this clearing now." John was already in the passenger seat. He slung both collecting bags over to the backseat.

The windshield was fractured into a million cracks, a piece or two had fallen out, and when the car started to move, another piece fell. Ducking her head, trying to find an area clear enough to see through, she drove forward. "A couple of miles," she muttered, "then I'll stop." At the moment she simply wanted to put some distance between them and the man with the gun.

She stopped at a place where the trees were close enough to touch the car. It was getting dark in the forest already. They picked glass out of one another's clothes, cleared glass from the seats, and inspected the damage. The headlights were smashed, taillights, all the windows. She and John finished taking out the windshield. Then he leaned against the front of the car, examining the road ahead.

"What's wrong?" she asked softly.

"Why didn't he just disable the car altogether?"

"I wondered, too. I'll drive, and you keep a watch. Okay?"

He didn't argue. As she drove slowly, he peered at the road ahead. Then he said, "We're coming to the turn."

She nodded and slowed even more. The car was hardly moving when she started the turn; then she hit the brake. "Easy," John murmured, his hand on her leg. She tapped the brake again and came to a stop before the turn was complete. On the narrow road were boulders and rocks, ranging from baseball- to basketball-size. The Land Rover had stopped only inches from the first of them.

For a moment no one spoke, then John said, "Looks like we get a real workout today, mining, hiking, road clearing. . . ." He opened his door.

No one stated the obvious: If they had come down in the dark with no headlights, or at a faster speed, hitting the rocks would have thrown the car out of control. They would have gone over the side. They rolled and carried the rocks to the side of the road and over the edge.

When she started to drive once more, Barbara stayed as close to the cliff as she could, now and then scraping the car against rocks or roots. At the next blind curve, she eased around and tapped the brake again. A pickup truck filled the road from side to side. She caught in her breath, expecting someone to open the door, step out with a rifle. . . . It was empty.

John laughed, a short ugly sound. "If there are keys in it,

we'll take it. If not, over the side with it," he said. "Come on, Teddy. You can help." They had to get out carefully, there was so little room on that side; there was no room to open the door on Barbara's side.

John was limping badly when they reached the truck. He spoke briefly to Teddy, then went to the driver's door and opened it. He looked back at Barbara and shook his head: no keys. Then, with him at the driver's side, steering, and Teddy in the back, they started to push. The truck began to roll, barely moving at first, then faster. Teddy stopped pushing and straightened up to watch. John stayed with it only a few seconds longer. It was rolling faster now. He jumped clear, and the front wheel went over the edge. It teetered, its forward momentum disturbed, then it seemed to shudder, and plunged over the side. There was a crashing, breaking noise that went on and on until there was a final crash. Teddy went to the edge to watch; John grabbed his arm and pulled him back.

"Let's get the hell out of here," John muttered when he climbed back into the Land Rover.

There wouldn't be any more traps, Barbara felt certain. That man had driven up, turned around, stopped long enough to smash up their car, and then driven out again, then he had returned on foot. He wouldn't have tried anything lower down; that had to be clear for his departure. Nevertheless, she drove very slowly, approaching each curve as if it held a new menace, when the only real menace now might be darkness. It was already almost too dark to see the road here on the east side of the mountain.

Beside her, John did not relax until they reached the last curve and spotted the little bridge. In the backseat Teddy was eating his sandwich.

"See how much distance we can make before it gets too dark," John said. She nodded and made the turn onto the real road.

But she couldn't drive fast; the wind in her eyes blinded her when she went more than fifteen miles an hour. Every time the road curved away from the west, the shadows were too deep to be certain where the edges of the road were. She slowed down more and more, straining to see. When they came to the crude shelter where Teddy had camped with Ted, she pulled in and stopped.

"I can't see enough," she said wearily. "I might run us off into the river."

"Let's make some coffee," John said. He looked up the mountainside.

Without a word Carolyn got out and started the little camp stove. She brought out a lantern and set it up, and in a few minutes the aroma of coffee was in the air. John went over to examine the lantern. It was the kind that could be a general camp lantern, or it could be hooded to become a spotlight. He shone it across the river; it cast a narrow beam, but strong for thirty or forty feet.

"It has a cord," Carolyn said, animated again. "It can plug into the cigarette lighter. Is it enough?"

John nodded. "We'll crawl, and we're going to be cold, but we'll be moving."

They ate candy bars and cheese and drank the coffee. Teddy wanted to camp here and fish, but he settled for a sandwich. Carolyn made another pot of coffee and filled both thermoses; they were ready to start again.

"I'll drive a while," John said. "We'd better take turns. It's going to be a strain either way, holding the light or driving."

"Are you all right?" Barbara asked.

He shrugged. "I wasn't sure my leg wouldn't freeze up on me, but it's okay."

They drove, taking turns. Holding the light, trying to keep it on the edge of the road, proved to be as difficult as driving. They made rest stops and drank the strong black coffee. In the backseat Carolyn murmured to Teddy, and before long he was snoring softly. She leaned forward then.

"Are we going back to Port Orford? We have to call home. They'll be frantic."

"Port Orford," John said, driving. "Barbara can call her father, and I'll call cops."

"State police," Barbara said quickly. "Locals might think a man has the right to protect his gold mine," she added bitterly.

* * *

They reached Port Orford at twenty minutes after twelve; they were freezing, exhausted, filthy, and hungry. The town looked closed for the night.

"What are we going to do?" Carolyn cried. She sounded very nearly hysterical.

"Someone will open up, or we'll break in," John said grimly. "Pull in there." He pointed to a motel with three cars in the parking spaces.

Barbara pulled in and stopped. She had no doubt he would break in if he had to. She leaned her head against the steering wheel. John got out and limped to the entrance door and pressed the bell. He kept pressing it. At last a disheveled man in a bathrobe appeared at the window and gesticulated angrily. "Closed," he mouthed. Then he looked harder and opened the door. "Good Lord, you folks have an accident?"

He opened rooms for them, made sure there was an open connecting door between Carolyn's room and Teddy's. She had to have a separate room, she had said. The motel owner, Mr. Luger, said he could make them some scrambled eggs, and mercifully he didn't linger to talk or ask many questions. In her room, Barbara sat on the edge of her bed and called her father.

"Bobby, for God's sake, where have you been? Where are you? What happened?"

"Dad, we're all okay. A guy ambushed us, but we're all right. John's calling the police right now. I don't know how we'll get home tomorrow; the car's a mess." She could hear her own voice rising, and she stopped.

"Bobby, are you hurt? Tell me where you are."

She told him the name of the motel and assured him again that they were all right. "We left all our stuff up there," she said in her strange high-pitched voice.

"I'll be there first thing in the morning," he said. "Eight. Get some rest, honey."

She continued to sit on the side of the bed after she hung up. Moving was too much effort; she was too tired. John looked in at the doorway.

"Come and eat something," he said gently. "The police will be here in fifteen or twenty minutes."

At first she thought she didn't want to eat, but when she took a bite, she thought there wouldn't be enough. Teddy was sleeping, Carolyn said when she joined them. She was very pale and unsteady.

Soon two state police officers showed up and listened with some skepticism at first to their story. Barbara told them the license number of the truck, and no one mentioned pushing it off the road. When one of the officers asked to see the fourth member of their party, Carolyn said simply, "You can't. Not tonight. He's very retarded, and he is sound asleep."

John went out with them to examine the car, and when they returned, he said, "Look at us. We're falling-down tired and sore. Let's leave it for tonight."

Suddenly Carolyn said, "What if he comes here? He'll see the car and know where we are." Her voice was shrill, and her pallor alarming.

"Take it easy," one of the officers said. "We'll hang around tonight. You just get some rest now."

She stumbled when she stood up, and Barbara went to her room with her, holding her by the arm. Carolyn was shaking. "I'll take a bath and go to bed," she said.

And cry your eyes out, Barbara thought, walking back to John's room. The police were leaving. They would come around in the morning, get a complete statement then.

For a moment she and John regarded each other, then she went to her own room, entered, and closed the door. When she took off her boots, bits of glass fell to the floor. She heard a soft tapping at the door between her room and John's. She unlocked her side; he was standing there.

"Are you all right?" he asked.

She shook her head. "No. Are you?"

"No."

She reached out for him.

TWENTY-EIGHT

PALE LIGHT WAS filtering through the drapes when she awakened. He was stretched out beside her, his arm bent, his cheek supported on his hand, looking at her, his face different again, soft and tender.

"It's seven," he said. "I have to shower. The cops will be here pretty soon."

She put her finger on his lips, then ran her hand along his jawbone. He leaned over and kissed her, drew back. "Let's have dinner later, someplace quiet."

She nodded and watched him roll over and stand up, then limp to the bathroom; his lower back was scarred, and a long scar ran down his right inner thigh. Both thighs had other scars where they had removed skin to repair his chest with grafts. She watched him until he closed the bathroom door; then she got up and went back to her own room, where she pulled the bedspread off the bed and crawled under the covers. Just for a minute, she told herself.

Realizing that she was drifting off, she forced herself up. It was eight o'clock. On the foot of her bed were her clothes; he had brought them back and closed both doors.

Under the shower, she became aware of her muscles, sore all over. Her raw, cut fingers stung under the water. Her back hurt. And she was starved. She toweled her hair and remembered she didn't have a brush or comb, no clean clothes, no toothbrush . . . not even an aspirin. When she opened her door to go outside, a paper bag fell inward. She pulled it in and closed the door again. Brush, toothbrush, toothpaste . . . and a note: "We'll be in the coffee shop around the corner, Belle's Café. F.".

Twenty minutes later when she entered the café, she saw John sitting in a booth with her father; in another booth were Teddy and Carolyn and also Gail and Reid. Carolyn and Teddy were in clean clothes; she was drawn and tired, but Teddy was talking animatedly to his brother and sister. Barbara waved to them and sat down next to Frank. He put his arm around her shoulders, drew her close, and kissed her wet hair.

"Morning," John said.

"Good morning. I think I won't take up prospecting as a full-time occupation. How about you?"

He smiled. "I've had it."

She became aware of the look Frank was giving her; then he turned the same look toward John. But it couldn't be helped, she thought. There it was.

Carolyn came to their booth. In a low voice she said, "Teddy has a secret, about the truck. His secret and ours, and the family's. He loves secrets."

Barbara caught her hand and squeezed it. "Right. You and Teddy were really great, by the way. I want you both on my next adventure trip."

Carolyn returned to her own booth and Frank cleared his throat. "The drill is that you stuff yourself and we wait here for the police to show up. Reid will drive Carolyn and Teddy back, and we'll take off as soon as they let us go."

She grinned at a hovering waitress. "Everything," she said, and placed her order.

The state police, two different officers, arrived before she finished her breakfast; they said they would wait.

They all returned to John's room to give their statements; Teddy talked a lot about the clown act he and Barbara had performed. No one mentioned pushing the truck off the road, or the black Ford that probably had followed them to Port Orford.

When they were done, Frank asked, "You trace that truck license yet?"

"Yes," one of the officers said. "Registered to Owen Praeger."

"Where did he come from?" Barbara asked.

One of them said, "Gold Beach area maybe. He's been staying down that way in a cabin."

They would be in touch, they said, as soon as they located Praeger and got his statement. Then they left.

Soon afterward, Frank, Barbara, and John were in the Buick, heading back to Eugene. The Wendovers were already gone. "You want to see a doctor?" Frank asked John.

"No. It'll be okay in a day or two."

"We'll get Bailey right on that Ford," Barbara said, and Frank gave her a searching look. "He didn't tell you?"

"I saved it for later," John said. "I should have called off the trip," he added bitterly.

"Will someone just tell me now?" Frank growled.

Barbara told him. He gave her another sharp look when she told about disabling the Ford. "Good God," he muttered.

"I didn't stop to think he might call someone else, that by stopping there we gave them our destination on a plate," John said.

"Neither did I," Barbara reminded him. "Bailey can get on it and find out who the guy was."

They all became silent then, and when Barbara looked back again, John had both legs stretched out on the seat, his head against the window, sleeping. She put her head on the side window and dozed.

Frank drove to the Wendover house to let Barbara retrieve her car. She felt she had left it eons ago. Reid's car was already there, but they didn't go in this time.

"Will you call Bailey, give him that license number, and get him over this afternoon sometime?" she asked Frank. His nod was resigned. Then she said to John, "We know some pretty good doctors."

"No. I'll call you at your dad's house later."

"Later," she said, and walked to her car in the drive, every muscle protesting with every step.

When she got to Frank's house that afternoon, she felt marginally more human. She had soaked for an hour, had taken two aspirins, put on clean clothes, put Band-Aids on three fingers where the cuts had opened. Her face was a mess, she thought glumly, red, windburned, sore. . . .

Frank opened the door and moved aside for her. "He said he's going to get some Epsom salts and soak."

Slowly she walked past him to take her jacket off and hang it in his closet. She had expected a lecture, a warning, something other than his apparent acceptance of the situation. "Did you get Bailey?"

For a moment there was no answer; she turned to look at him, caught his expression of great pain before he could put on his mask.

"He'll be around at four. Have you eaten anything?"

She shook her head. Standing at the closet door, she said, "Dad, if I talk a little, you promise not to lecture me?"

"Honey, that's the last thing on earth I would do now." He came to her and put his arm around her shoulders. "Let's sit in the living room. I'll rustle you up something in a little bit."

They sat in chairs opposite each other; a small fire was burning, not a serious fire. The kittens were tumbling in and out of the cat bed, growling ferociously at one another.

She realized she didn't know how to start. Gazing at a tiny blue flame jet, she said, to her own surprise, "When Mike died, I thought it was my fault. But you know that. I began to believe I couldn't love anyone again, I was afraid to." She had not looked at him, but she held up her hand, aware that he wanted to say something. "Wait. It's not the same with John. Different, but real. I love him. I won't hurt him, Dad. I swear I won't. No matter how hard things get. Yesterday, when I thought we might all die up there, I kept thinking, I've done it again. It just didn't seem fair. You know, I'd get a reputation, Typhoid Mary, something like that. I know why you were so furious when I asked him over for Christmas Eve. You saw ahead, and I didn't." At last she looked across at him. The hurt had come back to his face.

"I watched it happen, honey," he said. "With both of you. I don't think anyone or anything on God's earth could have stopped it from happening."

One of the kittens started to climb his leg. He reached down and gently disengaged its claws and put it on his lap. When the other one started up, he lifted it, too. "You Things don't show a bit of respect," he grumbled, stroking one, then the other.

The doorbell rang; she stood up, groaning melodramatically. "I'll get it."

It was Bailey, who was early. He gave her a swift scrutiny and said, "Wow!"

She motioned him inside, then stopped at the door to the living room. "Can I have a sandwich now while we talk?"

Frank put together the makings of sandwiches, brought over beer for Bailey and milk for Barbara, and they sat at the dinette table.

She told Bailey about their day, then said, "The guy in the Ford must have called someone. Who? If it was Praeger, okay, but it could have been someone else. Find out."

"Oh, sure," Bailey said. "Done deed. The guy's Michael Mayhew, a private investigator, works out of Portland. He'll open up like a rose in bloom if I ask him anything. And I can't get at the telephone company records. FBI can, cops can, I can't."

"A detective! Who hired him? Okay, no telephone company records, but maybe we can find out. If Praeger has an answering machine, there could be all kinds of interesting things on tape. He's holed up down in Gold Beach; they haven't found him yet, or they hadn't this morning. I bet he'll keep out of sight for a while again after this."

"Well, he didn't do Knecht," Bailey said, eating his ham sandwich. He had onions and pickles, mustard and mayonnaise, lettuce on it. Things kept falling out. He tucked a pickle back inside. "He was up at Warm Springs that weekend playing poker. Lost a couple of hundred."

"Where is he getting money?" she asked.

"When we catch up with him, I'll ask," Bailey said. "Good ham." He drank beer from the can and then said, "Your guy Wilmar Juret, president of Carlyle Mining Company has an office in San Francisco. And he doesn't talk to strangers or private detectives." He looked beseechingly at Frank. "Tell me it ain't so, it isn't coming down to gold mines."

Frank shrugged. "Ask Praeger when you catch up with him. He was ready to kill to protect his mine."

"It's just a hole in the ground," Barbara commented. "John's got samples for testing, but he thinks it's just a hole in the ground, too." She frowned. "Lois wrote, 'P says gold mountain is real, or will be.' Gold mountain, but there isn't any gold mountain." She kept frowning. "She also said the Chinese laborers who were brought in called America 'Gold Mountain.' " Her frown vanished. "That's it," she said. "Lois heard the phrase from someone else and must have brought it up with Praeger, skeptical maybe; that's what he would have said, it's real, or will be. Something ongoing, not done yet. What? And who mentioned it in the first place?"

Bailey said something that she didn't hear as she visualized again the few minutes she had spent with the waitress at Sky-View, Wanda Isleton. She had said Lois only talked to people who had something to contribute to her history dissertation. . . . She'd even gotten old Mr. Rowland to talk.

Barbara stood up and groaned slightly, unconsciously, on her way to the wall phone to call Shelley at the office. "Look, can you go through Lois Hedrick's manuscript again and see if you can find any reference at all to Arthur Rowland? And separate out every mention of gold. I know it's a real chore." She listened, then said, "Thanks, Shelley. I'll be there all day tomorrow."

"Mal Zimmerman has something for us," she said, returning to the table. "He'll be in the office around noon tomorrow."

"And what's that about Arthur Rowland?" Frank asked very mildly.

"He talked to Lois; she taped it. I'm willing to bet it's not there. I don't remember a mention of his name anywhere. The Rowlands, Carlyle Mines, Praeger are all together in a project of some sort. I think Lois found out about it and was killed. Knecht found out and was killed."

"And you damn near got killed," Frank said with a strain in his voice.

There was no possible response. Then John called and asked

almost formally if she would have dinner with him. She named the restaurant and gave the address, as formal as he had been.

In a few minutes Bailey got up to leave. "Don't break any laws," Barbara said.

He grinned. "You tell me that? Who drilled a hole in a radiator and pushed a truck off the road? By God, not me!"

"I know. I just want it on record that I told you to behave," she said sweetly, then smiled at him.

She arrived first at the Electric Station, a nearby restaurant where they knew her and had agreed to seat her at the rear of one of the railroad cars they had refurbished. It was a dimly lighted booth; no waiter would traipse back and forth. She saw John when he appeared at the front end and waved to him. His limp was not as bad as it had been earlier.

"Hi," he said, sitting opposite her. "Exactly the right kind of place."

"I thought it would be. How's the leg?"

"Coming along. Rest a couple of days, that's all it takes."

The cocktail waitress came and they ordered Bloody Marys; their waiter came to tell them the specials and take their orders. They talked about food until their drinks arrived. They touched glasses, tasted the Bloody Marys, and put them down.

"Now do we talk about the cats?" he asked.

She shook her head. "Last night," she started, but he reached across the table and put his finger on her lips.

"Not last night, not yet. I'll start somewhere else. See, I was in a coal-mining family—Dad, grandfathers, uncles, all miners. It's all I knew to do, all I thought about doing. And there was Betty. I was nineteen and she was seventeen when we got married. She's very pretty. We were going to buy a house. I made pretty good money; we were saving like crazy. Then the mine fell in on me." He shrugged. "Everything changed. It was as if the world turned upside down and I was tossed off. Hospitals, doctors, therapy, all of it. She stuck. I wouldn't have made it without her." His voice was low and easy; he might have been talking about his first bicycle or his first puppy.

"Later, when I was okay pretty much—not well, you understand, but okay—I told her I wanted to go to school. No one believed me at first, not my family or hers. She stuck again. She hated Arizona. God, she hated it! Anyway, next it was the BLM, the Denver office, and she hated Colorado even more than Arizona. She began to say I wasn't the boy she had married, and she had that right. Larry came along, but we knew it was over with us. She was so homesick, she couldn't sleep. She wanted her children to grow up with family, and I knew I could never live back there again. It was over, but she said what she wanted was another child, and then she wanted to leave me."

Their dinners came and they both played with their forks for a moment, then put them down.

"I knew she had to leave. That wasn't even a question. It was just that she had been put through so much, and all she wanted were the children, and her family, and to go home."

"You still love her."

"I'll always love her," he said. "Not the woman she is now, but the Betty who stuck by me when I was crazy. I owe her everything. After we talk about the children, we have nothing to say to each other, but I love the memory of the girl I married. She's very happy. They have a little farm with horses; he has a farm-supply store. It's exactly the kind of life she needed."

"And you? Do you have the life you need?"

"I have the life I chose."

"I don't think that's the same thing," she said after a moment.

"Barbara, I can never have the life I need. Not when I know I might fly apart anytime. If I hadn't been afraid I was being paranoid, I never would have taken you up that mountain. See, that's how it is. Is it paranoia, or is it real? I never can be sure."

"Bailey traced that license number. The guy's a private detective. It's a wonder you spotted him at all."

"For me to think I'm being followed is not a wonder," he said. His face twisted in a grimace.

The waiter was approaching, concerned. "Is everything all right? Would you like a different entrée?"

"It's fine," Barbara said, waving him away. She leaned across the table and said vehemently, "You weren't responsible for yesterday. Praeger was. He's the crazy one, not you."

"That really doesn't change anything. I know who I am, what I am. You don't need me, Barbara. Believe me, you don't. You've been like a magnet ever since I met you. Last night had to happen, I guess. But that's it. That's all. I'll wrap up my job here and head for home."

Slowly she said, "That's exactly what I want you to do. After all this is over, the trial, all of it, I'll call you."

"Don't. I saw what I did to one woman. I don't want to see it again. Betty was scared to death of me for years; that's not easy to take. I wasn't even grateful enough to give her what she needed after all that."

"She has your children. I think she's the winner."

He pushed his plate back an inch or two. "You really want any of this?"

She shook her head.

"Let's knock it off. I'll get the lab report in about week. It might need interpretation, so I'll hang around, take Teddy shopping, teach him a couple of tricks of the trade, do things like that." His gaze was steady and unreadable.

"You won't come back."

"No." He put a credit card on the table, and the waiter appeared as if by magic.

Neither spoke while they waited for the credit-card routine to be done with. He walked to her car with her and watched her fumble her keys from her purse and open her door.

"Yesterday, last night, I kept feeling your blood," he said then. "On the steering wheel, on the lantern. You never said a word." He lifted her hand and kissed it. "I'll never forget you. You need a heavier car, the kind of driving you do."

She knew that if she tried to speak, she would cry. She touched his cheek, his scar, and got inside her car to leave. He was still standing there when she pulled out of the lot.

TWENTY-NINE

MOST OF THE pain had left her muscles and now lodged behind her eyes by the time she walked into the office the next morning. That happened when she took sleeping pills, and last night she had taken two. Feeling sluggish and hardly conscious, she unlocked the closet to get to the files, then took the Stone Point folder to the round table, where she began to read Shelley's reports.

Shelley had talked to the occupants of all but three guest rooms on the second floor the day Harry Knecht was killed. Two couples had not answered their phones; she would keep trying to reach them. One couple was a no-show; their room had remained empty all weekend.

Barbara searched for the floor plan with room numbers and checked the vacant room, then leaned back. Knecht had had the corner suite, Benjamin and Tilly Rothman the next room, and next to them no one. She was still thinking about the no-show couple when Frank came in. Before he could ask, she said, "I'm okay, not very sore, just as if I'd gone a round with a sumo wrestler. John's going to finish his work here and head for home. And stay there."

He looked her over, then nodded. She knew he had not missed her puffy eyes, or anything else; he never did. "All right," he said.

She began to tell him about the no-show when his telephone rang. He answered. "Ah, Jeremy, what can I do for you?" Barbara felt herself go tense. He listened, then said in a silky voice, "Jeremy, get a Kentucky associate who can get a court order. We want those files. And I guarantee your fee. Just do it now."

He hung up and said to Barbara, "They're stonewalling back in Pikeville. The therapist is retired, doesn't want the bother. I'll show him bother," he added darkly.

Barbara took a breath; her gaze landed on a calendar in her notebook, the trial date circled in red. Five weeks. She resisted panic, but it was there.

What she needed was a link between Knecht and whatever project involved gold mines, and no link surfaced, no matter where she searched, except for John. Then, at eleven forty-five, Mal Zimmerman handed it to her.

He arrived with a woman, Polly Kratz. They made an interesting pair; he was so tall and spindly, nervous, wired; she was very compact, in her forties, with white hair, oversized glasses, and an air of efficiency. She had been the office manager in Harry Knecht's Eugene office. They seated themselves at the desk, with Frank behind it.

He had been sorting the congressman's papers, Mal reminded Barbara. Each piece had to be evaluated and cataloged.

"So after you came up, mining was on my mind, and when I came across this letter, I called Polly to see if she remembered anything about it. And here we are. I didn't want to put it in the mail, and since she lives down here, this seemed as good a way as any to show it to you."

He pulled an envelope from his pocket, withdrew a sheet of paper, and handed it to Barbara.

She read it swiftly, looked up, startled, then reread it.

Dear Congressman Knecht:

For my dissertation I have been interviewing many people, and I have learned of a massive gold-mining plan to take place here in the state. After reading your speech about the Denali road, I feel certain that you will want to know more about this and take whatever action is necessary. The project is called Gold Mountain, and I believe it involves wilderness areas. I haven't talked about this to anyone since I don't know quite what it all means. I am staying at SkyView Ski Resort for the purpose of completing my dissertation. I will be gone from today until the first of the year, but after that I can be reached here if you have any interest in this matter. Perhaps by then I will have found out more. Yours sincerely.

Silently Barbara handed the letter to her father. After he read it, he took off his glasses and polished them, then he read it again.

"Then what happened?" Barbara asked.

Polly Kratz answered crisply. "She sent the letter to Washington, and staff there forwarded it to the Eugene office. Congressman Knecht was in and out several times over the holidays. On December twenty-ninth, he dictated an answer. We gave her three dates on which he would be in the state and asked her to choose one and call the office for an appointment. I mailed it on the thirtieth of December. I made a copy for you." She handed Barbara her printout. "We never received a reply. I know her death was an item in the newspapers, but I didn't see it at the time. In February, Congressman Knecht brought it up himself, but when I called her at SkyView, I was told she no longer was there." She said regretfully, "The matter, of course, was dropped."

"What's the Denali road she mentioned?" Barbara asked.

"It's in Alaska," Mal said. "There's an old law on the books, from 1866, Revised Statute 2477, which has been an issue for a couple of years now. It was repealed in 1976 and then reinterpreted in 1988. Basically, the law allows states to maintain and improve traditional rights-of-way over public lands. And rights-of-way can be interpreted to mean a footpath, a horse trail, road, like that. Anyway, Alaska wants to build a three-hundred-mile road through Denali National Park, and that will open it to all kinds of development and exploitation, and in the end destroy the wilderness. Congressman Knecht gave a speech opposing it in the fall of 1992. He said rights-of-way should include only roads that are already used for vehicular traffic between public destinations."

Barbara asked them questions but got little more information. The congressman had not brought it up again, Mal insisted, and Polly agreed.

"But last June, he hired a mining consultant," Barbara said. "Something aroused his interest again."

Mal frowned. "You mentioned that before, so I looked it up. He was in Oregon in June, spent a day or two out at Stone Point, and then went to a conference in Denver, where I joined him. If he met with anyone concerning this, I don't know about it."

"What about August?" she asked.

He hesitated. "He went out alone a couple of hours in August in Portland."

She went over both dates with him, making notes as he talked, and then he and Polly Kratz left. Barbara reread her copy of the letter from Lois. "That's the missing piece," she said softly. "That ties Knecht to her, completes the circle."

"Now all you have to do is find a way to introduce it," Frank said thoughtfully. "They'll fight tooth and nail to keep it out as irrelevant."

"I know," she said. "There will be a way. Dad, I want a little brainstorming session." He nodded, and she buzzed Shelley and asked her to come in. Today Shelley was dressed in a dark blue skirt and matching sweater; she was wearing shoes with low heels, and her hair was tied back in a ponytail. She looked like a pretty little girl playing grown-up.

"Okay," Barbara said when they were seated in the easy chairs by the round table. "What do you do when you're planning a massive project?"

"Get backing," Shelley said.

"Check your bank account," Frank said almost simultaneously.

"Right. We know the Rowlands bought land first, then Connie Mines. Who put up money for Praeger? Then Carlyle bought land down there. How were they induced to go along? That's the question of the day."

"A presentation of some kind," Shelley said after a moment. "Risk analysis, projected returns, a schedule . . ."

Barbara grinned at her. "Right. Your department, Shelley. Find out how they advertise, who they use, and if there's anything on Gold Mountain in the files." She smiled. "And don't let them know you're poking."

Shelley nodded, dead serious.

"Next, I'll tackle the maid at Stone Point, and the reservation clerk." She looked at Frank then. "And someone has to talk to Wilmar Juret, at the Carlyle Company."

Frank was nodding unhappily. "Without mentioning Project Gold Mountain."

"You've got it. But as one affluent businessman dealing with another, you will get along swimmingly, I'm sure." Then she added, "No one is to mention Gold Mountain to anyone. Our little secret."

On Friday she had an appointment to talk to Nora Blake, the maid at Stone Point, and another appointment on Saturday to talk to the reservation clerk. Afterward, she added them both to her list of witnesses. On Saturday night she used the last of her sleeping pills. She slept little Sunday night, but she woke up without a head stuffed with cotton. Tired but functioning, she told herself.

On Monday John brought in the results of the laboratory work on the rocks. She was dismayed at her sexual response just from seeing him enter the office. He looked shaken, then his face tightened and became masklike.

"It's what I expected," he said, standing on the opposite side of the desk. His voice sounded husky; he cleared his throat. Only then did he become aware of Frank on the couch across the room. He nodded to him, and from that moment, he addressed his remarks to Frank.

"I had twenty-two pounds of rocks," he said. "The assay predicts one hundred sixty grains of gold to the ton. To be profitable, that number would have to be five hundred sixty grains, an ounce. It's approximately twenty-eight percent of what it would take to start mining. Anything under an ounce per ton isn't worth digging for. You can buy it cheaper on the open market."

He put a folder on the desk without a glance at Barbara, who felt immobilized, as if the air around her had become enormously heavy. "There's a certified lab report, and another certified report from me that states where the rocks came from and when I collected them. I guess now I'm done." Finally he looked at Barbara, his expression remote and strange. "I brought this out for you. You dropped it." He laid on the desk the rock she had picked up and discarded in her flight from Praeger's mine.

She tried to say thanks, to say anything, but the words stuck. He turned to leave, with Frank suddenly at his side. Barbara had not noticed when her father stood up and crossed the office. "I'll walk out with you," he said, reaching past John to open the door. They both walked out; Frank closed the door softly. She picked up the rock, still warm, and held it in both hands, her eyes tightly closed.

After that, time did its miraculous trick: It stalled entirely or the days flashed by faster than she could grasp the fact that they were gone.

Bailey brought in the tape from Praeger's place in Gold Beach. "Nothing to it," he said. "Slipped in, made a copy, replaced the original, slipped out."

They played it in Frank's office. They all recognized Praeger's voice, the voice on the tape Lois had made. For a moment Barbara was confused by the thick voice of the caller: "Damn it, Owen, give me a call as soon as you get in."

She exhaled. "Arthur Rowland," she said. The tape made clicking sounds; Praeger's message repeated, then the same voice came on again. "You idiot. Call me. What's going on?" After that was a call from someone who said he was Marvin; he announced that a game was on for Friday night. And nothing more.

"Arthur," she repeated.

"Are you sure?" Frank asked.

"Yes."

Three weeks to go. Still no Praeger, nothing yet on Gold Mountain. Two weeks. One week. They had prepared Ted as much as possible. Praeger was still among the missing.

The day before they were to start the trial, she realized how frightened she was, how poorly prepared, how desperate. She still didn't know how she could introduce the matter of gold mines; there was no certain bridge from Harry Knecht to mines without John's testimony.

And then it was time to start.

SPRING

THIRTY

JURY SELECTION, SHE had warned the Wendovers, could be both tedious and frightening. By the end of the week, they had a panel of seven women and five men, the youngest twenty-three, the oldest seventy-one. They would do, she assured Ted: a retired librarian, a computer programmer, a farmer, a sculptor supporting himself as a baker, two housewives, a carpenter, and so on.

Judge Jordan Ariel was fifty, a strict judge who believed in rules and decorum and would run a tight, no-nonsense court. That was fine with Barbara; what she found disturbing was the fact that he had been a prosecutor for twelve years before becoming a judge only three years ago. He was a hefty man with a florid complexion and gray hair.

When she asked Frank if he was a boozer, he had scoffed at the idea. "He's a God-fearing churchgoer with a wife and five children; he hasn't heard a joke in fifty years that made him smile. I reckon he's not in favor of having two women slug it out in his court."

Grace Heflin had a number of suits, apparently, in many shades of blue. She presented such an immaculate, well-groomed look that Barbara felt shabby in comparison. Assisting Heflin was Marcus Truly, who had been with the district attorney's office for six or eight months. He was a goddamn robot, Barbara thought, studying him. He always knew exactly what Heflin wanted next, and he had the right paper, the right questionnaire, the right pen to hand to her. Also, he made notes like a machine.

Frank was as comfortable and relaxed as his old disgraceful

chair, and only Shelley held up their side in appearance, with many new outfits, all very grown-up clothes, for this, her first court trial.

When court recessed on Friday, Barbara spoke briefly to Ted, who was grim and too rigid; she would have to talk to him about that over the weekend. Then she joined the three adult Wendovers for a moment. They all looked worn, despite the brave front they maintained.

The downstairs of the courthouse was crowded with reporters, television crews, onlookers. "Can't comment," Frank said again and again. "Judge's orders. No comment." He waved in a friendly fashion and got Barbara and Shelley through with enviable slickness.

As she and her father walked to his house, where she had parked, he said tentatively, "Bobby, I've been thinking. We work pretty well together, when we're in touch. You never know when something's going to break and we'll both be needed. And you sort of forget meals when you get preoccupied. Don't decide too soon, but it's worked in the past for you to stay at the house—"

She linked her arm through his and said, "Okay."

He stopped in midstride to stare at her. "Okay?"

"It's worked beautifully before, no reason it shouldn't this time. I'll move some of my gear over this weekend."

She recalled how her mother had watched over him when he was in the middle of a trial, how he had watched over her, Barbara, in the past. It was more than okay, she decided.

That weekend she moved many things to Frank's house, told her neighbors she would be away a few weeks, and settled in. Frank planted more of his garden; the cats were at his heels constantly. He murmured to them, scolded them, maybe discussed constitutional law with them, Barbara mused, watching them in the backyard. She felt almost bewildered at how far advanced spring was, flowers in bloom, lush grass, everywhere bushes and trees that had come into bloom, rhodies and azaleas. Spring. In her mind, she heard John's quiet voice: "Springtime in the Klamaths."

Then it was Monday and the actual trial started with the opening statements. Heflin said she intended to prove Theodore Wendover, deliberately and with malice prepense, had murdered Harry Knecht; that his motive had been jealousy and rage. . . . He had endured betrayal, had known his wife was having an affair with the man who destroyed his son, and for years he did nothing, until he finally reached the end of his endurance. He had made a threat, and with cunning and forethought, he had carried out the threat and murdered his wife's lover. It was a very simple case. And the proof, as they would see, was indisputable.

She still had the crisp edge she had shown before, but it was tempered with restraint, almost sadness. When she finished, she nodded to Barbara in a way that suggested understanding, as if to say she knew the defense was a necessary procedure but that they both recognized its futility.

Barbara approached the jury box; the jurors were rapt in their attention. "Ladies and gentlemen, there is no such thing as a simple structure. Behind every apparent simplicity, there is infinite complexity. Behind every human statistic, there are human beings, and no one can know the complexity of another human being. The state's case is indeed a simple one, but in the same way that a mountain range is simple, if you are far from it. As you draw nearer, the complexity becomes more and more bewildering. And in all creation, human beings are the most complex. Libraries are filled with volumes that try to explain human behavior, and year after year more volumes are added because we are still puzzled, still in wonder at the variety of actions and reactions people are capable of.

"This is not a simple case. The defense is joined to prove a negative, that Ted Wendover did not murder Congressman Harry Knecht. Ted Wendover did not have a motive, and he did not have the opportunity. We will show that Ted Wendover loves his son deeply, and he loves his wife. His life was one of contentment. In the days to follow, the defense will demonstrate that others had both motive and opportunity. . . ."

Grace Heflin's first witness was Winston Brody. Today, he was in a nice gray suit, his shoes were polished, he was so freshly shaven that he probably was still wet, and he had a neat haircut. He appeared comfortable, at ease as he recited details of his past experience and his present employment as chief of security at Stone Point. Heflin got to the point very quickly with a series of questions about his finding Knecht's body.

"Mr. Brody, can you identify the man you saw kneeling by Congressman Knecht's body?"

"Yes, ma'am. That's him, Ted Wendover." He looked at Ted and pointed.

Grace Heflin nodded. "Thank you. When you first made your statement, Mr. Brody, you said the person you saw was in blue jeans and a white shirt and that he carried a canvas bag over his shoulder. Can you tell us about that?"

He looked down at his hands and said in a low voice, "I made a mistake. When I realized I had made the mistake, I went right in and cleared it up." He looked up at her. "Can I add something?"

"By all means," she said.

"See, earlier I'd been down on the beach and I saw Teddy Wendover with his mother. That's how he was dressed, jeans and a white T-shirt, and he had a bag of rocks over his shoulder. Trouble, I thought. He's trouble. Later on I saw his mother in the hotel, and I thought he must be there, too. The first thing that flashed in my mind when I saw the congressman was that Teddy did it. I might have been in some kind of shock, seeing the dead man, all the rocks. Anyway, as soon as I knew that I made a mistake, I went in and told them."

"Why did you think of trouble when you saw Teddy Wendover?" Heflin asked.

"Well, he got in trouble over at the ski resort. They won't let him inside the lodge over there, or near the swimming pool, anyplace where there's little kids. I didn't think they'd want him at Stone Point, either. Lots of little kids wander around the beach or by the swimming pool."

Ted made a strangled sound; Barbara whispered, "Easy, take it easy."

Heflin finished with him soon after that. Barbara stood up

and walked to the center of the jury box. "Mr. Brody, you've been at Stone Point for nine years. Is that right?"

"Yes."

"Were you hired to be chief of security?"

"No, I was raised five years ago."

"Before Stone Point, you were a police officer in Dallas. For how long?"

"About six years."

"Did you do office work?"

"No. We cruised, me and my partner."

"Were you trained to use firearms?"

"Sure."

"Did you ever have to use yours?"

"Yes, a couple of times."

"Did you ever investigate a situation where there were violent deaths?"

"Objection," Heflin said. "This is getting off the subject."

"I don't think so," Barbara said. "He was trained to deal with violence, yet he said he went into shock at the sight of the congressman's body."

"Overruled," Ariel said. "But no more about the past."

"Yes," Brody said. "Sometimes."

"Who told you Teddy Wendover was trouble?" she asked, not moving from the rail.

"Mr. Rowland," he said promptly.

"You mean Brian Rowland, the owner of Stone Point?"

"Yeah, Mr. Brian Rowland."

"When was that, Mr. Brody?"

"When he hired me."

"Did he tell you what happened at the ski resort?"

"Not much. Just that he got in trouble with little kids."

"Did he warn you about other possible troublemakers?"

He hesitated, then said, "No. I don't think so."

"In your knowledge, have any of the Wendovers ever stayed as guests at Stone Point?"

"Not that I know of."

"Have you ever met any of them?"

"No." His face had taken on a set expression.

"Where were Mrs. Wendover and Teddy when you first saw them on September ninth?"

"Down the beach a ways. I went down the elevator and stopped at the landing, where I could see up and down the beach, just checking things out, and I saw them."

"How far away were they?"

He shrugged. "Not far. A couple hundred feet maybe."

"Were they on the north side of the creek?"

"No."

"Mr. Brody, the creek we're talking about is five hundred feet from the elevator, isn't it?"

"I don't know. I never measured it."

She nodded and went to the defense table and rummaged among papers, brought out a folded map. She identified it as a United States Geologic Survey map of Lane County and had it entered as evidence, then refolded it to show only the shoreline. She approached Brody with the map in her hand.

"Mr. Brody, this is the creek we're talking about, isn't it?" she asked, pointing to the map. He nodded, and she said, "Yes. And here is the landing for the stairs and elevator to Stone Point. Is that correct?"

"Yes," he said.

"Yes," she repeated. "According to this map, Mr. Brody, the distance from the center of the creek to the landing is six hundred twenty feet, and at that point the creek is fifty feet wide. And you say you saw Mrs. Wendover and her son on the south side of it. That would be six hundred forty-five feet. Were there other people on the beach that day?"

"A few."

"But you were able to see well enough to identify Teddy Wendover, someone you had never seen before, from that distance, and in spite of other people on the beach?"

"That's right," he said. "I spotted him."

"I see. From your original statement, Mr. Brody, let me quote your words." She handed the map to the jury foreman, Mr. Betz, and then went to her table to retrieve the statement while the jurors passed the map around. She waited until the clerk took the map and placed it on the exhibit table. Then she read:

" 'Question: Will you please describe the man you saw kneeling by Mr. Knecht's body? Answer: Yes. He was about six feet, one eighty pounds, brown hair, not very dark, with a little bit of wave. And he had this real goofy expression, like he's not all there. You know what I mean?' " She looked at Brody. Although expressionless, his face had reddened. "Mr. Brody, do you recall those words?"

"Yes. I said I made a mistake; he just flashed into my mind in the excitement of seeing the congressman dead."

"Since we now know you didn't see him at all in Stone Point, you must have seen his expression from six hundred and forty-five feet away. Is that what you mean?"

"I saw him on the beach," he said stubbornly.

"What does a 'goofy expression' mean, Mr. Brody?"

"He's retarded, maybe crazy, I don't know, just not right. You can see it in his face."

"From over six hundred feet away," she murmured, and shook her head. She picked up a large piece of graph paper and handed it to Brody. "Is that a fair representation of the suite Mr. Knecht occupied the weekend of September ninth?"

He examined it, shrugged, and handed it back to her. "It looks okay."

After having it admitted, she turned toward her table, where Shelley was setting up a folding easel where the jurors and the judge could all see it; she clipped the drawing to the easel. The rooms were drawn in heavy black lines.

Barbara walked to the easel. "This is the door to the hallway. You said this door was open slightly. Is that right?"

"That's right. A couple of inches—that's why I went in."

"Let's take it slowly this time, Mr. Brody. You pushed the door open. Did you close it again?"

"No."

"So it was against the closet door in the foyer. Did you at any time look inside the closet?" He said no. "All right. After you entered the foyer, what did you do?"

"I looked in the bedroom and the bathroom and then I went into the sitting room."

"Did you enter the bedroom?"

"No, I just looked in."

"From the doorway?"

"Yeah, from the doorway. I could see enough."

"Then what did you do?"

"I looked in the dressing room and bathroom."

"Did you enter the dressing room?"

"No, from the doorway."

Barbara looked from the drawing to him. "Did you hear anything when you entered the foyer?"

"Yes. It sounded like something dropped in the sitting room. Like rocks or something."

She nodded. "Were you armed, Mr. Brody?"

"Yes. I drew out my revolver when I heard the noise."

"All right. You were suspicious because of the open door; you entered the foyer, then you heard something drop in the sitting room, but you say you went to the bedroom door to look inside and then to the bathroom door to look inside before you entered the sitting room. Is that correct?"

"That's what I did," he said harshly.

She studied the drawing; then, using her pencil, she drew in a line diagonally through the bedroom. "From the open door, the line of sight would include this area," she said, pointing, "while this area would be out of sight. Is that right, Mr. Brody?"

"No, it isn't. I could see it all."

"Then you must have stepped inside the room. Did you do that?"

He was getting redder with each question. Patiently she asked questions and forced him to admit that without entering the room completely, he could not have seen the right quarter. She repeated this with the dressing room and bathroom. It was a laborious procedure.

Finally she said, "Mr. Brody, you could not really see the whole bedroom or the entire dressing room and bathroom, could you?"

"No, but enough to know no one was in there."

She shook her head. "If you couldn't see the space, you have no way of knowing if anyone was there, do you?"

He glared at her. "No."

"Now, you said you heard something fall in the sitting room. There is thick carpeting in all those rooms, isn't there?"

"Yes."

"So any object you heard fall must have been heavy, is that right?"

"Objection," Grace Heflin said. "Supposition."

The objection was sustained.

"All right," Barbara said pleasantly, "now let's follow your movements from the time you moved to the door of the sitting room. First, these double lines represent glass doors and windows, don't they? Eight feet on the south side, eight feet on the west?"

"Yes," he said.

"And according to the police report, Mr. Knecht's body was here." She drew in a line about five feet from the south doors and six feet from the west. "Is that how you recall it?"

"I don't know. I guess it was."

"We can look at the police photographs if you have any doubts," she said.

"That's how it was," he snapped.

"All right. His body was aligned east to west, with his head toward the west windows." She drew a small circle on the line, then studied the room. "The door is about fifteen feet down the room. Were the drapes all open, Mr. Brody?"

He said they were.

"So you stepped into the room. Exactly what did you do, Mr. Brody?"

"I told you. I saw him, Knecht, and Wendover bending—"

"One moment, Mr. Brody. You were here at the doorway. You saw a figure on the floor and another figure kneeling by him. They must have been silhouetted, with the sun streaming in the west windows behind them. When did you identify the figure on the floor as Congressman Knecht?"

"Right away. I yelled, 'Hey,' something like that, and took a couple of steps in—"

She stopped him again. "Please, just a little slower. From the doorway, you saw the figures, and you called out. Is that right?"

"Yes." He stopped this time and she nodded at him.

"All right. When you called out, what did the kneeling man do?"

"He looked up at me and got to his feet and ran."

"Which side of the body was he by, closer to you or to the windows?"

"Inside the room, closer to me, up by Knecht's head." He was snapping the words out sharply.

"All right. So from the doorway fifteen feet from him, with him against bright sunlight, you saw him clearly. Is that right?"

"Yes." Quickly he added, "His back was to me when he was down, but he looked up and I saw him."

"When he stood up, was he wearing gloves?"

"I didn't notice."

"Was he holding anything?"

"I couldn't see anything. His back was to me when he ran out."

"Then what?"

"I ran to Mr. Knecht and knelt down to see if he was alive."

"Where did you kneel, by his head?"

"Yes, so I could feel his carotid."

"Was that about where the other man had been kneeling?"

"Yes. I mean, I'm not sure. Maybe it was."

"All right. Then what?"

"I ran out to the balcony. I pulled my walkie-talkie off my belt and called Julio Martinez. The guy was going down a post to the ground, and he took off toward the cottages. I had to run all the way to the end of the balcony and down the stairs because my hands were full."

"So he climbed down a post. Was he using both hands?"

"He was at the bottom when I got out, just dropping to the ground. I couldn't see his hands."

"So you can't know if he was carrying anything, is that right?"

"Right."

"Or if he was wearing gloves?"

"I couldn't see his hands."

"From the time you first saw him, then saw him run, drop

down from the post, and cross the stretch to the cottages, did you ever see anything in his hands?"

"He could have had something, or he could have stuffed something in his pocket."

"But my question is, Did you see anything in his hands?"

"No."

"Why didn't you shoot him, Mr. Brody?" she asked softly.

He shifted in his chair, glanced at the jury, then glared at her. "My gun wasn't loaded."

"You carry an unloaded gun?"

"Yes. Sometimes, not often. When there's a political figure, a lot of enemies around, I carry it."

"But if you can't use it, why do you carry it?"

"It's enough just to have it. People respect weapons."

"Why is your gun unloaded, Mr. Brody?"

"It's just not necessary to use it except for show," he muttered.

"In your position as chief of security, are you authorized to bear weapons, to use them?"

"No," he said sullenly.

"So you carry it for show." She nodded. "Were there a lot of Congressman Knecht's enemies around that weekend?"

Heflin's objection was sustained.

Barbara had to go the long way around to get back to the question: "So extra security had been hired that weekend; you had several meetings about security operations and possible problems. You carried a gun. Did you believe Mr. Knecht had enemies who might cause trouble?"

"It was a possibility. With politicians, it's always possible," he added swiftly.

"I suppose," she said meditatively, "having a murder occur almost under your nose when you were chief of security was a shock. Did you follow the news stories, the television stories concerning it?"

He hesitated, as if trying to determine what she was getting at. Finally he said grudgingly, "A little."

She smiled and shook her head. "Mr. Brody, really? Just a little?"

"Objection," Heflin said. "Witness answered the question."

"Sustained."

Barbara nodded at the judge. "Well, did you see any articles concerning the detainment of Teddy Wendover?"

She waited for the objection; none came.

"I heard something about it," Brody said after a pause.

"And the articles that detailed his exoneration?"

"I heard something about it," he said again.

"Did you read it?"

"I might have. I don't remember."

She turned around to open a folder and bring out a newspaper. She had it admitted, then showed it to Brody. "This was the major story about him," she said. "Is this one you read?"

"I'm not sure."

She opened the newspaper partway to display the picture of Teddy making a castle. She started to cross to the jury to show them the paper, then paused. "Mr. Brody, when did you report the mistake in your description of the man you saw?"

"As soon as I was sure," he said sharply.

"What was the date?"

"I don't know."

"It's on the statement," she said. "Let me refresh your memory." She returned to her table to pick it up again, then said, "Your statement is dated December fifth. Is that right?"

"I don't know. I wasn't interested in the date."

"But I am, Mr. Brody," she said sharply. "I'm very interested in the date. This newspaper is dated December fourth. And this lower part has a picture of Teddy Wendover with his family, including Ted Wendover. And on December fifth, you changed your description to fit Ted Wendover." She handed the newspaper to Mr. Betz.

She waited as the newspaper was passed from hand to hand; one or two of the jurors looked up from the picture to Ted, back down again. When it was at last handed to the clerk, she faced Judge Ariel.

"Your Honor, I have no further questions to ask this witness at this time. However, I wish to recall him as a hostile witness for the defense at a later date."

Heflin objected. "Counsel can ask whatever questions she has now."

Reasonably Barbara said to her, "There has been no proper foundation for the questions I intend to ask. Without such foundation, you would have cause to object repeatedly."

Heflin's lips tightened. "May I approach the bench?"

Judge Ariel beckoned them both to come forward.

"Your Honor," Grace Heflin said in an intense low voice, "I have cause to believe that counsel will try to muddy this case beyond recognition. Mr. Brody has testified to what he knows about this, and to bring him back again is simply a ploy to confuse the issue."

"I believe it is my job to determine that," Judge Ariel said. "If at any time you think I'm not doing my job, let me know." He made a shooing motion at them. "Let's get on with it." He turned to Brody and said, "Mr. Brody, you will hold yourself in readiness to take the witness stand again. You will be notified of the time and date." Then he asked Grace Heflin, "Do you wish to continue with this witness at this time?"

She walked stiffly back to her table and consulted with Marcus Truly. Then she faced the judge again. "Yes, Your Honor. The state will continue. Mr. Brody," she started, without waiting for a response from the judge, "did you see the man clearly who was kneeling by the body of Congressman Knecht?"

"Yes, I did." His voice was confident again, his answer swift and sure.

"And was that man Theodore Wendover, the accused?"

"Yes, it was."

"Thank you. That's all." She sat down.

Judge Ariel then said, "The court will recess at this time and reconvene at two o'clock. I advise you to fortify yourselves. We will continue until five or after." He reminded the jurors that they were not to discuss the case with one another or anyone else.

After the judge and the jury panel left, Barbara turned to Ted, whose eyes were shining. "You were great," he said. His guard was at his elbow. He waved to his family and walked out, almost jauntily. The other Wendovers were nearly joyful. It was the first time Barbara had seen them all so radiant; she didn't have the heart to tell them what both she and Frank knew. The prosecution had used its weakest link first; from now on, they would be building a much firmer case.

She and Frank walked out into clamorous reporters and cameramen and continued through them with nods and smiles, not saying a word. They went through the tunnel under Seventh Street, emerged in the parking lot, and started the walk toward his house. They had agreed that if they had more than an hour for lunch, that would be the place for it, not a restaurant, not the office and deli sandwiches. At his corner they separated.

"I'll take a walk," she said. "Be back in an hour." He nodded, reaching for her briefcase.

She walked on the river trail skirting Alton Baker Park. The air was misty, the sky overcast, but not really threatening. Few other people were on the trail at this time of day; the river was swift and somewhat muddy from spring rains, and there were no traffic noises, no one asking questions, shoving a microphone in her face.

She thought about Grace Heflin. She had done two smart things: She had preempted Barbara's questions about the misidentification of the suspect and she had left the jury with two hours to solidify Brody's firm identification of Ted Wendover as the man he had seen.

THIRTY-ONE

JULIO MARTINEZ WAS a slim, handsome man, thirty-five, with abundant, shiny black hair. He was very nervous. Heflin led him through his history, his five years at Stone Point, and then asked, "Mr. Martinez, will you tell us about September ninth of last year in your own words, please?"

He swallowed and nodded. "Yes, ma'am. I was out by the swimming pool when I got the call on the walkie-talkie and Mr. Brody said Mr. Knecht was killed and I should get someone to call the sheriff and get a doctor to his room and keep everyone out and send the rest of the guys out to help him find the killer." He said this without a pause.

"What did you do next?" Heflin asked.

"I ran to the desk and told Gloria—she was on duty that day—told her to call the sheriff and get a doctor and call in the other guys and tell them to go help Mr. Brody. And Mr. Siletz, he came, and I told him and he said he'd call the sheriff and I should go up and watch the room. And I ran up the stairs—didn't wait for the elevator, just ran up the stairs and stood in the doorway, where I could see the windows, and he was on the floor."

Grace Heflin produced a brochure with the layout of the hotel and grounds; she showed it to Martinez. "You were here at the pool and ran into the hotel, stopped at the desk, and then ran upstairs. How long do you think all this took?"

"Two or three minutes maybe. I really ran."

"Did you see anyone on the stairs?"

"No, ma'am. Not in the hall, nowhere. Not until Dr. Vorlander came and he went in and squatted down and stood up again and stood by me. He didn't say a word to me."

"Did you enter the sitting room?"

He shook his head hard. "No, ma'am. I stood right by the door, where I could see the windows, and that's all I did."

"Did Dr. Vorlander touch anything in the sitting room?"

"No, ma'am. He just squatted down to get a good look and came right back out and he didn't say a word to me. And Mr. Siletz, he came to wait for the sheriff's deputies, too."

She finished with him quickly, and Barbara stood up at her table. "Mr. Martinez, who hired you at Stone Point?"

"Mr. Walleski—he's the personnel manager. Five years ago I answered the ad and he talked to me and Mr. Brody talked to me, but Mr. Walleski, he said I could start the next week."

"Did Mr. Rowland talk to you?"

"No, ma'am. I never talked to him, except maybe to say good morning or something like that."

"When Mr. Walleski hired you, did he warn you to watch out for Teddy Wendover?"

"No, ma'am. I never heard of him until all this started up. Mr. Brody, he didn't mention him, neither. Nobody did."

"Did they warn you about any troublemakers?"

"No, ma'am, not in particular, if that's what you mean, just what to watch out for by the pool and on the beach—you know, pickpockets, or rowdiness, drugs, things like that."

"Where did you stand to watch the sitting room?"

"In the foyer, right by the door, and Dr. Vorlander, he stood there with me."

She thanked him and returned to her chair.

Dr. Vorlander and a deputy sheriff took the stand and left quickly; they had nothing to add. Then Heflin called Sheriff Jackson Friess.

He was fifty-six, almost bald, with faded reddish tufts of hair over his ears. He was very tan and looked fit, as if he worked out regularly. He stated his background succinctly, obviously familiar with court procedures.

"Sheriff Friess, will you please tell us about that evening of September ninth?"

"I was at home when the call came through. I called the dispatcher and told her to round up the Homicide Unit and send them out, and I drove over to Stone Point, arrived at six forty-five. By seven-thirty, the whole unit was there and the technicians were at work."

He described the room, the pebbles, and the murder weapon, and identified it when it was produced. Heflin showed him photographs and passed them to the jury. Knecht was on his back, the left side of his head crushed and bloody, the right side of his head against the carpet. Other pictures showed close-ups of some of the pebbles that were all around Knecht's body. Another was a close-up of the murder rock on the floor near his head.

The sheriff stuck to the facts without a single conjecture, not even when Heflin asked about the position of the body.

"He fell and was moved to that position after he was down," he said simply.

"Can you say why?"

"No, I can't."

"Could you tell in what way he was moved?"

"It looked as if he had been on his side maybe and then was turned on his back. The carpet was scuffed by his shoes, and other scuff marks indicated that was the case."

She moved on to fingerprints, and he said there were none recoverable on the rock or the many pebbles; the bottle had a lot of smudges, and one recoverable print, which turned out to be the congressman's. All the fingerprints, he stated, were accounted for, left by people who had been in and out of the room earlier in the day.

"Did you identify Mrs. Wendover's fingerprints in the suite?"

"Yes. In the sitting room and the bathroom."

"Would you say, Sheriff, that the murderer wore gloves and that accounts for no unidentified fingerprints?"

"I would say that," he agreed.

"Did you find any other physical evidence that is unidentified?"

"Yes, we did. There were fibers on the carpet near Mr. Knecht's head. We have been unable to match them."

"Can you tell us what those fibers are?"

"Dark gray, almost black, cotton-and-wool blend, commonly found in lightweight menswear."

"Did you look through Mr. Wendover's wardrobe?"

"Yes. He had two pairs of slacks of the same fabric, the same blend, but one was lighter gray and the other was dark blue."

She finished with him soon after that, nodded coolly to Barbara, and sat down to begin a whispered consultation with her assistant, Marcus Truly, who made notes.

"Sheriff, you have been very helpful," Barbara said truthfully. "I have only a few questions. Were there any items from room service in Mr. Knecht's room?"

"No."

"Was there a tray?"

"No."

"In your experience, have you seen other head wounds similar to Congressman Knecht's?"

"Similar, yes."

"And have you determined how such a wound is administered?"

He looked at her shrewdly and nodded. "We always try to. Sometimes the suspect has confirmed our guesses."

"Can you tell us how you believe the congressman's wound was delivered?"

"Objection," Heflin said. "That's simple speculation."

Before Barbara could speak, Judge Ariel said, "Sustained."

"Exception, Your Honor," she said.

"Noted. Now continue, if you will."

"Sheriff, was there a great amount of blood under the congressman's head?"

"Yes. It doesn't show in the photographs very well because it soaked into the carpet."

"Was there blood anywhere else in the room?"

"No, just in the area of his head."

"From the scuff marks, could you tell how far he had been moved?"

"Not far," he said. "Maybe just rolled over, or shifted a couple of inches from where he landed."

She went to the exhibit table and lifted the rock with both hands, returned with it to stand before him. It was in a plastic bag, tagged. "This rock is almost completely covered with blood, isn't it?"

"Yes, it is."

"And the hand that held it must have gotten blood on it, too. Is that correct?"

"Objection," Heflin said. "Speculation."

"Overruled," Judge Ariel said.

Barbara thought she glimpsed a gleam in his eyes, but it vanished too soon to be certain. "Shall I repeat my question, Sheriff?" she asked.

"No need. That hand would have had blood on it. There's no doubt."

She replaced the rock. "Did your technicians examine the balcony, the rail, and the post?"

"Yes."

"Did you find any fingerprints?"

"No, just some smudges."

"Did you find any blood?"

"No, we didn't."

"Did the person who went over that rail have on gloves?"

They both waited for Heflin to object; she remained still.

"He must have worn gloves if that's where he went over."

"When your laboratory examined this rock, did they find anything else on it besides blood and the tissue from Mr. Knecht's head?"

"Yes, they did. A few particles of yellow rubber."

"Did you identify those particles?"

"They're the kind that would be in utility gloves, the kind cleaning people sometimes use."

She went to her table and produced a pair of yellow rubber gloves, elbow-length. "Would that be in this kind of gloves?" He said yes.

She nodded and walked to her table to retrieve a police photograph, then took it to the sheriff. "Is this your technician's photograph?"

He examined it and said it was. "Sheriff, do you see those indentations?" She pointed to three faint shadows on the carpet, evenly spaced to form a small triangle.

He took glasses from his pocket and studied the photograph. "I see them here, but I didn't see them before."

The lowering sun had cast them in relief. They were several feet from Knecht's body.

"Do you know what made those indentations?" she asked.

"No, I don't. As I said, I didn't see them before. It's the way the light falls that makes them show up here."

"Sheriff, will you please draw a circle around them?" She handed him a pen, and he drew the circle. She took the print to

Judge Ariel, who examined it briefly, and then took it over to
the jury box.

To her surprise, when the sheriff was excused, Judge Ariel
called for a fifteen-minute recess. She had expected to be kept in
court without a break. She was ready to relax a minute, she
thought, and turned to speak to Ted. He was pale and grim
again. She glanced over her shoulder and caught a glimpse of
Carolyn as she stood up and started to walk from the courtroom,
waxy-faced and very rigid.

"Try to relax," she said to Ted then. "It always gets worse
before it gets better. Hang in there."

He nodded without changing his bleak expression, then he
left with his guard.

Dr. William Tillich was sixty-seven, thin, and tired-looking. He
had been a medical examiner for seventeen years and had been
a rheumatologist in a Portland hospital for twenty-four years.
He had conducted the autopsy and prepared the autopsy report,
he stated.

"Dr. Tillich," Heflin said, when he had finished his résumé,
"the report is in highly technical medical terminology. Will you
kindly tell us in common terms what your findings indicate?"

He started with the physical description of the dead man,
giving his weight in kilograms and his height in meters. He
went on to say the health of the deceased had been excellent. He
had found two loose molars, upper and lower in the right jaw,
presumably loosened by his fall. There was bruising on the right
side of his face, from the forehead area to the chin, including his
ear, where capillaries had broken but no external bleeding had
occurred. He had died in the position in which he had been
found, on his back. The cause of death was a blow to the head
with the rock the state had in its possession.

Heflin nodded. "Thank you, Doctor. That's perfectly under-
standable. Can you determine if bruises are new?" He said yes,
and she asked, "Can you explain the bruises on his face and
ear?"

He nodded. "I found many fibers from the carpet embedded

in his skin on the right side of his face, and a slight abrasion along the jaw contained the same fibers. They are all from the carpeting under him. He was bruised in the fall to the floor."

She asked him to describe the wound itself next. He did so in highly technical terms, then concluded: "He was hit with enough force to fracture his skull in multiple places. Bone fragments were driven inward to the brain, and bones and brain tissue were embedded in the rock."

"Could he have survived a blow like that?"

"Absolutely not."

She finished with him soon after that and Barbara approached him slowly. She was aware that some of the jurors were looking squeamish, one woman looked positively ill, and she dreaded to think how Carolyn was taking all this. Tough, she thought then.

"Dr. Tillich," she asked, "could Mr. Knecht have moved after such a blow? Involuntary muscle spasms, something of that sort?"

"No, he couldn't. Muscle spasms are minute compared to the strength needed to move masses such as legs and torsos."

"Could you determine where the blow came from, if it was angled from front or back, for example?"

"It came straight in from the side," he said without hesitation. "The bone fragments were driven in without any lateral displacement."

"Was there any vertical displacement?"

"None."

"You said his height was one point eight meters. Is that about five feet eleven inches?"

"It is."

"Dr. Tillich, exactly what happens when a body sustains an injury like that?"

"First, a complete loss of consciousness. I would expect a relaxation of the involuntary muscles, loss of bladder control, bowels. The energy of the blow was absorbed mostly by the head of the deceased, of course, but there was sufficient energy to drive him so that he would not have fallen straight down, but with some momentum to one side."

Nodding, she walked to the defense table, where Shelley

handed her an artist's jointed wooden doll. It was maple, perfectly proportioned. She returned with it to the witness stand. "I wonder if you could demonstrate with this doll how such a blow would affect the victim."

He eyed it suspiciously. "It's too stiff," he said. Then he said, "Maybe it'll work." He handled it a moment, then held it upright. "See, first the head would be thrown to the side." He pushed it accordingly; it stayed where he put it. "The knees would buckle, and the hips. . . . The arms would be hanging, without muscle tone." He bent the doll as he talked and finally had it in a sprawl on its side on the witness stand. He frowned at it and moved the head, frowned again. The side of the face was not flush with the stand. The shoulder was in the way. He looked up at Barbara. She nodded.

"Would you use this pen and mark the doll's face in the same way the bruises showed on the deceased?" She handed him a red felt marker.

He marked the doll and she held it upright. "Let's assume this is a representation of a five-foot-eleven man. In order to hit him straight from the side without any downward or upward motion, the rock would have had to come in a straight line. How tall would a person have to be in order to deliver such a blow, Doctor?"

"Five feet nine or ten at the shoulder," he said promptly. He knew exactly where she was going now. "Probably six feet four or five inches altogether."

She laid the figure down before him and went to the evidence table to pick up the rock. "Doctor, how would such a man wield the rock? Like this?" She held it in both hands and raised her arms.

"No, that wouldn't do it. You'd have to hold it straight out at shoulder level and swing it in hard."

She tried to hold the rock out as he directed. It was too heavy to hold at arm's length; her arm began to sag. "Would there be enough force behind such a motion to do the damage you reported?"

"Maybe," he said. "You couldn't do it, but a very strong man could have done it that way. But what's the victim doing, just waiting?"

"Objection!" Grace Heflin snapped. "Strike the comment following his answer."

Judge Ariel told the jury to disregard the comment, a meaningless order; the idea had been planted.

"Doctor, the way you demonstrated the fall, the victim's legs and hips would have landed on the floor first, wouldn't they?"

"Yes, more than likely. It's possible that his shoulder hit first, and his arm, then the lower torso."

"Were there other bruises on his body?"

"None," he said firmly.

"Dr. Tillich," she said slowly, moving back a step or two to give the jurors a clear line of sight to him and the doll, "is there another way to account for the bruises on his face and ear, and his loose teeth?"

"Yes," he said without hesitation. He positioned the doll on its back and turned the head to one side. "Now, if you're on your knees and raise the rock with both hands and smash it into the cranium, you could inflict the damage to his head, and you'd bruise the opposite side of his face."

"Previously you said the bruises were caused by his fall. Is that still your opinion?"

He shook his head. "No. I don't believe so."

"Is it possible that the deceased was struck two times, the first blow knocking him out, and the second one with the rock?"

"It is. There was such massive damage to the skull, no trace of a first blow would have been detected. The blow with the rock was fatal."

"Could a blow be delivered with a hand or a fist to the skull with sufficient force to cause unconsciousness?"

He thought about this a moment. "Maybe," he said. "If you were lucky, but you couldn't count on it. And you'd probably do some damage to your hand. The skull's tougher than knuckles."

"Thank you, Dr. Tillich. I have no further questions." She returned to her chair. She had hoped for a flat-out no to her last question, but you can't have it all, she told herself.

Grace Heflin stood behind the prosecution's table to ask her questions then. "Let's examine another scenario, Doctor. If the victim had been seated, would there be any problem with delivering such a lethal blow?"

"No," he said.

"And if he was seated and such a blow struck him, he would have fallen sideways, wouldn't he?"

He said yes, and she continued. "Can you say his face would not have been bruised in such fashion?"

He said no.

Barbara was gratified then when Heflin continued instead of quitting when she had scored a point.

"Dr. Tillich, can you state without doubt that two blows were struck?"

"No, I can't."

She thanked him and sat down.

When court recessed, the Wendovers rushed forward for a moment with Ted; Gail and Carolyn both kissed him, and Reid clutched his hand a second before Ted had to leave with his guard. Carolyn said to Barbara, "It's going well, isn't it? You're doing a wonderful job!" She had lost the waxy look. Barbara suspected she had resorted to tranquilizers.

"Well," Frank commented, "you rattle their foundation here, there, and pretty soon people begin to think the whole structure's about ready to fall down."

"Yeah," Reid said. "She's really rattling the whole thing."

They all walked from the courtroom together. The mob today was worse than before—more microphones, more cameras, more shouted questions. Frank had Barbara's arm in one hand, Carolyn's in the other. "Where are you parked?" he growled at Reid. It was the lot across Seventh. "Come on," Frank said, walking briskly, not hesitating for people to move out of the way. They parted before the little group.

The press followed them downstairs, through the wide corridor to the tunnel under Seventh; several pursued them through it. No cameramen, however.

"No comment," Frank kept calling. "Judge's orders, no comment."

In the parking lot, he kept his firm grip on both arms and followed Reid to the car, where he helped Carolyn in, blocking her from the reporters who had tagged along. He moved only when Reid started the car and backed out.

"Is there anyone connected to the case who's over six feet?" someone yelled.

Another one said, "What difference does it make if the congressman was hit twice?"

Frank laughed and waved them off. "Come on, you guys. The judge said no comment. You want us to get slapped with contempt of court?"

"Wouldn't be the first time," someone called. But they began to drift away.

Frank and Barbara had cleared the parking lot and were walking toward his house when she heard, "Hey, remember me?"

She spun around, to see Gregory Leander, almost close enough to touch. He was wearing jeans, a denim jacket, and running shoes.

"Hi," he said. "Got a present for you, over dinner. Deal?"

"What is it?"

He shook his head. "Over dinner. My God, you scared me in court today. You're a bit of a tiger, you know? I want you to take my next case."

"I don't do divorces," she said, grinning.

"Okay, I'll knock off one of the exes and you can defend me."

She laughed. Frank cleared his throat, and she said, "Come with us. We're heading for home and a drink or three. Then we can talk about presents and dinner."

He took her briefcase, linked his arm through hers, and said, "Deal."

THIRTY-TWO

WHEN THEY ENTERED the house, both kittens raced through the hallway and came to a dead stop, arching their backs at the sight of a stranger. Gregory laughed. "This is all perfect," he said, taking off his jacket. "The neighborhood, this house, the cats. Perfect."

Huffily, Frank said, "Make yourselves comfortable in the living room. I'll bring some wine and cheese. You want something besides wine?" he asked.

Gregory shook his head. "Even that's perfect. Wine and cheese. Believe me, I meant that in the best possible way. You have no idea how much pretentious bullshit I have to put up with. This is perfect."

Almost as huffily as her father, Barbara said, "Maybe I can poke the fire into life. Sit down, Gregory."

Frank walked out toward the back of the house and the kitchen. Gregory shook his head at Barbara. "If I weren't here, what you'd do is run upstairs, or wherever your room is, change your clothes, put on comfortable old shoes, and sprawl. Right?"

She shrugged.

"Just go do it," he said. "I'll poke a fire into life." She was almost rigid in her stance. He laughed again. "I wonder if you have any idea how like him you really are. I bet not."

"Neither of us has had much experience dealing with a guest who mocks us in our home," she said.

"Barbara, up to now I have not mocked you, or him. Believe me, I have not. No guarantees about the future, you understand, but I have a clear conscience about the past. Go change your clothes. Then we can talk about John Mureau."

She felt a spasm in her midsection, almost as if she had been threatened, or even hit.

He studied her for a moment, then said softly, "I missed the boat, didn't I? Too little, too late, something like that?"

Silently she nodded.

"Oh darn," he said, smiling gently. "It would have been fun. I'll make the fire, then we'll sit and have wine and talk like grown-ups. Okay?"

She went up to change. Her hands were shaking. When she returned to the living room, dressed in jeans and running shoes, a sweatshirt, Gregory nodded approvingly.

"I was telling your father I grew up in a house so much like this one, it's uncanny, not the same layout or furnishings, of course, but the same kind of house. My dad was an ophthalmologist, made bundles of money, and friends would nudge him from time to time to go out to one of the expensive suburbs, out by the country club, where the people like him lived. He never argued, never said a word, just let them talk, and he died in that house seven years ago. He was ninety. Mother sold the place and moved to a posh retirement community, all glass and chrome, that kind of thing. She died six months later; she was only seventy-one. She should have stayed in the house where she belonged."

For a moment Barbara disliked him intensely. He was so clever; he knew exactly how to mollify Frank. She poured herself wine and shook her head at the cheese, then sat down near the fire. Gregory was standing at the fireplace, where he had a nice blaze going. Of course, he would be able to make a fire like that, she thought bitterly. She asked her father, "Has he told you about John Mureau yet?"

Frank shook his head. He was on the couch, where both kittens were racing up and down the back.

"I was saving it for you," Gregory said. "What are their names?" He pointed to the kittens, then laughed when she told him. "You named them," he said. Then he sat down opposite her in a matching chair. "Your potential witness, John Mureau, suffered transient iatrogenic psychosis off and on over a period of four years."

"Iatrogenic? Caused by his doctors? Medications?"

"Prescription drugs," he said, "in combination with medically approved and administered narcotics during his periods of rehabilitation therapy. I have the details in the car. That's the summary."

"Didn't the fools know what they were doing to him?" Frank demanded.

Gregory shook his head. There was no trace of humor on his face now; if anything, he looked grimmer than Frank. "No, they didn't," he said. "There was no communication between his surgeon in Lexington and his primary physician in Pikeville, and very little between the physician and the therapist, and it appears none at all between the psychiatrist at the mental-health clinic and anyone else. It happens," he said. "I've been fighting this sort of thing all my professional life."

Barbara drank her wine and went to refill her glass. Too much, she knew, too fast, but she needed something. "They put the label on and then treated him as if the label was correct."

"Exactly," Gregory said. "The first episode was treated with tranquilizers, with no effect, or, more likely, with deleterious effect, I imagine. They went to antipsychotics and continued the narcotics and muscle relaxants. It's a wonder he survived. Then, as the pain lessened, the dosages were reduced, and lo and behold, another psychiatric miracle cure. The following years, the entire sequence was repeated, until he refused to be treated further and shucked them all."

"His face," Barbara whispered.

"Yes, and more surgery on his hand. They had him sign a waiver that he accepted their diagnoses, that he had refused additional surgery and recommended treatment, and that he held harmless his doctors, the insurance company, and the mining company from any future actions."

"Who stonewalled?" Frank asked in a mean voice.

"The therapist and the mental-health facility. The therapist was a hack; he's retired, and he simply didn't want to go searching through old records. He had no business administering narcotics, but he did. The clinic labeled Mureau a violent, paranoid schizophrenic with acute onset, and it treated him in a way acceptable to some of the psychiatric community at that time."

"At least they didn't go to lobotomy," Frank said harshly.

"The psychiatrist recommended it," Gregory said. "It was at the time his other medications were being reduced, and he was pronounced improving before they got around to it. He never went back."

Barbara drank the second glass of wine, keeping her back to them. No one spoke. Finally she returned to her chair. "You can document all this?" she asked.

"Yes, but, Barbara, that's part one; let me tell part two. Every bit of his treatment can be defended by someone, and will be if you use him. You'd be trying to get a wedge into a closed society, and they won't let you."

She looked at him with sympathy now. "That's what you've tried to do, make them open the door to that society?"

"That's what I'm still doing," he said. "I know how they will fight."

"I wasn't thinking of the trial," she said. "For him. He needs to know."

"He should know," he said somberly, his gaze steady on her. "I'll be going now. I'll drop the report off before I leave town, half an hour or so."

"No dinner?" she asked.

Frank stood up. "Dr. Leander, you're welcome to stay and have dinner with us. I don't believe we'll be going out tonight."

He said no, then walked toward the hall and the closet to get his jacket. Barbara followed him as Frank went back toward the kitchen. Gregory pulled on his jacket.

"Where is your car?" she asked.

"At the Hilton."

"Oh," she said in understanding, and ducked her head. "I'll drive you over."

"I don't think so. You know, every time I found the right woman, we could talk and talk, up to the time the ring went on and the papers were signed; then there didn't seem to be much to say. Maybe you and I can talk now and then. Deal?"

She held out her hand and they shook, then he laughed and

took her in his arms and kissed her. When he drew back, he said regretfully, "Test drive. Okay, I give. But I still say you were a tiger in court. I'll be back in a bit with the opinion. See you, pal."

After he left, she returned to the living room and sat on the couch. Thing One and Thing Two scrambled up onto her lap and began hitting each other. "Behave yourselves," she whispered, lifting one, holding it for a moment against her cheek.

She wanted to run to the telephone and call John, tell him he was as sane as she was, although at the moment she felt a little bit crazy. She dumped both cats and stood up to pace. Not like that, not a call. She would deliver the papers in person, she decided. But not now, not until the trial was over.

Gregory was right: It would be doctor against doctor, a fight she had seen too many times, with never a winner. But first they would rip John into shreds that possibly no doctor could piece together again.

She was pacing through the hall when she almost bumped into Frank. He looked troubled. "Guess I'm not in the mood for cooking," he said. "Let's go to Martin's, someplace good and quick."

His thoughts had paralleled her own; they so often did. "As soon as Gregory comes back with his report," she said.

"Good a time as any."

"Right." She started up the stairs to wash her face, and the doorbell rang. Frank emerged from the living room to answer it. After a moment, he came to the bottom of the stairs with a manila envelope and held it out. She took it, hugged it to her chest, and went up. In her room she stood a moment with the papers hard against her body, her eyes closed. "Now there's nothing in the way," she said under her breath.

THIRTY-THREE

WEEKS EARLIER BARBARA had told Ted what to expect. "They'll attempt to prove a motive. Be warned," she had said, "it's going to be tough. They'll use Teddy and Carolyn. You're going to have to sit there and take it. If anyone says anything you disagree with, make a note of it. Tell me right away."

And now it began. The state called Mrs. Pamela Dyson, who was fifty-six and had been a teacher for thirty years. She was a pleasant-faced woman, plump, with gray hair and no makeup. She exuded kindliness, and it was evident she was not happy with her role on the witness stand. She had been on the field trip with Harry Knecht on the occasion of Teddy's accident. She kept looking at the jury almost apologetically, and turned the same hesitant gaze toward Ted, toward his family, seated behind him.

"Will you tell us what happened that day?" Grace Heflin asked her.

Her account of the accident was long and detailed.

"When the boys started to run, did Mr. Knecht make any effort to stop them?" Heflin asked when she finished.

"Oh yes. He called out instantly. Harry couldn't have done any more than he did. He was too far from them to reach Teddy. We lectured them all beforehand, of course, but boys will run sometimes."

"Did you know Teddy before the accident? Can you tell us about him?"

"Oh, he was a beautiful child." She turned her anxious gaze toward Ted, then past him to Carolyn. "He was gifted. Very intelligent, well behaved, but lively."

"And did you have any occasion to see him after the accident?"

"Yes, two times. Once in the hospital in Portland. He had just come out of a coma, you see. He was dazed. So I went to his home later on, but he didn't know me."

"You had been his teacher for that year?"

"Yes. And he didn't remember me at all." Her face was crinkled, as if she had to fight tears. "It was a shame," she said. "Such a shame. He was so different. He was playing with some little cars, like a little boy, a much younger child."

"Was it Mr. Knecht's idea to go to Malheur that year?"

"Yes. He suggested it three years before the accident, and that's when we began to go out there. He wanted children to experience the environment in all its forms—forests, the coast, the high desert, and especially geology. That was his specialty, you see; he had a doctorate in geology."

Heflin finished with her soon after that, and Barbara approached the witness stand.

"Mrs. Dyson, do you believe that accident could have been prevented?"

She shook her head. "I don't believe it could have been prevented."

"Did either Mr. or Mrs. Wendover ever imply that anyone was at fault?"

She shook her head again. "No. They knew that it was an accident. They never blamed anyone that I know of."

"Do you know the other two Wendover children, Gail and Reid?"

"Oh yes. They both have been my students."

"And have they gone on field trips with you?"

"Yes. Every year we take our children out several times. They both participated."

"Did you take them to the Malheur Station?"

"Yes. We've never had another serious accident."

"Have Mr. and Mrs. Wendover ever done or said anything to make you believe they harbor any ill feelings toward you or the school?"

"Never."

"Did either of them ever say or do anything that you're aware of to make you think they harbored ill feelings toward Mr. Knecht?"

"No," she said firmly.

The state's next witness was Peter Hoffman. He was twenty-eight, muscular and tanned, with close-cut blond hair, blue eyes, and luxurious eyelashes.

"Were you a lifeguard at SkyView ten years ago?" Heflin asked.

"Objection," Barbara said. "Irrelevant."

"Overruled."

"Were you a lifeguard at SkyView ten years ago?" Heflin repeated.

"Yes, I was."

"Do you recall an incident that involved Teddy Wendover while you were on duty?"

"Yes, Ma'am. You want me to tell about it?"

"Yes, Mr. Hoffman, please tell us what you saw."

"Well, a lot of the little kids were playing a game, tossing a penny and diving for it. He, Teddy, was playing along with them, like he was little, too. And one of them came up bawling, and they said Teddy was bothering them underwater. And his sister began to yell, and a couple of kids were crying, and it looked like a fight might start, so I told him, Teddy, to get out of the water, and Mrs. Wendover came down from the terrace and said what was going on. About then, Mr. Rowland came to see what was going on. So I told him, and he said for Teddy to go home until they decided what to do. So they had a meeting and the next day Mr. Rowland said if Teddy came back to swim without his mother or father stayed with him, I should let him know right away, and we'd get rid of them."

"Did Teddy come back to swim after that?"

"Not without his mom or dad stayed with him."

When Barbara stood up, Peter Hoffman seemed to stiffen. She smiled at him. "That was a responsible job for you at eighteen years of age, wasn't it?"

"Yes, ma'am."

"Had you held other jobs before that?"

"No."

"How many people were in the pool that day?"

He shook his head. "I don't know. About like usual, couple of dozen maybe."

"Were there many small children in the pool?"

"A bunch," he said.

"So it must have kept you busy watching out for them. Were there teenagers swimming, too?"

"Some," he said.

"Four, five? More than that?"

"I don't know. Six maybe."

"When the smaller children were diving for the penny, what were the teenagers doing?"

He stiffened even more. "They were all over the pool."

She nodded. "Were they near the children diving for the penny?"

"I don't know. A couple of them maybe were."

"All right. So small children were playing their game, and the teenagers were all around. Is that how it was?"

"Yeah, except for Teddy—he was playing with the little kids, and he was a big guy."

"Did you ever talk to him, Mr. Hoffman?"

His answer was fast and sharp. "No."

"Did he usually play with the younger children?"

"Yeah, he hung out with them."

"Let's take your earlier statement a little at a time, Mr. Hoffman. You said a bunch of little kids were playing with the penny, diving for it, and one came up bawling. Is that right?"

"Yeah, that's how it was."

"Then you said they said he was bothering them underwater. Who do you mean by 'they'?"

"The little kids."

"All of them?"

"No, the one that was crying."

"He stopped crying to point to Teddy? Is that what you mean?"

He began to speak, stopped, and finally said, "No, not with

his finger or anything, but that's who he meant. One of the other kids said so."

"One of the little kids?"

"No, one of the teenagers. He said it was Teddy that was bothering the kid underwater."

"You said Gail was yelling. What was she saying?"

"Like she always did, taking up for him. Saying Kenny did it, not her brother."

"Was Kenny the one who accused Teddy?"

"Yeah, he was hanging out, watching them play."

"Was he diving along with them?"

"Yeah, not playing, just watching them."

"I see," she said; she walked to the jury rail, stopped. "Was Teddy bigger than you in those days?"

"Yeah, he was a big guy."

"You were both eighteen that summer, weren't you?"

"I don't know how old he was. He was just big and he acted like a little kid all the time. I was eighteen."

"Did the smaller children play with him?"

"Yeah, they didn't know no better."

"Mr. Hoffman, did you see Teddy do anything wrong that day?"

"No, not with my own eyes. But I know he did."

"When Mr. Rowland came, what did you tell him?"

"Just what happened, Teddy was bothering the little kids."

"Is that what you said, he was bothering the little kids?"

"Yeah."

"Did you mention that Gail said Kenny was the one bothering the child?"

"No. It was Teddy."

"Which Mr. Rowland came out?"

He looked surprised. "The old m—I mean, Mr. Arthur Rowland."

"Who told you that Teddy was to be accompanied by a parent in the pool after that?"

"When I came on the day after, Dora in the check stand, she said Mr. Rowland wanted me in the office and I went and him and Brian Rowland were both there. I guess Brian Rowland was the one who told me."

"He told you to let him know if Teddy came alone, and your words, I believe, were, 'we'd get rid of them.' Is that right?"

"Yeah, something like that."

"Was Brian Rowland the one who said that?"

"No, his father. Brian said he had to be with his mom or dad, and his father said they'd get rid of them."

"Did Teddy come back to swim after that day?"

"Yeah, but his mom or dad stayed with him."

"You said Mrs. Wendover came down from the terrace the day there was trouble. How far away is the terrace?"

"Right next to the pool. It's got an awning. Parents like to sit there in the shade."

"Did you ever have trouble with other children? Or teenagers?"

"Well, sure. They get to horsing around sometimes."

"Did you ever have any trouble with the boy Kenny?"

"I don't know. Maybe. He was in the bunch that got rough sometimes, just showing off."

"Did you ever have occasion to throw anyone out with the same restrictions Teddy had? That they had to be accompanied by a parent?"

"No, just him."

"On any occasion have you ever spoken to Teddy, said hello, or anything?"

"No."

She nodded and went to her table. "No further questions."

It was quarter to twelve when Judge Ariel called for the luncheon break. "Be back at one-thirty," he said after his little set piece about not discussing the case.

"Did you have to let that cretin go on like that?" Ted asked Barbara in a low voice as the jury filed out.

"I couldn't have stopped it," she said. "I wouldn't have, in any event. We have to let them show the bias, the prejudice their witnesses have. And I had to let them bring in Brian Rowland's name again. I'm sorry, Ted." She put her hand on his arm, which was rigid. "You've got to grit your teeth. But keep listening hard, make notes. Okay?"

His guard was hovering. Wearily he stood up. "Sure," he said. "Notes." She watched him being led away.

Later, leaning against a tree, watching the river rush toward its rendezvous with the sea, watching a heron step delicately in the shallow water on the opposite bank, Barbara acknowledged her awareness that not very long ago she would have made the same assumption that Peter Hoffman had made: The idiot boy did it.

He's not on trial, she reminded herself, and knew that was irrelevant. They would come to see Ted and Carolyn both burdened with a retarded son who was more and more trouble as the years went by.

Barbara admired Grace Heflin's wardrobe; today she was wearing a blue suit that shaded into black when she moved, then became almost teal blue in the shifting play of light. Grace Heflin was as businesslike as her assistant, Marcus Truly. She called Lorraine Poster.

She was a pretty woman in her forties, with carefully styled hair that looked as if a hurricane would not disturb it. Her clothes, an ecru-colored silk suit and matching blouse, were elegant and expensively simple. She lived on Bear Hollow Road, she said, with her husband and two sons, aged fifteen and eighteen. They had occupied their house for eight years.

"Do you know the Wendover family?" Heflin asked.

"Yes, of course."

"Are you friends with them, neighborly?"

"In the beginning we tried; they came over and introduced themselves—Carolyn and Ted, I mean. And we went to their house once. Then Reid came over to play with my boys and I saw Teddy lurking behind him, and I said I didn't let my boys play with men. Reid left with him. He never came back, and, naturally, I wouldn't let my sons go over there. My sons were very afraid of Teddy. He was always watching them. They were frightened. I had to take them inside when he was about."

Ted was scribbling furiously at Barbara's side. Behind her, she could hear Reid's whisper, then Gail's. Judge Ariel looked at them sharply and they subsided.

"Mrs. Poster, was there any one event that sticks in your mind that concerned Teddy and his family?"

"More than one. The first one was Teddy watching them all the time, from down by the creek. I went to Carolyn and told her how that frightened them, and she said, more or less, that Teddy thought of himself as a child about their age and just wanted to play. I told her that was out of the question, and the next day I saw Ted with Teddy, walking down the creek bank. When they got to the edge of our property, Ted put a big flat rock in the water and they stepped on it and crossed to the other side and continued on that side. I think he lectured him about moving on, not stopping there again."

"Did that resolve the problem?"

"No, it didn't. He would move on after that, but at a snail's pace. It was as bad as ever. And one day, he threw rocks at my boys. My husband and I both went to talk to the Wendovers that night. Ted offered to put up a fence at the back of our property, but, obviously, that was not a solution."

"Was the matter resolved?" Heflin asked sympathetically.

"Finally. The next day, I saw Ted going to other neighbors on both sides of our property. Neither of them had small children to protect, I might add. They agreed to let Teddy cut through their yards from the creek to the road whenever he wanted to. And that's what he did. Ted took him by the hand, literally took his hand, and walked the path with him. He could walk along the creek to the next yard over, then go to the road and cross it to pass our property, then go back down to the creek. It was not a perfect solution; he was still very close very often, but that's how it finally worked out so my children could play in their own yard without fear."

"Did you talk to the neighbors who allowed Teddy to use their property that way?"

"Yes, I did. The ones on both sides had lived there a long time, and they had no small children. They let their sympathy for the Wendovers go too far, although some of the neighbors on the road believe, as I do, that Teddy should be in an institution, for his own good."

"Mrs. Poster, was it Ted Wendover who tried to resolve this matter?"

"Yes, it was. He suggested the fence, and he took Teddy around to show him where he could walk. When we went over to discuss the rock-throwing incident, Carolyn Wendover wouldn't say a word; in fact, she left the room altogether, just left it up to him."

Ted touched Barbara's arm. She read the note he had written: "She was too mad to speak. T had bruises from being hit."

"Mrs. Poster," Grace Heflin asked then, "just from your own personal observations as a neighbor, would you say that it was Ted Wendover who had to deal with complaints concerning his son?"

"Objection," Barbara said. "That's a leading question, conjectural."

"Overruled," Judge Ariel said, frowning slightly at her.

"Exception," she snapped.

He nodded, then nodded at Heflin. "Continue, if you will."

"Would you like to hear the question again?" Heflin asked.

"There's no need. Yes. It was always Ted Wendover. She had nothing to do with resolving anything, as far as I could see."

Heflin was finished then. Barbara walked around her table and stopped in front of it.

"Mrs. Poster, who owns Bear Hollow Creek?"

"Why, nobody owns it. It's public, county property."

"How far up the banks does public ownership extend?"

"I don't know. Ten or fifteen feet."

"So for ten or fifteen feet on both sides, it is public property, and the creek itself is about four feet wide. Is that correct?"

"Yes, about that."

"Did you see any of the incidents your sons reported?"

She hesitated a moment, then said defiantly, "My sons have always been extremely truthful. They had no reason to lie."

"Did you see any of the incidents?" Barbara asked again, speaking slowly, as if to a person unfamiliar with the language.

"No!"

"Did you warn your sons about Teddy when you first moved into your present house?"

"Yes, as soon as we realized what the situation was. We told them to keep away from him. They knew strange men could be dangerous. And especially men with mental illness can be very dangerous."

"Has Teddy adhered to the rules, to stay on the opposite side of the road when he passes your house?"

"Yes."

"Your sons were seven and ten when the rock-throwing incident occurred, is that right?"

"Yes."

"Did you learn how it started?"

She hesitated, then said, "He called to them to come see his rocks, something like that, and they said no, for him to go away."

"He offered to show them his collection. Where were your boys when that happened?"

"On our property, in our backyard."

"Did they throw any rocks?"

"They might have. Few boys will take something like that quietly. They throw back. He ran away, crying."

"Would you say they drove him away?"

"Yes, they were very small children protecting themselves from a large mentally ill man. By the time I got out there, he was running home."

"Where were they all?"

"He was on the other side of the creek; they were in our yard, where they belonged."

"Do you have loose rocks in your backyard, Mrs. Poster?"

She hesitated again, then shook her head. "A few perhaps."

"Mrs. Poster, is it possible that your sons gathered rocks before Teddy appeared, that they were lying in wait for him?"

"Absolutely not!"

"What name did your sons use for him in those days?"

Lorraine Poster's lips were very tight now. "They called him names, I have no doubt. Boys will do that."

"What name did they call him?" Barbara asked coolly.

"I don't know."

"Mrs. Poster, don't you know they called him 'Rockhead' every time they saw him?"

"I don't know. Boys can be cruel sometimes."

"Your sons are fifteen and eighteen now, aren't they?"

"Yes, they are."

"What do they call him these days?"

She shook her head. "I have no idea. He is not an item of conversation in our house."

"Mrs. Poster, don't you know that every time they see him, they yell out 'Rockhead'?"

"Objection," Heflin called out. "She already answered the question. Counsel is badgering the witness."

"Sustained. Get on with it, Ms. Holloway," Judge Ariel said impatiently.

"Mrs. Poster, what other neighbors complained to you about Teddy Wendover?"

"It was general talk, that he belonged in an institution."

"But I want you to tell us specifically who said that."

"It was a long time ago, when we first moved in. I don't remember."

"Do you know of any specific complaints, other than your own?"

"Not that I can remember. I just know there were."

"Does that mean that in your case Ted Wendover tried to find a solution to a problem, but you don't know of other instances?"

"There were others; I just can't recall exactly what they were," Lorraine Poster said angrily. "I don't make notes of what neighbors talk about."

"All right," Barbara said. "Perhaps a list of neighbors on Bear Hollow Road will refresh your memory."

"Objection," Heflin said. "Counsel is trying to intimidate the witness."

"Your Honor," Barbara said swiftly, "this witness has made what amounts to an accusation against my client, saying there were complaints about his son that he was forced to deal with. We have every right to ascertain the substance of those complaints."

"Overruled," he said. His face was more florid than it had been earlier, a darker red. He looked as if all he wanted was to be done with this matter, to get on with the case, be done with it.

Barbara turned at her table and took the list Shelley had waiting for her. "This is a list of the residents of Bear Hollow Road. Mrs. Poster, I'll read from this list. Will you simply say yes or no if anyone I name voiced a complaint to you concerning Teddy that his father had to deal with? Mrs. Olivia Halstead." She looked from the list to Lorraine Poster, who was glaring at her. "Well?"

"No," she snapped.

"Mr. Warren Halstead."

"No."

Barbara deliberately read out the full names of the three Halstead children; each time, the answer got harsher. She moved on to the Petrovsky family. There were four children. When she started with the Larkins group, Lorraine Poster's nerves failed.

"No one told me in so many words. It was just in the air, the way they looked at him, the way they didn't say anything directly. It was just in the air."

"You have no direct knowledge of any other complaints. Is that right?"

"It was in the air," she said sullenly. "Everyone knew."

"Do you have any direct knowledge of other complaints?" Barbara demanded.

"No!"

Barbara looked her over with contempt. "No further questions."

Heflin's redirect was exactly what it should have been, Barbara told herself. Had Mrs. Poster felt Teddy was a threat to her children? Had they been afraid of him? Had Ted handled the matter?

Judge Ariel said they would take a ten-minute recess, and he stalked out. He looked very angry, and Barbara had no idea why.

"How's the jury reacting?" she asked Frank in the attorneys' lounge a few minutes later.

"The fat one, Sproul? She's on Poster's side, I believe. She wouldn't want someone like Teddy hanging around, either. The computer nerd keeps eyeing Ted as if he's trying to figure out how much of a trap he's in. Most are deadpan."

"What's eating Ariel?"

"Don't know. Lunch didn't settle well, maybe. I'll mosey on out and see a couple of folks. Catch up with you in a couple of minutes. You're doing great, honey, by the way."

She grinned. That was strictly Pop talk. Shelley asked if she wanted anything. Barbara said no. Shelley said, "Wow! Just wow!" And Barbara realized again how much the young woman had yet to learn.

When they resumed, Heflin called Mrs. Mildred Villard, a former housekeeper in the Wendover home. Beside her, Barbara heard Ted groan.

THIRTY-FOUR

MRS. VILLARD WAS sixty, with glossy black hair and dark eyes. She was a widow, she said, with two grown children. She had worked as a housekeeper for thirty-six years, for some of the best families in town, she added.

Grace Heflin asked her to describe her experience working for the Wendovers.

The picture that emerged was one of a stressed family, with Teddy a problem from her first day.

"Mrs. Wendover told me to treat him like a little boy at the start, but how could I do that, with him a grown-up man? Then she said I should just leave his room alone; she'd take care of it. He had toys and junk scattered all over it all the time; no one could get in there to vacuum or make up the bed, or anything else. He was always dragging in junk—rocks, tree branches, pinecones, and it all made a mess. And he left toys in the bathtub, even after I asked him not to. I mean, I had to pick up after him all the time."

"Was Mr. Wendover home much of the time?"

"In and out, in and out. He'd be gone two or three days at a time, then be there for weeks. He had associates come to his office in the house a lot, or he'd have to go to town or something, but he was there a lot."

"And Mrs. Wendover? Was she there most of the time?"

"Yes. She had committees she went to, but usually only when Mr. Wendover was home. Then he had to baby-sit. A lot of times she'd make him take Teddy with him on his business trips, get him out of her hair, and then she'd be off to Portland, or to the coast or something."

"Can you tell us what happened over the Christmas season in 1988?" Heflin asked then.

"Yes. Her parents came for the holidays, Mr. and Mrs. Nye, lovely people, both of them. They gave the children lovely presents, a beautiful gold chain for Gail, and one of those headphones the kids all liked for Reid. A Walkman. Such nice presents. Well, they gave Teddy a nice present, too, an expensive microscope. He broke it right away. And they all had a fight—not Mr. Wendover—he wasn't there when it started—but Mr. and Mrs. Nye and her. Mrs. Nye was saying they were just trying to help him develop, and Mr. Nye was saying it wasn't fair to keep him where he didn't fit in, he belonged with others like him, for his own sake, so he would have some self-respect. And she was saying, stop it, just stop it. You know I won't send him away. That wasn't a proper present for a child. See, she treated him like a little boy, but he was a big grown man, and her folks wanted to help him. And it was like that until she came marching out of the living room and started upstairs, spitting mad, you could tell. That's when Mr. Wendover came home, and he said what's going on, and she said, ask them, and went up the stairs. Well, he went into the living room and they all talked in a civilized way. I couldn't hear what they were saying, and I went on about my duties. The next day he took

Teddy off somewhere for a few days. He had to get him out of there, away from the screaming and yelling."

"Did Mr. and Mrs. Nye suggest it would be in Teddy's best interest to have him in an institution with other handicapped people?"

"Yes, they did. Just for his own good."

"And Mrs. Wendover reacted with anger? Is that right?"

"Spitting mad, she was spitting mad."

"Did Mr. Wendover agree with them?"

"He never said much, but you could tell that's what he wanted, too. And I heard him trying to tell her they just wanted to help Teddy, they wouldn't do anything to hurt him. But she wouldn't listen to anything like that."

"Was Mr. Wendover angry when he went to talk with Mr. and Mrs. Nye?"

She looked puzzled, then said slowly, "He never was angry. He was more like resigned, and real sad."

When Heflin finished, Judge Ariel recessed until nine the following morning. Barbara was seething as she stood up for his departure.

Behind her, Gail muttered, "We should have dropped the house on her when we had the chance."

"I'll be in to talk with you after your dinner," Barbara told Ted. She spotted Patsy Meares speaking to Shelley, who was nodding vigorously. Shelley kissed her cheek and Patsy waved to Barbara and left. Slowly Barbara began to gather her materials together. When she glanced at her father, his expression was unreadable. That bad? she wondered. She forced a smile for Carolyn and her children as they started out.

"Ready," she said then. But Shelley was almost jumping up and down in excitement.

"Daddy called and said he's sending a video from one of the ad agencies. They sent it to him. I'll pick it up at the airport at nine. Should I bring it over to your house then?"

"What video?" Barbara asked.

"See, I had to look at dozens of them when I was pretending Daddy wanted to do some modern advertising, and this one place wouldn't let me see much, but they must have sent it on to him."

"Let's get out of here," Barbara muttered. "Then you slow down and start way back and tell me what you're talking about."

Frank moved Shelley and Barbara through the waiting reporters and cameramen with his usual slickness and got them through the tunnel to the parking lot across the street. They came to a halt near Shelley's car.

This time Shelley started way back. "When I was trying to find out about possible advertising, I sort of hinted that my father might be interested in doing some videos, something like that. He builds boats, you know."

Barbara laughed. Her father indeed built boats—yachts, cruisers, speedboats.

"Okay, so they showed you videos?"

"Some of them did, but this was the company that handles the Rowland stuff. They were reluctant to show me anything, except old videos, training films, that sort of thing. I said my father was interested in more modern presentations, maybe with computer animation, some morphing, things like that. I said he might go for animation showing a lot of different kinds of places, lakes, rivers, the ocean, whatever. They showed us a snippet, on a videotape, along with other things, and I said that wouldn't persuade him. I gave them his name and address and said if they were interested in showing him more, to send it down to him. Bill began to talk about some of the other videos we'd seen, how they weren't so old-fashioned, and about a company down in L.A. that does videos for promotion, and he said we should hop down there to see it." She blushed. "Bill Spassero was with me. He drove his Jaguar up, and they got a glimpse of it, and I wore some jewelry and acted pretty dumb. Anyway, they sent it to Dad, and he called and told Patsy he'd put it on the plane this evening."

Barbara stared at her in awe. Pretty dumb blonde with an adoring rich boyfriend, helping out Daddy. She began to laugh again, and Shelley and Frank did, too.

"Bring it over to the house," Barbara said after a moment.

"We'll watch TV tonight. Thanks, Shelley. Maybe it's exactly what we need."

At home, she changed her clothes and went back out, this time taking her car; it had started to rain. When she saw Ted in the conference room, he was despondent.

"They're tightening the noose, aren't they?" he said.

"She's being methodical," Barbara said. "She started with the accident and now is working her way to the present, step by step. I'd like to go over those next few witnesses again, if you're up to it. All we can do at this point is try to deflect some of the damage point by point. Let's get at it. Okay?"

At nine-fifteen that night Shelley arrived with the videotape.

"Pray," Barbara ordered, sliding it into the VCR.

The video started with panoramic shots of mountains, mountain lakes, white river rapids, while the sound track played a jazz version of "America the Beautiful." The music faded to a trumpet solo that stopped abruptly as a gold mountain appeared against a cerulean sky, and a voice-over said, "Welcome to Gold Mountain."

After that it was very good computer animation. People in rubber boats shooting rapids, others climbing mountains, taking pictures of wildflowers and butterflies, a group in single file with llamas on a trek, others on horseback, people playing golf, fishing, swimming in pools and lakes, panning for gold in streams. . . . The voice said, "Explore over a hundred thousand acres of wilderness, surrounded by hundreds of square miles of wilderness on three sides and the Pacific Ocean on the fourth." It was obvious that a lot of editing had been done. Aerial photography pulled away to show the entire region, the endless mountains, rivers, and finally the coast. The camera came in close again, on a river. People were getting into rubber boats. They went down a river, through a canyon pass that Barbara recognized as Hell's Gate on the Rogue River.

"Try your hand at gold mining. Over twenty million dollars' worth of gold has come from this area; many, many times that much remains. If you find it, you keep it." The computer animation now was of a disparate group of people wielding picks and hammers in a brightly lighted mine. A man found a rock with a gold streak and held it up. The camera ranged over many such rocks, each with visible gold. It played over a nugget the size of a hen's egg.

Barbara heard Frank grunt when a gondola appeared, suspended on a cable that stretched across the river. The camera followed the passengers when they stepped out and walked toward a mammoth hotel. Then another hotel in a different setting was displayed, and a third one; a cabin in the woods was next, and the voice in sepulchral tones said there would be over fifteen hundred rooms, a hundred individual cabins. Trees morphed into a brilliantly lighted amusement park. . . . An information center would be staffed with trained geologists, botanists, biologists; mining experts would lead groups to mine for gold, the voice-over said. A telephoto lens zoomed in on a bear sow with two cubs at a riverbank.

The video ended with a jet launch going down the river to another hotel overlooking the ocean, where whales sported and a deep-sea fishing boat was coming to a dock. One of the computer-animation figures was smiling broadly, standing by a salmon bigger than he was. Then the dazzling gold mountain filled the screen. The trumpet came back, and sound and image faded out together.

"I'll be damned," Frank muttered. He didn't move.

Barbara whispered, "Gold mountain is real, or will be."

Shelley's eyes were wide, almost perfectly round. "They can't do that, can they?"

Frank was frowning, his eyes unfocused. "I don't know," he said. "I sure as hell don't know. But I reckon we'll be finding out."

"I want Bailey," Barbara said. She turned to Shelley. "That was great work. Congratulations."

Shelley blushed.

By the time Bailey arrived, Barbara had watched the video two more times, the second time with a stopwatch in her hand. She had sent Shelley home, after telling her again what a wonderful job she had done. She suspected Shelley had flown under her own power.

"Okay," she said to Bailey. "First you watch, then we talk."

He watched without a motion or sound. When it ended, he said, "So you struck gold after all!"

Frank handed him a drink, and Barbara rewound the video. "This time I'll stop it here and there. These are the places we need to identify beyond doubt, starting with the location where they're putting in the rubber boats." They watched; she stopped the tape; then they watched some more. "Can do?"

Bailey nodded. "Yeah. Some of that footage is probably from a film library, complete with longitude and latitude. I know guys who will pinpoint the rest of it."

She nodded, satisfied. "It's a rush, Bailey. Prod them."

He lifted his glass in acknowledgment.

"And find out who owns that landing site on the Rogue."

He nodded. "You know how they manage a wild river like the Rogue? They issue permits for so many trips down, and no more. It's a raffle. You don't get picked, you wait a year and try again. How do you suppose they intend to get around that?"

"Good question," Barbara said. "Let's do some digging."

THIRTY-FIVE

THE NEXT MORNING Barbara started tearing down the ugly scene Mrs. Villard had painted of life in the Wendover house.

"Did you ever hear Mr. Wendover say or imply that he wanted his son to be institutionalized?" Barbara asked.

"Not in so many words," Mrs. Villard said placidly.

"My question is, Did you hear him say that?"

"No. Not if you put it like that." She said it in such a way that it was obvious she had not changed her mind. She remained placid, sure of herself.

"Did he ever imply that he wanted his son institutionalized?"

"I said no, not if you put it like that."

"You guessed his intentions. Is that what you mean?"

"I don't know. I'm sure that's what he wanted."

"Were you ever left in charge of Teddy?"

"Yes. Several times. Once when Reid got sick and she had to go pick him up at school. And another time Gail had to have her eyes examined. That was longer, at least two hours. And all day one time."

"What happened that day?"

"It was raining and she didn't want to take him to the airport when her parents were ready to fly home again."

"That was following the visit you told us about earlier, when they had the argument?"

"Yes. They stayed over the holidays and then flew home."

"Wasn't she getting ready to take her son along, Mrs. Villard? Wasn't that the original plan?"

"Yes, but Mr. Nye said to leave him at home. And she did."

"All right. Then what happened?"

"She called and said the flight was held up because the rain was freezing in Portland, where the plane was coming from."

"How long was Teddy in your charge that day, Mrs. Villard?"

"From ten in the morning until a little after four," she said coolly. "All day."

"Where did he stay?"

"In his room."

"Did you order him to his room as soon as his mother was out of the house? Isn't that what you did on all three occasions?"

"He wanted to stay in his room," she said.

"Did he have lunch that day?"

"He wouldn't come out for lunch."

Barbara nodded and walked to the rail of the jury box. "When did you start work at the Wendover house?"

"In July 1988."

"And when did you stop working there?"

"In January 1989."

"Were you fired?"

"Yes. She had a temper tantrum and fired me."

"Did Mrs. Wendover give you severance pay of thirty days' wages?"

"Yes, she did. It was the least she could do."

"Did she give you references?"

"No."

"When did she fire you, Mrs. Villard?"

"In January. I already told you that."

"In fact, the day after her parents left, didn't she meet you at the door with the check made out and tell you she wouldn't have you in her house again because you treated her son like an animal that had to be kept in a cage?"

"All right, I said she was mad. She made a fool of herself over him, and him a grown man. I couldn't have him messing up while I was trying to clean up."

"Did you ever hear Mrs. Wendover use the expression 'to get him out of her hair'?"

"No, not in those words."

"Those are your words, aren't they? You wanted to keep him out of your hair. You kept him locked in his room, didn't you?"

"He wanted to stay in his room as much as I wanted him to," she said defiantly.

"Did you ever hear Carolyn Wendover order, ask, or even hint to Mr. Wendover that she wanted him to take Teddy on a trip?"

"Not in those words."

"Did she in your presence ever ask, order, or hint that she wanted Mr. Wendover to take Teddy away?"

"I told you, not just like that."

Judge Ariel leaned toward her. "Mrs. Villard, will you just answer the question so we can get on with this. A yes or no answer will be sufficient."

"No," she snapped.

Barbara nodded to the judge. "Thank you, Your Honor. I have no further questions." She did not glance at Mrs. Villard when she returned to her seat.

Gail put her hand on Barbara's shoulder and whispered, "You dumped the whole house on her. Thanks."

While Grace Heflin was doing her redirect, Barbara studied the jury. They would believe one side or the other, and she had no way of telling which side that was.

The afternoon held no surprises. Heflin began calling businessmen who had used Ted's services. They testified that their deals were lost because of Teddy's presence. Barbara undid much of it, but in each case Heflin had the last word. Her questions were to the point: Had Teddy's presence been a factor? How much commission had Ted lost? In one case it was $2,500; in another it was $4,000. . . .

Ted's expression was bleak when he was led out. Barbara turned to speak to Carolyn, who was pale with anger. "How can they do that to Teddy?" she asked. "How can they despise him so much?"

Two more businessmen were called the next morning. There was nothing new; Teddy had caused the deal to go sour, one said. A man shouldn't take his retarded son along on business trips. It had cost Ted five thousand dollars last April. Barbara forced him to admit he had raised his price two different times, until the prospective buyer had backed out; he said it was Teddy's fault, nonetheless.

Then, after a short recess, Heflin called Hank Versins. He was stout, with long gray hair in a ponytail. He looked uncomfortable in a sports coat, shirt, and tie.

"He's a good kid," he said deliberately. "A good worker, easy to get along with. Does what he's told and does it well."

"Why don't you use him full-time?" Heflin asked.

"Well, it's kind of hard, you know, keeping an eye on him. I mean, he's a good worker, but he's like a kid. He gets bored and is off doing something else after a while. Not that he doesn't do what I tell him to," he added quickly.

"What kinds of things is he off doing then?" Heflin asked. She was being kind and understanding; she smiled a lot at him.

"You know how kids are, after a garter snake, or poking around looking for a rock, just kid things."

"But you have to keep an eye on him so he won't get hurt or cause damage? Is that it?"

"He wouldn't do any damage," he said swiftly. "It's just that kids don't pay much mind to the difference between flowers and weeds sometimes. And he's got pretty big feet. So I keep an eye on him and after a couple of hours I'll say, Well, Teddy, you've done a good day's work, time to go home now. And he takes off on his bike. He just helps out on Bear Hollow Road," he said. "He rides his bike to work and then back home."

"Mr. Versins, you pay him five dollars an hour, don't you?"

He nodded, then said, "He makes that, yes."

"Do you pay him out of your pocket?"

He glanced at Ted with a pained expression. "I give him the money," he said slowly.

"Out of your earnings, do you give him five dollars an hour?"

"Not exactly," he said with obvious reluctance. "His dad, Mr. Wendover, he said one day that Teddy loved to help me when I worked in their yard, and would I let him help out now and then in other folks' yards. He said it made Teddy feel proud to have a job and be able to buy comic books and toys now and then."

"Does Mr. Wendover pay the five dollars an hour?" Heflin asked gently.

"Yes. But Teddy doesn't know that. He thinks it's a real job with real pay. And it is," he said. "He's a good worker. I'd be willing to pay him myself if I could afford a helper."

She thanked him and nodded to Barbara, who was enraged. Ted hadn't told her that. She doubted that Carolyn had known.

"Mr. Versins, do you talk with Teddy when he's helping out?"

"Sure," he said. "He's got a lot of things on his mind. We discuss them."

"How would you describe Teddy?"

"He's a sweet-natured, good-tempered kid. He's got more love in him than most. I never heard him bad-mouth anyone or anything."

"Do you think of him as happy and secure?"

"All the time. You don't show the kind of love he does unless you've had it yourself. It's like he's reflecting back what he knows best."

Efficiently, Grace Heflin returned to her two points: Versins never kept Teddy around more than an hour or two because it was a strain to keep an eye on him; Ted Wendover had made the arrangements for Teddy to work with him.

That afternoon Heflin called Dr. Virginia Janec.

Virginia Janec was as blond as ever, her glasses were oversized, her hair short and straight, almost a classic Dutch boy's haircut. She stated her credentials rapidly.

"Have you examined other adults with retardation similar to Teddy Wendover's?"

"Yes, many times."

"Will you tell us something about the procedures you use to determine the psychological and intellectual development of such individuals?"

She told about the four days of testing, starting with a complete physical examination. "He is physically quite healthy, and severely retarded," she concluded.

"Is there a classification for his degree of retardation?"

"It used to be called 'within the moron range': that is, an adult with intelligence equivalent to that of a child between eight and eleven years of age. We rarely use that term any longer because it is so censorious. We prefer to say 'severe retardation.' "

"Are people with that degree of affliction difficult to manage?"

"They can be extremely difficult," she said.

"What is the prognosis for his future recovery from the retardation that afflicts him at present?"

"The prognosis has not changed. It is absolutely negative. He will never recover."

When Barbara started her cross-examination, she was deliberately casual, without a trace of the briskness that had been shown by both Janec and Heflin. "Dr. Janec, can you give us an example of when retardation might present behavioral problems?"

"Yes. If it happens that other physiological processes have continued, without the corresponding development of a superego, and the person has fully developed libido, it can be extremely difficult."

"Dr. Janec," Barbara said, "in the simplest possible terms, what is the superego?"

"We mean the division of the psyche that accommodates standards of moral behavior, usually based on community or religious standards."

"Is that sometimes called the conscience?"

"Yes, it can be."

"When does this development normally occur in human beings?"

"Between seven and ten years of age."

"Does Teddy have a developed superego?"

"He has the superego we would expect of a child of about eight years of age."

"Does that mean he has a developed conscience?"

She hesitated, then said, "Well, yes."

"What does libido mean?" Barbara asked.

"That's the division of the psyche responsible for the development and manifestation of sexual impulses."

"Called the sex drive by some, I believe. Is that right?"

"Yes."

"What determines the development of the libido, Dr. Janec? For instance, is it age alone?"

"Of course not. There must be physical changes, such as occur in puberty. The gonads, the hormonal system, the secondary sexual characteristics, and the libido develop all together."

"And where is Teddy in this development?"

Janec shrugged slightly. "He has had no development of sexual attributes."

"No raging hormones, no secondary sexual characteristics, body hair? None of the signs of approaching puberty?"

"None."

"I see. Dr. Janec, a person with adult strength and adult sex drive and without a developed conscience might present behavioral problems, is that correct?"

"It often is the case."

"What about a person with adult strength and a developed conscience but no sex drive? Would such a person present similar problems?"

"It would be rare," Janec said.

"Dr. Janec, from your tests and your personal observations, would you say that Teddy's behavior is consistent with that of any well-adjusted, secure, happy eight-year-old child?"

She hesitated a long moment before she said, "Yes."

"You stated that you had access to all of Teddy's medical records. Is that right?"

"Yes."

"Did those reports all conclude year after year that Teddy has the cognitive, emotional, and psychological development of a well-adjusted, normal eight-year-old child?"

"Yes."

"Just from reading his test results and the expressed opinions of many experts over the years, did you see any reason to differ in any way with their findings?"

She hesitated, then said, "No. The tests were all thorough and rigorous."

Barbara looked at her with puzzlement. "Then why did you put Teddy Wendover through four days of additional testing?"

"As I already testified, I am an independent contractor for the state. My duties include—"

Barbara held up her hand. "You are correct, you did state your connections with the state. I'm asking, why Teddy? Surely you don't haul people in randomly and subject them to intensive testing, as you did with him."

"Objection," Heflin snapped. "That's an improper question and counsel knows it."

"Sustained," Judge Ariel said sharply. "Counsel will refrain from including comments in her questions."

Barbara nodded, then turned back to the witness stand. "Dr. Janec, why did you put Teddy through four days of testing?"

"Objection," Heflin said. "This matter is irrelevant to the trial we are considering here."

"But it is relevant," Barbara said easily. "The prosecution has introduced the topic of Teddy's mental health and has elicited from the witness a number of statements with no foundation. It is necessary to explore in some depth those areas that have been mentioned more or less in passing."

Judge Ariel looked as if he had a bad taste in his mouth. "Overruled," he said. "Answer the question," he said to Janec.

"I was charged by the Court to conduct an evaluation of Teddy Wendover concerning his ability to aid in his own defense, and determine his mental development through an independent examination."

"Was your charge in writing?"

"Of course."

"Dr. Janec, is there a phrase in that charge that reads: 'Because of certain repetitive and aberrational aspects of all three deaths, the possibility exists that the suspect is of unsound mind'?"

"Yes."

"So Teddy was suspected of having committed three murders?"

"Yes."

"When did you receive your charge?"

"November seventh."

"At that time, did you receive his medical file?"

"Yes."

"After reviewing the file, what was your recommendation?"

She lifted her chin and said clearly, "I recommended that established routine should be followed and that he should be placed in custody at Fairview State Hospital for a complete psychiatric examination."

"Is that a hospital for mentally disturbed adults?"

"They could have kept him isolated from the adult population for the purpose of the psychiatric examination," she said coldly.

"Is it for adults?" Barbara asked again, and Janec said yes.

Step by step, Barbara led her through the following weeks, until the final interrogation on the beach.

"So, from November seventh through November thirtieth, Teddy was incarcerated. And from the thirtieth until December third, he was in the custody of his parents, with orders not to leave the state. Who paid for his incarceration?"

"His parents paid. They were not willing to place him in the state institution."

"Was he ever charged with anything?"

"No."

"Dr. Janec, what does *aberrational* mean in the context of your original charge to examine Teddy?"

"Well," she said slowly, "murder is aberrational in itself."

"In the context of your charge, what did it mean?"

"The macabre placement of rocks—strewing them about was considered aberrational," she said even more slowly, after glancing at Grace Heflin.

"All right. What was the meaning of the word *repetitive*?"

"Objection!" Heflin said sharply. "Your Honor, may I approach the bench?"

He motioned to her and Barbara both. His face was very red; he looked as if he was suffering. "I'm calling a recess," he said, "and I want both of you in chambers." Before either moved away, he banged his gavel and said, "Sustained. We will have a fifteen-minute recess." He stamped out without a glance at anyone in the room.

Ted looked bewildered, but Frank's hand on her shoulder was warm and reassuring when they all stood up and the jurors filed out. "Chambers," she said in a low voice to Frank after Ted had gone out with his guard. "Wish me luck." He patted her arm.

She met Grace Heflin in Ariel's anteroom. They waited in silence until a buzzer on the secretary's desk sounded; the secretary, a pale middle-aged man, motioned them toward the door.

Judge Ariel's room was large, as were all the judges' chambers; it was furnished with brown leather-covered chairs that looked as if his grandfather had donated them for the cause.

They were very ugly and oversized, inhumanly sized. His desk was a rich dark wood with a high gloss; it appeared fragile compared to the chairs. He was seated in a high-backed chair behind the desk; he did not invite them to sit down.

"Ms. Holloway," he said, "I find your line of questioning about Teddy Wendover objectionable, and inadmissible. Teddy Wendover is not on trial. In investigating serious crimes, the state follows many leads, most of which subsequently prove to have no merit and are dropped, and henceforth are irrelevant. Your client is charged with the murder of Congressman Knecht, and that's the only case we are trying in this court."

"Your Honor," Barbara said carefully, "if Mrs. Musick had not come forward, Teddy would be in an institution today, and three murder cases would be closed. I believe it is in my client's interest to make that clear. The state's witness—"

"I warn you, Ms. Holloway, do not pursue this line. It is inadmissible; whatever probative value you may think it has is far outweighed by the probability of confusing the issue and misleading the jury. I will not permit any further questioning or comments concerning the investigation of Teddy Wendover. Do you understand?"

"Yes, sir," she said slowly. Then she asked, "Your Honor, may I ask if this warning is on record?"

His eyes narrowed. "It will be on the record, Ms. Holloway."

They both understood quite well that she had met his threat with one of her own.

"Now, get out of here, both of you. We'll resume in fifteen minutes." He glared at them until they walked from his chambers.

Grace Heflin looked as shaken as Barbara felt. They walked without speaking down the wide steps to the second floor, where Heflin went one way to consult with Marcus Truly and Barbara went the other way toward Frank and Shelley.

"Take this down," she said to Shelley. Her own hands were shaking too hard to write at the moment, she was so enraged. She repeated the conversation as Shelley wrote.

When she finished, Shelley whispered, "What does it mean?"

Frank answered in a harsh voice. "It means the son of a bitch thinks Ted's guilty and he's going to run his court on that assumption. And another step or two like this one means we'll have cause for a mistrial."

At least an appeal, Barbara thought, but the idea of putting Ted and Carolyn through a mistrial or an appeal was disheartening. Would either of them be able to stand it? She knew she had to be careful. Judge Ariel might charge her with contempt; he could order her to jail, and in that event her father and Shelley would have to take over.

Frank patted her shoulder. "Honey, you filled the bucket and carried it most of the way; if the jury doesn't have enough sense to get it home, you might as well give up now."

When they went back to court, Barbara stood up and remained at her chair. She looked at Ted, then let her gaze move over the jurors, to Dr. Janec, and finally she said to Judge Ariel, "I find I have no more questions to ask of this witness." Her nod to him was almost a bow.

He got the message, she knew; she could only hope the jury did also. She had been forbidden to continue this line of questions and none other was worth pursuing.

THIRTY-SIX

FRIDAY MORNING WAS as bad as Barbara had warned Ted and Carolyn it would be. Testimony from three witnesses in a row put Carolyn and Harry Knecht in the same hotel or motel at the same time, having dinner together, coming in late together, or just registered for the same day or two. A hotel maid testified that they had had two rooms but one had not been used. Someone else had a snapshot of them together, with Knecht's arm around Carolyn's waist. There was little Barbara could do to temper the testimony; it was all true.

That afternoon Grace Heflin called Ruby Crispin, who was dressed in a black linen suit, white blouse, black shiny beads, black hose and shoes. Her black hair was in a severe chignon. As slim as a pencil, as elegant as a queen, she walked with a model's confidence and poise, seated herself gracefully, tilted her head as if for a cameraman, and appeared as languid and unself-conscious as a dream nymph.

She stated that she had known Carolyn when they were both in school; Carolyn had been a gifted musician. "She had to give that up, of course," she added regretfully.

"So you've been a family friend for many years, is that right?"

"I never knew Ted that well," she said. "He didn't approve of me; he was cold and distant. Or perhaps it was our friendship, mine and Carolyn's, that he disapproved of. I had the impression he was jealous of our friendship."

"Ms. Crispin," Heflin said then, "going back to before the death of Congressman Knecht, on what occasion did you last see Ted Wendover?"

"In June of last summer. My house is not far from Stone Point," Ruby Crispin said in a low voice. "That day last June, I had been swimming earlier, and I was on my way out through the lobby when I saw Congressman Knecht. I stopped to speak to him a moment near the registration desk. As we spoke, he began to look upset, and I glanced back over my shoulder to see what was the cause. Ted and Brian Rowland had just come from Brian's office, and Ted was glaring at the congressman. I heard Ted say, 'You take care of your affairs, and I'll handle mine. By God, I'll take care of mine.' "

Ted whispered urgently to Barbara, "That's a lie! I never saw her or Knecht that day!"

She nodded at him. "Let's just listen."

"Then what happened, Ms. Crispin?" Heflin prompted.

"Well, Brian put his hand on Ted's arm, as if to restrain him, and Congressman Knecht was walking away from the registration desk, very stiffly, as if . . . I don't know, as if he expected to be attacked or something." She looked at her hands on the witness stand. "I moved away, too. If there was going to be a fight or anything, I didn't want to be in the middle of it. Ted stamped out and the congressman nearly ran through the lobby, toward the stairs. He was pale and agitated. I went over to Brian. He was strained, too. I said, 'He must know about Harry and Carolyn.' Brian just laughed." She looked up from her hands and said softly, "I didn't see Ted again from that day to this."

"Exactly what did you mean, 'He must know about Harry and Carolyn'?"

Her voice became even lower. "That they had been having an affair for a very long time."

"How did it come about that Mrs. Wendover stayed in your house over the weekend of September ninth?"

"When I read that Congressman Knecht would be speaking, I asked her if she planned to be on the coast. I invited her to stay with me, but she said no, she already had a reservation for a cottage up at Newport. Then about a week or two before he was due, she called and said her plans had changed, she would have Teddy with her, and was the invitation still good. Of course, I said it was. I told her I would be gone, but I'd leave the key so she could help herself to the house."

"Had your own plans changed also?" Heflin asked.

She shook her head. "Not really. I just decided not to be there, and I visited friends in California."

"Was there a reason for your decision?" Heflin asked, more insistently this time.

After a pause, Ruby Crispin said, "I had started to regret my invitation. I thought if there was trouble between Ted and Harry over Carolyn, I didn't want it to happen around me. But I couldn't very well turn her down, so I just went away myself."

"Did Mrs. Wendover ever talk to you about Harry Knecht?"

"No."

"How did you know she was having an affair with him?"

Ruby Crispin glanced at Carolyn, then turned her gaze back to her hands. "About ten years ago, she stayed with me a couple of days. One morning she went out riding with him and didn't return until dark, and when she did come in, I could tell. She was flushed and happy, the way a woman is afterward."

When Heflin finished with Ruby Crispin, Barbara had a whispered conference with Ted. "Write your version of that

June meeting," she said. "We'll get it in later." He looked ghastly, pale, near tears, his face rigid.

"Ms. Crispin," she said, walking toward the witness stand, "you and Carolyn were friends years ago, is that right? When you were both in school?"

"Yes. We were in college together."

"Did you graduate together?"

"No, I dropped out after the first year. I got married and moved to New York."

"That's when you began your modeling career?"

"Very soon after I went to New York."

"Did you know Ted Wendover when you and Carolyn were freshmen together?"

"Yes, she was engaged to him. I met him a couple of times."

"Did you keep in touch after you moved away?"

"A Christmas card a few times, that was all."

"So for over twenty years you had no real contact with her. Is that right?"

She shrugged. "Yes. We both had our lives, and we lived on opposite coasts."

"Of course. Were you surprised to find her still married to Ted Wendover when you met again after so long?"

She hesitated, then said yes.

"I believe you've been married three times and divorced three times. Is that correct?"

She glanced at Heflin, as if inviting an objection. Then she said, "That's right."

"How long were you married the first time?" Barbara asked.

Heflin objected.

"Your Honor," Barbara said, "the witness has made a character assessment of my client, intimating that he was cold and distant and that she believed him to be jealous of her friendship with his wife. I believe we should know the basis of her understanding of men, and relationships."

Ariel nodded. "Overruled. You may answer the question," he said to Crispin.

From his frown, Barbara was beginning to get the impression he disapproved of the witness as much as he disapproved of her.

"I was married five years the first time," Crispin said coldly.

"And the second time?"

"Three years."

"And the last one?"

"Two years." Her eyes were shining with anger.

"I see. Do you have any children?"

"No!"

"Is Brian Rowland a neighbor and friend?"

"Yes. He lives on my road."

"Do you get together over coffee, chat? Do neighborly things like that?"

"We see each other fairly often. I like to swim at Stone Point. He passes my house every day."

"And you chat, the way neighbors do?"

"Yes, we talk."

"Gossip?"

"No, I don't gossip. We talk about books, magazine articles, movies, that sort of thing."

"When you plan to go away for a few days, do you ask him to keep an eye on your house?"

"Yes. If he's going to be gone, he mentions it to me. We are the only two residents on our road. We watch out for each other."

"So you find him friendly, easy to get along with?"

"Yes."

"Have you ever tried to talk to Ted Wendover in a similar manner, about books, or movies, or articles?"

"No. He won't talk to me."

"Did you talk in a friendly manner to Congressman Knecht when he was at Stone Point?"

"Not really. He was always busy. We said hello, but that's about all."

"Did you find him cold and distant, too?"

She narrowed her eyes and said, "No. He was simply busy."

"When did you become reacquainted with Carolyn Wendover?"

Crispin made a shrugging motion. "I'm not sure, about ten years ago."

"You just happened to run into each other?"

"No, I called and told her I was in town, and she asked me out to her house."

"Is that when you became reacquainted with Ted also?"

"Yes. I had dinner with them."

"I imagine you and Carolyn had a lot to talk about—your career, college days, life in New York. Is that right?"

"Yes, of course. Her daughter, Gail, was very interested in what it was like to be a model."

"Was Ted Wendover interested in your talk that night?"

She hesitated, then said, "Not at all. He left almost as soon as he finished eating. He said he had some work to do."

"When was the next time you were in Ted's presence?"

"About three years later. I visited them again, and he came home late and just went to bed."

"How late did he come home?"

"I don't know. After eleven."

"Do you know where he had been?"

"Eastern Oregon somewhere; I don't remember."

"I see. So he came home tired and went to bed, again demonstrating a cold and distant attitude. What about later? When were you with him again?"

Angrily she said, "I don't remember."

"Did he ever come to visit at your house?"

"No. She brought the children twice, but he was off on a trip each time."

"So you've seen him with his family only two times in the past ten years. Is that right?"

"No. It was more than that, but I can't remember when."

Barbara looked at her pityingly. "You've described him as being cold and distant, and possibly jealous of your friendship with his wife. Please try to remember when you think he displayed that attitude." She moved toward her table, as if prepared to wait.

After a moment, Ruby Crispin said, almost sullenly, "I can't remember when."

"All right," Barbara said then. "When Carolyn Wendover called you this last time, did you mention to Brian Rowland that she would be there?"

"I don't know. Perhaps I did."

"Did you and Brian Rowland discuss a possible relationship between Mrs. Wendover and the congressman?"

"Well, everyone did. We all knew."

"But did the two of you discuss it?"

"I don't remember. Perhaps in passing we mentioned it."

"You said last June, 'He must know about Harry and Carolyn.' Were those your words?"

"Yes, that's what I said."

"And that would indicate you had talked about it previously, wouldn't it? I mean, you didn't have to explain what you meant."

"Yes, we talked about it! Everyone did."

"What did he say when you told him Carolyn Wendover and Teddy would be staying in your house?"

"He said he didn't blame me for leaving. He just hoped she'd keep the idiot out of sight in his hotel."

"Had Carolyn Wendover ever left Teddy alone in your house, or with you?"

"No. I think she realized that most people are uncomfortable with him. We didn't talk about it; it just never came up as an issue."

"So you assumed she would keep Teddy with her that day?"

"Yes."

"Ms. Crispin, why did it surprise you to find Carolyn and Ted Wendover still married after so many years?"

She made a shrugging motion again. "I didn't examine why. I didn't think of it much one way or the other."

"Did Ted Wendover ever do or say anything specific to make you believe he was jealous of you?"

"I said I can't remember the incidents."

"Ms. Crispin, are you, in fact, jealous of Carolyn Wendover and her relationship with her husband, the fact that they've been married thirty-one years?"

Heflin yelled out an objection, and it was sustained almost before Barbara finished the question. But it was out there, she thought, satisfied. "No further questions," she said coolly, and sat down.

It could have been worse, Barbara knew, when Judge Ariel said they would adjourn until Monday morning. At least the jury had a little more to consider than merely the love affair between Carolyn and Harry. Nobody loves a gossip, she told herself, but looking at the jurors when they rose to file out, she thought maybe a couple of them did.

That night Barbara and Frank went to a small Italian restaurant for a fish stew that he said was a bouillabaisse with more soul than the French version. It was a slow meal; each mussel, clam, and crab had to be confronted individually, with care. Sipping Soave, Barbara said, "That's what I needed. What a rotten day."

"You're doing a good job," he said thoughtfully, "considering what you have to work with."

"It would be nice if Carolyn and Harry had not been a thing," she agreed, "but there it is." She poked around in her bowl for another bit of crab. There was none left. She settled for another glass of wine.

"I'm really bugged by the timetable," she said then. "Harry got the letter from Lois over two years ago. They dropped the matter in February, and there it lay until last June, over a year later. Something made him pick it up again. He knew a lot to tell John when he met him the first time. What made him connect her letter and Gold Mountain to the Rowlands?"

"He could have seen Ted with Brian Rowland in June, even if Ted didn't see him," Frank said, then shook his head. "Won't work, will it? He went straight on to Denver and got in touch with John, with his questions already at hand."

"I know. Something happened before June. He had time to do some digging before then. He saw Carolyn in March, in the Eugene office, with several others present." She frowned. "I'll have to ask her if there was anything said at that meeting to revive his interest in Gold Mountain." She did not relish the thought of cross-examining Carolyn right now. Carolyn had been devastated by the day's testimony, her betrayal by Ruby Crispin.

She narrowed her eyes, remembering what Carolyn had said about that day. She had met with Polly Kratz, the Eugene office manager, at ten to discuss the speeches, the timing, invitations, all of it before Harry even arrived. He had said hello, then had gone into a second office to use the telephone. Carolyn and Polly had chatted until he was ready to look over the schedule; he had okayed it, and Carolyn had left five or ten minutes later. They had not been alone at any time that morning. Polly, she thought then. She would call Polly Kratz.

It was pouring rain when they left the restaurant. She had a jolting flash of memory of the time she and John had left a restaurant and he had placed his hat on her head, pulled up his jacket over his own head, and they had run like rabbits to her car. She drew in her breath. Frank opened an oversized umbrella, and they walked to his Buick in silence.

At home a few minutes later she called Polly Kratz. After apologizing for disturbing her, she asked about that day, listened, then said, "Can you recall anything you chatted about while you waited for him? Take your time. Maybe I should call back. . . . " She listened again.

"I recall quite clearly," Polly Kratz said. "We talked about the weather. It was a day like this one, raining hard, and I said something about not wanting to go to the coast if it was still pouring the next day. She said her husband and son had been down in the Rogue River area about half a dozen times over the past year, and it was always different weather down there. Up here it rained; down there it was sunny and pleasant. She said they had just returned from a trip, sunburned. I remember exactly."

"Ms. Kratz," Barbara said, "is it possible that Congressman Knecht heard your conversation?"

There was a pause, then Polly Kratz said, "It's possible. He didn't refer to it, but he was in the doorway for part of it, and after she left, he went to stand in front of the map. We had a large map of Oregon on the wall. I remember I had to speak to him twice before he noticed. I thought at the time he might be considering a trip down that way. But he never mentioned it to me."

"Where would his telephone records be?" Barbara asked then.

The pause was longer. "If anyone has them, it's Mal. But he wouldn't let you examine them, not without a court order, I'm sure."

When Barbara hung up, she let out a long breath and nodded to Frank. "That's when it happened," she said. "He heard that Ted had been down in the Klamaths a lot, around the Rogue River, and he must have looked into it without telling a soul."

"He could have called the county clerks' offices," Frank said after a moment. "Just to see if there'd been land transfers involving a lot of acreage."

"Right. Let's hope Mal Zimmerman is still being cooperative." She called him.

He wanted to cooperate, he said several times, but he absolutely could not let her browse in the congressman's telephone records. "You don't realize what you're asking," he said plaintively.

"I do, though. Look, if I can't see them, will you do me a favor and just see if he made some calls? That's all I need to know, if he made the calls, and when. Between the middle of March last year and June."

He couldn't do it, he said over and over; then he said he'd try. "I'm being called on Monday," he said, "so I'll have to be down there. If I find anything like what you're after, I'll make a record of it. But just that."

She told him the prefixes she was after and hung up after another few minutes. "He'll find them," she said confidently. "That's the missing link, Dad. I know it is."

"You may be right," he said. "It sounds like it may be. Now, we have some serious talking to do about Judge Ariel. Scuttlebutt has it that what you're seeing is what he is. He doesn't like complications; he doesn't believe the cops arrest innocent people, and the prosecution tends to get convictions in his court. He slammed the door shut on you over Teddy. I believe he'll decide anything to do with Mary Sue or Lois Hedrick will be inadmissible, too. He wants a clean, neat little trial without any irrelevancies."

"And a quick verdict: Guilty as charged," she said glumly.

THIRTY-SEVEN

ON SUNDAY BARBARA put on her poncho and her waterproof boots and walked for miles along the Willamette River in the rain. She met only three others on the bicycle path. When Frank regarded her ruefully on her return, she laughed. "I needed that more than you know."

At ten-thirty that night the phone rang; it was Mal Zimmerman. "Congressman Knecht called three numbers with those prefixes twice each," he said without preamble. "County clerks' offices in Curry, Coos, and Josephine counties. The first calls were short, a couple of minutes, all on April twenty-first. The second ones were longer, ten or twelve minutes each, on May third. And that's all I know about them." He sounded resentful.

After hanging up, Barbara sat at the telephone in thought. Harry Knecht had called first, she decided, to ask questions; the second call was to get answers.

Mal Zimmerman was Heflin's first witness on Monday. Dressed in a proper gray business suit and tie, he didn't appear as thin as before. He looked like an up-and-coming MBA. He was a good witness, concise and to the point. Heflin got right to the afternoon of September ninth.

"What was his schedule from four on?"

"He had a few phone calls to make; then he was to have a short meeting with Mrs. Wendover, rest, review his speech, and get ready for the dinner that night. He planned to be back down in the lobby by six for a reception."

"Did you see him again that evening?"

"Yes. At five-twenty he called and asked me to come to his room. I went right up. He said he might be a few minutes late getting to the lobby. He hadn't changed clothes yet. And he asked if I had plans for that night. He said we might be working late. I stayed no more than five minutes, and probably not that long."

"Was he alone?"

"As far as I know, he was."

"Did he have any appointments for the period between four and six besides the one with Mrs. Wendover?"

"No."

When Heflin finished with him, she hadn't left much room for Barbara to maneuver in. She simply had not wandered from the point; nor had he.

"Mr. Zimmerman," Barbara began, "was the congressman's schedule printed out?"

"Yes."

"It was a busy day for him, wasn't it, breakfast meeting, riding with a group, the luncheon. . . ? Did he stick to a schedule like that?"

"Yes, he wanted scheduling and he stuck to it."

"So Mrs. Wendover's meeting with him that day was an official meeting? Is that right?"

"Yes."

"Did the congressman tell you anything about the phone calls he wanted to make or receive when he went to his room that day?"

"No."

"Did you usually keep a log of phone calls, who called, and what about?"

"Yes."

"Is there a record of any calls that afternoon?"

"No." For the first time he volunteered information. "He wouldn't have logged personal calls."

"You said you kept track of his official appointments and schedule. Did you keep track of any of his personal appointments?"

"No."

"Did he indicate what you both might be working on that evening?"

"No."

"At what point would his personal interest in a project become official? Would there be a lag?"

He said carefully, "He was interested in many problems, but until he thought there was a reason to pursue them officially, they would have remained personal interests. He didn't confide in me regarding his personal affairs and concerns. However, many of his official concerns about the environment began as personal interests."

"Can you give us an example?"

She wanted him to loosen up, to talk about Knecht as a man of passion where the environment was involved. So far he had been little more than a robot answering questions. Now, as he began to talk about a hydroelectric dam and its effects on salmon, a project that Knecht had become interested in, Zimmerman got animated and even fierce.

After this she said, "So it was nearly four months from the time he became aware of the problem before he involved his staff. Was that fairly typical?"

"Yes. He knew how hard it was to keep anything secret in Washington," he said with some bitterness. "He wanted to make certain he knew where he was going before he started, in order to gauge what roadblocks he'd encounter, what opposition would arise."

"Who had copies of the printed schedule last September?"

"I did, his staff in Eugene, Mr. Rowland, Mrs. Wendover, Mr. Brody, the security chief. There may have been others."

"Were you expecting any trouble?"

He paused, considering, and then said, "We always acted as if we did if any environmental issue was under discussion. The dinner that night was to be with a forestry group. It could have been trouble."

"Did Mr. Knecht have enemies?" she asked then.

"Yes, he did."

"Did they threaten him?"

"Yes! They sent him dead owls, and threats written in crayon on butcher paper smeared with blood. They called him in the middle of the night." He clutched the edge of the stand before him with both hands. "Governor McCall had been his idol, and Congressman Knecht was determined to continue his mission, to preserve the state and the country, and the same people and more were determined to stop him."

"Objection," Heflin said then. "Please, no speeches from the witness."

"Sustained," Ariel snapped. "Just get on with it, Ms. Holloway. Mr. Zimmerman, simply answer the questions."

Mal Zimmerman's face flushed and his lips tightened.

"So he had enemies, and his schedule was not a secret," Barbara said. "Is that right?"

"Yes!"

"When he called you to his room, did he say anything he couldn't have said on the phone?"

He hesitated, then said, "No. Nothing."

"Do you know why he didn't just tell you by phone what he wanted?"

"I think he was waiting for a call. He glanced at the phone while we were talking."

"Objection," Heflin said. "Speculation."

"Sustained."

"Did you see the bottle of Wild Turkey when you were in his room?" Barbara asked then.

He shook his head. "No."

"Do you know if he brought that bottle with him?"

"No."

"Did you always come to Oregon with the congressman?"

"No. He was back and forth a lot. I came with him when there were important conferences or speeches, like in September."

"How did you keep track of his official business when you weren't with him?"

"Either his Eugene office manager, Polly Kratz, kept a record, or he did. Then we had a staff meeting in Washington to discuss whatever he had talked to people about. He kept a business diary, with dates, times, who was present, what the meetings were about, everything."

"Were you with him in June when he stayed at Stone Point two days?"

"No. I met him in Denver for the mining conference that followed."

"Did he keep a record of his meetings at Stone Point or anywhere else for that period in June?"

"No."

"So you assumed it was a personal concern that brought him here that time. Is that right?"

He hesitated, then said slowly, "I don't know. He canceled a meeting in Washington in order to fly out to Oregon before the Denver meeting. He never did that for personal reasons."

"Mr. Zimmerman, do you have reason to believe the congressman was engaged in a preliminary investigation that involved his primary interest in the environment?"

Heflin objected, and this time Ariel said, "Overruled."

"Yes, I do," Zimmerman said. He told about the calls to Curry, Coos, and Josephine counties. "That's how he would do things, find out as much as he could while he was thinking about it and then call for a staff meeting." He looked at Barbara, glanced at the judge, and said quickly, "I looked through his diary for the time of those calls, and there is a note that says, 'Lois Hedrick.' Just that. But she had written to him—"

"Objection!" Heflin cried. "Your Honor, counsel is simply muddying the waters, dragging in conjectural material that is not relevant to this trial."

There was a commotion in the rear of the court as several reporters made their way out in a hurry.

Judge Ariel banged his gavel, scowled at Barbara, and said, "I will rule on the objection after lunch. We will be in recess until one-thirty."

Frank took charge as soon as the court began to clear. Ted was gone; the jury was gone. Carolyn and her two children stood bewildered, uncertain what they should do. "Reid," Frank said, "watch me and do exactly as I do. Let's go." He took Barbara's arm in one hand, Shelley's in the other; Reid took his mother and sister in the same way. Frank led the way out, through the mob of reporters, all yelling questions. He ignored the cameramen, ignored anyone directly in front of him, and kept moving steadily, this time toward the Eighth Street exit. Reid followed with his mother and sister.

They went out to the street, and Frank marched them at a fast clip down the block to the office. The reporters ran along with them all the way. Barbara had to resist her impulse to stick her tongue out at the camcorders. At the office, they all crowded into the elevator, leaving no room for anyone else. When they got out, Frank said to Pam at the reception desk, "Lock the stairway." She ran to do it. Then she closed the doors to both corridors, effectively turning the reception area into a tiny space with doors and walls and a glass expanse, with her desk on the other side. This was all very swift and efficient.

Frank led the way to the spacious room where clients and attorneys could spend time waiting for verdicts. The room was outfitted with game tables, couches, comfortable chairs, many magazines, and games to play. Most people simply sat, staring, waiting. Frank turned on a television and said, "We'll make the twelve o'clock news, I expect. You folks can decide if you want to eat here or take your chances with the bloodhounds outside. Patsy Meares will be along in a minute to take orders. Meanwhile, we have some work to do."

Reid and Gail were breathless with excitement, their eyes shining, high color on their cheeks. Carolyn was breathless, too, but from excitement or the pace of their escape from the courthouse was not apparent. She sank down into a chair in front of the TV. "I'll stay here," she said.

Barbara was at the door when Reid asked plaintively, "Will someone just tell us what happened? Why everything boiled over?"

Frank looked at him gravely. "Yes. Thought you knew. She just got a state's witness to make the connection between Harry Knecht and one of the other murders. Not only a connection, but complete with the name, Lois Hedrick. Watch the noon news."

In the corridor on the way to his office, Frank stopped off to speak to Patsy; Barbara and Shelley continued on. When he joined them a minute later, he was carrying a portable television.

He plugged it in, got the channel he wanted and muted the sound, and then glanced at Barbara, who was on the couch, her legs stretched out in front of her. She grinned, and he burst into laughter.

Patsy came in to take lunch orders; the news came on; Patsy left. No one spoke as they watched the segment concerning the trial: Outside the courthouse, Mal Zimmerman looked like a martyr, his hands spread helplessly. "No questions. Please, no questions. The judge ordered me not to discuss my testimony." There was Grace Heflin, flanked by Marcus Truly and another assistant from the DA's office. She smiled graciously and shook her head. "We'll have a news conference later today," she said. There were many shots of Frank rescuing his flock. Barbara grimaced at her own image on the screen: Her clothes were rumpled, her hair yucky. Shelley looked like a doll, of course.

The newswoman recapped the details of Lois Hedrick's death. "Her head was crushed with a rock," she said in a melo-dramatic tone. "Congressman Knecht's head was crushed in a similar fashion, and so was Mary Sue McDonald's. Is this the work of a madman, a serial killer? We will have a full report of the trial of Theodore Wendover, accused of murdering Congressman Knecht, as well as the story about the other two similar deaths immediately following the six o'clock news tonight. . . . "

Frank turned it off when the coanchor began to talk about other events. "Okay," he said. "We need to get that diary. The state will beat us to it, and in that case, a motion to force them to turn over a copy. My department."

"Ariel will sequester the jury," Barbara said. "And, no doubt, I'll be lectured again," she added with a grimace. Frank nodded, unconcerned.

As before, Judge Ariel did not invite Barbara or Grace Heflin to sit down. They stood before his pretty little desk like two schoolgirls before a headmaster out of Dickens.

"Ms. Holloway, I warned you before, and I warn you once more. You will not ask questions of witnesses that lead to monologues and conjectures. What might have been, what anyone suspects could be in the future are both beyond the scope of this trial. I will so advise the jury at the time I instruct them. I shall instruct your witness that he is to answer questions directly, without speeches, and without speculation. I so instruct you now. Is that clear?"

"Your Honor," Barbara said, "may I remind the Court that Mr. Zimmerman is the state's witness, and that my cross-examination was properly conducted only to develop more fully matters he already had testified to?"

His eyes narrowed; his face grew redder, a dark shade, which made his lips look pale. "Ms. Holloway," he said softly, "I remind you that I will not tolerate any further attempt at obfuscation. This case will not be tried as a media event, or in the newspapers. To this end, I shall sequester the jury as of now." He turned his dark gaze to Grace Heflin. "Ms. Heflin, I also instruct you that there will be no press conferences by any of the principals concerning this trial as long as it is in progress. That applies to both of you and everyone in your offices. You are both excused. Get out of here."

Again they walked out silently. Near the bottom of the stairs, Grace Heflin whispered, "I think he found his wife in bed with the plumber."

"Or his mother made him eat lumpy oatmeal three times a day," Barbara whispered back.

They both kept a serious demeanor as they were enveloped by a cloud of reporters and a roar of questions.

It was close to two before they resumed. Zimmerman was reminded that he was still under oath before he took his seat in the witness box.

"The Court sustains the previous objection," Judge Ariel said then. "Mr. Zimmerman, the Court orders you to answer the questions directly, without speeches, without conjecture, or what you imagine. You may testify only to facts that you know directly." He nodded coldly to Barbara. "You may continue."

She had Zimmerman tell about Knecht's trip to Oregon in

June and to Denver following it, then about his conference in Portland in August.

"So he broke an appointment to fly to Oregon; he broke appointments in Denver in June and in Portland in August, and each time he was out alone for two hours. Is that correct?"

"Yes."

"Were those unusual occasions, for him to break appointments, to go somewhere not previously planned on trips like those?"

"Extremely unusual."

"Mr. Zimmerman, you've told us that Congressman Knecht received numerous threats, dead owls, blood-smeared notes, things of that sort. What did he do about them?"

"He shrugged them off, said it went with the territory. I took them all to the FBI in Washington."

"What do you mean, 'it went with the territory'?"

"He was a staunch environmentalist, dedicated to environmental causes; he knew many people were opposed to his views. He was willing to risk everything for what he believed in."

"Objection," Heflin said wearily. "The witness is making a speech again."

"Your Honor," Barbara said quickly, "the witness is responding directly to a question of relevance. The congressman had enemies who threatened him. We have a right to know what was done about those threats, and why they were issued."

"Overruled," Judge Ariel said. Then he added, "Ms. Holloway, I suggest you get on with it. You have belabored this point overlong as it is."

She turned again to Zimmerman, who was angrier than ever. His thin face was rigid, his lips compressed until they were pale. "What happened when the FBI investigated? Did they find a suspect?"

"I don't know," he said tightly. "I don't think they found an individual, or they would have told us. That's what they said at the beginning."

"Do you have direct knowledge of those threats, Mr. Zimmerman?"

"Yes. I saw the ones that came in the mail or appeared on his car or at his house. He made notes about the phone calls and gave them to me to deal with."

"Were any of the threats of a personal nature?"

"No. Absolutely not. They were all connected to his work as chairman of the Natural Resources Committee, or some of the other committees he served on as an environmentalist."

She thanked him then and took her seat.

THIRTY-EIGHT

WHEN BARBARA GOT downstairs the following morning, she found Frank in the kitchen, looking mad as hell. "Go listen to the message on the answering machine," he said.

She went into his study and pressed the message button. "Good morning. This is Ronald Boyington, clerk to Judge Ariel. Judge Ariel requests the presence of Mr. Holloway and Ms. Holloway in chambers at eight forty-five."

It was ten after eight. She returned to the kitchen, where Frank had poured coffee for her.

"If he thinks that's the proper way to get in touch with attorneys in his court, he's got another think coming!" he said furiously. "What if we hadn't noticed the message? A contempt citation?"

"Well, I'd better finish dressing," she said, not even making an attempt to soothe Frank, which would have been impossible. She took her coffee upstairs with her and got ready for court.

This time Judge Ariel's room had more people in it. Heflin and Marcus Truly were there, the judge's clerk, and Brian Rowland with a stranger. They had all arrived more or less simultaneously. Barbara nodded at the others; no one said a word.

Judge Ariel entered and motioned them all to sit down. Barbara perched on the edge of an oversized chair, noting with satisfaction that Grace Heflin was equally uncomfortable.

Ariel sat behind his desk and introduced the stranger with his usual charm: "This is Marvin Cramer, attorney representing Mr. Rowland. Yesterday, after court adjourned, Mr. Cramer petitioned the court concerning a matter of interest for his client." He held up a paper, slapped it down again. "Mr. Cramer, summarize what you're asking as briefly as possible."

"Yes, Your Honor," Cramer said smoothly. He had a good voice. He was tall and heavily built, with gray hair, and eyes so dark, they appeared black. His eyebrows were bushy and black and nearly met in the middle. "Last week in court, we heard how adroitly counsel"—he bowed slightly to Barbara—"wrung an admission from a witness that he would have raised the price of property he was selling if he had known the buyers were from California. My client is in the middle of delicate negotiations for property in the Gold Beach area, and he is using the services of an intermediary. If it becomes known that Mr. Rowland plans another of his resorts on the coast, there is no doubt he will be forced to pay many thousands of dollars more than the actual market value for various parcels of ground. What we are requesting is that no mention be made in court of any of his land purchases, which, of course, have nothing to do with the case being tried."

He was masterful, Barbara noted distantly; it was clever of him to use her own cross-examination in this way. The witness he was talking about had become angry when he learned the real purchaser of his tract was a Californian.

Grace Heflin had been taken by surprise as much as she herself had been by this meeting, Barbara felt certain. Brian Rowland was tense, anxious, following his attorney's words with close attention, as if he was checking off points, making certain the ground was thoroughly covered. Cramer went on and on.

"To this end of protecting my client's business interests, I have delivered to the Court a complete list of Mr. Rowland's land transactions over the past several years, as well as a summary of proposed transactions. Every completed transaction, of course, is a matter of public record. . . . "

Although he was anything but brief, Judge Ariel did not protest his statement. After Cramer finally finished, Judge Ariel said, "The Court grants Mr. Rowland's request to keep his private business out of the public record in connection with the trial of Mr. Wendover."

Brian Rowland sat back in his chair, visibly relieved.

"Your Honor," Barbara cried, "I object to the preclusion of testimony that has not yet been heard!"

"Ms. Holloway, I told you the Court will not tolerate any further obfuscation, and it is the Court's opinion that to bring in testimony that is as irrelevant as Mr. Rowland's land transactions is inadmissible. The Court has examined the land transfers and finds them to be in good order. They are not to be referred to in examining or cross-examining Mr. Rowland. If questions arise in the future concerning whatever development he has in mind, that is outside the jurisdiction of the Court and has no relevance to the trial we are hearing. The trial of one individual is not to become an occasion to bring financial burdens to another in an attempt to confuse the jury. I did not bring you here to argue this point. I have stated my opinion, and I expect you to adhere to it."

"Your Honor," Frank said, as smooth as Cramer, "the courts have ruled that the possible distress of a witness is insufficient cause to restrict counsel from seeking testimony from that witness."

"Don't quote law to me, Mr. Holloway. I keep a clerk to serve that function. This meeting is adjourned. Court will reconvene at ten o'clock."

When they reconvened, Judge Ariel introduced Marvin Cramer to the jury, and they began.

Cramer had a chair close to the prosecutors' table; he appeared complacent and comfortable. Grace Heflin called Brian Rowland.

After he had filled in the usual background, she led him to the present. "Are you and the defendant friends?"

"Not really social friends," he said. He was at ease now, as comfortable as Cramer. "Ours is a business relationship. Mr.

Wendover has acted as a land agent for us many times over the past sixteen years, or even longer. And I have recommended him to others."

"Has this business relationship always proved satisfactory?"

He hesitated a moment, then said, "Yes. I've always personally felt well served."

"Will you please tell us about what happened last June tenth?"

"Ted, Mr. Wendover, came to Stone Point for a business meeting that morning. We had concluded our business and he was ready to leave when I felt obligated to mention that I had heard complaints concerning the presence of his son at business meetings. I simply asked him not to take the boy along on any business he was engaged in for us." He paused a second, then said, "He became furious. We left the office, and it happened that Congressman Knecht at that moment approached the front desk. Ted stopped and said in a fairly loud voice for me to take care of my affairs and he would take care of his. Then, almost whispering, he said, 'That son of a bitch has screwed up my life long enough. So help me, God, I'll take care of him.'" He stopped again, as if recalling exactly what had happened. "I put my hand on his arm, but he didn't pay any attention to me; he was staring at the congressman. Mr. Knecht turned and hurried away through the lobby, and Ted pulled away from me and stamped out the other way, out the front entrance."

Barbara could feel the tension in Ted almost as a palpable wave in the air. She leaned toward him and whispered, "Relax. Write your version, word for word, if you can." He began to scribble.

"Mr. Rowland, why did you put your hand on his arm?" Heflin asked.

He shrugged slightly. "I don't know. He was usually very self-contained, very calm. In all the years I'd known him, I never had seen him angry. I didn't know what to expect, what he might do. I didn't want trouble in my hotel."

"Then what did you do?"

"I went back to my office. Oh, first Ms. Crispin came over and said something about Ted knowing about Harry and Carolyn."

"Did you laugh when she said that?"

He shrugged again, a slight motion, as if he had to adjust the way his suit coat lay on his shoulders. "I might have," he said. "I don't remember if I did. But it was ludicrous for her to say that. She only heard half of what he said, an innocent part."

When Heflin was through, Barbara turned in her chair and motioned Frank forward, and then whispered, her hand over her mouth, "If you have any business to attend to, more garden to plant, wash the car, you might as well go on and be about it." He nodded gravely.

She approached the witness stand. "Mr. Rowland, in answering many of the state's questions addressed to you individually, your reply has been plural: We think this, or he has done that for us. Exactly whom were you referring to?"

He answered carefully, described the Rowland Company, the three resorts they owned, how long they had been in business. Barbara hung on every word attentively. Then she asked about his brother, and he was off again, this time explaining why Cyrus was not a member of the company—he wasn't interested in the business end.

"So if you make a decision, you can refer to it as a joint decision, a company decision. And if your father makes a decision, he can refer to it the same way. Is that right?"

"We confer regularly, and I go to SkyView at least once a month for a few days. There is no dissension."

She kept at this until Cramer objected; his objection was sustained. She asked Brian Rowland about his relationship with Ruby Crispin, and was still asking about this when lunch recess was called.

Barbara, Frank, and Shelley made their way through the onlookers and the press to the street, then started toward Frank's house. Timidly Shelley asked, "What's happening?"

"A war of attrition, I believe," Frank said.

She considered this for another half block, then asked, "Isn't there a danger that the jury will begin to sympathize with the witness?"

Frank laughed. "They will, absolutely. For a time. Then they'll be bored, and finally they'll begin to wonder what he's hiding, why he needs an attorney, why the focus of her questions is so narrow, all sorts of things. And, of course, he may even blurt out something he never intended when his temper's up high enough."

At the next corner, Barbara veered off toward the river trail without a word. She had paid no attention to their conversation; she walked, deep in thought, until it was time to go back to the house, have some lunch, then head back to court.

She took up her questioning of Brian Rowland exactly where she had left off, until once more Cramer objected.

"Counsel is harassing the witness, Your Honor. There is nothing more to be learned about his relationship with Ruby Crispin."

"Sustained," Judge Ariel said wearily. "Ms. Holloway, just get on with it."

"Thank you, Your Honor," she said. She started on Rowland's relationship with the Wendover family, and made it clear from the first question that she intended to ask about each member of the family. She was not yet through with them when Judge Ariel called for a fifteen-minute recess.

In the ladies' room she surveyed herself and nodded. She was still okay—not frazzled, not tired-looking yet, not even vindictive, just determined.

When they resumed, Judge Ariel beckoned her and Grace Heflin to the bench. "Ms. Holloway," he said in a mean voice, "my patience is wearing very thin. You will please get on with your cross-examination and stop playing this game."

"Yes, sir," she said, lying.

She turned to Brian Rowland, who looked a bit refreshed from the break, but his air of complacency was gone, and the looks he shot toward his attorney were not friendly. "Mr. Rowland," she said, "has Mrs. Wendover ever stayed as a registered guest at Stone Point?"

"No," he said sharply.

"Did Teddy ever go to Stone Point?"

"No."

"Why did you mention him specifically to Mr. Brody as someone to be watched out for?"

"It was still on my mind, the incident at SkyView."

"Did you ever see him alone after that incident?"

"No."

She took him through the family members one by one, and his answers grew even sharper. He was looking at his lawyer more and more frequently now, ignoring the jury altogether.

"How many times did Congressman Knecht stay as a registered guest over the years?"

"I don't recall exactly, several."

"Three? Four? Something like that?"

He hesitated, then said, "I think so. I would have to check the records to come up with an exact number."

"All right," she said agreeably. "How many of those visits were on official business, such as the September dates?"

"I can't remember without checking."

"Let me see if I can refresh your memory. I have here Mr. Knecht's office records that list his official speaking dates at Stone Point. The first date at Stone Point was ten years ago, May tenth, eleventh, and twelfth. Do you recall that time, Mr. Rowland?"

"Vaguely," he said. "It was a long time ago."

She nodded, and went on to the next two dates listed, and again he said he recalled them only vaguely. "And, of course, the last date was this past September," she said. "That makes four business meetings, and of course there was the June stay, which was apparently not for official business. Mr. Rowland, was there a great deal of advance preparation for his meetings at your hotel?"

"Yes. Meetings like that are always planned months in advance."

"And is the hotel usually filled for those times?"

"It's filled most of the time," he said.

"I see. So if I called today for a reservation for tomorrow, I might be turned down?"

"You would be," he said.

Someone laughed, and Ariel looked around sharply. Barbara smiled and said, "Let me put that another way. Would someone be likely to get a reservation for tomorrow, if that person called today?"

"Probably not."

"When did Congressman Knecht make a reservation for June ninth and tenth?"

"I don't know," he said angrily. "I can't keep track of the daily operations; I leave that up to the reservation clerk and my general manager."

"But he was able to get a room with no advance reservation. Is that right?"

"I don't know when he made the reservation. When I said the hotel is usually filled, I should explain that we almost always keep a few rooms open in case of emergency, or if an important guest wants a room. He wouldn't have been turned down."

"Did you know he was coming?"

"No."

"When did you find out?"

He glanced at Cramer, who, it was clear, would have objected if he thought he had cause. He didn't move.

"He had already registered when I learned he was there," Rowland said.

"Did you alert your security chief, Mr. Brody?"

"No. There hadn't been any publicity; there was no reason to."

"Did you talk with Congressman Knecht that day?"

"Yes, as a matter of fact, I went to his room to see if there was anything we could do for him. We had a drink together."

"Did you order the drinks—on the house, so to speak?"

"It's possible. I don't remember who paid for them."

"I think I have a copy of his bill for that stay," she said easily, moving toward her table.

"He paid for them," Rowland snapped.

"When you had a drink with him, did he seem upset, or worried?"

"No. He was perfectly normal, maybe a little tired."

"Had you seen him upset or worried at other times?"

"I don't know. I didn't know him that well. I don't know what he was like when he was upset or worried."

"But you said he wasn't that day. How could you tell?"

Cramer objected, and the objection was sustained.

"Did you have lunch with him the following day?" Barbara asked then.

After a swift, bitter look at Cramer, he said coldly, "Yes. In his room. And we went for a walk."

"Did he pay for the lunches?"

"Yes! He wouldn't accept any favors. He made an issue of it, not accepting anything."

She nodded. "Do you know if he had appointments with anyone else?"

"I have no idea what else he did."

"Let's see if we can piece it together," she said. "We know his arrival time from Washington into Portland was two o'clock; we know he rented a car and drove directly to Stone Point, arrived there at three fifty-five." She picked up the bill and scanned it. "His bill here shows room service at four-fifteen and again at four forty-five. It shows four drinks altogether. Is that right?"

"I don't remember."

"Um," she said, still studying the bill. "I see that he had breakfast alone in his room at eight-thirty, then lunch for two in his room at twelve-thirty. And you said you went for a walk afterward. His check-out time was five P.M."

"Objection," Heflin said. "Does counsel have a question?"

"Yes, in fact, I do," Barbara said. "Mr. Rowland, we've heard testimony that Mr. Knecht broke an appointment in order to catch that flight to Oregon and go to Stone Point. Do you know of anyone other than yourself whom he saw when he was there?"

Cramer stood up then. "I most strenuously object, Your Honor. Counsel is simply harassing this witness. What Mr. Rowland remembers from last June is completely irrelevant."

"Your Honor," Barbara said, "we have heard testimony that Mr. Knecht received numerous threats and also that he often worked alone while gathering information. This unplanned trip appears to have been carried out with some urgency. If Mr. Rowland can shed any light on the substance of Mr. Knecht's purpose for this trip, it is not irrelevant."

Impatiently Judge Ariel said, "Overruled. But Ms. Holloway, just move along, will you."

"Yes, sir," she said. "Shall I repeat my question, Mr. Rowland?"

"No. I don't know who he saw. We had a short lunch, and a very short walk; he was free all the rest of the afternoon. I didn't keep tabs on him."

"Did you have drinks in his room and then lunch in his room for the sake of privacy, Mr. Rowland?"

"No! We had no private business to discuss. The hotel was crowded, the dining room was busy, and service gets a little slow. He said he didn't want a two-hour luncheon, so we ate in his room."

"But then he had time for a walk. How long was the walk?"

"A few minutes. I don't know."

"You said you had no private business to discuss, and you also said you didn't know him very well; he had been in the hotel on business previously, and we've seen what kind of schedule he maintained on an occasion like that. Mr. Rowland, what did you two have to talk about if not business or personal affairs?"

"Nothing in particular," he said, glancing at Cramer. "He just wanted to chat. I can't remember what we talked about."

"For an hour the first day, and at least two hours again the following day, you simply chatted. Perhaps about movies, books, magazine articles?"

"Objection!" Heflin cried.

"Sustained," Ariel snapped.

"All right," Barbara said. "Who issued the invitation to have lunch together?"

"I as—no, he asked me."

"When?"

He drew in a deep breath and looked again at Cramer, who remained silent. "I don't remember," he said then. "Sometime that morning."

"Oh? You had a third meeting?"

"No! I happened to see him in the lobby, just in passing."

"He had breakfast in his room at eight-thirty and went riding from nine until ten-fifteen. You were closeted with Mr. Wendover from ten until eleven forty-five, then returned to your office. When did you manage to cross paths with Mr. Knecht in the lobby?"

"I said I don't remember! I can't keep track of details like that from months ago!"

"All right. But was it before your meeting with Mr. Wendover?"

"Yes!" He was staring at her with open hostility, his face flushed and tight.

"Was it possibly the day before, when you had drinks together? Was a suggestion made that you should sleep on whatever it was you talked about and have another talk the next day?"

Heflin and Cramer both objected. Cramer's voice overrode Heflin's. "The witness has answered that question several times. Counsel is simply badgering him."

For a moment Judge Ariel hesitated; then he sustained the objections.

Slowly Barbara walked toward the jury box. She had been keeping track of the time; it was a few minutes before five. She turned back to Rowland.

"Mr. Rowland, no one has come forward to indicate that Congressman Knecht met with anyone but you on that trip in June. You had two lengthy conferences with him in private. Isn't it a fact that the sole purpose of that urgent, unplanned flight was to meet with you? Weren't you, in fact, the only person he had any interest in talking to those two days?"

Cramer and Heflin were on their feet objecting before she finished the question, but she persisted; her voice added to theirs did create a bit of bedlam, she had to admit—especially since Judge Ariel was also banging his gavel with some enthusiasm.

He sustained the objections, which he couldn't have heard any more than she had, and he lectured everyone about talking, dismissed the jury, demanded they all return at nine the next morning, and stalked out without a pause.

Ted looked completely bewildered. "I'll come around and talk to you in a bit," Frank said. They hadn't had a chance yet to tell him about the morning meeting in Judge Ariel's chambers.

When Ted was taken away and the courtroom was clearing,

Shelley asked, "How much longer can you keep him on the stand?" Her eyes were wide.

"All day tomorrow," Frank said without hesitation. "She hasn't even got to the meeting with Ted yet."

His face was sober, but Barbara knew he was laughing inside; she could tell from the way his hand on her arm was shaking slightly.

Frank continued, speaking to Shelley: "See, they tried to gag her, and this is what they get. Reckon they won't try that again anytime soon." His hand was shaking harder, but his face was perfectly serious.

"Do you want me to come over?" Shelley asked.

"No need. I'm taking her home, putting her on the couch with her feet up and a glass of wine in her hand; then I'll go talk to Ted, bring him up-to-date. And later on I'm taking her to dinner."

Barbara did not mind at all that they were talking about her as if she had already left. In a way she felt she had; she felt distant, unconnected, and exhausted.

Frank got Shelley and Barbara out with his usual skill, bantering with reporters, never slowing his forward progress through them. A block away from the courthouse, he began to laugh softly. "Ah, Bobby," he said after a minute, "I wish you could have seen Cramer's face. He was looking at you the way a snake charmer might look at a hungry wild cobra that somehow got in his basket."

That night when they got home from the restaurant, the message light on the telephone answering machine was blinking. They listened together to Sheriff Tourese's voice: "Ms. Holloway, we found Owen Praeger. He's dead. His car ran out of gas and he started walking, died of exposure, froze to death. Just thought you'd want to know."

She gazed dully at the machine as the realization hit her of how much she had counted on finding him, on somehow forcing him to talk. Dead, the man who had heard gold calling him, singing to him, a chorus of gold singing to him. Dead.

THIRTY-NINE

BARBARA STARTED HER questioning of Brian Rowland where she had left off the day before. Today Cramer was on his feet, objecting nearly as often as she asked questions. Heflin seemed content to let him play the heavy. After an hour Barbara got around to Rowland's June meeting with Ted.

"You said you heard complaints about Mr. Wendover's son Teddy. Is that right?"

"Yes." He made his characteristic shrugging movement. "People talk. I heard that some deals fell through because of him."

"Who told you?"

"I don't recall exactly who it was, more than one, but I don't remember names."

"I see. Yet on something as nebulous as rumors of unnamed clients who might or might not have had unfortunate dealings with Mr. Wendover, you felt strongly enough to mention it to him?"

"Yes. I brought it up."

"When did you hear those rumors?"

"For a number of years—they've been circulating quite a while."

"Did you ever mention them to Mr. Wendover before last June?"

"No." He seemed on the verge of erupting, but he controlled it. He kept glancing at his attorney.

"You said your dealings with him had always been satisfactory over a period going back sixteen years. Apparently, whatever the basis of those rumors was, it had not affected your dealings with him. Is that right?"

"We never complained about his work for us."

"Then why did you pass on a rumor last June?"

He paused, with another glance at Cramer. "I just thought it was something I should do, warn him there was talk."

"But you went beyond that, didn't you? You stated that you also told him not to take Teddy on any project that concerned you. Didn't you?"

"Yes! I agreed that it wasn't proper to take his son along on business trips." He was biting off his words.

"You thought that in June, but did you not think that when you first heard the rumors? Why didn't you warn him then?"

"Objection!" Cramer shouted. "Your Honor, counsel is engaged in simple persecution of the witness. This matter is irrelevant, besides."

"No it isn't," Barbara said. "He stated that his comments to Ted Wendover made Mr. Wendover furious. I am trying to find out what those comments were and what inspired them."

She was allowed to continue.

"I ask again, Mr. Rowland, why didn't you warn Ted Wendover when you first heard such rumors?"

"It wasn't any of my business," he said sharply. He started to add something more, but she cut him off.

"If it wasn't your business earlier, what made it your business in June?"

"I happened to know the person involved. It wasn't just a rumor anymore."

"Did you discuss it with Mr. Wendover, tell him the source of your information?"

"Yes," he snapped. "He knew it was true."

"Who was the person who complained?" she asked then.

"Owen Praeger, just a man I happened to recommend Ted Wendover to."

"Mr. Rowland," she said, "why didn't you just come out and say that an hour ago?"

"Objection!" Cramer said sharply. "Counsel knows that's not a proper question."

"Sustained," Judge Ariel said, then added, "But I think it's a pretty good question. Get on with it, Ms. Holloway."

"Was Mr. Praeger an associate of yours at the time?"

"No."

"A friend?"

"No, just an acquaintance."

"Isn't it a fact, Mr. Rowland, that you took Mr. Praeger to Ted Wendover's home and introduced them, and sat in on the business they were discussing?"

He hesitated, and this time Cramer objected. "Your Honor, all this is irrelevant. Mr. Rowland's business, Mr. Praeger's business—none of it has anything to do with the trial under way here."

"Sustained," Judge Ariel said. "I quite agree. You wanted the name of the person who informed on Mr. Wendover, and you have it, Ms. Holloway. Now let's move on to something else."

She nodded agreeably, then asked, "Was Mr. Wendover the only land broker you dealt with over the past fifteen or sixteen years?"

"Yes."

"And he was always satisfactory, you've stated. After your warning in June, did he continue to be satisfactory?"

He hesitated. "Actually, we haven't had any business dealings since then."

"Oh? Were all your transactions concluded last June?"

"With him? Yes."

"Are you using the services of another broker now?"

"No—that is yes, we are."

"When did you engage a new broker?"

"Objection!" Cramer cried. "Irrelevant."

"Sustained," Judge Ariel snapped. "Ms. Holloway, I remind you that you are not to stray from the point of the trial before this Court."

"Yes sir," she said. Very blandly she then asked, "Mr. Rowland, where were you when Congressman Knecht was killed?"

He started and his mouth tightened to a thin line before he answered. "I was out on the patio at Stone Point."

"Were you with other people out there?"

Angrily he said. "No! I was just strolling around, looking over the crowd, on my way to a back entrance of the hotel so I could go change my clothes before the reception at six."

"Did you see Mr. Martinez hurry into the hotel?"

"No," he said wearily. "I didn't know anything had happened until I got inside, and my manager spotted me and came running to tell me about the tragedy."

"Then what did you do?"

He drew in a deep breath. "He told me they had called the sheriff, and he was on his way up to make sure things were under control. I went on to my office and washed up and changed my clothes. I put on a suit and tie because I knew we were in for a bad night with our guests, and I wanted to present a more formal appearance than a sports shirt and slacks." He said this with exaggerated patience. It sounded rehearsed.

Judge Ariel called for the lunch recess then.

Barbara leaned against a fir tree and watched muddy water swirl and foam over a rock. It made a mess, she thought, but it got over one way or another. Abruptly, she turned and began to walk briskly back to Frank's house.

Frank had put together a beautiful salad, greens from the garden, scallions, strips of sweet pepper, and crabmeat. She ignored it.

"I'll keep Brian Rowland on the stand until we adjourn," she said to Frank and Shelley, who had both eaten already, "but tomorrow there will be Anna Leiter, and she's going to be tough, maybe too tough." She looked at Shelley. "This afternoon, I want you to call Mal Zimmerman and Polly Kratz. If you can't reach him, at least try to get her. Tell them we know what the congressman was involved with, and we would like to see them both tonight. Around nine."

Frank held up his hand. "Wait up, Bobby. You're playing with fire and you know it. Ariel will slap a contempt citation faster than you can duck."

"He can't make it stick. I was ordered not to talk about the trial, and I won't. He's ruled all the Rowland business irrelevant. If it's not connected to the trial, by God, I'll talk about it."

"Why?" Shelley asked. "The jury won't be able to hear anything about it."

"I want to put a scare into Brody. Remember, he's due back. I want him to think a long time about Praeger, and Knecht, and Lois Hedrick, and Mary Sue McDonald. He's dumb, but maybe it will sink in that his skin might be at risk."

"Bobby—" He stopped, then growled, "For God's sake, eat something. We have to leave in a minute."

She picked up a piece of crab, put it down again. "Dad, get hold of Bailey, will you? I want to know if Connie Mines was transferred to anyone, and when, and if money crossed hands. And I bet if you put in a call to Juret at Carlyle Mining Company—leave a message if you have to—that all hell's going to break loose over Gold Mountain, I bet he'll call back." So far he had not taken a call or returned one.

"I'm going to get the car out," he grumbled. "What's the point of a decent watch if you never look at it?" He went out the back way to the garage.

Shelley snatched up the bowl of salad and shoved it in the refrigerator, and they went out the front door to meet Frank in the driveway. "You won't miss anything in court," Barbara reassured Shelley as they got in the car. "I'm just going to keep pounding on him and make him wish he'd fired Brody a long time ago, if I get lucky."

She started back with the incident in the swimming pool at SkyView and worked to the present; it took all afternoon. Brian Rowland didn't say a thing she hadn't already known.

"Did you know Mrs. Wendover would have Teddy with her on September ninth?"

"I thought he wouldn't be far away; he never was. Ruby Crispin might have mentioned it."

"Did you advise Mr. Brody that Teddy might be around that day?"

"No—maybe. I don't remember. I might have mentioned it."

"Why did you keep Mr. Brody, after such a glaring mistake, misidentifying the person he claimed he saw?"

He shrugged. "He was sorry, more than I can even express.

He just made a mistake. He had seen Teddy earlier, and my warning flashed into his mind, he said. I believe in giving people a second chance if they are truly sorry."

He was smooth and easy now. She had gone into another area where he had rehearsed his answers, she felt certain.

When she said she was through at last, Heflin cut through all the testimony of two and a half days. Had he ever had any official or business relationship with the congressman? Had he known about the affair between Carolyn Wendover and Congressman Knecht? Did others know? Had his warning about Teddy being a hindrance to business, coupled with Ted's seeing Knecht, caused Ted to blurt out a threat? Had he believed it was a threat? Did he still believe that?

After court adjourned, Shelley whispered that Zimmerman and Kratz would be at the house at nine. "They're dying of curiosity," she added.

"Great," Barbara said. "You go on and rest, have dinner, whatever. Come back at nine if you want to; you don't have to."

"I'll be there!"

"I have to talk to Ted," she told Frank as Shelley hurried off. "Then I think I'll want a couple of aspirins and maybe a real drink."

"What you'll want is food," he said. "Come on, let's do it."

This time the reporters' shouted questions were mostly about Praeger. "Who was he?" "Did you know he's dead?" "Why was there an arrest warrant out for him? You signed a complaint. Why?"

"You guys know I can't talk about any of that," she said.

"Then it's connected to the trial, right?"

"No comment. No comment," she said helplessly.

"What was his connection with the congressman?"

"No comment," she said again. "I'm really sorry, but I can't comment. Orders."

Then they were through the tunnel and in the parking lot and Frank hurried her to the Buick and they left.

"Sometimes you can say as much with 'No comment' as you can with a speech," he said, driving. "I'll go with you to see Ted, and then we eat. Pronto. Wonder you didn't faint in court."

* * *

Their three guests were early. Polly Kratz and Mal Zimmerman arrived together, followed within seconds by Shelley. Frank showed them into the living room, shooed cats off chairs, and offered something to drink, which they refused. Mal was back to his scarecrow look, in jeans, a close-fitting sweater, boots. Polly Kratz was slightly less informal; her gleaming white hair was hairdresser-perfect, and her jeans were pressed. Even in jeans and running shoes, she gave the impression of efficiency; it was due to her alertness and her lack of fidgeting. She was one who listened closely and then acted. Mal was a foot shuffler, a gesturer. Now he was in a state of nerves that made his hands appear to have a life of their own, in his pockets, reaching for one of the cats, smoothing a wrinkle in his jeans. . . .

"Thanks for coming," Barbara said. She was on one end of the couch, Frank on the other. "I have to say a couple things before we get into the purpose of this meeting. First, we can't talk about the trial, none of us. Next, there's no doubt you'll be questioned about tonight, closely questioned, certainly by the press, perhaps by the judge. If you're not ready for that, I quite understand and we can call this off. We need to know up front if you're prepared to take on what Congressman Knecht was investigating. Carry on where he left off, in a way."

"You know I am," Mal said. "Let them ask questions."

Polly Kratz nodded. "No one worked for him who wasn't dedicated to his causes," she said. "No one."

"Okay. You may have questions to ask that we can't answer, not because we want to hide anything, but because we can't. That has to be understood also."

They both nodded. "I know," Mal said impatiently. "I saw it in operation; the gag order's in effect."

Barbara didn't respond, and he nodded again.

"Okay, let's just watch this," she said then, and pressed the play button for the VCR. No one spoke as the gold mountain appeared and the voice-over started.

"I don't believe it," Mal whispered when it ended. He was pale and a nerve in his cheek was twitching. "I just can't believe it!"

"I know," Barbara said quietly. "Let's go in to the table. I have a lot of material to show you, then another video. First, the paperwork." She got up and led the way to the dining room.

She showed them the map and the land-transfer copies, then they all went back to the living room, where she put a second video in the VCR and started it. It began as the first one had, but then it stopped; a scene froze on the screen. The screen split into halves, and in the second window the same view appeared, this time with red dots on many features, and the longitude and latitude of each one clearly marked. There was no unctuous voice-over in this video, and hardly a sound in the room as a scene froze, the screen divided, and the location was identified.

When it ended, Frank said, "Maybe now we'd all like some coffee, or wine, or something."

"That's what those red dots on the map meant, isn't it?" Mal asked. "Can I go see it again?"

"Coffee," Frank muttered, and left the room.

The others returned to the dining room to study the map spread out across the table. Barbara and Shelley stood back as Polly and Mal located each site marked with a red dot. All three parcels of land had red dots on them.

"Let's sit down in the dinette and have coffee and talk," Barbara said a little later. They followed her to the dinette, where Frank had out mugs and the carafe. A plate of cookies was on the table; almost absently, Mal picked one up and ate it.

"I don't think there's any danger in knowing this, or having those materials," Barbara said. "But I don't know that. There could be."

"That's what he was going to work on that night, isn't it?" Mal demanded. When she remained silent, he nodded. "That's it. He had learned enough to staff it out."

"How much of this did he actually have?" Polly asked. "You must have found a lot of the material."

"He didn't have the video," Barbara said. "We dug that up. He would have had the locations of the land sales by that night, a rundown of who had bought land, a lot of it. He probably wouldn't have suspected the intended use of that land yet." She lifted her coffee, and added to Polly, "I won't be calling you as a witness."

Polly considered this. "All I could have testified about was the letter from Lois Hedrick. You're not allowed to bring that up?"

Barbara remained silent.

After a moment Frank asked, "What would the congressman have done with this material?"

"At this point?" Mal said. "A big news conference. He would have gotten in touch with a lot of environmental groups, briefed them, and held a joint news conference. He would have shown the videos, of course, and copies of the map would have been handed out. . . . "

He looked at Polly, who nodded. She said, "He would have given copies of everything to a lot of people, started a mass protest. Held hearings." She looked stricken. "No one will hold hearings about this now."

"Maybe, maybe," Frank said.

They talked for a while, then Barbara said, "You understand we're not advising you about what to do with the materials. We simply feel it's proper to turn it all over to those who are still interested in continuing the congressman's work. You shouldn't contact us about what you decide to do. We are in no way part of your staff, nor are we your advisers in this matter."

Mal was studying her shrewdly. "I understand," he said. "I didn't hang out in Washington for six years for nothing. Gotcha."

Polly Kratz was looking thoughtful. "The sooner we distribute some of the material, the better," she said. "Just in case someone hits us with a restraining order or something."

Good girl, Barbara thought, but she did not say a word.

"There's an all-night Kinko's, and we can buy a dozen video cassettes in a supermarket," Polly went on. "There's probably a late-night video store open where we can rent a VCR and start making copies."

Barbara held up her hand. "Don't tell us your plans," she said.

"We'd better get started," Mal said, and stood up. "You have room for an overnighter?" he asked Polly.

"You can have the couch," she said; then after a glance up and down him, she shook her head. "I'll take the couch, you can have the bed."

They gathered everything together and left then.

"You go on, too," Barbara said to Shelley. She studied the young woman a moment; Shelley was flushed and excited. "You're really sure this is the line of work for you?"

"Are you kidding! Bill's just green, absolutely green. He says every younger attorney around town is green because I'm on the inside of this one. I can't wait until I can talk about it a little with him!"

"Is he asking questions?" Barbara asked curiously. She remembered walking on the beach with Bill, answering question after question.

"No way. He knows better. But after it's all over, I'll be able to talk about it a little with him, won't I? At least some of the things I understand."

"Shelley," Frank said, "after this is over, I'll personally walk you through the transcripts and explain every bit of it. And you can do the same with him."

She looked overwhelmed, as if he had promised to escort her through heaven. Barbara laughed. "Maybe it *is* your line of work. Go on, beat it now. Morning comes earlier and earlier these days."

After Shelley was gone, Barbara and Frank cleared the table, put the mugs in the dishwasher, and she went back to the living room and sat before the smoldering fire, no more than embers now. Both cats scrambled for her lap. They were getting too big to occupy a single lap. Often she couldn't tell them apart: just Thing One and Thing Two. Golden clouds.

Frank came in and sat opposite her. "Want a brandy or anything?"

She shook her head. "She's so young, isn't she? Excited. I remember once when I was excited like that; you lectured me that a man's life was at stake, it wasn't a game, if I wanted thrills to take up skydiving or something. Remember?"

"Yep. Notice you didn't lecture her."

"Not yet. She doesn't realize how bad it is. She sees me turning witnesses inside out and thinks we're winning." She stroked Thing One, then Thing Two. "Heflin's good. She doesn't let herself get distracted." One cat decided that was enough cuddling and started to bite the other one in the ear. She put them both down and watched them roll over and over.

"Ted's going to be a lousy witness," she murmured. "He never quite got the hang of talking about himself, his feelings. I imagine he was freer talking with Teddy than with anyone else."

Frank nodded. He would be a lousy witness.

"What are the odds around town?" she asked, keeping her gaze on the mock battle of golden clouds.

"Don't know," Frank said.

She knew he was lying, because he always knew things like that. She nodded. "If we lose, there's appellate, and maybe even a mistrial after the shit hits the fan, but . . . I think Carolyn will break, and if she goes, so will Ted."

"Bobby," he said gruffly, "knock it off. You haven't lost yet. And don't underestimate Carolyn or Ted. They're both tough; they've had to be."

"Ah, but guilt is so powerful, isn't it?" she murmured. "It can corrode the toughest hide, get right down to the soft parts and eat away at them." Abruptly she stood up. Both cats fled as if they had been attacked. "Go on to bed, Dad. I'll have a glass of milk and turn off lights in a minute."

He stood up, too. "Bobby, don't underestimate the jury, either. They have eyes. They know something's going on, doors are being slammed in front of your nose every time you turn around. When they get around to talking about it, they'll wonder about those doors, what was on the other side. Give them a little credit."

"Right," she said. "See you in the morning. Good night." She left to wander about the downstairs a few minutes, to have a glass of milk, to try to consider what the jury was thinking along about now. She smiled as Thing One and Thing Two twitched their ears when Frank's bedroom door opened; they both raced down the hallway toward him.

Then she found herself thinking about guilt again, and it was a long time before she was ready to try to sleep.

FORTY

ANNA LEITER WAS forty-nine, a little overweight, with a smooth round face, round blue eyes, and pale brown hair with henna highlights, probably covering gray hair. Everything about her was modest, her navy blue dress, a simple strand of pearls, and her wedding and engagement rings.

Her husband was an orthodontist, she said, and she stayed busy with the school board and church committees. They had two grown children.

"Mrs. Leiter," Grace Heflin said, "will you just tell us in your own words what you were doing on September ninth at Stone Point?"

"Well, Henry, my husband, you know, he played golf all afternoon, and he wanted to take a nap before the reception, so I went out for a walk. I didn't want to go back to the beach because I had a touch of sunburn from being down there before, so I just walked up the other way, toward the highway, looking at the hostas and toad lilies." She was talking fast, with quick glances at the jury, then at Barbara, back to Grace Heflin. "I was getting ideas for a shady corner of our yard. And I saw the man I thought was a waiter walking on the road toward the hotel. I couldn't help but see him, you know. The path curves back in the rhodies and azaleas, then out to the road, and back and forth like that. I was at the road part when I saw him, and I thought it was a waiter going to work for the reception maybe. So I looked at my watch to see if I should go back yet. It was five-thirty. Then the path wound back in the trees again, and I didn't see him anymore. After five more minutes, I did go back to our cottage."

"Was he carrying anything?"

"Oh, I nearly forgot. Yes, he was. A brown paper bag."

"And you were able to see him clearly?"

"Yes. The sun was in his face—you know, he was walking toward the hotel. He might not have seen me, what with the sun in his eyes like that. But he was clear."

Heflin produced a layout of the area, plainly showing the path Mrs. Leiter had taken, and the road. "You were on this stretch of the path?"

"Yes. I had just come to the edge of the road when I noticed him. I was almost even with him."

"Where was he?"

"Not far. Just across the road. About from here to the rail by the jury away from me by the time I turned in again."

"So he got within fifteen feet of you. Is that about right?"

"I think so."

"Can you tell us how he was dressed?"

"Well, like I said, I thought he was a waiter, because he had on a long-sleeved white shirt and black slacks, or very dark gray maybe. They looked black. And no one except the waiters wear long-sleeved shirts like that at a resort."

"Did the police ask you to try to pick out the man you saw that day in a lineup?"

"Yes. There were twelve or more men. I picked him out."

"Is the man you picked out here in court, Mrs. Leiter?"

She pointed. "Yes, it's him, Mr. Wendover."

"Is that the same man you saw at five-thirty on September ninth?"

"Yes."

Grace Heflin walked toward her table, then paused to ask, "Do you wear glasses, Mrs. Leiter?"

"I have reading glasses," she said.

"When was your last eye examination?"

"In December. He said I was doing fine and to come back in two years."

"Did your doctor prescribe new lenses for you?"

"No. He said I was fine."

Heflin nodded. "Thank you, Mrs. Leiter. No further questions at this time."

Conversationally Barbara asked her, "Mrs. Leiter, has it ever happened that you saw someone you thought you recognized, only to have it turn out to be someone else?"

Anna Leiter hesitated, her forehead wrinkled a little; then she said, "I think so. I think it happens to everyone."

"Yes. It's a common occurrence. Do you subscribe to a daily newspaper?"

She looked confused, then nodded. "Yes. The *Oregonian*."

"Having a congressman murdered at the resort during your visit there must have been a terrible shock. Did you follow the developing story in the newspapers?"

"Well, some, I guess."

"When did you tell the police about the waiter you saw walking toward the hotel?"

She looked nervous again and began to twist her rings. "On Monday, December fifth," she said in a low voice. "I just didn't think anything of it before. I mean, he was like a waiter, and I didn't think to tell them sooner. At first they said they were looking for someone in blue jeans and a T-shirt, not a waiter."

Barbara nodded reassuringly at her. "What did you do on the fifth of December?"

"I talked it over with Henry—he's my husband—and he said I had to call the police and tell them, so I did. They sent two detectives up to ask me questions, and I signed a statement for them, and then later that day, they asked me if I could come down to look at a lineup. And I said yes."

"But what made you think it was important then, since you hadn't given it a thought earlier?"

"Well, the newspaper said the young man hadn't done it, and they were looking for someone dressed in black pants and a white shirt, and I remembered him, and I thought maybe I should tell someone."

"Had you thought about him at all from September until then?"

She shook her head. "Not at all."

"Was that the same day you called the police, when you read the newspaper story?"

"No. That was on Sunday. I waited until Monday. I was so worried about it, I couldn't sleep that night, and Henry said I had to tell them."

"So you saw the story in the Sunday *Oregonian*," Barbara said. She went to her table and Shelley handed her the newspaper. "This is the Sunday edition of the newspaper you read, isn't it?"

Mrs. Leiter glanced at it, then said, "I guess so."

"Take your time, Mrs. Leiter. Do you want to put on your glasses to make certain?"

She groped in her purse for her glasses and put them on to examine the paper. "That's the one," she said.

Barbara opened it to an inside section with the story and two pictures, one of Teddy playing with two children on the beach, building a castle, and the other of the Wendover family.

She showed it to Mrs. Leiter. "Did you also look at the pictures?"

She shook her head. "I don't remember ever seeing them," she said. "I really don't recall seeing the photographs. I was just so upset about the story, and the man I saw."

"You said, Mrs. Leiter, the man you saw was carrying a brown paper bag. Can you tell us a little more about that?"

Again she shook her head. She was almost whispering when she said, "I can't. They asked me, too, and I just can't remember much about the bag. Just that he had it."

"Which hand was he carrying it in?"

"I don't know. It might have been both hands, but I can't honestly swear to it."

"Was he carrying it up near his shirt or down by his slacks?"
She didn't know.

Barbara went to her table and picked up a grocery bag, held it up. "Was it like this one?" She held up a second one, much smaller. "Or like this?"

Mrs. Leiter shook her head. "I'm not sure."

Silently Barbara walked to the exhibit table with both bags and started to put the rocks in the smaller one. The pebbles were in a tagged plastic bag. She put the big one, also in a plastic bag, in first, then tried to stuff the other bag on top. It didn't fit. "Your Honor," she said then, "if the rocks are loose, perhaps they will fit into the bag. May I try?"

"No, no," he said irritably. "You've made the point. Get on with it."

She nodded, then placed all the rocks in the bigger bag. She picked it up and had to hold it with both hands. "This weighs twenty-one pounds," she said. "Mrs. Leiter, does this look like the bag the man was carrying?"

"I just don't know," Mrs. Leiter said. She looked to be near tears.

Exasperated, Barbara said, "Mrs. Leiter, you've made a positive identification, yet you can't say anything about what he was carrying. Are you sure you got a good look at him?"

"Yes," she said. "I really did. I saw him all over—you know, his whole body, the black pants and white shirt, but then I guess I really only looked at his face. That's how I am."

Barbara worked at it a little longer, but Mrs. Anna Leiter did not budge. Then Heflin brought her back to her positive identification and she was excused.

During the recess, Frank said to Shelley, "She's the worst possible witness. Honest, no ax to grind, no hidden agenda, just a good American housewife, who happens to be wrong, and will go to her grave convinced she's right."

"She reminded me of my mother," Shelley said.

Barbara grinned. "If I'd been allowed to use a two-by-four, pounding might have done some good. But the jury would have been sore. You don't beat on everyone's mom."

The state's next witness was David Siletz, the manager of Stone Point. He was a tidy little man, five seven or eight, fifty years old, slender, with black hair that looked dyed, and peaked eyebrows. His eyes were pale blue, and red-rimmed, as if he suffered from allergies.

"Mr. Siletz, will you tell us what you were doing from about five-thirty to six on the afternoon Congressman Knecht was murdered?" Grace Heflin asked.

"I was back and forth a lot between the front desk and the Orca Room. That's the function room where the reception was to be held. At five thirty-five I was at the front desk. I was keeping a close eye on the time because they hadn't finished setting up for the reception, and people were arriving and milling about in the lobby. One of the guests approached me, and we were chatting when I noticed one of our waiters in gray trousers. Not black, but dark gray. Then I saw that he had on brown shoes. At first, I couldn't see more of him than that— trousers and shoes; there were many people in the lobby at that time. Just before he passed the desk, he looked toward me, and I got a look at his face. I was looking hard, because I was going to fire him. He turned down the corridor that leads to the elevators, and as soon as I could leave the guest—it was several minutes later—I hurried after him. But he was out of sight."

Heflin interrupted him then. "Mr. Siletz, you say you got a good look at his face. Can you identify that man?"

"Oh, yes, it was Mr. Wendover."

"Then what did you do?"

"I looked around in the corridor, and then I returned to the front desk. It was fifteen minutes before six, and by then our security man had come in from the pool and was talking in an excited way to one of the clerks there. I hurried over and learned about the tragedy. I sent Martinez on up to keep watch on the room and I called the sheriff myself, and told the clerk to ring Dr. Vorlander." He paused; then when Heflin didn't interrupt, he continued.

"After I got the sheriff on the phone, I went through the lobby to the back corridor, where the service elevator is, in order to go up to the room myself. Mr. Rowland was just coming in a back door, and I told him what happened. He told me to go on up, and he went toward the front desk. I went upstairs in the service elevator and stood with several others until the sheriff and his people arrived."

She didn't keep him long after his statement.

"Mr. Siletz," Barbara asked then, "why did you assume the person you saw was a waiter?"

"The white glove," he said promptly. "No one would be wearing white gloves except our waiters."

"So you saw his hand also?"

"One hand, with a white glove, and a little bit of shirtsleeve."

"Which hand was that?"

"His left one. He seemed to have come in by the front entrance, which is not allowed, either," he added primly.

"So you thought he was a waiter improperly dressed. After he looked your way and you got a good look at his face, did you recognize him?"

"No. I don't know Mr. Wendover, and I don't know all the waiters; they come and go."

"You still thought he was a waiter?"

"Yes, it just didn't cross my mind to think otherwise."

"Did you call the waiters together and lecture them about proper apparel after that incident?"

He looked uncomfortable and said yes.

"When was that, Mr. Siletz?"

"It was more than a week later," he said. "Ten days perhaps. In the excitement, I forgot the incident, and when I remembered, I had the meeting."

"Did you fire anyone during that meeting?"

"Yes, I did, but not for that reason. He was simply incompetent."

"Didn't you state in the presence of eight waiters that your reason for firing Mr. Jerry Bruckner was that he had failed to observe the dress code and, in fact, had appeared in gray slacks and brown shoes?"

"I said it, but I didn't mean he was the one I saw."

"You fired a waiter for improper dress, isn't that what you told the assembled waiters at that meeting?"

"Yes, but—"

"Yes is sufficient," she said. "When did you notify the police that you had seen the waiter in the lobby?"

"The day after I read the article about Teddy and I saw the picture of him and his father, and I realized that's who I had seen."

"Did you talk to Mr. Brody about his mistaken identification when that article appeared?"

He shifted uncomfortably. "We talked about it a little," he said.

"Did he tell you he had identified Mr. Wendover?"

"He might have, but I knew when I saw the picture, not because he said that was the man he saw."

She looked at him pityingly. "You said you saw the waiter's hand. Was he carrying anything?"

"Not in the left hand. I couldn't see the other hand."

"You said at fifteen minutes before six you returned to the reception desk and Mr. Martinez was talking to the desk clerk. Then, of course, he had to explain to you what had happened. Is that right?" He said yes, and she asked, "That took a minute or two, didn't it?"

"I don't know," he said miserably. "He was excited. I couldn't understand at first what he was telling me."

"All right," she said kindly. "You sent him to the congressman's room. Where was Dr. Vorlander when the clerk called him?"

"In the lounge. She tried his room first, and then had him paged."

"So that was another few minutes before he actually went up, is that right?"

"I guess so. I was on the phone to the sheriff, not paying much attention."

"All right. You used the service elevator. That's on the opposite side from the room the congressman had, isn't it?"

"Yes."

"Were there people milling about there also?"

"No," he said. "It's a little out of the way."

She brought out the floor plan of the hotel, then asked, "Can you identify some of these rooms for us? This one, for instance, on the second floor. What is that?"

"Janitorial supplies," he said.

"Midway down the corridor there seems to be an exit. Is that right?"

"Yes, to the stairs. And the room next to it is a lounge for the staff."

She studied the layout. "There are the two corner suites, and twelve rooms between them on the west side. Is that right?"

"Yes. They are the largest rooms we have—minisuites."

"Ah. I see. And the stairs are nearly centered, convenient for them all. The service elevator is here next to the stairs." She pointed. "What's this space, Sunset Room?"

"A lounge," he said. "Bar. The entrance is in that corridor." He indicated it on the layout.

"And this is the rear door where you met Mr. Rowland?"

"Yes."

"The hotel was very full that weekend, wasn't it?"

"To capacity," he said. "We had to turn people away."

"No vacancies at all? Not even emergency rooms?" she asked, smiling.

"Not that weekend. We had to turn people away."

"I have a guest list for that period," Barbara said, picking it up at her table. "Do you recognize this list, Mr. Siletz?" She handed it to him. He looked it over and said yes. "When guests call for reservations, do they also reserve space for other things—deep-sea fishing, for example?"

"Yes, many of them do. We arrange it all for them."

"Objection," Heflin said then. "This is irrelevant."

"No, it isn't," Barbara said. "It appears that the guest list furnished by Mr. Rowland may be in error, and there were two empty rooms in a row next to Congressman Knecht's room that day."

Judge Ariel looked as flushed and impatient as ever, but he overruled the objection. "Up to a point, Ms. Holloway," he said, "you may continue."

"Thank you, Your Honor," she said politely. Then she said, "So Mr. and Mrs. Rothman had Room Two Twenty-one, next to the congressman's room, and they were out fishing all day on a planned expedition. Is that right?"

"Yes. They were gone until seven."

"Next to them the list says Mr. and Mrs. Wylie had Room Two Twenty-two. Is that right?"

He hesitated and shifted in his chair. "They were no-shows," he said then.

"Will you explain what you mean?" she asked.

Siletz explained about a mix-up in the reservation of Mr. and Mrs. Wylie. He looked more uncomfortable talking about this than he had when talking about the death of the congressman.

"So their reservation was in the computer, and their cancellation never made it to the computer. Is that right?"

"Yes. I don't know how it happened. A clerical error, that's all."

"Did they reserve a minisuite?"

"They must have," he said. "That's what they were given."

She smiled at him. "Do you know if they reserved a minisuite?"

"No. The reservation clerk might know, but I don't."

"When are rooms actually assigned to guests? Is that done in advance?"

"Just the suites and minis. The others are given when they arrive."

"Mr. Siletz, when a guest checks in and is given a key, is that information also in the computer?"

He squirmed again. "Yes, it is. And when he checks out, the time is entered. Mr. and Mrs. Wylie were entered as having checked in and then checked out. No one can account for it."

"So the computer showed that room occupied from Thursday night until Sunday afternoon. Is that correct?"

"Yes," he said miserably. "They were billed on their credit card for those days."

"Were they also billed for a fishing expedition?"

"Yes, unfortunately."

"Who has access to your computers, Mr. Siletz?"

He blinked. "Why, management, of course. And security. The reservation clerk." He paused, then added, "The bell captain. Housekeeping."

"In fact, most of the people who work there, is that right?"

"Many of them," he said with a sigh.

"Did the maid who cleaned that room report it unoccupied?"

"She said she did, to the head housekeeper, on Saturday. She left her a note, since it was the head housekeeper's day off and everyone else was so upset with the investigation, but her note was lost and the billing went out automatically. As soon as the

Wylies brought it to our attention, of course, we put through the credit."

"Mr. Siletz," Barbara said slowly then, "can you explain why the list of guests still has Mr. and Mrs. Wylie listed as occupying Room Two Twenty-two?"

He shook his head. "It must have come from the computer before the correction was made."

"The Wylies found the charge for the room in October, when they called you. What did you do following that call, Mr. Siletz?"

His discomfort was painful to watch as he squirmed in his chair, darted glances at the jury, then at Judge Ariel, who was frowning. "I went to the reservation desk and checked the computer," he said. "They were still listed then. We, the reservation clerk and I, discussed it, and I questioned the night clerk, who said they had not checked in that night. Obviously, the Wylies had not been there, so I put through the credit and called them back and apologized for the error."

"Did you make the correction in the computer at that time?"

"Not personally. I assumed the reservation clerk corrected it, but I didn't watch him do it."

"Who prepared this list of guests and their rooms?"

"No one prepared it," he said, almost whining. "It was just in the computer. My secretary called up the three days the police were interested in, and made a copy. Later, Mr. Rowland said you wanted a copy, and she made that one. She didn't have to prepare it, just call it up. It was already there."

"Did you look it over?"

"No. I wouldn't have remembered any of those names or numbers. There wasn't any point in looking it over. It was in the computer."

When Barbara finished with him, Grace Heflin made it clear she wasn't interested in guest lists or empty rooms. "Mr. Siletz," she asked briskly, "why did you fire the waiter, Mr. Bruckner?"

"He was incompetent. It was a lot of little things that added up to too much."

"Why did you say your reason for firing him was his failure to dress properly?"

"I wanted to put a scare in them all, make them realize it's important to appear for work in the proper clothes."

"Was the man you saw in the lobby on September ninth at five thirty-five the defendant, Mr. Wendover?"

"Yes! It most certainly was."

And that made it full circle, Barbara thought. First Brody had identified Ted as the man kneeling by the body and then running away; fifteen years of his life had been filled in, giving him more than enough motive, and he had been identified approaching the scene, closer and closer. A real pulp-fiction treatment: Open with the cliffhanger, flash back to causes, close with him drawing near the victim.

Now Grace Heflin said the state rested, and Judge Ariel turned his dark face to Barbara. "We will have the lunch recess until two-thirty. Will defense then be prepared to present its case?"

She would. "Present our case," she said gloomily to Frank when court cleared. "A bunch of character witnesses, a couple of doctors, Ted."

"Come on," he said too heartily. "You've got the maid and the reservation clerk, don't forget. Enough to cast a serious doubt." He crossed his fingers. "And who knows, maybe Brody will come through."

She told Shelley which witnesses to get in touch with and then walked out with Frank. Bailey was lounging against the retaining wall of the tunnel, looking as disheveled as usual. He raised two fingers in a wave and shuffled out, then let them catch up in the parking lot across Seventh.

"Is it lunchtime yet?" he asked.

"Do you have something for us?" Barbara asked in turn.

"Yep. But you won't like it."

FORTY-ONE

THEY ORDERED SANDWICHES at the office, where they sat around the low table as Bailey reported.

"Okay," he said, "it seems that the day after Praeger ambushed you at the gold mine, he showed up in Agness. It's not too far from the mine to the Illahe Road, and he might have hitched a ride. Anyway, he got to Agness and put in a call to Brody. Told him to come pick him up. Brody drove down on Thursday, got him, and headed back to Stone Point. They got back real late Thursday, midnight or after. Early Friday, Rowland bought out Connie Mines, lock, stock, and all that. Praeger wanted a cashier's check, so they went to the bank in Florence and got it. Don't know for how much. Then Praeger borrowed Brody's car and took off. He told them he intended to go to SkyView to get stuff from his cabin and he'd bring the car back in a few days."

Their sandwiches were delivered, and Bailey paused while he doctored his with pickles and mustard.

"Talk first, eat later," Barbara said impatiently.

"Okay, right. Anyway, he left in Brody's car, and next thing, his body turned up." He took a bite and chewed deliberately.

Barbara glared at him. He swallowed, then went on. "The sheriff had someone primed to give him a call if Praeger showed up at SkyView, and he never got the call. What they think happened is that he drove on through Sisters, out to the old McKenzie Highway, and from there onto a Forest Service road that led to an abandoned shack in the woods. The highway's still closed for the winter, but there's just a chain anyone can

364

undo and fasten up again. It looked like he ran out of gas and started to walk to the shack, and bingo, he bit it."

Barbara shook her head. "I don't believe it."

"Neither does the sheriff, but that's the story for now."

"Any sign of the cashier's check?"

"Nope. And he wasn't packing in food for a stay."

They ate in silence then. Frank spoke first. "He was an outdoors man. He could have survived a month in the woods in the winter."

"That's what the sheriff said," Bailey commented. "He didn't have any matches for a fire, though. And he wasn't dressed for a hike in the snow. His heavy jacket and gloves were in the car. It was twenty, twenty-five degrees and windy back then in February. With windchill, he wouldn't have lasted long, way he was dressed."

"Good God," Frank muttered.

Bailey got up to take a map from his coat pocket. "See, here's Sisters, and this is the McKenzie Highway. The service road's up two, three miles. And the cabin he was heading for is about five miles up the service road. The highway department sent in a crew to check snow conditions and they spotted his car, out of gas, a couple hundred feet from the highway. There's a lot of melting on that south side, so they decided what the hell, they'd check out the service road, and they found him about two miles in from the car."

"It stinks," Barbara said. "Any idea when he died?"

"Nope. Could have been Friday night after he left the coast, Saturday, a week later. It snowed off and on through February; no one was in there until last week, when the crew checked out the roads."

"Did Brody file a stolen-car report?" she asked, scowling.

"Nope. Praeger was his other boss, remember? If he wanted to use the car, that was okay with Brody." He picked up the last pickle.

She began to move around the office restlessly, and Frank said, "Go on and take your walk. I'll fill Bailey in. See you back in court."

She fled. Not to the river this time, but downtown Eugene,

past restaurant windows, the inoperable fountain in the center of the mall, where a gang of teenagers was whizzing around and around on in-line skates, past a sidewalk sale of sweatshirts and running shoes. It was a pleasant day; people were sitting out on benches, eating lunch. Food wagons were doing a good business. The food smelled disgusting to her. Present your case, she thought bitterly. Right.

That afternoon she called two of the Wendover neighbors, who painted a different picture of the family, one which she knew from her own observations was the accurate portrayal. Whether the jury bought it, she couldn't tell. The many good times, the easy times, might, in their opinion, be vastly outweighed by the bad times. Wisely, Heflin asked few questions. It was never wise to savage character witnesses; it was enough to imply that they were biased in their own way.

That evening she and Frank conferred with Carolyn at the office as soon as court adjourned. "It's going to break wide open in the press and television," Barbara told her. "Are you up to holding a news conference?"

"Whatever is necessary," Carolyn said quietly.

"They'll ask you about the attempted murder at the gold mine, who was involved, what all you can tell them about it. Are you up to that?"

"How much should I tell them?"

"Not our secret about the demise of the truck," Barbara said with a faint grin. "Everything else. What you know, what you suspect, all of it."

"If I show them Teddy's rock with the gold in it, they'll want to ask him questions," Carolyn said after a moment. "I can't let them. I just can't let them get at him!"

"Don't," Barbara said. "Tell them no."

"What about John Mureau? What should I say about him?"

"What do you know about him?" Barbara asked.

Carolyn looked puzzled and thoughtful. "Actually very little. He's a geologist, a mining consultant, an expert in mine safety, something like that. He lives in Denver. That's about all."

"Then that's all you can tell them, isn't it? But, Carolyn, you realize they won't stop with the Praeger mine incident. They'll press you about Harry Knecht, too."

Carolyn nodded. "I know. I'll tell them the truth: Harry was a very dear friend I saw privately once or twice a year. And that's all I'll say about him."

Frank patted her hand, and Barbara remembered what Gregory Leander had said about her: She was a survivor.

"Okay," she said. "I hate to put you through this, but I don't see how we can avoid it. You set the time and place and duration, and stick to it, and then no more comments. Have your attorney, Clayton Worth, arrange it and stay with you. His office would be ideal. When he sets it up, will you ask him to give us a call? And it should be after the Gold Mountain story breaks. Okay?"

"Okay," Carolyn said firmly. She looked terrified.

"Poor Mr. Worth," Barbara said after Carolyn left.

"It'll do him worlds of good," Frank said. "Shake him out of his complacency a bit."

When they walked home from the office, it was not yet dark. She had hardly been aware of the lengthening days, or the progress spring had made. At their street, Frank said, "Ah," and gazed with contentment at the shrubs, the rhododendrons, azaleas, all in bloom. When had all that happened? she wondered, and then forgot it again. In her mind she was starting to work on her closing argument.

She was at her computer in the upstairs office when it grew so dark Frank had to stop puttering in his garden. She looked up in surprise when he cleared his throat.

"I said dinner's ready. And so am I."

She followed him downstairs. He had brought in spinach and lettuce, scallions, and he said the asparagus was looking good, too bad they couldn't cut any this year, but by next spring—

"Dad, what does a big corporation do when they invest in something that doesn't work out? Just cut it loose, or hang in with it?"

He sighed, aware that his culinary skills were being wasted

again. "Might as well feed you bologna sandwiches and let it go at that," he grumbled. "If they have enough invested in time and/or money, they might hang in and try to make it work. If the CEO says I want it, they hang in longer. Otherwise, they take a tax loss and get out. But it can change with each and every project. You're thinking Carlyle Mining Company and Wilmar Juret?"

"They can afford to cut loose. But can the Rowlands? They must have a bundle tied up in all that land by now."

"Probably mortgaged to the hilt," he said. "Have you tasted the casserole yet?"

She looked at her plate in surprise; it was almost empty. She had eaten everything. Ah, she thought, he said "tasted." "Sorry," she said. "It's wonderful, as always." They both knew she would have been unable to say exactly what she had eaten.

"They must have needed the Carlyle bunch for leverage," she said then. "Would they have signed contracts, things like that already?"

"Maybe. Letters of intent, at least, probably pending acquisition of the land and title searches. You can work out all kinds of deals, with a lot of different hurdles to leap before you make them formal or even binding."

"Let's pretend for a minute that you're Wilmar Juret. I'm Brian Rowland. It's February. I call you and say, Hey, I've got all the land now. Let's finalize our deal. What do you say?"

He narrowed his eyes in thought. After a moment, he said, "I say, Let's wait until the trial's over. If Wendover really did it for personal reasons, we go forward."

"The parent corporation would insist on that much, at least, wouldn't they? No murder of the environmentalist still hanging fire. Tidy that up first, then move forward." She thought for a moment. "When you called Juret, who did you get?"

"You know damn well. Three numbers, two manned by secretaries, who were very polite. One answering machine that takes a message and says, 'Thank you for calling.' Period."

"That's the one," she murmured. "Let's try once more."

They went into the study, where she sat at his desk and made the call. When the machine came on, she said crisply, "Mr.

Juret, this is Barbara Holloway, defense attorney for Ted Wendover. I would like to speak with you about the news story that will break in the next day or two concerning Gold Mountain. Four murders will be linked one to another, and to the project Gold Mountain. There is a rapidly diminishing possibility of protecting the Carlyle Mining Company and the Lockner Corporation from some of the controversy the stories will engender and the notoriety that is certain to ensue." She gave her number and then said, "Thank you."

That night, helping Frank clear the table and do the dishes, she kept having the uneasy feeling that the ground was not as firm as it had been; the air felt more unsettled, with a strange heaviness all about her. She wondered if that was how animals felt before an earthquake; she had read that many animals became nervous hours before an earthquake happened. Birds flew away; fish swam erratically; horses didn't want to be stabled. If she were a bird, she thought moodily, she would fly away; if she were a fish, she'd swim backward or something; and the house felt like a cell, confining and smothering.

Saturday she was too restless to stay up in the office and do the work she knew she had to do; she was up and down the stairs so many times her legs began to ache. She stood watching Frank out in his garden. He even looked like a dirt farmer, she thought. Old baggy pants, a heavy plaid shirt hanging out, boots, wide-brimmed hat. The two cats ran and jumped and tumbled joyously. Now and then, he stopped whatever he was doing to watch them. She suspected he was talking to them, although she could not hear a sound. At eleven the phone began to ring. She ran to the study to listen to the caller. A reporter. As soon as he hung up, the phone rang again. Now she ran to the radio in the kitchen and turned it on to a local news station. *Ah!*

She hurried to the back door and yelled for Frank to come in and then went to stand by the radio, listening. Mal Zimmerman and Polly Kratz were being quoted extensively. Mal's voice was broadcast then: "Nationwide, one percent of the population visits a wilderness area each year. In Oregon it's five percent.

Of course, Oregon won't let the entire southwestern quadrant be turned into an amusement park." Then the newscaster was back, summing up. In the study the phone kept ringing. "We'll have a full report on the twelve o'clock news, and we'll show the video on our noon telecast."

Barbara turned the volume down when a commercial came on. She and Frank regarded one another for a second, then he said, "Well, you did it, Bobby. The hornets are out buzzing."

She grinned. The telephone was ringing again, and now the front door bell was ringing also. "Bailey, I hope," Frank said, and went to peep out the window before he approached the door. He opened it to admit Bailey and two other men he sometimes employed, Hank Belusco and Alan Macagno.

"Hank, you're the backyard," Bailey said, and waved to Barbara. "Shit hit the fan, didn't it?" he said cheerfully as they all escorted Hank Belusco to the back door. "He'll keep them out of the garden," he said to Frank. "And, Barbara, I hope this is the last time you'll ever see Alan. But he'll be with you until this thing's over. Boss's orders," he finished, saluting Frank.

Barbara started to protest, but Frank shook his head. "Orders," he said sternly. "There are four dead people out there, and four more who damn near ended up dead. That's enough."

She eyed Alan Macagno. He was thirty to thirty-five, five feet ten, dressed in a windbreaker, jeans, running shoes. His dark hair was a touch long, and he was lean and looked like a cyclist, or a runner. Reluctantly, she nodded. "I like to walk," she said.

"Me, too," he said; then he grinned at her, appearing almost boyish. No one would give him a second glance: he was a Eugenean to the nth.

"He has a bike, but the damn thing keeps breaking down or something. Broken down right now, matter of fact," Bailey said, still cheerful. "Barbara, you won't be going out alone at night, will you, for the next few days? That would make it hard."

"No," she said, feeling the house shrinking all around her.

"Good. Okay, Alan, off you go."

He nodded, grinned at Barbara again, and went out the front door. Barbara watched him glumly. She couldn't blame Frank for wanting someone out back; the last time they had been besieged, reporters had come over the fence and trampled his garden mercilessly. But a bodyguard! "Too damn much," she muttered under her breath, and went to the study to listen to messages.

When she returned to the kitchen a few minutes later, she told Frank, "Clayton Worth called."

Frank was washing lettuce. "I'll call back," he said. "He might want a bit of jollying. And he'll sure need a pointer or two. Wonder when's the last time he even talked to a reporter." He dried his hands and walked out.

She finished washing the lettuce and put it in a colander, then stood gazing out the back window at his pretty yard. Hank Belusco was playing with the cats, dragging a length of string through the grass. She shouldn't be doing this to her father, she thought suddenly. He should be out there contentedly digging or doing whatever he always found to do, talking to his two cats. . . . He came back, grinning.

"He's hopping. Prima donna stuff. What should he wear, for God's sake! Conference room, his offices," he said to Bailey. "Two o'clock. He'll tape it, but I want you to tape it, too. That son of a bitch just might decide to protect his client from us."

He was laughing, and that made Barbara feel even glummer. He should be retired, not enjoying himself like this. If he wanted thrills, he should take up skydiving or something. The doorbell rang. Frank went to answer it, and she could hear the cadence of his voice, bantering, joking. . . . Reporters, she knew. It had started. When he came back, grinning, she said, "What if someone tries to come over the back fence? What's Hank supposed to do?"

"Keep them out," Frank said mildly. "He has my permission to shoot to accomplish that. Lettuce ready yet? How about a chicken salad for lunch? Think I have some leftover chicken."

Throughout the afternoon Barbara went to hear the messages on the machine, then erased them, again and again. No one she wanted to talk to called. No Juret, damn him, she thought, erasing the last batch. Then Bailey came back with the taped news conference Carolyn had held.

They listened in the study. She was very good, cool, calm, apparently not rattled at all by the questions. She explained Ted's role as broker for most of the acreage on the Gold Mountain video, told about the adventure at Praeger's mine, and answered questions about why they had gone there. She was good with John Mureau questions, too, kept it brief and to the point. If her voice faltered when they started on Harry Knecht, it was not noticeable on the tape. Bailey said she had been pale, and composed. She sounded almost serene.

"They took hundreds of pictures of that hunk of rock," Bailey said. "She let them pass it around to look at, and she said absolutely no, they couldn't ask the kid anything at all, and that was that. She was okay," he said judiciously.

"She was wonderful," Barbara said. "That was perfect."

"Well, it's all out there now," Frank said. "Just wonder how Ariel is going to handle this."

No one mentioned that by Monday Barbara could be in jail for contempt of court.

FORTY-TWO

"WE'RE SPLASHED ALL over the front page," Frank said the next morning when she went down to the dinette in a fuzzy blue robe and slippers. He was finishing eggs and toast. She poured juice and sat down to scan the papers. There were Mal and Polly, and some stills from the video under a banner headline: RAPE OF THE WILDERNESS? There was Carolyn sitting at a desk covered with microphones. Her headline was: AMBUSH AT GOLD MINE. And there were Barbara and Frank on the front steps of the house, parrying questions, with the headline ATTORNEYS CON-FIRM MURDER ATTEMPT.

"Oh my," she said in mock dismay. "And after the judge clamped the lid down on all that. My, my."

"More in the local-news section," Frank commented. He drank the rest of his coffee and poured for both of them. "Ariel will run a tighter ship than ever, won't allow even a hint of any of this in testimony."

"Um." She turned to the continuation on page four. Mal and Polly had done a great job. Every environmental group she could think of had been represented. The doorbell rang, and she was barely aware when Frank got up to see who it was. No statement had been available from the Rowland Company or the Carlyle Mining Company, the article said. Wilmar Juret, president of Carlyle, would issue a statement later in the day. She nodded. Right.

She heard Frank's study door close, then looked up to see John Mureau in the doorway. The paper slid from her fingers and she jumped to her feet, knocking over her chair. "No," she whispered. "Why did you come back?"

"You knew I would," he said, not moving. He was as stiff as a wooden man, his face rigid; only his eyes seemed alive, and they were fixed in a gaze so steady on hers that she felt immobilized. Then she ran to him. For a moment, he resisted.

"Christ!" he whispered. "Oh Christ!" His embrace and his kiss were almost brutal. She heard herself moan when he released her. She drew back, took his hand, and led him to the stairs and up.

In her room she closed the door and pulled off her robe and nightshirt; this time he moaned, undressing.

Later he tasted the tears on her face, and she trailed her fingers over his scarred chest. "You're smiling," he whispered.

"I kept thinking something was going to happen, something like an earthquake. Intuition's up and working just fine."

"I kept telling myself I was making it up," he said. "It hadn't been that good, I was fantasizing. Dreaming. I haven't been able to think of anything but you, how you move, how you eyes go a little crossed when you're thinking hard—"

"They don't!"

"But they do. And the little shake of your head when you're impatient. Remember the heron we watched at the restaurant the first time we were together? I think I knew then. That heron flies in my dreams and you're by me watching it, too." He kissed the hollow of her throat.

"Remember when you put your hat on my head and we ran in the rain? I think I knew then."

He pulled the blanket over them both. "You're so sweaty, you'll get chilled."

She laughed; she felt feverish. "We both could use a shower."

"What's your dad going to say about all this?"

She put her finger on his lips. "Nothing. Not a word." He began to nibble on her fingers, and she gasped. "My God, you've found another erogenous zone!"

He laughed.

Later, showered, dressed, they went downstairs. There was a note on the table: "Gone dinner shopping."

"See," she said, smiling. "Now, food. I am starved."

She made scrambled eggs and toast, and they ate ravenously in silence, even though the eggs were overcooked. Then, with coffee, he said, "You've been making the news. CNN even."

She shrugged and pointed to the newspapers. "That's the real story, not what's happening in court."

"How's it going in court?"

She told him everything. Gag order be damned, she thought.

He nodded when she finished. "I've come to testify, you know."

"No. I don't want you to."

"I intend to. What else do you have?"

"Look, you understand your field, you're the authority. I'd defer to you in anything concerning geology or mining. Why not grant me the same expertise in my field?"

"I've thought about this a lot," he said slowly. "I know what they'll say about me, how they'll make a fool of me, discount everything I can testify to, all because I was crazy twenty years ago. But don't those twenty years in between count for anything? Won't the jury consider them, too?"

"You weren't crazy," she muttered. "Wait here a minute." She went upstairs to her office and got his file from her cabinet, then stood holding it a few moments. It wasn't supposed to happen this way, she thought despairingly. She was supposed to deliver this personally in Denver after the trial was over, after it was too late for him to be called in court. She closed her eyes hard for a minute before she went back down.

"Read it," she said, and started to clear the table. When she returned from loading dishes into the dishwasher, he caught her wrist in a hard grasp.

"When did you get this? Why didn't you give it to me?" His face was contorted in a grimace of anger. "You thought I'd stay out of sight a while longer, and then you'd let me in on my case history, didn't you? My God, I've got to call Betty!"

He released her wrist and hurried from the dinette to go to Frank's study. She sank into her chair, rubbing her wrist; she wanted to scream and throw things. Call his ex—his first thought was to call his ex! She heard his voice in her head: "I'll always love her."

Slowly she got to her feet and finished clearing the table; then she made a fresh pot of coffee and stood at the back window waiting for it, waiting for her blood to start flowing again, for the ice to melt.

She heard him approaching the dinette and busied herself getting out clean mugs, filling the sugar bowl, getting cream from the refrigerator. Not looking at him, very aware when he entered the room, she said coolly, "Since I won't be calling you, there's little point in your staying, is there?"

He ignored her words. "You don't know what it's like thinking you were insane, and might be again at any time. A little headache and you wonder if it's starting again. You think someone's watching you. Is it starting again? A bad dream. Maybe it's starting again." He rubbed his hand over his eyes, then regarded his hand. "Watching someone else watching you, watching her go pale, knowing she had a suitcase packed at all times. I was afraid I might hurt someone, hit someone, kill someone. I was afraid of my temper, even when I knew it was okay, under control. I couldn't trust myself when I knew we were being followed on the coast. I couldn't be sure it wasn't starting again. We've watched those kids like hawks, ready to pounce into treatment at the first sign of anything wrong. But they're okay. They'll be all right. No inherited madness to worry about. My God, they're all right!" He looked as if he wanted to cry.

She held on to the counter as relief swept through her. Then, as soon as she could trust her legs, trust her hands, she began to carry the coffee things to the table. "What about the twenty years, didn't they count for anything?"

"Not when it's your kids you're worried about," he said. "You should have told me. You could have saved us both weeks of worry."

"I should have," she said. "I'm sorry. But don't you hear what you're saying? You think a jury will discount those episodes because of a piece of paper? You couldn't discount them with the evidence of your life."

"I can't be responsible for the jury," he said. "Only for me. You have to call me."

"I won't! Here, take the carafe to the table. Let's talk about it like reasonable people."

"Fuck the damn carafe! I won't have you manipulate me, decide what's best for me. I've had that."

"You don't know shit about what would happen! They might even accuse us all of collusion. And no one will believe you. You won't do any good, and you could do damage. Do you understand that?"

"You're lying. You kept the report back; you didn't want me to come here again. You want to run the show your way, and after it's all over, then what? What if you lose Wendover because you won't use what little you have? Can you live with that?"

"I have enough! Just go home where you belong! Go visit your kids. Go anywhere!"

"They can't hurt me, Barbara. Can't you trust me, believe me? They can't hurt me."

"They can kill you!" she yelled. "Ruin you professionally. Wipe out the last fifteen years. You want to start over, with people whispering that maybe you're not quite all there? Is that what you want?"

He shrugged. "So I start over. If you don't call me, I'll go public with my story, and I'll tell them the DA tossed me out, and you did, too. It'll still be out there, just not where the jury can hear it."

"What's the matter with you? You want a halo? Be canonized? Be a goddamn martyr? Not on my turf!"

"Ahem, I said," Frank said from the doorway. They both started in surprise. "Is that coffee, or just a tease? If it's coffee, I brought home some apricot Danish that would go fine with it."

Silently Barbara picked up the sugar and cream and took them to the table. After a moment, John followed with the mugs and carafe. Frank washed his hands, then brought the bakery bag to the table and opened it. "Plates," he said, and went back for them. He poured coffee for everyone and helped himself to a Danish. "That's good," he said after a bite. Neither Barbara nor John had touched the coffee or made a motion toward the pastries.

"Way I see it," Frank said meditatively, "if John testifies, you've got to notify the DA in advance, and the judge. Heflin will make a fuss, want to bar him altogether, probably file a motion or two, but the way this trial's heading, I think Ariel will have to admit John, and then try to curtail what he says as much as he can. God alone knows how he'll instruct the jury later on. He could tell them none of John's testimony is admissible." He took another bite and a sip of coffee, apparently finished talking for now.

"If he does that, do they automatically have a memory wipe?" John asked bitterly. "How can they not consider something they've heard?"

"Juries are a strange and wondrous institution," Frank said. "No one knows what goes on in the deliberation room until after the fact. There's an old saying, 'Hang the prisoner that the jurymen may dine.' They've been known to do that, make snap judgments and get on with their lives. Or they could stay out for days, with one or two holdouts on either side. What they'll think about privately, only they know."

He was watching Barbara, who sat immobile, her eyes narrowed, thinking. He pushed the plate of pastries toward John. "Try one. They're really very good. What's happened in this particular trial," he said then, "is that Bobby's gone way out on a limb, stirring up a lot of fuss outside of court. Sometimes when that happens, not saying that's the case here, but sometimes it means that if you get a hung jury, the district attorney goes back to basics and starts looking at some of the dirt that's been stirred up. If you get a guilty verdict, and you've been attentive and made the proper objections and exceptions to rulings, you have a good case for appeal. But the problem is that when there's a gag order, you've put yourself at risk. You don't want to rile a judge too much, or he can slap you in jail, or fine you right down to your gold fillings."

John was listening hard, his gaze intent on Frank. "You don't think you can win this case?"

"Didn't say that," Frank said, holding up his hand. "Didn't mean to imply it even."

"If I put him on," Barbara said, addressing her father, "I won't call Ted. We have to act as if there's no doubt whatever that John's testimony is the deciding factor." Abruptly, she stood up, glaring at John. "You asshole, why didn't you stay where you belong?" She ran from the room.

She walked the length of the upstairs hall, back and forth, back and forth, but that wasn't enough. She had to get out and walk, rethink her entire case from this moment on. She pulled on a jacket, slipped a notebook and pen in her pocket, tied a scarf on, and picked up her sunglasses, ready.

"I've got to get out," she said curtly to Frank, still in the dinette. She ignored John. "Back in a couple of hours."

Frank nodded. "In disguise?"

She walked out. Alan was not in sight, and she didn't care. Some guardian angel, she thought derisively, probably tinkering with his stupid bicycle somewhere. It was a beautiful day, crisp, cool, and sunny, with cumulus clouds drifting here and there in no hurry, not going anywhere. And that summed it up for her, too, she thought. Not going anywhere, just around in circles.

A few clouds would discover the Coburg hills and settle in there; a couple probably would anchor themselves on top of Spencer's Butte. A few would hover around Skinner Butte, but they wouldn't stay, not yet. By evening, nightfall, they might decide it was a good place to perch, but not in daylight, with brilliant sunshine. She was already at the river, and there were too many people on the path today: kids on bikes, joggers, dogs, couples, a group of tourists exclaiming over the flashing river.... She crossed the grassy park to the foot of Skinner Butte and headed for the trail up to the top.

There were a few others making the climb, but they were separated from her by the curves in the trail, and she could not hear their voices. Gradually, surrounded by fragrant fir trees, she did start to think. By the time she reached the top, she was breathing hard; the trail became steep as it wound its way upward and she had passed two different groups of dawdlers. She stood at the low stone wall at the parking area and gazed at the town below. It looked very small. To the south, Spencer's Butte had snagged a passing cloud, which was strung out like a pennant. She turned her gaze to the east, where the Cascade Mountains were clearly visible, fifty or sixty miles away, the peaks frosted with snow, dazzling in sunlight.

A car filled with teens pulled in and the kids began to point out buildings and streets to one another. She moved to the far end of the parking lot and sat down on a stone ledge in the sun, still looking at the high Cascades. The snow was perfect for skiing, the newspaper had reported, and the weather was perfect, warm and sunny. Skiing in shirtsleeves. That always seemed incredible, but that's how it was at this time of year.

She smiled to herself, remembering the high color on Vicky Tunney's cheeks, the sparkle in her eyes up at SkyView, and the near reverence on Cy's face as he gazed out at the world of snow. They must be having a ball today. They both lived to ski; that summed them up. The ideal couple, one as good as the other, or close enough. Then she thought of Arthur Rowland, waving his cane, his misshapen hand grasping the chair back, and his ugly words about Vicky. And Vicky's words—the day after he died, she and Cy would be married. Ugly.

And what are you going to do with John Mureau? she asked herself then, almost mockingly. She had told her father a long time ago, a lifetime ago, that she wouldn't hurt John. She had sworn it. He had known better even then. "All right," she muttered. "He didn't have to come back." And that was a lie, she knew. He had to come back. He had always had to go back. So now what?

Each trial had its own rhythms, its own shape. Usually, she had a vague idea of the shape of her case when she started working on it, and as she filled in blanks, asked and answered questions, the shape became clearer, until the shape determined finally what had to come next. She couldn't have explained exactly what she meant by that, but she needed the shape in her mind in some form before she could move, and the shape of this trial had altered beyond recognition with the return of John Mureau.

But she never had worked with a judge who was so inflexible in his determination to control her defense. And she didn't know what he would do in the morning—a summary judgment against her, banish her from his court, send her to jail. . . . She also didn't know if he would decide John's testimony was incompetent, inadmissible. She drew in a breath and shook her head. She had to go on the supposition that she would have John on the stand. She couldn't wait for the judge's decision and then improvise. Finally, she pulled out her notebook and started to write.

Later she realized with a start that her feet were cold and her bottom on the rock was numb. Clouds had moved in from the west, bringing the ocean air to smother the sun. She stood up stiffly and stretched, then began the hike back down the trail, still deep in thought. Few people were around now, no one else on the trail, and only two or three cars in the parking area that bordered the street. She didn't return to the river trail, but stayed on the sidewalk and returned home. She had been out for four hours.

*   *   *

Frank walked out from the kitchen when she entered the house, studied her briefly, seemed satisfied, and asked if she wanted a drink or wine.

"In a few minutes," she said. "John, there's something you can do, if you will. Go make copies of all your medical records, the whole file, including Gregory Leander's report. Four copies. Okay?"

"I asked John to stay for dinner," Frank said.

"Well, he can do this and come back. It won't take long," she said impatiently. She caught a flicker of a grin on John's face and scowled at him. She was certain she had not shaken her head with impatience.

"Point me in the right direction of the nearest copy shop," John said. He put down a sheet of paper.

She realized he had been reading Frank's manuscript, his book of cross-examinations. There was the ream box and a stack of papers on the couch where John had been sitting. She told him how to find the Kinko's on Thirteenth and Willamette, then said, "I have to call Shelley. What time's dinner?"

"Seven," Frank said, and started back toward the kitchen.

"Think you'll be back before six?" she asked John. He nodded. "Okay, I'll ask her to come around then if she can. Send her up when she gets here, will you, Dad?" She started up the stairs without waiting for an answer.

Frank grinned at John and spread his hands as if to say, I can't help it, that's how she is.

FORTY-THREE

ON MONDAY MORNING Judge Ariel was choleric, Grace Heflin icy, and her assistant, Marcus Truly, stiff with indignation. They were all seated as before in the uncomfortable oversized chairs, the judge behind his desk, his clerk behind him, and a stenographer against a wall.

"Ms. Holloway," Judge Ariel said, "did you deliver to Mr. Zimmerman and Ms. Kratz materials concerning land purchases with the understanding that they would make them public?"

"Yes, sir," she said. "For the record, I want to state that the Court has ruled that for the purpose of this trial those materials are irrelevant and inadmissible."

"And did you advise Mrs. Wendover to hold a news conference concerning other matters not directly related to the trial before us?"

"Your Honor," she said slowly, "the press knew about the complaint we signed against Mr. Praeger; it is a matter of public record. And the press is aware of Owen Praeger's unexplained death. I advised her that since the Court has ruled Mr. Praeger's affairs inadmissible, it would be proper for her to explain the incident."

His dark face turned even darker red; he appeared to be choking. "The Court finds you in contempt for deliberately violating the spirit, if not the words, of admonition concerning the disclosure of land purchases and other business of parties not directly involved with the trial we are charged with hearing. Land purchases and the intended use of that land will be dealt with in other hearings, under other jurisdictions, and will not be used as devices to bring disarray to the trial of Mr. Wendover. In respect for your father, Mr. Holloway"—he nodded to Frank—"I won't remove you from this case at this time. But if you step over that line again, I will most certainly remove you as Mr. Wendover's counsel and bar you from further proceedings in this trial. Furthermore, if through leading questions you coax any witness to cross that line, I'll hold you personally responsible, just as if you had done it yourself. We are hearing the trial of Mr. Wendover, accused of murdering Congressman Knecht, and that's all we are hearing. Do you understand?"

"Yes, sir," she said.

He turned his glare to Grace Heflin. "You filed a motion to protest the appearance of a witness. Why?"

"Your Honor," Heflin said, "counsel has notified our office that they intend to call a Mr. John Mureau. Mr. Mureau came forward earlier to make a statement concerning the congressman's death, and in our investigation of his statement and of him, we determined that he is non compos mentis. As you know, every murder brings forth some unfortunate people with mental illness who make many claims. Our investigation of Mr. Mureau proves beyond doubt that he is an incompetent witness."

Before Ariel could speak, Barbara said, "They didn't do a thorough job investigating him. We had to get a court order to have some of his records released to us, and we have an independent opinion concerning his past and his present mental health. I can produce a psychiatrist who will state definitely that Mr. Mureau suffered an iatrogenic illness brought about by his medications, and that when the medications stopped, he was completely well."

"You want to bring in a shrink to prove your witness is sane?" Ariel asked in amazement. "Then she'll want to bring in another one to prove he isn't. Then you'll want witnesses to prove your shrink is better than hers. And we're in an infinite regression, another merry-go-round that has nothing to do with this case."

"It has everything to do with it!" Barbara exclaimed. "I have here Mr. Mureau's complete, I emphasize the word *complete*, medical records, and the opinion of a renowned psychiatrist who has studied the records." She pulled a folder from her briefcase and stood up to approach his desk. "The competence of a witness is not to be judged a priori to the examination of all pertinent information concerning that witness." She placed the folder on his desk. His stare was so sharp and mean, she felt burned by it. "I have another set of the records for the prosecutor." She brought out a second folder and handed it to Grace Heflin, then sat down again. Ariel's dark gaze was still fastened on her.

"I'll make my decision concerning this witness by

Wednesday morning," he said in a thick voice. "Now, I think
we've delayed today's court long enough. We will convene in
half an hour."

"Could have been worse," Frank commented in the lounge a
few minutes later. He waved to Shelley, who hurried to join
them. "You want anything?" he asked Barbara.

"No. Worse would be slamming me into the slammer.
You're right, could have been worse."

Shelley sat down and Barbara filled her in. "So from now on
I have to tippytoe all the way. What a bummer this case is."

When it was time for her to go upstairs, back to the courtroom, and start a new day, Frank left to tell John what had happened in chambers.

Throughout the day, Barbara brought in character witnesses,
ending the afternoon with a businessman who said about Teddy,
"He wasn't any bother at all. In fact, after we wrapped up our
business, I hung out and fished with them a couple of hours in
the John Day River."

But again, Barbara could not tell how the jury was taking all
this. Good days, bad days, which had more weight? She knew
the jurors were getting tired, and they were not happy being
sequestered. They must be wondering what was going on in the
world they were barred from, why the need to keep them virtual
prisoners, why the influx of reporters and onlookers, why the air
in the courtroom seemed to vibrate with expectancy and excitement. A little while longer, guys, she thought, just hang in there
a few more days.

Change of game plan, she and Frank had decided the night
before. Bailey was to keep John out of sight, away from the
press, away from everyone until they knew if he would be
called. Bailey's associate Hank Belusco would take over for
him in carting materials from the office to the courtroom,
leaving Frank's backyard unguarded. The worst is over with the
press, they had told each other, hoping it was true.

Now they were both going to see Ted. She did not look forward to the visit.

The reporters were as bad as ever; more spectators had gathered, sensing perhaps that the end was coming fast. They got through the mass of bodies, out to the street, and started to walk toward the jail.

"He'll be sore," Frank commented.

"Oh boy, will he ever," she said.

And he was. "What do you mean I can't testify?" Ted yelled. "I've made notes from day one, things that are lies, mistakes, my side. You kept saying I'd have a chance to tell my side."

"Ted, you haven't been listening," Barbara said. "Just sit down and let's try again."

They were in the small conference room, which always was crowded with two, and nearly impossible with three people in it. Frank was at the table, close to the wall; she was in a chair next to him. And now Ted was standing opposite them both, his hands opening and closing spasmodically.

"Ted," Frank said then, "you don't have to prove anything. The state has to prove its case and it can't. But neither can you prove you didn't do it. That would take a bunch of witnesses putting you somewhere else, and you don't have them."

Ted was glaring at Barbara, paying no attention. "You've lied to me from day one. You said I could tell my side. Why are you doing this to me?"

"How did you feel knowing your wife was in the bed of the man who destroyed your son, your namesake?" She snapped the question harshly.

He turned white and his hands bunched into fists. He made a low noise deep in his throat and looked ready to lunge across the table at her.

"That's what you'd face on the stand," she said very quietly then. "It would all be on that order. 'When did you stop beating your wife' questions. When did you stop hating the congressman?" She reached out and put her hand on his. "Sit down, Ted. We were going to use you out of desperation. We might still have to. But those questions are going to be asked if you testify,

and you can't answer them. You deny you hated the congressman and they brand you a liar. You admit it and there's
your motive. You go all to pieces over your love for your son
and they call you hysterical, out of control. You stay calm and
cool and they call you cold-blooded, maybe even psychopathic.
How could anyone stay cool talking about his wife's lover and
his irredeemably damaged child?"

He sank down into his chair and stared at her hopelessly.
"My own worst enemy," he said bitterly. "I can't explain it
because I don't understand it myself. But I've always loved
Carolyn, and I love her now. We weren't hurt by what happened with her and Knecht. That's what they won't believe,
isn't it? It had nothing to do with the two of us."

"That would get twisted out of recognition," she said. "And I
might still have to call you. You have to be prepared, just in
case. But only as a last resort. We'll know Wednesday morning.
If you testify, it will be on Friday. No sooner. Wednesday and
Thursday nights I'll prepare you, if that happens." She looked at
him sadly. "And I'll have to ask the questions I'm sure Grace
Heflin will ask in court."

He flexed his hands, made fists, and nodded. "You plan to
call Leander?"

"Yes. He's known about your family, everything about you
all, for a long time. He'll be a good witness for you. Maybe he
can explain you better than you can."

They left him soon after that and walked home silently. Explain
the human being, she thought. Right, I'll get to it immediately.

She worked late that night, preparing two different scenarios for
the next days. If A, then fork one; if B, then fork two.

On Tuesday she called more character witnesses, who were
unchallenged by Heflin, and after lunch she called Gregory
Leander.

He gave his background in some detail; it was impressive. He
was impressive—well dressed, in a gray suit that looked very
expensive, polished shoes even, very much the successful psychiatrist. When he smiled, his crooked teeth strangely gave him
another dimension, a very human dimension.

"How long have you known the Wendover family?" she asked.

"Thirteen years. I was consulted two years after Teddy's accident, and I have seen them all many times since then."

"Have you consulted with the family members individually?"

"Yes. I told them in the beginning I would have to know them first as a family and then individually in order to assess their son. They accepted that without any question."

She had him talk about the family as a whole, then asked him, "Why did you advise them to consider Teddy to be an eight-year-old child instead of a retarded adult?"

"In every way except size and chronological age, he is a child. As soon as they came to accept that instead of the label 'retarded male,' they made the final adjustment in their lives and every sign of a dysfunctional family vanished and has never reappeared."

He had been on the stand over an hour before she brought up the subject of Ted Wendover and his passivity about his wife's affair. "Did Mr. Wendover consult you professionally?"

"We talked several times, yes."

"I understand Mr. Wendover has given you permission to reveal the substance of those talks. Can you tell us how the tragic accident affected him and his life?"

"He withdrew from life temporarily," Gregory Leander said, addressing the jury directly.

He spoke well, with no jargon at all. He would be a good therapist, Barbara realized, in spite of himself. He spoke with compassion and understanding, and not a hint of condescension or moral judgment.

"He went through denial about the magnitude of his son's injuries, but when the prognosis was clear, he became isolated in his own grief. He could not speak about it, or weep, or react, except through silence. He blamed himself for failing Carolyn, for not being able to comfort her or share her outwelling of grief. He fully understood that her need for an emotional release was overwhelming, but he couldn't respond to that need. Later, when the most devastating phase of grief evolved into acceptance, he realized a new configuration had been formed. After some months of renewed grief and guilt, he accepted that. The new accommodation meant that three people could cope with a grievous tragedy and its lifelong aftereffects, where one or more of them might have been destroyed by it individually."

"Was Ted Wendover vengeful concerning Congressman Knecht?"

"Never."

"Did he feel threatened by the congressman?"

"In no way. He came to understand the triad was a necessary emotional crutch, just as a tripod on a cane is a physical crutch. He never felt his marriage was at risk after that first year of isolation. It is a very strong marriage, a stable marriage."

"Did you ever recommend to either of them that they seek other professional help, a counselor?"

He shook his head. "No. They had a problem and they found a solution that worked for them and hurt no one. Teddy is a happy, secure child; the other two children are very well-adjusted young adults; Ted and Carolyn have led productive, useful lives, and the congressman will long be remembered for the good work he accomplished."

When Heflin had her turn, she asked furiously, "Dr. Leander, did you advise Ted Wendover simply to tolerate the immorality of an adulterous wife?"

"No to the first part, and I don't agree with the second part of your question."

"You don't agree that she was having an affair?"

"Yes, I do."

"Then you don't think it was immoral, is that it?"

"Exactly," he said. "Morality is established by community standards, and it shifts from one community to another, from one situation to another."

She turned her back on him and went to her table to pick up a book. She opened it and read: " 'There is no such thing as insanity. Banish the very word from consciousness.' Did you write that, Dr. Leander?"

"Objection," Barbara said. "Improper cross-examination."

"Dr. Leander has come forth as an expert witness," Heflin

said sharply. "He listed a number of books he has written. It is proper to explore some of the words he has written."

The objection was overruled.

"Did you write those words?" she asked again.

He smiled and said yes.

"So you don't believe in morality and you don't believe in insanity, either?"

"I believe very much in morality, and not a bit in insanity," he said easily. "The word *insanity* has become a generic catchall for any behavior that is unacceptable to the one who uses the word to describe such behavior. Eccentricity can be called insanity; extreme bashfulness can be so labeled; a secretive person can be labeled insane—"

"Dr. Leander, please simply answer the questions without lecturing," Heflin said sharply. "Do you believe in violent behavior that can resemble a psychotic episode?"

"Yes."

"Do you know that people can endure torment for a long time and then erupt with violent behavior in order to escape the torment?"

"If you qualify the word *people*," he said. "Do you mean some people?"

"Your Honor, please direct the witness to answer the question asked," Heflin said.

"Objection," Barbara said. "The witness is asking for clarification of the question."

"No, he isn't. He's playing word games," Heflin snapped.

Judge Ariel banged his gavel and glared at everyone before him. "Sustained. Rephrase your question."

She rephrased the question and Gregory smiled approvingly at her and said yes.

"Can you tell in advance who those people are who might erupt into violence?"

"You mean, just by looking around?" He glanced at the judge.

"No, I don't mean just by looking around," Heflin said furiously. "Among your friends and acquaintances, can you predict who might erupt into violence?"

"Probably, and no."

Suddenly she relaxed; by what effort, it was impossible to tell. She even smiled slightly. "All right, Dr. Leander. Can you tell among your friends who might become violent?"

He nodded. "Some of them, if I know enough of their backgrounds, but one doesn't always know enough, even about friends."

"Can you tell among your acquaintances who might become violent?"

"No," he said promptly.

"Do you consider Ted Wendover a friend?"

"He's more a client than a friend."

She picked up the book she had referred to earlier and said, "In this book of essays, you outline a case involving a Mr. X, who after twenty years of marriage turned on his wife and killed her. Everyone who knew them was astonished and bewildered by his sudden act of violence; he was judged insane—excuse me, incompetent—and institutionalized. Is that a fair summary of the incident you describe in the book?"

Barbara objected and was overruled.

"Yes."

"But you argue here that Mr. X's act of violence was not only predictable but inevitable, and that he was not incompetent at all. You argue that he had reached the limit of endurance and acted in the only way he could to extricate himself from a life of torment. Is that a fair summary?"

"Are you going to fill in the rest of the details?" he asked her.

"Just answer the question, please," she said. "Is that a fair summary?"

"Only if all the details are known. Then it is."

"I just want a yes or no answer, Dr. Leander. Is that a fair summary?"

"No. A summary without context is empty."

"Your Honor, please direct the witness to answer the question yes or no."

"Objection," Barbara said. "He answered the question."

"Overruled," Judge Ariel snapped. "Just answer the question without a comment attached."

"No, then."

"Let me read the passage I referred to," Heflin said easily. " 'Mr. X acted, finally, in the only way left for him. Fifteen years earlier there were other choices, and fifteen years earlier, when he failed to make those choices, this act of homicide became predictable and even inevitable. He acted with reason, not from a psychotic, uncontrollable impulse. He had what appeared to be an insoluble problem, but one that he finally solved in the only way left to him.' Are those your words, Dr. Leander?"

"Yes." He was regarding her with an interest he hadn't shown before, as if appraising her in a different way.

"So you wrote that murder was his only option in solving a problem. Is that so?"

"I wrote those words," he said, "but out of context, they can mean a lot of things."

"I think we understand exactly what they mean, Dr. Leander."

"I think you might," he said, "but I don't think you've given the jury enough information to understand them."

"Very well," she said, almost smugly, as if this was what she had been aiming at. "Can you give us a brief summary of the case of Mr. X?"

"Objection," Barbara said. "This is irrelevant. Mr. X is not a participant in this trial."

Judge Ariel was regarding Gregory Leander with a fierce frown. "I think it's relevant," he said. "Overruled."

"I can be brief," Gregory Leander said cheerfully. "Mr. X was totally dominated as a child by his mother, who used a serious illness of his as a continuing threat against him. If he didn't obey her every instruction, he would become ill and have to return to the hospital. She picked out the woman for him to marry. The woman seduced him and claimed falsely to be pregnant, and both women forced him into marriage. His mother lived with the couple, and both women worked together to dominate him in every way. His opportunity to escape the situation occurred when his mother died, after he had been married for five years. However, he failed to understand that his mother's death had altered the pattern sufficiently for him to break it the rest of the way."

He was sitting back in his chair, comfortable, at ease. He spoke so smoothly, he might have been reading from a prepared text. "He failed to act," Gregory Leander continued, "and gradually his wife became, in effect, his mother. She ruled him totally, bought his clothes, drove him to work and picked him up afterward, went to lunch with him, made all his appointments for the dentist and doctor and went with him to the appointments. She kept him on a diet, which she supervised, selected his books and magazines, and even the articles he was permitted to read, and, of course, the television he watched. To all appearances, she was the perfect wife who took extraordinarily good care of her husband. Then he decided he'd had enough and he plotted for several months and finally killed her. The jury said it was an irresistible impulse that drove him to murder. He stayed in an institution for a year and a half, and today he is a single man, living contentedly by himself."

No one in the jury box moved during his recital of the story; no one moved now. It was as if he had hypnotized them all.

"So you think it's inevitable that a man who has endured torment for fifteen years will eventually lash out at the tormentor?" Heflin asked.

"No," he said equably. "It's that qualifier again. 'A man' implies all men, and the answer must be no."

She shook her head, as if she had to clear it. He continued to watch her with a bright-eyed gaze.

Suddenly Barbara was astounded to realize he was eyeing Grace Heflin like that because he was interested in her. She ducked her head and coughed to hide her near laughter. That idiot, she thought, that crazy idiot! When she looked up again, he was regarding her, and she knew he was aware of her understanding. She had to duck her head again.

"Dr. Leander, how many times have you met Mr. Wendover in your professional capacity?" Heflin asked then.

"I'm afraid that's a difficult question," he said. "Do you mean alone, or in various family combinations?"

"Altogether," she snapped.

"Ah." He thought a moment, then said, "Probably twenty or twenty-two."

"And you feel you have come to know him well, as a client?"

"Yes."

"In your professional judgment, is Mr. Wendover capable of erupting in violence?"

"Yes."

"That's all," she said curtly, and sat down. There was high color on her cheeks; his gaze followed her to her chair.

"Dr. Leander," Barbara said then, "what is the title of the book the prosecution quoted from?"

He smiled slightly. *"I'm Okay, My Cat's Okay, But You're a Loon."*

Someone in the courtroom behind Barbara sniggered, and Ariel used his gavel.

"And who wrote the introduction to the book?"

"Dr. Amory Love, president of the American Psychiatric Association."

She picked up the book from her table and held it up, then opened it to the introduction. "Dr. Love wrote: 'In this current collection of essays, Dr. Leander, with charm and sometimes savage wit, brilliantly analyzes the repercussions in our society brought about by the misuse of poorly understood terms borrowed from the literature of psychology and applied by lay persons and professionals alike. . . .' What was the purpose of this book, Dr. Leander?"

"It's a popular book intended for people who believe they have some understanding of psychology and psychiatry. I attempted to demonstrate how a little knowledge can lead to grave errors."

Oh God, she thought, no puns, please no puns. He remained sober-faced, but she suspected he was laughing inside.

"Also," he continued, "to demonstrate how the misuse of certain terms tends to eradicate all meaning for them, as happened with the word *insanity*."

Barbara nodded and replaced the book on the table. She crossed her arms and asked, "Can you explain very briefly what you meant by writing that Mr. X's act of homicide was predictable and even inevitable?"

"Yes. He was caught up in a pattern that he couldn't find a way out of. He had tried to leave his mother when he was sixteen, but she found him and took him home again, then punished him by purging him frequently, claiming his illness was coming back. So, as far as he was concerned, leaving was not an option, since his wife had replaced his mother as the authority in his life. He believed that the entire world was on her side, that she was perceived as the perfect wife. He had no friends of his own choosing, no one he ever talked to in a confidential manner, and he had been denied when he suggested he might need counseling. He had abandoned his free will for the pattern, and it came to rule him."

"What made him finally act?" Barbara asked.

"She took away his salt," Gregory Leander said with a straight face. "She decided it was bad for him. That was in February, and he killed her in May."

Barbara's mind was racing. She didn't believe he was deliberately trying to scuttle her case, condemn Ted, but the parallels were there for everyone to see. He could have dodged Grace Heflin's questions with ease if he had chosen to do so. He had played games with Heflin, and he was still playing games.

Slowly she said, "Dr. Leander, you said that you don't think it's inevitable for a tormented man to lash out at his tormentor. Yet you say it was inevitable for Mr. X to do so. Can you explain the difference?"

"Objection," Heflin snapped. "This is becoming a class in freshman psychology."

Judge Ariel turned a disbelieving and angry gaze to her. "Overruled," he said sharply. "You brought it up, Ms. Heflin."

Barbara decided the judge was beyond her understanding.

Without prompting, Gregory Leander said, "When we say a man, we imply everyman, mankind in general. Naturally, not every man will lash out in violence; some men will—very few, actually. It was inevitable for Mr. X because he had not exercised his options in the past, and he had no belief in other options he could choose. He had become blinded by the pattern of his life. He was too weak to attempt anything except murder, the only way finally he saw to free himself from her daily, even hourly, torment. For him it was a reasonable choice, not an act of psychosis, or an irresistible impulse. It was well reasoned, and well executed. It is highly unlikely that anything else would have worked for him."

"You said that Ted Wendover is capable of erupting in violence. Can you explain that?"

"Everyone is capable of it," he said easily. "It's part of the human survival mechanism, which he shares along with the rest of us. I also said few people actually do become violent, and that's because few are presented with sufficient provocation to unleash a violent reaction."

She felt as if she was wading blindfolded in a swamp where the next step might be into a bottomless hole, but she had to ask a few more questions, close the door on Heflin's argument as much as she could. She simply did not know what this incredible man would say next, where it might take them.

"Dr. Leander," she said then, "do you see similarities between Ted Wendover and Mr. X?"

"Absolutely not. None whatever. Mr. X was a tormented man, hour after hour, day after day. He dreaded the rising of the sun, the start of each day. Ted Wendover has been blessed with contentment, even happiness. Mr. X was desperate to change his life. Changing his life was the last thing Ted Wendover wanted, with the exception of the restoration of his son's mental capacity. There are no similarities."

She didn't dare breathe out her relief at his answer. "What, in your professional opinion, would it take to make Ted Wendover erupt into violence?"

"A direct and immediate threat to his family," he said promptly, and then added, "As it would be for most of us."

After court, the usual crush of reporters was waiting. Gregory Leander was the center of attention today; he was not at all hesitant about being spotlighted. Barbara and Frank said good-bye to Shelley and walked home.

"That was quite a show," Frank said. "You reached in bare-handed and pulled it right out of the fire. Good job."

And that wasn't Pop talk, she knew. "Thanks. I'm pretty wrung-out."

"You have a right. Let's go out to eat later. I'm pretty wrung-out, too."

At home they laughed as Thing One and Thing Two tried to squeeze through the cat door simultaneously; they wouldn't learn that only one fitted at a time, or else each was determined to be first. Then Frank went out to look at his garden—not to work, he said, just look. And she went to listen to the telephone messages.

"Junk," she muttered, fast-forwarding one message after another, mostly from the press. Then she stopped all motion. A man's voice said, "You've been trying to reach me for weeks. If you will reserve a table in your name in the lounge on top of the Hilton, I'll find you at six-thirty." Juret, at last. She called the Hilton to make the reservation, then hurried to the back door to tell Frank.

Wilmar Juret turned out to be a short, fat man, five feet six at the most, and over two hundred pounds. His eyes were shrewd, very dark, and his hair was thick and dark. He didn't offer to shake hands when he was shown to their table by a waiter who was already carrying a tray with mineral water and a glass. He placed them in front of Juret and took Barbara's and Frank's orders for wine.

"I've been following your trial closely," Juret said as soon as the waiter left. "What else do you have beside what you've already released to the press?"

Frank smiled. "You want an inventory of my house, my office, my correspondence? What?"

"You know what I mean. What do you want from me? What do you have for me?"

"No deals," Frank said genially. "We thought we could do you a favor, and as we're gentlefolk, that seemed our Christian duty."

"Bull!" He drank his water thirstily.

"Mr. Juret," Barbara said then, "what I really want from you is information. In return, I won't tell the press my suspicions. But you should know what they are. I know a lot of what's gone on about the land deals. One thing eludes me. What made you risk your reputation, and a long, involved court hassle over environmental impact, things of that sort? What I suspect is that the Rowlands guaranteed that Knecht would be gotten rid of and his replacement would be friendly to your enterprise. But you see, that could well implicate you as an accessory before the fact."

He studied her for a moment. "You don't have a damn thing. You come out with a story like that and I'll show you what the courts can be used for."

She shook her head. "No, the story will stick. We already gave you something, a warning in advance, enough for you to get your staff to work untying knots, or else tying them even tighter. The fact that you're here now suggests you're severing connections, not digging in."

She paused briefly. When he remained silent, watching her, she continued. "Wendover didn't kill Knecht, or Mary Sue McDonald, or Lois Hedrick, or Owen Praeger. I'll tie them all together. And the minute I do, Wendover's a free man. But there will still be four murders to investigate, a killer to apprehend and try. I can say you were appalled when we discussed the various possibilities, that you were eager to cooperate in any way, that without your help it would have been a bigger muddle than ever. Or I can say you were throwing dust in our eyes along with everyone else, stonewalling at every turn. I can mention your terrible thirst, how nervous you were when we met, how you tried to find out what I knew in order to hide your tracks even more. I can say a lot of things that your lawyers will have trouble finding actionable, especially after the police start asking their questions."

The waiter brought their wine. No one spoke for a minute or two.

Juret drank more water, his gaze fixed on her. Then he said, "Ms. Holloway, if you ever want a job, come to me. What happened was, Rowland presented a pretty package. A legitimate deal for a grand wilderness resort, complete with gold mines. They needed financing, and they had a beautiful project. If gold was found in any significant amounts—a real possibility, you understand—my company would become active; otherwise, we were to be silent partners and help with financing eventually."

He paused, eyeing her. "Do you know what a goldbug is?"

She nodded. "Owen Praeger."

"Of course," he said with a little nod. "He was a bit crazy, but he had the talent, the gift, whatever it was when it came to locating gold. We investigated him thoroughly; he was as close to infallible as a mortal can be in his own area of expertise. The Rowlands have the expertise in operating successful resorts. Our expertise would have been utilized only after a long time, and by then, with the resort up and operating, with roads in place, no practical purpose would have been served by prohibiting real mining. If it doesn't work out, we write off a small loss and that's that."

"How did Rowland guarantee that Knecht would not butt in and stop it cold as soon as he learned about it? He would have, you know."

"Knecht was going to lose his election. Everyone knew a mammoth change was overdue, liberalism is out, conservatism in, environmentalists out, property rights in. And so on."

"No, Mr. Juret. Knecht would not have lost, and everyone knew that. He was immensely popular. And against a man like Brownley? That's a real joke."

He studied her some more, drank the rest of his water, glanced at Frank, and then back to her. "He would have lost," he said flatly. "Brownley was going to wait until October and then smear him with his illicit affair, for openers. That was going to happen no matter what our company did. It's been in the making for over a year, two years even. Brownley was determined to have that office, and he would have been elected. After your senator raised the consciousness of everyone in the country the way he did, a smear campaign, complete with informants and pictures, would have been plenty coming in a timely fashion, before the election."

Barbara thought as she sipped her wine. "Are you involved with their financing yet?"

"No way." He hesitated, then said, "There are several others involved who do have financial concerns. I imagine they're pulling out. Eventually, we would have contributed financially. But the Rowlands had to show good faith first. They bought land; we bought land. They used our name to interest other investors. But, understand, everything was on hold until after the election, then until after the trial. We are not foolhardy. Rowland was confident that the retarded boy had done it, that the affair would be concluded swiftly, with little publicity. Then he was persuasive in assuring us that Wendover had done it for personal reasons. But with all the publicity about the wilderness park, plus the inevitable insinuations, we'll bow out. We're not committed enough for a long, protracted battle. It was a lovely dream, that's all. The land's still there; we'll unload it in due time bit by bit."

"You'll walk away from it, just like that?" she asked curiously.

"Ms. Holloway, the park idea was splendid, if they had brought it off without a lot of trouble. My company isn't looking for a lot of trouble or a lot of bad publicity. There are other mines, other deals."

"You've been very helpful," she said then, quite honestly. "I'll do what I can to keep you out of it in any unfavorable light."

He nodded, and without another word, he rose to his feet ponderously and left. When they were alone again, Barbara asked, "What do you think?"

"It's probably as much of the truth as we're likely to get. A smear campaign, by God. It would have worked."

"But someone jumped the gun," she murmured.

"And I think the Rowlands are going to be mad as hell." He was starting to gather himself together, prepared to leave, but she was gazing out the windows abstractedly. He settled back in his chair.

Dusk had fallen over the city; everywhere lights glittered and glowed. Moving lights, white and red, made patterns that dissolved as new patterns were made, over and over. Patterns, she was thinking. Mr. X had succumbed to the pattern of his life for years, then had broken the pattern irrevocably. She was startled by the waiter's voice asking if there would be anything else. Frank told him no. He looked troubled, as if he had been in deep thought as much as she had been.

"If Ted found out about the smear campaign, and he might have, wandering around the state the way he did, would that have been a direct and immediate threat to his family?" she asked in a low voice.

FORTY-FOUR

BEFORE SHE FELL asleep that night, Barbara thought about the myriad twists she was trying to follow simultaneously: What were the Rowlands doing? What would Ariel decide? Had Ted learned about the smear concerning Carolyn and Knecht? If Ted had to testify, would Heflin be aware of that new development? How vicious would Heflin get if John testified? And where was he? Out getting drunk with Bailey, she thought, tossing, twitching, unable to find a position where her legs felt comfortable, where her elbows didn't rub against the sheet, a place where the pillow didn't feel like a rock. . . . Think of wind in fir trees, she ordered herself, fir trees murmuring, whispering, rustling. . . .

"Bad night?" Frank asked the next morning.

She didn't bother to answer. When they got to court, she was summoned directly to Judge Ariel's chambers. She and Grace Heflin entered together, and once again they stood before his desk like two truant schoolgirls.

"You can call Mureau," Ariel said without preamble. "He

will be treated exactly as any other witness. You are not to elicit information from him concerning land sales or land usage."

"Your Honor," Barbara said, "if Mr. Mureau's testimony is to be censored in advance, I will be compelled to move for a mistrial. Are you instructing me to coach him? Tampering with a witness is a serious offense. I can't guarantee what he will testify to."

"Ms. Holloway," he said softly, and, strangely, he seemed more ominous, "let me tell you something. People buy and sell land for a multitude of reasons—some you approve of and some you don't. But if those sales are legitimate, and concluded, they are public record, and there is no motive to conspire to keep them secret. In referring to them obliquely and slyly, you have implied that they are illegal and even evil. You've managed to bring great embarrassment to legitimate businessmen who were well within the law in their transactions. But I won't let you air your philosophy concerning land use in this court, during this trial. That's where I stand. I am not censoring Mr. Mureau's testimony; I am telling you not to start down that path."

She remained silent, and he turned his gaze to Grace Heflin. "Since this witness has been called after the state concluded its case, I will allow certain latitude in your cross-examination, but don't try me too far. I'm also taking into account the fact that you've had his statement for months and that you already had him investigated."

"Yes, sir," she said. "And, Your Honor, since I did not anticipate this witness, I request that during my cross-examination I be allowed to read statements from others who would have testified if Mr. Mureau's name had been put forward earlier."

"Your Honor—" Barbara started, but he cut her off.

"You're the one who introduced this irregularity," he said sharply. "Live with it. Whose statements?" he asked Heflin.

"Leigh McDonald, Dr. Harvey Lowenstein, and Michael Driscoll."

"Who the hell is Michael Driscoll?" he demanded.

"He's one of the security people at Stone Point."

Ariel shrugged. "You can read their statements." He turned

his glare to Barbara as if daring her to object. "We convene in ten minutes," he said.

Barbara didn't budge yet. "Your Honor," she said, "defense has a right to examine the statements prior to their being read in court."

"I'll get them to you," Grace Heflin said.

"When?"

"Tomorrow morning."

"That's too late. My witness will be on the stand tomorrow morning."

"This afternoon, then," Heflin said irritably.

"That's settled. We resume in ten minutes," Ariel said, with even more irritation.

"That man's incompetent," Frank muttered after she reported the session in chambers. They were standing in the second-floor corridor, not far from Courtroom A. "He's sitting in two chairs, one on the bench, one at the prosecutor's table."

"Just from day one," she said. "Shelley, see what you can dig out about Lowenstein, and see if there's a Driscoll statement in the file."

She looked at her watch, then said swiftly, "Dad, do you know where Bailey is? Ask him if he can go back to Stone Point, with a camera. If he and John could get pictures, without being seen, especially by Brody—maybe the security guy he knows can help . . . God, it's time. See you later." She nearly ran to make it inside the courtroom before Ariel appeared.

Stuart Kirsten was her first witness. He was the reservation clerk at Stone Point, a job he had held for four years. Thirty-two years old, with a receding hairline that made him look ten years older than that, a bit paunchy, with a manner both obsequious and hesitant, he was a frustrating witness.

"Mr. Kirsten," she asked, "what do you do precisely when a person calls for a reservation?"

"I, uh, well, we have a screen we can call up to see, uh, it shows all the room numbers, you see, and I can glance at it, and I, uh, I just make the reservation."

Patiently she had him start over. "What is the first screen you call up on the computer?"

"Well, that's the opening screen, uh, you know, the reservation screen."

"Mr. Kirsten, is this a printout of that screen?" She handed him the printout he had provided her with weeks earlier. It was incomprehensible. He hemmed and hawed and finally said it was. "There is a list of numbers in three columns. Are those room numbers?"

"Well, there are blocks, you see, the suites, and minisuites, and . . ."

It was so laborious and painful that she began to ask questions that even she found objectionable because they were so leading. All she wanted from him now was a yes or no. Neither Heflin nor Ariel made a peep.

"You have this screen filled with symbols that tell you if the room is available. The check means it's reserved, the asterisk means it's reserved with special requests—a golf reservation, riding privileges, late arrival or departure, whatever—and the cross means it is actually occupied. Is that right?"

Eventually, he said it was. She went to her next question. "Then you switch to the other screen, where you enter names and addresses, telephone numbers, credit-card information. Is that where you enter the special requests—for example, the fishing trip the Rothmans reserved?"

When he admitted at some length that that was correct, she continued. "So just by glancing at the first screen, you know space has been reserved. Is that right?"

"That's all I would need to know," he said hastily. "That is, in the beginning. I mean, if you want a minisuite and I can see they're all reserved, that is, I might suggest something else, like a, uh, double with two queens, or a, you know . . ."

It took a long time, but eventually she summarized for him: "If you make a reservation for a minisuite, the computer assigns a room, but you can override that with a command and lock that room for a certain guest. You can lock as many rooms as you choose that way. Is that right?"

It was.

"Looking at the reservation screen, you have no way of knowing if rooms and guests are locked in, do you?"

"No," he said after a long hesitation.

"All right. Anyone employed by the resort, who understands the symbols used in this program and has access to a computer in the resort, can lock in a room and guest. Is that right?"

He hesitated a longer time, puzzling over the question. "You could, I guess, but you shouldn't. I mean, that, uh, is what I'm ... I mean, it isn't anyone else's duty to do that, and uh, I mean ..."

"Could I access the computer and lock a room and guest so that no one would change that reservation?" she asked more sharply.

"Well, yes," he said unhappily.

"And even if the computer had already assigned rooms, with access could I make changes, lock them in a different way?" After his reluctant yes answer, she continued. "Would there be any way of knowing that had been done?"

"Well, not really, uh, that is ..."

It was a long time before she could get to the questions about the no-show couple, Mr. and Mrs. Wylie. "When they called to complain about the charge, what did you do?"

"I, uh, called up the guest list, and I called Mr. Siletz to show him, and, uh, we talked and, uh ... I deleted them again. I took the cancellation call," he said, almost moaning aloud. "I canceled their reservation."

"Did you check back with the guest list when you saw the rooms were all reserved?"

"What for?" he asked. "I never did that. I mean, that's why we have the reservation screen, so we can tell with just a glance if we have—that is, I mean, if there is a room ..."

Before she let him go, she asked, "Did you take the reservation for Mr. and Mrs. Wylie? Did you cancel their reservation? Did you delete their names?" He answered yes each time. "Did you lock in Mr. and Mrs. Rothman in the minisuite Two Twenty-one?" He said no. "Did you lock in Mr. and Mrs. Wylie in the minisuite Two Twenty-two?" He said no. "Did you make a reservation for Mr. and Mrs. Wylie to go fishing on the ninth of September?" He said no. "Were both Two Twenty-one and Two Twenty-two locked with guests for the days from September ninth to the eleventh?" He said yes. "Who else could have done that?"

He began to name what seemed to be the entire staff at Stone Point. She let him go on until he came to a hesitant stop.

"You mean that almost anyone who worked there and knew the codes could have done it?"

"Except me," he said hastily. "I didn't do it."

"But almost anyone else there could have assigned those rooms, put the lock code in place, and be assured that they wouldn't be assigned to someone else?"

Miserably he said yes.

When Heflin started her cross-examination, she stood at her chair to ask, "Mr. Kirsten, just a simple yes or no, if you will. Have you ever made a computer error?"

"Well—" he started.

"Yes or no, please," she said.

"Well, then, yes."

"Have you ever deleted something by mistake?"

"Sometim—"

"Yes or no, Mr. Kirsten."

"Yes, just like eve—"

"Have you ever found something in a file that you thought you had deleted?"

"But this wasn't like—"

"Just yes or no, if you will."

"Well, yes."

"No more questions," she said coolly, and sat down.

Barbara smiled encouragingly at him. "Mr. Kirsten, did you take the call from Mrs. Wylie to cancel their room? Yes or no will do."

"Yes."

"Did you make the cancellation on the computer?"

"Yes."

"Do you know how the Wylies got back on the guest list?"

"No."

She thanked him, grateful to be done with him. He looked bewildered that it was over, and Judge Ariel said, "Step down, step down."

Frank had returned during the questioning of Stuart Kirsten. Shelley was still out when Judge Ariel said they would take the lunch recess.

"Let's go to the office and see how Shelley's making out," Barbara said when they left the courtroom. "Talk about pulling teeth!" she exclaimed in disgust. "I mean Kirsten."

A light rain was falling when they left the courthouse. They paid no attention to it and started to walk. "I think Brody's skipped," Frank said casually.

"Oh no," she said. "Another one?"

"Well, I think he's just lying low. I wonder who he's more afraid of—you, or the sharks in the water all around him? He didn't respond to the summons to appear this afternoon, and no one seems to know exactly where he is. I alerted Ariel's clerk. They'll issue a bench warrant if he doesn't check in today."

Shelley was in her tiny cubicle of an office, with the phone at her ear, when they got there; she waved as Barbara paused at the door to mouth at her to join them when she was done.

Frank ordered a Greek salad for three, and by the time it arrived, Shelley had come into the office. "Dr. Lowenstein's been an expert witness for the state of California a lot of times," she said. "He's head of the psychiatric unit at UCLA Medical Center."

They ate in silence for several minutes; then Barbara said, "See if you can get hold of Gregory Leander. Tell him about Lowenstein's statement that will be read and ask him if there are any questions I should ask John to counter them. It's a long shot, but maybe I can get in something in advance."

Shelley nodded. "Driscoll's statement was on file connected with the Mary Sue McDonald murder. The district attorney's office said they won't get a new statement, just use the one they already have. I can pick it up if you want."

"Let them send all the stuff together," Barbara said. She

pushed her plate away, the food on it hardly touched. "I'm going to stretch my legs a bit. See you back in court, Dad."

"Take an umbrella," Frank said.

Nora Blake was in her thirties, slender, with frizzy dark hair, lovely brown eyes, and skin that looked like mocha-colored silk. She had worked as a maid at Stone Point for seven years. While she was giving her background, Hank Belusco arrived and set down two golf bags, one of them on a piece of carpeting. He laid a second piece of carpeting on the defense table and left again. Nora Blake watched him intently.

"Ms. Blake," Barbara said then, taking one of the golf bags to her, "is this your bag?" It was blue and gray, with large Stone Point letters *S* and *P* in dusty rose on the side.

"Yes."

"And the other one just like it, is that yours also?"

"Yes, they both are. I put my initials and dates on them with a laundry marker."

"And do you recognize this piece of carpet?"

She nodded. "Yes, it's from Stone Point. That's what's in all the rooms there."

Barbara replaced it on her table and then ignored it. "When you worked on the second floor at Stone Point last September, how and when did you become aware that the minisuite Two Twenty-two was empty?"

"Well," she said slowly, "the couple who were there on Thursday checked out and I cleaned the room the way I do, the bathroom and everything. I thought the new people would get there real late that night. So on Friday when I got to that room and there wasn't a Snooze card on the door, I went in to clean, and I saw that no one had come in yet. It was just like I left it Thursday. I didn't pay much attention; sometimes people get there later than they think they will. When I went in on Saturday, it was still empty, and I left a note for the head of housekeeping, saying it was empty. But somebody had been in there."

"What do you mean?"

"Well, I put towels in there on Thursday when I cleaned, and I put the little bottles of lotion and shampoo, all that stuff on the counter in the bathroom, like I always do. But they had been moved; nothing was missing, but somebody moved them. They weren't like I put them, and the towels were pushed back too far and the washcloths were moved. I always leave them folded up on the counter, with the bath mitt across them from corner to corner, in a certain way. It looks nicer that way. They were moved. I put everything back like they should be. And I had to get my cleaner and polish the sink because it had some water spots in it, and on the handles. They're really particular that everything should be sparkling clean, no water spots or anything."

"Was there anything else different?"

She frowned slightly and nodded. "Dents or depressions in the carpet. You see, when we vacuum, we always end up sweeping in one direction, so it lays smooth, without lines. I notice things like that. And there were these three marks in the carpet. They weren't there when I vacuumed. I scuffed them out as much as I could with my foot. I didn't want to have to vacuum again if no one was in the room."

"Where were the marks?" Barbara asked her, walking toward her table.

"Near the door to the next room, the connecting door."

"Was the connecting door locked?"

"I don't know," she said. "I didn't try it. When the bellboys take guests up and turn on lights, they're supposed to make sure the doors are locked, and when I cleaned on Thursday, it was locked, but I didn't try it again."

"Was there anything else missing or out of place?"

"A tray was in there," she said. "Like from the bar, a little round tray they carry stuff from the bar on? I know it wasn't there when I cleaned on Thursday. I would have taken it out. It was on the dresser. I put it on the cleaning cart with a couple others."

Barbara nodded and picked up one of the golf bags. "How did you get this golf bag, Ms. Blake?"

"Well, you see the top part of it? It's been broken, like it was run over or something. The pieces that make different sections were broken out, and they were going to throw it away, and I asked if I could have it. The manager of the golf shop gave it to me for my little girl. She keeps toys in it."

"And the other one? How did you get it?"

Nora Blake looked slightly embarrassed. "I found it," she said. "See, I have two daughters, six and eight. After I gave Patricia her bag, Susan wanted one, too, so I was keeping an eye out for another broken one. The Saturday after the murder, I found that one in the supply room. It was broken like the other one, the dividers were gone, and somebody had tossed it, so I took it home with me."

"Where was it in the supply room?"

"In the big plastic trash bag. See, we empty waste cans and pick up papers and stuff in the rooms and put it in small bags, and then we put them in a big bag to carry it all out late in the day, about five or six. When I was putting my trash bags in, I saw this little bit of blue, and like I said, I was keeping an eye out for another bag, and I pulled it out."

"When could the golf bag have been placed in the trash bag?"

"It had to be after five or six on Friday, and before about eleven, when I spotted it, on Saturday."

"Is the door to the supply room kept locked?"

"Most of the time it is. While we're cleaning, we don't lock it because we might be in and out, but other times it is."

Barbara found the hotel layout on the exhibit table and showed it to her. "Is this the room you're talking about, the janitorial supply room on the second floor?"

Nora Blake looked at it and nodded. "Yes."

"What time did you check Room Two Twenty-two on Friday?"

"About nine. I try to get through before noon every day."

"And again on Saturday?"

"The same, about nine. And about nine on Sunday."

"How do the locks work on the connecting doors? Are they locked with the computer keys?"

"No. They have real keys—I mean metal keys. If you want connecting rooms, you have to get a regular key for both sides."

"And all the minisuites and the suites have connecting doors?"

"Yes. You could rent the whole lot of them and get back and forth if you wanted to and could afford them."

"Ms. Blake, can you describe the marks on the floor that you tried to scuff out?"

She tilted her head, as if in thought. "Well, there were three places where the carpet was sort of indented. Not far apart. I've seen them before," she said then.

"Where?" Barbara asked.

"When people bring their golf bags to their rooms—the hotel bags, I mean—they leave marks like that. Other kinds of bags leave other kinds of marks—some have the little legs like those; some have ridges, different bottoms. Sometimes they're hard to vacuum out."

Barbara picked up the bag again and took it to her. "There are three knobs on the bottom, aren't there? Would they have left indentations like the ones you saw?"

"Not empty, it wouldn't," she said. "That bag doesn't weigh much, nylon or something, like it is. But when their bags have a lot of clubs—you know, thirty or forty pounds—then they mark up the carpet."

Barbara returned to her table and regarded the second golf bag. She took from it a square of cloth, unfolded it, and spread it out on the floor, then lifted the golf bag and dumped out its contents on the cloth: twenty-one pounds of rocks that matched the murder weapon and the pebbles on the exhibit table.

She ignored the uproar in court, people standing up in the viewers' section, jurors leaning forward, Heflin yelling objections, Ariel banging his gavel furiously. She picked up the square of carpet, walked to Nora Blake, and held it out.

Nora Blake's pretty brown eyes widened; she nodded. She said, "Just like that."

Heflin was yelling that this was improper, no preparation had been made for a circus act like this, no one knew what those rocks weighed. Ariel was yelling, too, mostly at Heflin. Barbara didn't move. Finally, Ariel instructed the jury to disregard the dramatic bit of action, and he glowered at Barbara and ordered her to get on with it and to forego future demonstrations without proper preparation.

"Ms. Blake," Barbara continued then, "do these indentations look like the ones you saw in Room Two Twenty-two on Saturday, September tenth?"

"Yes, exactly like that."

Barbara found the photograph of the room where Knecht had been killed; she showed it to Nora Blake.

"Will you examine the area circled on the photograph," she said. "Can you identify those three marks on the floor?"

"Well," she said hesitantly, "they look like the marks a golf bag would leave." She looked from the photograph to Barbara. "They don't look deep enough, though."

Barbara nodded and took the photograph. "If you don't vacuum out the indentations, what happens to them?"

"Oh, eventually they fill in again. The carpet's springy, sort of, but if they're deep, we try to get them out before new people show up for the rooms."

Barbara didn't keep her much longer; then Heflin tore into her statements, trying to get her to admit she was not as precise as she claimed in her arrangement of articles on the counter, the placement of towels, that the indentations, if there had been any, might have been there for days. Nora Blake did not budge from her statements. She knew what she knew. Watching and listening to her, Barbara would have bet that Nora Blake never had a broken pair of socks in her life—her washing machine wouldn't dare eat a sock.

While Barbara was doing her redirect, Frank opened a big grocery bag and put it on the floor near the rocks. She did not mention it again, but the inference was clear. It would take a large heavy-duty bag to hold and carry them. Twenty-one pounds of rocks was not an insignificant load.

Very deliberately, she called Winston Brody next, and when he failed to appear, she asked that a bench warrant be issued. Again, the implication was clear. She knew several members of the jury, at least, had been impressed by today's evidence, and now again by the nonappearance of a witness. She was convinced that several of the jurors had made up their minds a long time ago and that nothing she did would shake them: Mrs. Sproul, Mr. Abenz, and possibly the youngest one, Janice

McClaren, who had regarded Gregory Leander with loathing, as if she had encountered someone like him and lost. . . . They knew what they knew, also; their own experiences would color everything they saw and heard. And tomorrow, with John's testimony, with Heflin's cross-examination of him, she might lose a few more jurors. But she might gain some, too, she told herself firmly, watching them file out of court for the day.

FORTY-FIVE

FATIGUE WAS SLOWING her down, she thought in the shower the next morning. Last night they had watched a special on television about Gold Mountain; the Rowlands had issued a statement in which Brian said that the video was pie-in-the-sky dreaming. They were planning another resort on the south coast, no more than that. Juret's office had issued a statement: They often bought land with gold mines, investigated them, and usually sold them again, as they probably would do in this instance. Brody was still missing.

She dried her hair and dressed. Later, in court, an adrenaline rush would override the fatigue, but at the moment she simply felt tired. She had been up very late again, working.

She went downstairs to the dinette, and came to a stop. John had stood up at the table at her entrance. It wasn't an adrenaline rush, she knew, that made her knees go funny and the pit of her stomach lurch and feel hot. She became aware of Frank's close scrutiny as she started to move toward the table.

"Bobby, tell me the truth," Frank said gruffly, "are you up to it today? Do you want me to take over?"

She shook her head, her gaze on John. "Do you want him to?" she asked.

"No."

"He's good. He taught me everything I know, and he has stuff left over that he hasn't even gotten to yet."

"You'll do fine," John said gently. "We'll be on our way now."

She hadn't seen Bailey until then. "We got the pictures," Bailey said. "John has them, and your dad has copies. See you in court." He nudged John's arm.

"See you in court," John said, and walked out with Bailey.

She sank down into a chair and drew in a deep breath. "Thanks, Dad," she said then.

"Right," he said. "Cheese omelette coming up."

She hadn't noticed how John was dressed at the house, but as he was being sworn in, she did: a good charcoal suit, discreet maroon tie, black shoes. He looked prosperous and sophisticated, in an unexpected way. Of course, she thought, he was used to testifying before congressional committees; he knew about things like that.

He recited his background, education, and experience, clearly and succinctly.

She showed him the printout of the *Congressional Record* that included his testimony and asked if he had appeared often on such occasions. He said yes, half a dozen times; he listed the committees he had testified before.

"Who do you work for, Mr. Mureau?" she asked. She was amazed at how they could look at each other without revealing by a flicker anything at all. At least she hoped she revealed as little as he did. He could have been a polite stranger.

"I'm a private consultant," he said. "Sometimes I work for a federal agency, or an individual company—an insurance company, a mining company. Sometimes for a local governing agency, occasionally for an individual person."

She picked up the newspaper article about the Kentucky mining accident in October. "This is from a local paper in Pikeville, Kentucky, dated October twenty-third, 1994," she said. "This article states that at that time you led an investigation into an accident at Milrose Mines. Who hired you to do that?"

"The Kentucky State Mining Commission," he said.

"Were you acquainted with Congressman Knecht?" she asked finally.

"Yes. I met him twice."

"Please tell us about the first meeting with him," she said. She didn't glance at Judge Ariel, but she sensed that he had stiffened, ready to cut John off if he felt he had to. John was very good, however; he described the June meeting in Denver without going into the particular details of names and companies. It was almost exactly the way he had talked about it the first time at Frank's house, months ago.

She asked about his second meeting. He told about being summoned to Portland to meet with Knecht in the Rose Gardens in August. He spoke carefully. "He wanted me to look into vast land acquisitions that included abandoned gold mines. He wanted to know who had purchased those tracts of land, to determine who the actual owners were." He thought a second, then continued, looking at the jury now. "He said he would be at the Oregon coast on September ninth, and asked if I could have a report ready by then."

"Please tell us what you did on September ninth."

No one moved, coughed, whispered, or made any other sound as he described his day, flying in from Denver, renting the car . . . finding Knecht's body, stumbling over pebbles, and finally running away, back to Denver.

"Will you please identify these various receipts for us, Mr. Mureau." She had the airline receipt, the car rental, motel, everything except the bottle of Wild Turkey. One by one, he identified them and she had them admitted. "What happened to the receipt for the Wild Turkey?" she asked then.

"The clerk put it in the paper bag, and I forgot to take it out when I put the bottle on the tray and tossed the bag in an ashtray."

"Will you describe the bag the bottle was in, please."

"A regular liquor-store paper bag, big enough for one bottle only."

She picked up a bag. "Is this like it?"

"Exactly."

She put an empty bottle in the bag and held it up. "How did you hold it? Do you recall?" She handed it to him. "Please, stand up so the jury can see how you carried it."

He held the bag around the neck of the bottle, in his right hand, swinging down at his side. She took it back and had it entered.

"When did you put on the gloves?"

"At the entrance to the hotel. I took them off while I was running toward the cottages."

"Why did you leave the scene of the murder?" she asked then.

Looking at the jury, he said, "I knew he had been alive only a few minutes before I found him. I was shocked, and then someone came in with a gun, and I assumed he was the killer. I didn't stop to think. I just ran out the door, over the side, and toward the nearest cover."

She took him back over parts of it in minute detail; he was very good with his answers, never hesitated or wavered. She asked him what color shoes he had worn and he said brown. She asked him if anyone had spoken on the drive from Stone Point to Florence.

"The old woman told her granddaughter to slow down once. And then she said something like, 'Lady, I'll make it up to you. We'll go somewhere else and stay, somewhere even nicer.' The granddaughter said, 'That's all right. Don't worry about it.' "

"Mrs. McDonald called her granddaughter Lady?" He hadn't mentioned that before.

"Yes."

"Mr. Mureau, why did you wait until December to come forward to tell your story to the police?" She moved to the rail of the jury box and stood there as he answered.

"I thought the police wouldn't believe me," he said quietly. "Between 1974 and 1978, I had four episodes of mental illness, which I have now learned were caused by prescription medications. I didn't know that until very recently. I knew the police would investigate me, and they would discover those episodes and discount whatever I said. No one else knew the congressman had hired me—not his staff, no one. He paid me with a personal check. At first, I even thought they might accuse me of the congressman's murder, since I was on the scene."

"Why did you change your mind and take your story to the police?"

"After Mrs. McDonald's murder—"

"Objection!" Heflin cried. "Irrelevant, and prejudicial to the case we are hearing."

"It's not irrelevant," Barbara said. "He had a reason to change his mind. We have a right to know that reason."

"Sustained," Ariel said. "Rephrase the question in such a way that it won't be prejudicial."

"Exception," Barbara said sharply.

"All right," Ariel said.

"Mr. Mureau, did you follow the progress of the investigation back in Denver?"

"Yes. I subscribed to a local paper from Oregon and read everything they printed about it. I knew the man the security guard had seen was myself, not Teddy Wendover, and not his father, Ted Wendover. Finally, after Ted Wendover was arrested, I decided I had to come forward."

"Before you went to the police, had you ever examined your own medical records?"

"No. I never had seen them."

"Why not?"

"I trusted my doctor. I didn't realize there was a reason to look into the records. I just never thought of it."

"After you went to the police, did you get your medical records?"

"Part of them," he said slowly. "I thought they were complete, but I learned later that the physical therapist was not a medical doctor and he had not released his records. We had to get a court order to force him to open his files and release the records to me."

"When did you finally see the complete medical files?"

"A few days ago," he said.

"When did you start the process of collecting your own medical records?"

"In December," he said promptly.

"So from December until late March, the records you were aware of were incomplete. Is that right?"

"Yes."

"When you went to the police in December, what happened?"

"They held me as a material witness until they investigated my background and my story; then they told me to go home and not bother them again."

"They didn't believe you," she said softly. "Just as you feared would happen. Is that right?"

"Yes," he said. He sounded despondent, even a bit tired. "Just like I thought it would be."

"Before 1974, had you ever experienced any symptoms of mental illness?" she asked then. Her stomach was hurting, she realized. He said no. "And since 1978, have you ever experienced any symptoms of mental illness?" He said no in a firm voice.

"What happened in 1974?" she asked. She was resisting the impulse to start pacing back and forth before the jury box. Her stomach hurt and her legs were starting to feel twitchy. He must be getting tired, she thought then. It was nearly twelve, nearly time for the lunch recess. Hang on, she thought, just hang on.

He described the mine accident in a very abbreviated way and did not mention his own actions.

"That was April ninth, 1974. You were rescued on April eleventh, and on April twelfth, did you have surgery?" She took him through the surgery, the care under his physician in Pikeville and into therapy. "So your surgeon gave you a supply of the medication diflunisal MSD to control pain, five hundred milligrams every eight hours, according to the medical report. He released you on April twenty-sixth with a thirty-day supply of the medication. Did you continue to take the tablets when you were returned to Pikeville?" He said yes. "Did he talk to you about possible side effects or adverse reactions?" He said no. She nodded and moved to her table. "This is the *Physicians' Desk Reference,* commonly in use all over the country. Concerning diflunisal MSD, it says it may cause ' . . . insomnia, dizziness, nervousness, hallucinations, confusion, disorientation, paresthesia. . . .' Did your doctor mention any of these possible effects?" He said no again.

"Then, your physician gave you hydrocodone bitartrate, five

milligrams every six hours. According to the *Physicians' Desk Reference,* 'Patients receiving other narcotic analgesics . . . may exhibit an additive CNS depression. When combined therapy is contemplated, the dose of one or both agents should be reduced.' Did your physician ask if you were taking other medications?"

"No."

"Next, we have the physical therapist, who, although not a medical doctor, nevertheless prescribed cyclobenzaprine HCI, a muscle relaxant, prior to starting therapy. Did he ask about other medications you were taking, or talk to you about possible side effects or adverse reactions?" When he said no, she turned to the entry and read from it: " ' . . . should be used only for short periods, up to two or three weeks. . . . may enhance the effects of alcohol, barbiturates, and other central-nervous-system depressants. . . . It may cause vertigo, disorientation, abnormal sensations, anxiety, agitation, abnormal thinking and dreaming, hallucinations, excitement. The normal dosage is ten milligrams three times a day.' According to your medical records, the dosage you were given was twenty milligrams three times a day, and for a period of five weeks."

She knew she was pushing her luck with such a long commentary without a question. Now she asked one. "Mr. Mureau, did any doctor talk to you about the effects of those various drugs either alone or in combination?"

"No, never."

Before she could continue, Ariel said they would take the lunch recess. When she glanced at Heflin, the prosecutor simply looked bored. What Barbara wanted to do was take John's hand and walk out with him, stroll along the river with him, have a sandwich together. Instead, she watched him walk away, meet Bailey in the rear of the courtroom, and vanish as he passed through the double doors into the waiting crowd of reporters.

She walked fast enough and long enough to make her legs burn and throb; then she returned to the house, washed her face, refused food, and was ready to start again.

She finished summing up the medications John had taken from April 26 to July 5, 1974, and then said, "When you were hospitalized in the mental-health clinic, were you still taking the medication your surgeon provided?"

"For several days, yes."

"Your records indicate that your physician, Dr. Smith-Fielding, reduced the dosage of hydrocodone bitartrate from five milligrams every six hours to five milligrams twice a day after the fourth day of your hospitalization, and on the eighth day, he discontinued it. He also continued the medication prescribed by your physical therapist for the first four days in the hospital. Three days later, on the seventh day of that stay, you were reported to have no symptoms of illness and twenty-four hours later, you were released. Did you have any medications after that?"

"The psychiatrist at the hospital gave me tranquilizers, but they made me dopey, and I only took them one day."

"Did you have any further symptoms of confusion, or hallucinations, anything of that sort?"

"No. Not until the following year, after the next surgery."

She reviewed the next three years, with surgeries followed by therapy and mental illness. She named the drugs he was given and read from the *Physicians' Desk Reference* for each instance.

Then she asked, "How old were you when you started working in the coal mine?"

"Eighteen, three months after I graduated from high school."

"How long had you known Dr. Smith-Fielding, your primary physician?"

"All my life. He was our family doctor."

"You trusted him?"

"Absolutely."

"You never sought a second opinion about your mental illness?"

He was becoming stiffer, his face set, the scar livid on his cheek. "It never occurred to me," he said slowly. "I know now that I should have thought of it, but I didn't. I accepted his word."

"Did you sign a waiver when you refused further treatment in 1978?"

"Yes. I hardly even looked at it. Dr. Smith-Fielding said the insurance company needed it."

"Why did you refuse additional treatment?"

"I was afraid of the doctors," he said slowly. "Afraid of more surgery. I was functioning, and I didn't want any more than that. I wanted to be done with it all."

"Who paid for your many surgeries, the extended treatments you received?"

"The mining company's insurance carrier."

"Who paid for your education?"

"I did," he said sharply. "When I signed the waiver, or disclaimer, whatever it was, I released them from any further obligation to me."

"In fact, Mr. Mureau, didn't you receive two different awards for heroism, one in 1975 and another in 1976? The first from the governor of Kentucky for five thousand dollars and the second from the Carnegie Hero Fund Commission of Pittsburgh Award for two thousand five hundred dollars?"

"Yes." His face flushed, and the line of his jaw was tighter than ever. Now the scar was drawing up the right side of his face in a grimace.

"According to the governor's citation for bravery, you were not injured in the original cave-in. The rest of your group all escaped unharmed, but you returned to the cave-in section three times, without regard for your own safety; twice you rescued others, and the third time you became a victim yourself when there was a new cave-in. Is that correct?"

"Yes," he snapped.

"You suffered grievous injuries that required years of surgery and therapy. Your back, your leg, hand, chest, and face were all badly hurt. Did you also suffer a head injury?"

"No."

"Thank you, Mr. Mureau," Barbara said quietly then. "No further questions at this time." Don't look at him; don't smile at him; don't let your gaze linger. Just sit down. She could almost hear the words in her mind. She clamped her lips to make certain no sound emerged and took her seat again. Her hands were trembling; she put them in her lap.

Grace Heflin stood up. "Your Honor, at this time, I request permission to read into the record statements that unfortunately were not presented in due course, since the present witness came forward at a late date."

Ariel nodded at her and said to proceed.

The first one was from Michael Driscoll, security man at Stone Point. He said he stopped the car with Leigh McDonald and her grandmother, looked inside, and then, on a signal from his superior, waved it through. No one was in the back, he said. He looked; there were only the two women in the car.

The second statement was from Leigh McDonald. "Question: Could you see the hotel from the cottage? Answer: Not at all. There are too many bushes and trees screening the cottages. You have the report of what she told the police. She was on the deck. She couldn't have seen anything. Question: Could anyone have been hiding in the back of the car? Answer: Absolutely not. I looked in when I went around to the driver's side, and I put my purse on the backseat. I would have seen anyone back there."

Barbara was seething, but there was not a thing she could do about this, since Ariel had ruled in advance that the statement, unchallenged, would be admitted.

The third statement was from Dr. Lowenstein. Finally Marcus Truly had his day in court as he read the statement. He had a good reading voice, deep and resonant. He had practiced the statement, evidently, and never stumbled over a word or phrase, although in places it was highly technical. Lowenstein described the symptoms of acute-onset paranoid schizophrenia. It was very textbookish until the questioner drew him back in.

QUESTION: In your opinion were John Mureau's symptoms typical of acute paranoid schizophrenia?

ANSWER: Absolutely. He was under tremendous psychological and emotional stress and he had very serious physical injuries with a great deal of associated, intractable pain—the ideal situation for a latent instability to manifest. The paranoid schizophrenic shows hostility, fear, disorientation; he builds a fantasy world to live in, and during the time he inhabits his fantasy world, he believes in it totally. Mr. Mureau believed he was being persecuted, hunted, in danger; he became afraid his doctors were harming him; he also exhibited extreme guilt feelings, another typical manifestation. He heard voices and had visual hallucinations, all quite typical.

QUESTION: Would the medications he was given account for the schizophrenic episodes?

ANSWER: Highly unlikely. Many people tolerate higher dosages than he was given. It is more probable that the drugs acted in the same way alcohol does in many people, in that it lowers the threshold of inhibitory behavior. In the case of instability such as he displayed, the action of the drugs might well have been simply to facilitate the latent mental illness, not cause it. If that is the case, then extreme stress, or alcohol, pain, or perhaps simple fatigue, could also act to release the latent psychological condition, as, in fact, was the case in subsequent years.

QUESTION: Could you offer a second opinion concerning his mental health today based on the records from 1974 to 1978?

ANSWER: No, I couldn't. I would have to have him under observation for an extended period, administer tests, evaluate him in a clinical setting to do that.

QUESTION: Would a person with such a latent psychological problem be able to function in the real world on a day-to-day basis?

ANSWER: Indeed he would. They often do for extended periods. But if the proper stimulus is applied, the latent condition may well surface again. Mr. Mureau evidently was in remission each year following his illness, until he was once more subjected to extreme stress and pain, and once more the latent psychological condition became

manifest until he was stabilized with psy-
chotropic agents. He was not in any sense cured;
his illness was controlled.

Barbara's hands were clenched; her fury was cold and complete. Every eye in court was fastened on John, still on the witness stand, pale and motionless. His face was expressionless; he
was controlling his cheek muscles so the scar did not cause a
grimace. She could imagine how he must be biting his cheek,
drawing blood. Lowenstein's statement went on for several
more minutes, but it was more of the same. She thought suddenly she wanted to kill him; she would rejoice in his death. The
thought shocked her.

Finally it ended; Marcus Truly sat down, and Heflin approached John. "Mr. Mureau, is it possible you were driving
toward Stone Point when you heard a news bulletin announce
the murder of Congressman Knecht?" she asked coolly.

"No," he said. His voice was firm, his gaze on her steady.

"Can you be certain of that?" she asked.

"Objection!"

"Sustained."

"Did you have discussions with the defense attorneys before
you talked to the police?"

"Yes."

"And you followed the developing story through the newspapers. Is that correct?"

"Yes."

"Mr. Mureau, isn't it possible that from what the defense
attorneys discussed with you, taken in association with the stories you read, you began to imagine that you had been the man
seen at Stone Point, that you imagined yourself in that role—"

"Objection!" Barbara cried.

"Sustained."

"When was the last time you were in the town of Florence?"

"In early January," he said. He sounded wary now, watching
her closely.

"These two receipts aren't dated, Mr. Mureau," she said,
holding them up. "You could have made those purchases at any

time. Wasn't it, in fact, in January that you went to that department store and bought gloves and a tie to corroborate your story?"

"Objection!" Barbara was crying out before the question was finished, but Heflin did not stop until the end.

The objection was overruled.

"I bought them on September ninth," John said evenly.

"Are you certain?" Heflin asked. "Sorry, withdraw the question." She walked to her table and picked up a folder, opened it, then asked almost casually, "Who was Robert Lee Staley?"

John paled visibly, but his voice continued steady as he said, "He was a clerk in a store in Pikeville, Kentucky."

"Did you kill him?" Someone behind Barbara gasped, and some of the jury members looked startled. One or two leaned forward.

"No."

"Did you confess to killing him?"

He hesitated momentarily, then said, "I don't know."

Heflin nodded and took a sheet of paper from the folder. "I have here a police report dated June first, 1974, Pikeville, Kentucky. 'Subject John Mureau forced his way into Police Chief Obert's office at nine-twenty, demanding to be arrested, tried, convicted, and executed for the murder of one Robert Lee Staley. Subject Mureau was highly agitated, incoherent, crying. On investigation, it was determined that Robert Lee Staley had died of a massive stroke three months earlier in Our Lady of Peace Hospital. Subject Mureau was detained twelve hours and released in the care of his physician, Hadley Smith-Fielding, M.D., who admitted him into Mt. Sterling, a mental-health clinic.' " Heflin put the sheet of paper down and looked at John sadly. "Did you make that confession?"

"I don't know," he said in a thick voice. "I can't remember that period."

"Did you kill John F. Kennedy?" This time someone sniggered, then turned the sound into a cough.

"No," John said.

"Of course not," she said. "You would have been eleven, wouldn't you? Mr. Mureau, did you confess to his murder?"

"I don't know," he said. He was very pale now, and the scar looked redder than Barbara had ever seen it. He looked mean and dangerous, his face twisted, his body too rigid.

Heflin read the police report and asked if he had made the confession; he said he didn't remember that period.

"Did you kill Martin Luther King, Jr.?" No one laughed this time; there was a deadly silence in the courtroom.

She went down the list in exactly the same way, first the name, then the question "Did you kill him?" then the police report and his admission of no memory of that period. It was brutal, and he was suffering, but he maintained his control.

Grace Heflin returned all the papers to the folder and closed it, her back to him. Then she turned to face him again. "Mr. Mureau, did you kill your father?"

He looked stunned for a moment, then he blinked rapidly several times. He cast darting glances all about, not as if searching for anything in the courtroom, but as if he was searching himself, his past, something invisible.

"Yes," he said in a voice that was nearly unrecognizable.

Barbara was aware of Ted's groan, of Carolyn's gasp, of other buzzing commotion among the spectators, but dimly, as if she were a great distance from it all. Frank's hand on her shoulder brought her back almost instantly, and she looked down to see a broken pencil in her hand. Carefully, she put the two pieces in her pocket.

Grace Heflin looked as taken aback as everyone else. She hesitated, then lifted both hands in a gesture that seemed to imply there was no point in continuing. "I have no more questions," she said.

Judge Ariel called for a fifteen-minute recess then. The first hint of humanity he had shown, Barbara thought.

Ted caught her arm as his guard approached. "We have to talk," he said harshly.

She watched John walk out stiffly without a glance to either side. "I know," she said to Ted. "As soon as court is over, not now. I want Carolyn there, too."

"I have to take the stand," he whispered. "I have to!"

"I said later. Take a break now. We'll talk later." Her voice was as harsh as his had been.

She fled to the ladies' room and locked herself in a stall, where she stood with her forehead pressed against the door. *Think,* she ordered herself. Where was that other Barbara, the courtroom persona, the one who didn't tremble, who didn't break pencils, who didn't want to run away and hide? She drew back from the door and rubbed her forehead. She'd appear in court looking as if someone had slugged her. Then she remembered her own words; they had to act as if they believed totally that John was the deciding factor in this case. They could show no doubt, no hesitation, no fear of his breaking. She nodded. Right. Her stomach spasmed; she drew in a deep breath, another.

When she joined Shelley and Frank in the main corridor outside Courtroom A, Shelley examined her anxiously.

"Is there anything I can do?" she asked.

Barbara nodded. "Find Lowenstein and tie him up, then begin cutting him to pieces. Tell him what you're going to do, then do it, and then explain what you've just done. Start at his toes; take off half an inch at a time, no more than that."

Shelley looked bewildered, then she grinned. "You're okay. I wasn't sure."

"She's fine," Frank said. "Told you so. You want anything, Bobby? Coffee, a Coke?"

She shook her head. "Afterward. A double something or other. Not now."

John was composed and very remote when they resumed. His face was almost blank, it was so expressionless; it was as if he had gone somewhere else and left a shell to finish the ordeal for him.

"Mr. Mureau," Barbara started crisply, "was your father killed in the mine accident in which you were so grievously injured?"

"Yes," he said distinctly, looking through her, not at her.

"Will you tell us how the men were distributed that day?"

"We were in three groups, thirty of us," he said after a slight pause. "The first group had nine men, including my father. They were in the deepest shaft. The second group had fifteen men; they were in the shaft just beyond the one I was in. My group had six men."

"Out of the thirty men, nine survived: the six in your group, and three you rescued from the next group. Is that right?"

He nodded, then said yes.

"Did you think the mine was unsafe?"

He looked surprised, and now his gaze seemed to focus on her. He nodded again. "Yes."

"Did you tell your father you thought it was not safe?"

He hesitated. "Yes."

"You were eighteen when you started working in the mine. How long had your father been a miner?"

"Twenty-six years."

"What did he say when you told him the mine was not safe?" She kept her tone conversational and easy.

His hesitation was longer this time. He was looking at her as if he was seeing a stranger; his brow wrinkled the way it did when he was puzzled by her. Then he said, "He told me I'd get over that. He said everyone felt that way when they started."

"Mr. Mureau, is there anything you could have done or said to convince him the mine was not safe?"

He looked away, stiff again, remote again. "I don't know. I doubt it."

"When did you decide to go to school and study geology and mining?"

"When I got the check for five thousand dollars," he said.

"So you used your awards for heroism to become a mining expert. Do you go into deep mines as part of your job now?"

"Sometimes."

She walked to the jury rail and stood there. "When you tell people now that mines are not safe, do they listen to you and take action?"

"Yes!"

She nodded and walked to her table. "Earlier, we heard statements from several people. Mr. Driscoll said he looked into the car when Leigh McDonald was leaving Stone Point. Can you tell us what you recall of that?"

"She was driving slowly," he said. He looked relieved that they were off the subject of mines. "She slowed even more, but she didn't come to a complete stop, and then she sped up some and drove to the highway."

"All right. Leigh McDonald said that the hotel was not visible from the cottage, that it was hidden by shrubbery and trees. Can you tell us anything about that?"

"Yes. I read that in the newspapers, and I kept wondering how that could be, when it was obvious that the old woman had seen me. Yesterday, with three other people, I went to Stone Point and we took pictures from the cottage walk. I have them. The hotel is visible."

"Who were the other people?" she asked. Bless Bailey, she thought, he had taken charge.

"One is a photographer, Ralph Suchet, who took the photographs with a Polaroid camera. One is a notary public from Florence, James O'Bannon, who certified the photographs. One is a man named Bailey Novell, and I was the fourth. We all initialed the pictures as they were taken."

"Did you give the photographer any special directions?"

"No, I just told him Mrs. McDonald had been four feet eleven inches. He adjusted his tripod accordingly to shoot his pictures where she would have been able to see."

He handed the pictures and the letter of certification to Barbara. Heflin objected; no one knew anything about those pictures, she said, except this one witness. Barbara said she would be happy to call the other three people who had been present. Judge Ariel looked at both of them with displeasure and overruled the objection. Barbara glanced at the pictures, showed them to the judge, then to Heflin, had them admitted, and passed them to the jury.

After this was done, she continued. "Leigh McDonald's other statement was that she looked in the back of the car and even put her purse on the backseat without seeing you. Can you explain that?"

He shrugged. "I was on the floor, under a cover. She opened

the front door on the driver's side and tossed something back, maybe her purse, then got in and started to drive. No one opened the door to the backseat after I got inside the car."

"Mr. Mureau, is your work stressful?"

He looked wary again. "It can be," he said.

"Are you ever in pain?"

"Yes, sometimes." He was reverting to the stranger once more.

"Do you ever drink alcohol?" He said yes. "Would you classify yourself as a light, light-to-moderate, moderate, or heavy drinker?"

"Light-to-moderate," he snapped.

"Do you ever become extremely tired?"

"Yes."

"Have you ever had lapses of memory besides those which occurred from 1974 until 1978?"

"Never."

"When you entered Congressman Knecht's room and discovered his body, did you drop a tray with a bottle of Wild Turkey on it?"

"Yes, I did," he said without hesitation.

"When you first went to the police in December to tell them about that day, did you believe the diagnosis that had been made concerning your mental health, that you had suffered from paranoid schizophrenia in the past?"

"Yes," he said wearily, gazing past her again.

"Do you believe that today?"

"No!"

"Do you believe today that there was anything you could have done at the age of nineteen or twenty, or even twenty-two, to prevent the death of your father?"

He closed his eyes a moment, then said in a very low voice, "No. Nothing."

"Thank you, Mr. Mureau," she said. "I have no further questions."

When he was excused, he walked out as stiffly as before, without a glance to either side.

Barbara stood up then and asked if she could approach the bench. Judge Ariel motioned her and Grace Heflin forward.

"Your Honor," Barbara said, "defense had counted on the appearance of Mr. Brody to conclude today's testimony. If we call him and he fails to appear, I request adjournment for the day in order to consult with my client and make adjustments in our defense."

He looked at Grace Heflin, but she simply shrugged. "He won't show," she commented. "I have no objection."

He nodded. "All right. Call your witness, and if he's skipped, we'll adjourn. We can all use a little rest," he added.

His second show of humanity, Barbara thought. She thanked him, and the bailiff called for Winston Brody, who did not respond. Court was over for the day; it was four o'clock.

FORTY-SIX

BARBARA DUCKED OUT an exit to the skywalk that led to the Federal Building, around the block, and on to the jail. She waited in the conference room for Frank and Carolyn to arrive and for Ted to be brought out. They all appeared almost simultaneously.

The door had not closed on the guard yet when Ted cried, "You have to put me on the stand! It's *my* neck!"

Carolyn touched his arm. He jerked away from her, glaring at Barbara.

"Sit down," Barbara said tiredly. "Just sit down, and let's talk." She and Frank sat down; Carolyn sat across the table.

"Sit down," Ted yelled, "be civilized, be polite! Bullshit! They're going to hang me, and you know it!" After a moment he took the last chair. He was shaking and red-faced, his stare still fastened on Barbara.

"Why did you bring him in?" he demanded.

Barbara ignored him and asked Carolyn, "What did you make of John's testimony?"

Carolyn said without hesitation, "I think he's a man who escaped a terrible accident, then escaped doctors who might have killed him. I believed everything he said."

Barbara turned to Ted. "And you?"

"He's crazy! You heard the statement from the psychiatrist. He's schizo, a nut. My God, maybe he killed Knecht himself! Who knows what he did? Who can believe anything he says? He's crazy!"

Barbara nodded. "That's what we're faced with," she said quietly.

"No!" Ted yelled, rising to a crouched position. "Not me! Not what I'm faced with! My life in that maniac's hands? No! If you won't put me on the stand, I'll yell to the judge, the press, the jury, anyone who'll listen, that you refused to let me speak. Do you get it? I won't be gagged! I'll take my chances with Heflin." Abruptly, he sat down again.

"You have the right to move for a new attorney at any time," Barbara said. "But hear me out first. Tuesday night Dad and I had a talk with Wilmar Juret, the president of Carlyle Mining Company. He was assured that Knecht would lose the election in November because Brownley was going to launch a smear campaign to begin in October. It would have started with documentation and photographs of Carolyn and Knecht, and gone on from there. Juret is not naïve; he would have been shown enough to believe it would be effective. He believed it would work, that Brownley would win the election."

For a time no one moved or made a sound. Carolyn looked frozen, her gaze straight ahead; her face had the sheen and color of old ice. Ted stared at Barbara, all color gone from his face.

Barbara waited until the full implication sank in; then she said, "Juret knew about the campaign; he was told by Brian Rowland. If Brian knew it, so does the district attorney's office. So far, there hasn't been any opportunity to introduce such material, but if you're on the stand, undergoing cross-examination, there will be. If you had found out about such a campaign, it would have been motive enough for you to kill the congressman.

They'll say that even if you were willing to live with the status quo, such a smear would have brought it all crashing down, ruined all of you. And it would have," she added soberly.

Ted shook his head. "I didn't know," he said, defeated.

"I believe you," Barbara said. "But what would the jury believe? You can't prove you didn't kill him, and you can't prove you hadn't learned about the smear." She paused a moment, then said even more quietly, "Whether it was brought out in October, or tomorrow in court, it's the same smear, the same photographs, the same documents. I don't know what all they have, but enough to convince Juret that Knecht would lose the election. We all know that would have taken a lot."

The silence extended. No one moved until Ted shook himself, glanced at Carolyn, then reached for her, put his arm around her shoulders, and drew her to him.

He looked at Barbara and nodded. "Do what you think is best," he said, then leaned in toward Carolyn. "Honey, why don't you start looking into flights to Hawaii, a condo or apartment or something. Just the three of us. Gail and Reid will be in school; we can duck out for a long vacation." He was stroking her back gently, his face bleak with despair. To no one in particular, he added, "Teddy swims like an otter. He loves it."

Bailey and a couple of reporters were tossing pennies on the front walk, using the step as a backboard, when Barbara and Frank arrived home. Someone started a camcorder at their appearance. Barbara smiled and made a zipper motion across her lips. Frank waved, grinning, and did not say a word. Today the questions were all about Mureau. Where was he? Were they hiding him? Did he have an agent? Would he give an interview?

They went inside the house, with Bailey at their heels. Before Barbara could ask, Bailey said, "He ditched me. We got to the parking lot; he got in his car and took off. I guess I could have tried to keep hold of the handle, but I thought that would not be a smart thing to do."

Silently Barbara started up the stairs, then paused to say, "That was good work with the pictures. Thanks." In her room, she changed into jeans and then sat on the side of her bed. She should rest a while, she knew, and she had to look over her clothes, make sure she had something clean to wear the next day. She had to go over all her notes; once she rested the defense case, it would be too late to add anything. She had to finish work on her summation, try it out on Frank. Her stomach still hurt; she should eat something. . . . Where had John gone? How badly hurt was he? Abruptly she stood up and walked into her office.

She was too restless to stay at her computer. She went downstairs and met Frank, who evidently had intended to come up.

"Let's have a bowl of soup," he said. "I'll make something real after a while. Just a little something to hold us over."

It was a clear chicken soup with a few snap peas floating on the surface. Frank went out to see to his garden after he finished his soup; Bailey went out to keep him company. Barbara stood at the door watching her father, watching the cats play. The sun was very low; the cats were tawny. Peace and tranquillity, she thought then, and wanted to weep. She went back upstairs, back to work.

"I'll wrap it up tomorrow," Barbara told Bailey that evening. "Dump it into the laps of the gods, make a sacrifice or two, and start praying."

"Maybe I'll hang around," he said, helping himself to more potatoes. "Just in case something turns up."

"I know you will," she said. "You're not all bad."

He looked embarrassed.

Later, going over her summation with her father, she was jolted by a sharp memory of his doing it this way with her mother. He had always maintained that Barbara's mother was his best critic; he was Barbara's. She wondered if that was really why he had given up trying criminal cases; he had lost his best critic. She excused herself and got a glass of water in the kitchen, then returned. He had a few suggestions, nothing serious; she listened carefully and made notes.

Much later, in her office, she looked up to see him in the doorway, dressed in his robe and slippers. He didn't enter.

"Bobby, whatever happens, you've fought a hell of a fight. I'm very proud of you." He left swiftly.

Frank had made waffles with strawberries for breakfast; they had always had waffles with strawberries when he rested a case. Barbara ate little, however.

In court, with all the players at hand, she consulted briefly with Ted. "Are you sure?" she asked him. He nodded. She looked at Carolyn, who nodded. Carolyn's hair had become much grayer over the past months; she had aged. Barbara stood up and said the defense rested.

It was a surprise to Grace Heflin, who asked for a fifteen-minute recess, and a surprise to the jurors, who looked confused. Some reporters hurried from the courtroom. They had the recess, and then Heflin started her final arguments, her summation.

She was very good. She dwelled on the pain and the burden of a retarded child grown into adulthood, who would be forever dependent, forever a problem. She spent a lot of time on the business Ted had lost, how much it had cost him financially. She used the phrase "a normal man" often: "Wouldn't a normal man have felt humiliation knowing his wife was in the bed of the man who had destroyed his son?" "Would a normal man simply accept the situation of an adulterous wife?" She savaged Gregory Leander. "He's a psychiatrist who doesn't believe in insanity, and who wrote that murder was the only solution available to the mysterious Mr. X, who killed his wife. He denied that the adulterous affair of Mrs. Wendover and Congressman Knecht was immoral. Can we accept his word that Ted Wendover was complacent and contented with his life?"

As she continued, Barbara resisted the impulse to look out over the spectators to see if Gregory Leander was among them. If he was, he would be laughing, she knew.

When Heflin got around to John Mureau, her scathing, scornful tone changed to one of great sadness. "Three people saw the man dressed as a waiter that day; none of the three mentioned a scar. He isn't to be condemned as a false witness," she said. "He believes in his story, exactly as he believed in his confession that he murdered John F. Kennedy. He believed in his fantasy world then; he believes in his fantasy world today. You heard the statement of Dr. Lowenstein. . . ."

Later she said, "In June, Mr. Wendover was confronted by an important client of many years standing; he was given instructions not to take his retarded son along on business trips. A man who was known to be calm, never angry, always resigned, even sad, he snapped; he became enraged. Then he saw his enemy, Congressman Knecht. And it was too much to bear. He made an overt threat, and in September, at his first opportunity, he carried out that threat and murdered Congressman Knecht. He had tolerated the intolerable for fifteen years; then he could tolerate it no longer. He deliberately murdered Mr. Knecht and did it in such a way that his own son would be implicated, charged, and, if found guilty, put in an institution. He knew his son would not be punished; he would be found incompetent. And he would have lived the rest of his life in an institution, where he would have been tended and cared for, exactly what Mrs. Wendover's parents had urged for many years, a humane solution of a heart-breaking problem that his wife would not agree to."

She got around to the empty rooms, the maid's testimony. "Frankly, ladies and gentlemen, in this flawed world, there always will be mistakes. Mistakes in billing, mistakes in memory, mistakes by human beings, and by computers. We live with them daily. The defense will always draw attention to them, try to make common errors appear to have criminal intentions, to cast doubt." She proceeded to cast doubt on everything the maid had said, everything the manager and reservation clerk had said.

When she finished, she had talked for over three hours, summarizing the state's case and tearing down the defense. She had explained, defended, or dismissed every point.

Barbara walked and thought; she played with a salad without tasting a thing, and then she was back in court, the two-hour lunch recess a blip in her awareness.

"Ladies and gentlemen," she said, standing in front of the jury box, letting her gaze roam over the attentive faces, strangers all, "think back to a day or a night when you were entirely alone. Maybe in your garden, maybe taking a long walk, driving, or simply at home watching television. Alone, with no one to pay any attention to you. If you were accused of committing a crime during the hours you spent out of sight, by yourself, how could you prove you had not committed that crime? That is a dilemma, the dilemma my client, Ted Wendover, faces. It is impossible to prove a negative. Ted Wendover made a statement to the police; he signed it, swore to it, and he could do no more than that. If he were to testify here, he could do no more than that. He swore under oath that he did not murder Congressman Knecht, and he did not. He told where he was on September ninth, and that is all he could do.

"The state's case relies on the evidence of three eye-witnesses. But how reliable are those witnesses? Consider Mr. Brody. . . ." She talked about Brody at length.

"The second witness who identified Mr. Wendover at first appears to be more difficult," she said. "Mrs. Leiter had no reason to pay any particular attention to a waiter arriving for work. After she read about Teddy's exoneration, she remembered the waiter. Three months had passed; he had not existed in her consciousness for that time. Could anyone have read that account without looking at the photographs? It is well-established police procedure never to show a potential witness photographs of suspects before they participate in a lineup. The police didn't show Mrs. Leiter a photograph; the newspaper did. She then saw a familiar face in the lineup and made the identification."

Barbara was studying the jurors as she spoke, addressing them individually. "Little has been said about how the rocks were transported to the hotel that day," she said. "Mrs. Leiter was vague about a paper bag the waiter carried. She could not describe it, how big it was, how he carried it. But you saw the pile of rocks that weighed twenty-one pounds. Think, a ten-pound bag of potatoes, ten pounds of sugar, a pound of butter. That is not a small load to carry. Not a load you would carry in one hand for very long. The bag probably would rip, to begin with. You would use both hands and support the bag from below. And it would be noticeable." She paused, then said, "But Mrs. Leiter might not have noticed a small liquor-store sack with a single bottle in it, carried in the right hand of a walking man. She did not mention a scar, because she could not have seen it. When she first saw him, he was too far away. When he drew nearer, he was in profile. She saw the left hand and arm, the left side of the man; Mr. Mureau's face is scarred on the right side."

She walked to her table and stood there, regarding the jurors soberly. "The hotel manager saw a man he assumed was a waiter; what drew his attention was the waiter's clothing. He saw his left leg and arm, his left hand in a glove, and he glimpsed a face in a crowded lobby. You are asked to believe someone was carrying twenty-one pounds of rocks in a grocery bag in one hand, out of sight. Why did no one else notice him?" She shook her head. "Ten days after he saw a man he thought was a waiter improperly dressed, Mr. Siletz fired one of his waiters, giving as his reason the improper clothes he had glimpsed on September ninth. Only after discussing the newspaper article with Mr. Brody, seeing Ted Wendover's picture, did he identify Ted Wendover as the man he had seen."

Slowly then, emphasizing every word, she said, "And that is really all the evidence the state can present to link Mr. Wendover with the murder of Harry Knecht. An eyewitness account by a man who has failed to respond to a summons to reappear in court, and who made an earlier different identification; an eyewitness who must have seen Ted Wendover's photograph in the newspaper before she picked him out of a lineup; and an eyewitness who saw only part of a person he assumed was a waiter and in fact, acted on his belief by firing a waiter. Everything else the prosecution has stated as fact is in truth only one assumption after another."

She walked back and forth slowly. "The first assumption the state made was that Teddy Wendover killed Congressman Knecht. Why? Because he is severely retarded, he was in the area, and Mr. Brody identified him. Let's examine that assumption. . . ."

She drew a vivid portrait of Teddy and his family, friends, and neighbors. She used words from the testimony they had heard and drew conclusions from it. She concluded: "If Mrs.

Musick had not been wise and kind, if she had not been able to
see past the exterior into the heart of a child who wanted only to
play with her children, to build a castle on the beach, the prosecution of Teddy Wendover would have gone forward, because
without her he could not prove, nor could anyone else prove, the
negative, that he had not killed Congressman Knecht. Mrs.
Musick saved him that day. I have no doubt she saved his life."

She paused, then went on. "The next assumption the state
made was that a normal man would have found Teddy an intolerable burden." She talked at length about the outings the Wendovers had taken as a family, the times Ted had taken all three
children with him, then just Reid, and finally only Teddy. "The
other two children are grown," she said. "They are university
students with their own lives to lead, but Ted Wendover still has
Teddy. He was never forced or coerced into taking any of them
on his many trips; he is not forced now to take Teddy with him.
He chooses to take him because he enjoys the companionship of
his son.

"The next assumption is that a normal man would have found
his wife's affair unbearable. Ladies and gentlemen, examine
your own lives. Has your father ever done anything you considered a mistake, something you would not have done? If you
consider yourself normal, would that make him not normal?
Has your mother ever done something you know you would not
have done? Is she not normal? In fact, hasn't everyone you
know at one time or another done something you would not
have done? Wouldn't they all say the same thing about you?
Who is normal? The word we need here is not the word *normal*,
but the word *different*. And yes, certainly, we are all different.
Our reactions to tragedy are different. The way we deal with
adversity, with happiness, with every aspect of life demon-
strates the differences among us."

She talked about the tragedy of Teddy's accident, the turmoil
in the household, and the relationship that developed afterward.
"Unless you have walked in their shoes, you can't judge his
actions or hers," she said. "That he chose to accept the situation
is one of the imponderables of the human condition.

"During the year of crisis, Ted and Carolyn failed each other;

the family could have disintegrated completely, but they found a solution they could live with, and as a result they have three fine children, and a closer family than ever today. . . ."

She examined the jurors' faces as she spoke softly now. "However you judge them on moral grounds, remember the witnesses who have testified that theirs was a kind and loving relationship, a loving family. Remember that Ted accepted the situation; he was not a bitter, vengeful man. Remember that if a price must be paid for moral transgression, they have paid that price many times over. If suffering is demanded of them, they have suffered."

She went to her table for a sip of water. Ted was sitting with his head lowered; in the seat behind him, Carolyn had lowered her head, but tears were visible on her cheeks. Gail had her arm around her mother's shoulders.

"The next erroneous assumption the state made, and on which this case depends, was that John Mureau is not a reliable witness. With incomplete medical records, and without a thorough investigation, the state dismissed him and his story, and as a result they failed to investigate every aspect of his story, even those that might have been easily proven. Was a bicycle stolen in Florence on September ninth and later found at the wayside park a few hundred feet north of Stone Point? Did Mrs. McDonald ever call her granddaughter Lady? The prosecutor said the hotel was not visible from the cottage; we proved it would have been to anyone as short as Mrs. McDonald was. Did they question any clerks in the department store where Mr. Mureau bought gloves and a tie? Did they try to learn if anyone in Florence had bought a bottle of Wild Turkey that day?

"Let's examine the evidence of his unreliability. We all know, to our dismay, that narcotic drugs can cause hallucinations and psychoses. Mr. Mureau was given massive doses of prescription narcotic drugs. . . ."

She summarized John's history and then said, "By the time the psychiatrist saw Mr. Mureau, he was hallucinating, irrational, psychotic. Instead of inquiring about his medications, the psychiatrist diagnosed paranoid schizophrenia, and after that the doctors and the therapist were without blame. Mr. Mureau had been labeled and from then on they saw him in terms of the label that had been applied. An entire life of service and hard work can be ignored just like that, because a label has been applied."

Careful, she warned herself. She could hear the indignation in her own voice, and knew everyone else heard it, but that was all right. Indignation was called for, to a point. She walked the length of the jury box. "Put very simply," she said then, "Mr. Mureau was a healthy, well man; he was given prescription drugs and he became ill; he stopped the drugs and he was well again. Who among us hasn't known someone who suffered a reaction from medications? Anything from a slight rash, to incapacitation, to death can result from an adverse reaction to medication. Aspirins, penicillin, antihistamines, any drug can be dangerous to some people. For most people, the remedy is to stop that medication. Mr. Mureau found that remedy by refusing to continue with further surgeries.

"As a boy, he tried to inform a man with decades of experience. He didn't know enough to say why he was afraid the mine was unsafe. The day of the accident he saved three lives and was awarded for bravery. Since then, how many lives has he saved through his investigations, his testimony before committees? We'll never know. But does he still harbor a residue of guilt over not saving his father? Yes. Children, even without cause, feel guilty when their parents die. If he had known enough, if he had argued enough, if he could have pointed to a structural flaw—if, if, if. Yes, I imagine he torments himself with it. Is that a symptom of instability? No, ladies and gentlemen. It's a sign of humanity."

She changed her tone then; leaning slightly against her table, she said conversationally, "What happens when the prosecution becomes committed to a particular scenario is that anything that doesn't fit into that scenario is dismissed as irrelevant. It's like the menu; you can have one from column A or one from column B, but you can't have both. Briefly, let me mention some of the items left behind in column B, dismissed as irrelevant. First, we know Congressman Knecht had political enemies; he received threats. We know he often worked alone on a project, investigated it himself, before he put his staff to work on it. We knew he broke an appointment to come to Oregon, to Stone Point, in June. The only person we know he saw then was Mr. Rowland. We know he met with Mr. Mureau in Denver, again breaking an appointment to do so, and that he did this again in August in Portland."

She spoke quickly, very brisk now, businesslike. "Mr. Knecht's reservation was locked in for the corner suite months ahead of time. Then Mr. and Mrs. Rothman's reservation was locked in for the next room. No one takes responsibility for doing that. Mr. and Mrs. Wylie canceled their reservation, but it mysteriously reappeared on the reservation screen, locked into the next room over. So we have three adjoining rooms with connecting doors, and reservations locked so that none of them would be changed. No one knows how that happened. We have the Rothmans, whose original reservation included a fishing trip that would keep them out from early morning until seven that evening. The false reservation for Mr. and Mrs. Wylie indicated that they would be out on that same fishing expedition. Room Two Twenty-two was empty for several days, even though the hotel was so filled that people requesting reservations were turned away."

She walked up and down along the jury box, almost as if inviting a comment. "Somehow," she said, "the rocks have to be accounted for. A man's life is at stake, and it isn't good enough to say Mrs. Leiter might have seen a man with a paper bag. A bag big enough to carry the murder weapon and the pebbles, twenty-one pounds of rocks, would not be an inconspicuous object. But no one saw anyone carrying such a bag, not approaching the hotel, not in the lobby, nowhere."

She smiled slightly. "Next, let's look at what the maid saw. If someone enters your house and moves anything, aren't you aware of it? If someone moves anything on your desk, don't you notice? Well, Nora Blake knew she had vacuumed the carpet in Two Twenty-two and that she had finished it in a certain way so that the nap would lie flat. She knew how she always arranged things in the bathroom, the shampoos and lotions and towels. She knew at a glance someone had moved things. She saw water spots; someone had turned on water and splashed it. And she saw indentations in the carpet like those left by the hotel golf bags. Sometime after she inspected the room on Friday morning and before she returned on Saturday morning, someone else had been there, had moved things, had used water in the bathroom, possibly had put a golf bag down near the connecting door to Room Two Twenty-one. And someone had left a tray in the room. Later, she found a discarded golf bag in the trash; the bag was damaged, the dividers broken out.

"Now all that might be innocent; we could have a series of mistakes being made, starting with reservations, continuing through the maid's observations. Or someone might have gained access to the room. We don't know because the state did not investigate what the maid saw. They had her statement, but it was in column B; they dismissed it."

She stopped her slow pacing and regarded the jurors soberly. "All right, now for the room of the murder. There are questions about that room and how things could have happened there.

"How can anyone account for a single fingerprint on the bottle of Wild Turkey? And what happened to the tray? Since the state dismissed Mr. Mureau's story, they can also dismiss the tray and claim it never was there. But the single fingerprint remains a problem. If Mr. Knecht unpacked the bottle and carried it from his suitcase in the bedroom to the sitting room, he should have left many prints, not only one. If Mr. Mureau handled the bottle while wearing gloves, as he stated, he might have smudged all the prints on the bottle, but again the question is, How did Mr. Knecht's single fingerprint get on it?"

She paused to let them ponder this for a moment, then said, "The next unsolved problem is in the photograph that shows indentations in the carpet that look like the kind left by the hotel golf bags. Mr. Knecht did not play golf. Someone else must have set a golf bag down there and then removed it again."

Some of them were really getting into it, she thought with satisfaction. The foreman, Mr. Betz, and the computer man were both following avidly, leaning forward slightly. Another man was nodding, his eyes narrowed in thought. The fat woman, Mrs. Sproul, looked bored.

"Then there is the problem of the blow itself. You saw the marks on the doll's face, where bruises occurred, and you heard that the fatal blow had come straight in from the side. If Mr. Knecht had been seated, then the chair had to have been moved, since his body was moved only enough to turn him over. And what was he doing, sitting down in the middle of the room waiting for someone to hit him in the head? But sitting or standing, would he have failed to see someone holding a rock raised to strike him? No, it's another problem," she said. "Unless," she added slowly, "the first blow was with a weapon that had some reach, a weapon that looked innocent until it became a lethal weapon."

The man who had been nodding with his eyes narrowed, Mr. Ackerman, she remembered, suddenly opened his eyes wide, blinked a time or two, and then sat back in his chair. Good, she thought. She had wanted at least one of them to get it before she spelled it out more. That one could become her ally.

"Ladies and gentlemen," she said then very quietly, "I will propose an alternate scenario to the one the state has prepared. If the new scenario answers more of the unanswered questions than the state's, you must consider it when you start your deliberations. In my scenario, the killer has to be in the hotel, has to have access to the computer and understand the codes. He has seen to it that two adjoining rooms will be empty, with an entrance into and an exit from the congressman's room. On Thursday night he places a golf bag in the closet of Room Two Twenty-two, out of sight of the maid who will be there in the morning. In the bag are the rocks, soap, a towel, gloves, maybe a clean shirt, and a few golf clubs. He has the congressman's schedule and knows he is expected to be in his room alone between five and six on Friday. Sometime during the day on Friday he enters Room Two Twenty-two and puts the towel and soap in the bathroom, rearranging things slightly as he does. He sets the golf bag down near the connecting door, where it leaves indentations. He unlocks all the connecting doors. After Mr. Zimmerman has come and gone, he enters the congressman's

room, taking the golf bag with him. He removes a club and
starts to swing it the way a golfer might do. But the telephone
rings, and Mr. Knecht tells someone to come on up. He strikes •
as soon as the congressman is off the phone. He turns the body
over to the right position, dumps out the contents of the golf
bag, the murder weapon and pebbles, and the long yellow
rubber gloves. He puts on the gloves, picks up the murder rock,
and smashes in the congressman's head. He has to act very fast
now. He strips off the bloody gloves, probably tosses them in
the golf bag, opens the sliding door to the balcony, still framing
Teddy. Everyone is supposed to think Teddy entered and left
that way. He picks up the golf bag and opens the door to the corridor before he leaves through the connecting door to the next
room."

The courtroom was so still, it was as if the moment had been
plucked out of time, frozen. A soft, audible collective exhala-
tion ended the moment when she moved to talk directly to the
jury as a whole.

"He opened the door to the corridor so whoever came first
could enter, discover the body, and set up a hue and cry for the
killer, before Teddy had time to get off the beach. Then he
stepped behind the door to the adjoining room, Two Twenty-
one, and waited. But Mr. Mureau showed up with his tray and
bottle, and closely behind him came Mr. Brody, and suddenly
there were new factors to consider—a strange man, the tray and
bottle. Obviously Teddy would not have brought them. So, as
soon as Brody ran out after the waiter, the killer returned. He
removed the tray, but for some reason he decided the bottle
could stay. He tried to imprint Mr. Knecht's fingerprints on it,
and succeeded in getting only one. Then he fled."

She spread her hands. "The rest follows naturally. He locked
doors behind him and used the bathroom in Two Twenty-two to
clean himself up. No doubt he wiped the sink, but he was not
the fastidious housekeeper the maid is. And he forgot the tray
and left it on the dresser. He had more than enough time.
Remember, Mr. Martinez was still at the reservation desk at five
forty-five, and when he went to the suite, he stood inside the
foyer, not out in the hall. When Dr. Vorlander arrived some

three or four minutes later, he also stayed in the foyer. No one was in the hall for many minutes. The killer had time to wash his hands, possibly even change his clothes. Then, clean, he left the room, probably used the nearest stairs to go to the main floor, and it was done. Sometime before nine the next morning, he put the golf bag in the trash in the supply room, got rid of the gloves and golf club, and no one ever asked him a serious question. The police were looking for a man in jeans and T-shirt, a man with a canvas shoulder bag. A man whose description was furnished by Mr. Brody."

She walked slowly the length of the jury box, regarding each one in turn. "Ladies and gentlemen," she said, "you are not required to solve the mystery of who murdered Congressman Knecht. But unless you are convinced beyond a reasonable doubt that it was Ted Wendover, you are expected to consider any possible alternatives. . . ."

She talked about reasonable doubt, about the lives in their hands, about assumptions that rested on generalities. Then she said, "Thank you for your patience and your attentiveness," and she was done.

FORTY-SEVEN

JUDGE ARIEL DISMISSED everyone immediately after Barbara sat down. He would instruct the jury on Monday morning. As soon as the jury filed out, Ted embraced Barbara. "Thanks," he said. "Just thanks." His voice was thick, choked-sounding.

"Try to rest this weekend," she said. "It's going to be hard again next week, waiting for them to bring in a verdict."

He nodded, looked yearningly at Reid and Gail, gazed longer at Carolyn, and left with his guard. Barbara repeated her advice to Carolyn. Then Frank herded her and Shelley out through the reporters. As soon as there was a verdict, he said, they'd have a press conference, nothing until then. The questions persisted anyway. In the parking lot, Barbara said to Shelley, "You're off for the weekend, too. Rest, relax, have fun."

"There's nothing else to do, nothing for me to do?" Shelley looked lost.

"Now's the letdown time," Frank said. "You and that young man of yours ought to go off somewhere, to the beach maybe, and fly kites or something."

Later, in her comfortable slouch clothes, a glass of wine in her hand, Barbara sat on the back step in the sunshine and watched Frank work, or play, in his garden. She should have an engrossing hobby, she thought. Not gardening; she had proven to be an inept gardener a long time ago; immature weeds, vegetables, they all looked the same to her. Not needlework—she detested doing it. The cats stalked invisible somethings in the grass, pounced, tumbled over each other. Lapidary work might be interesting; take a rough stone, cut into it to discover its secrets, polish it. It would be fun for her and John to scour creek beds, camp out in east Oregon. . . . She bit her lip and closed her eyes.

When she opened them a few minutes later, Frank was standing upright, regarding her with a strange reflective look. It seemed a lonesome look, which vanished quickly; he rubbed his back.

"Dad," she said softly, "no matter what happens now, I'm not going anywhere. I mean, the trial, or with John, anything. Just thought I'd mention that." She drained her wineglass and got up to refill it. He had brought out a tray with two glasses and the bottle but had not touched his.

He left his garden, came to the porch, and propped his hoe against the rail, then sat down on the top step. "Want to pour some for me? Those fool cats—" Thing One and Thing Two were digging where he had just weeded.

She brought the wine and sat down again with her back against the rail post. "I always felt I had to just get away when things didn't go right. Doesn't work, though."

"Nope," he agreed. "I ran away from home once when I was, oh, ten maybe. I wrote a good-bye letter to my folks and left it on the kitchen table and took off. Got a mile away, maybe a little more, and began to wonder if my letter would sound silly, if I'd misspelled 'condemn.' See, I'd written that I wasn't trying to condemn them for beliefs they couldn't help." He chuckled. "I ran all the way back and got hold of that letter first. Misspelled it, too."

"I remember Grandma and Grandpa," she said. "They were more tolerant than you are. You had a nerve!"

"Well, they mellowed some as they grew up," he said complacently. They were silent a minute or two. Then he said, "What made you say that? That you'd stick around?"

"Things," she said. "You know what I said in court about Ted enjoying the companionship of his son. You're pretty good company."

"Yeah, and what else?" When she didn't answer, he said, "Bobby, you can't hang around because you'd feel guilty if you left. That's clearly not a good reason."

She said, "When Mother died, I was nearly overwhelmed with guilt. I hadn't done enough, hadn't done anything I might have done, hadn't been there for her. . . . Guilt of the survivor? I don't know. But I had it for a long time, years even. I failed her, and then I ran away and failed you, too. Then Mike . . . I said I wouldn't hurt John. . . . I'm just tired of failing people I love."

Frank held up his glass to the sunshine and gazed at it. "Bobby, if I dropped dead before I finished this wine, you'd feel guilty as hell, and you know it. If you got run over by a truck tomorrow, I'd feel the same. It's our lot, I'm afraid. As for John, you know there was no way on God's little green ball of earth that you could have kept him off that stand. If he were fragile, he'd have self-destructed a long time ago. Don't go masochistic on me; that's hard to put up with."

She laughed. "That's a hoot. But anyway, whatever the reason, when Ted hugged me after court today, the thought popped into my head that if I lose him, I'll take off, and it was overtaken and killed by the next thought that no, I won't. I'm done with running away. And that's all I know about that," she added firmly.

He looked at her with a curious expression. "The day all this started he was lost, but now? Let's wait and see. You don't know how good you were today, do you? You're just feeling the letdown. The adrenaline's dried up, you're tired, and you'll probably get even lower. Happens."

"I'm scared," she said, and finished her second glass of wine. "We don't know how much Ariel will tell them they can't consider, how much he'll say is inadmissible. He's still a goddamn prosecutor at heart."

"Now, Bobby. Tell you what, I've been itching to try out that new restaurant that's been getting raves. Florios, something like that. I'll give them a call, say about seven-thirty. Let's go for it."

"Will you tell me some more about your miserable childhood?"

He chuckled and pushed himself up from the step. "Deal."

Saturday was bad. She got up at ten and felt dopey, although she had gone to bed early. Eleven hours of sleep, and she felt dopey, she grumbled to herself. She needed a haircut again, she thought, toweling her hair dry, and she really had to shop for some clothes. She was sick to death of everything she owned. When she made her bed, the rock fell to the floor. Holding it, she sat on the side of the bed, remembering when John handed it to her. She had gone to sleep holding it. Did it have gold? Just a rock? She held it tighter a moment before she replaced it on the nightstand.

Laundry, she told herself, tackle the mess in her office, heaps and stacks and piles of stuff to be sorted. File her nails.

The day dragged. Every time the telephone rang, she hurried to the study door to listen to the message. Frank asked if she wanted to go out to the Arboretum, roam a little, and she said no. "Someone has to stay home and listen to the goddamn telephone," she muttered, and went back to her office.

Sunday was bad, too. If she didn't get out and move, walk, climb a hill, do something, she'd start screaming, but what if he called, or came to the house? She went up and down the stairs over and over. In late afternoon, she listened to yet another message, and this time she hurried to lift the receiver.

"Sheriff Tourese, I'm here."

"Ms. Holloway, how are you? Been following the trial; looks like a real humdinger."

"I'm fine," she said. "What's happened?"

"Well, just thought you'd want to know that more than a little hell's been breaking out up at SkyView. Brian and his brother and father seem to have had a blowout. Brian and Cy both took off, and then Vicky Tunney, why she took off, too. None of them paid much attention to the speed limits, I hear."

"Do you know what they were fighting about?"

"Nope. Brian came in late Friday night, fighting mad. They were holed up most of yesterday, storming around, yelling, but nothing that my contact could make out. Then, this morning, they blew altogether and three of them peeled out." He cleared his throat very audibly, then said, "Ms. Holloway, if what I see in the paper's what really happened in court—course, we all know you can't pay much regard to what they print, but still—some folks might say you pinned the tail on Brian. That right?"

"Not really," she said. "The reports might be a little exaggerated."

"Uh-huh. Well, just thought you should know all three Rowlands have blood in their eyes, and two of them are out racing around."

"Thanks, Sheriff. I really do appreciate this. After we have a verdict, I'd like to come over and talk."

He laughed. "I think that's a fine idea, Ms. Holloway. I surely do."

Neither Frank nor Bailey was inclined to joke about the Rowlands, and, Frank reminded her, there was Brody out there somewhere, too.

"For the time being," Frank said, "no walks, no wandering around alone. Not until they all light and we know where they are."

They were in his study, and already Barbara was feeling the

pressure of walls too close, ceiling too low, not quite enough fresh air.

"Alan can be your chauffeur for the next few days," Bailey said.

"If you can find him," Barbara said.

Bailey grinned. "Whistle and he'll be here."

"Ariel will take a couple of hours, and then the jury is out. We'll have a lot of waiting to do," Frank said meditatively. "We could haul the Wendovers over here; not any farther from here to court than from the office, if we drive. Which is best for you, Bobby? Here or the office?"

She shrugged indifferently. "If we hole up here, I'll want all the files brought over."

"Okay," Frank said. "Shelley can gather stuff and she and Bailey can bring it over. What else?" he asked Bailey.

Barbara stopped listening. All those files: material on Lois Hedrick's death, Mary Sue McDonald's, Harry Knecht's. Nothing on Praeger. So much material that she had not had time to think about for weeks and weeks. Carolyn would do needlework. Reid and Gail would play games, play with the cats, watch movies; they would find something to do while they waited. Frank would work in the garden. And she would start sorting files. Good enough.

Judge Ariel was fairer than Barbara had expected, and tougher than she had hoped. He talked at length about reasonable doubt, what it meant under the law, and then he sent the jurors out to deliberate.

As soon as Ted left with his guard, Frank talked to Carolyn and her children in Courtroom A. "Nothing's going to happen this morning. Then from twelve-thirty until two, they'll take a lunch break. Anytime after two, we might get a call to return. So you're pretty much free until then."

He gave them the option of house or office to wait in and they accepted his house without hesitation.

"We'll go home until two," Carolyn said. She looked as if the weekend had been hard; the hollows under her eyes were deep and dark.

"All right," Frank said. "You might want to bring something to wile away the time. Guess all I've got at the house is chess and playing cards, and lots of books. Movies might be nice."

Barbara told Shelley what she wanted her to do, and said yes when Shelley asked plaintively if she could help with the files. Then they left. This time, they went out the front entrance at the exact moment Alan Macagno pulled up to the curb in the Buick.

Waiting one day was more exhausting than a month in court, she decided that afternoon. Shelley was working on the files upstairs; the Wendovers were in the living room watching a movie; Frank was in the backyard. Alan was reading in the dinette. She was everywhere, nowhere more than a few minutes. If she had a lapidary setup, she would have bushels of rocks, and if she had bushels of rocks, she would be throwing them. If she had a mess of entrails, she would be trying to read them. She returned to the upstairs office.

Heaps, piles, stacks of stuff, she thought gloomily, unable to concentrate on any of it. She counted floorboards, counted stairs, counted knots in the wood doors; when she found herself counting seconds to make up a minute, she fled to the backyard.

Then it was time for Frank to change back into court clothes, to return to Courtroom A. The jury had not reached a decision; the judge dismissed them for the day.

Alan drove them again, then Frank told him he was off until morning. "We'll stay here," he said, ignoring Barbara's groan.

Late that night she stared at the material on her desk. All right, she told herself, do something. She went back to the beginning, Lois Hedrick's death.

At her computer, she began to make two columns, one headed "Facts," the other "Speculation." Under "Facts" she wrote, "Someone told Lois about Gold Mountain." "Speculation: Arthur Rowland. Fact: Praeger confirmed it. Fact: Lois wrote to Harry Knecht and told him she would try to learn more. In the first week of January someone killed her, probably in the early afternoon." Fact or speculation? She had a vivid memory of Arthur Rowland's gnarly hand grasping the chair back as he swung his cane. And his ugly words about Vicky

Tunney: "I've got the hots for her pussy!" She shuddered and stood up.

Something's crazy, she thought then, starting to walk the length of the upstairs hall. Why hit her again when she was already dead? She visualized the cane, a simple crook-handled cane. A blunt instrument, easily replaced if it had a mark on it. The first wound would have been called death by a blow with a blunt instrument. A piece of wood, or a club ... Already framing Teddy? She shook her head. That was too fast; the second blow had been struck very soon after the first one, too fast for such an elaborate frame-up to be concocted.

If he called Praeger to help, as he must have done, how had Praeger managed in daylight to get her body out of the hotel up to a higher level where she would freeze within hours? She went back to the office to examine the SkyView layout.

She found the resort material all together: Stone Point, SkyView, and Columbia Falls, and spread everything out on her desk. Columbia Falls was by far the largest, and from all appearances the most expensive; it catered to big conventions, probably made a bundle. SkyView was tiny in comparison with it and Stone Point. She studied the layout of SkyView: Lower Loop One, Upper Loop, what they called the ridge, where the Wendover house was, the train to the chairlifts. There was no way anyone could have carried a body out without being seen, she told herself glumly.

She stood up, feeling stiff and sore; it was one o'clock. A soak first, then bed, she decided, although she did not feel sleepy, only tired. Shelley had made a separate stack of books and pamphlets; on top was Gregory's book *I'm Okay, My Cat's Okay, But You're a Loon*. She had skimmed it; now she picked it up to read in the tub, smiling slightly as she remembered his blatant appraisal of Grace Heflin in court. She wondered if he had sent her a funny present yet.

During the night, she dreamed of playing in the snow with John, throwing snowballs, laughing, and then she was dreaming of Vicky Tunney and Cy Rowland playing in the snow, and the images became confused, the dream frightening. She woke up, hearing a hard rain outside her window. She had to close the window, she thought, groping around for her rock, reluctant to leave the warm bed. When she forced herself to get up, close the window, she stood looking out at a few lights shimmering in rainfall. "Where are you?" she whispered, holding the rock very tightly.

Tuesday was a repeat of Monday; they appeared in court and were sent away again. Stay within call, free from twelve to one-thirty, return at five if not called before that. It was raining. Barbara caught Frank's enquiring gaze in court, and again when they reached the house.

"As soon as Carolyn and the kids get settled down, let's talk," she said. The Wendovers were already on the front porch, shaking water from raincoats.

"Me, too?" Shelley asked, not quite begging.

Barbara nodded. "Of course. You're part of the team." At Shelley's smile, she felt as if she had bestowed her allotment of happiness for the day.

Frank was a genial host again with the Wendovers. He took their coats, put on coffee, pointed to the refrigerator, and told them to make themselves at home. Then he, Shelley, and Barbara withdrew to his study. She stood at the window overlooking the back garden. The rain was very heavy.

"I was wrong about Lois Hedrick's murder," she said, looking out. "It couldn't very well have been Arthur. He needed to balance himself when he wasn't using his cane. And there's the problem of moving the body. Try this instead. Lois already had talked to him, and she had talked to Praeger. I doubt she would have gone back to either for more information. But she might have gone to Cy Rowland."

She turned away from the rainy landscape and sat in a nearby chair. Frank was at his desk, Shelley in another chair, both silent and intent.

"It kept raining in January two years ago," she said. "Hardly anyone was trying to ski. They put the artificial snow down at night, and the next day it got rained on and melted. But Cy was up at the shack most of the time. She could have gone up to talk to him. He could have killed her up there where it was freezing, where her body would freeze in a few hours, and where he had the chance to hide her body."

"Why the rock?" Frank asked, not disputing her, but not agreeing, either.

"If he hit her with a ski pole, that would have left a distinguishable pattern. I think he had to hide that wound with something else massive enough to cover it up."

Frank was thoughtful, not convinced. "From all reports, including yours, he had nothing to do with Gold Mountain, or any of their other enterprises. Why would he even care if she knew about it?"

"He didn't want to be part of it," she said. "All he wanted, all he ever wanted, was SkyView. Vicky said that, and she spoke truer than she realized. She said the day after Arthur dies, they'll be married. Why wait? I think Arthur wouldn't permit it. He kept Cy from trying out for the Olympics; he reined him in at SkyView until he was forced to yield a bit. Not altogether—Brian is still in charge, actually. Cy just has the ski business. But he has two bosses, father and brother. Last night I read Gregory's account of Mr. X. Cy Rowland is Mr. X, not Ted Wendover. If word got out about Gold Mountain, and if it got stalled, as it has now, and if they're strapped for money, I imagine SkyView would be down the drain. It's not a big moneymaker, not like the other resorts, but it's all Cy Rowland wants. You said it, Dad, that they're probably mortgaged to the hilt. Juret said other backers are pulling out; he's pulling out."

As Frank mulled this over, she said, "I saw and heard how Arthur treated Cy and Vicky Tunney, how he talked about her. And Cy just stood there and took it. I think he took a lot for a lot of years. But if SkyView itself was threatened by Lois Hedrick's going to Knecht, starting an investigation, he couldn't take it. SkyView might be the last straw, taking away his salt."

"And no way on earth to prove anything," Frank said. "Even if you're right, getting anything concrete now is impossible."

"I don't know," she said. "Right now, I wonder if Vicky isn't in danger. She talked about how excited they were when the snow finally started, but he was up in the snow every day. I think he was excited because at last he could get the body down the mountain and into the streambed. He led the searches up around the shack, and no doubt he was damn careful where he had his team search. And she might know exactly where he was or wasn't the day Owen Praeger was killed." She thought a moment, then said, "If she starts, or already started, to ask questions, the whole thing might fall apart. She knows better than anyone else how he feels about SkyView."

This time the silence stretched out, until finally Frank grunted. "I don't know if there's anything to it, but just in case, maybe it would be a good idea to call the sheriff over there and have a talk with him. He might know where Vicky is."

She took his place at the desk and he stood at the window with his hands clasped behind him, gazing at the rain. There was a long wait for Sheriff Tourese.

"Sheriff," she said at last, "Barbara Holloway here. I think we have to talk now, not later. Can you tell me something—was Owen Praeger murdered?"

He took his time answering. "I'm sure he was," he said then.

"I think Vicky Tunney is in danger," she said. "If you know where she might be, maybe someone could talk to her, warn her. I think she knows more than she might realize about Lois Hedrick's death, and maybe Praeger's as well."

There was no delay at all in his response now. "Why don't you just tell me what you suspect, and what you know."

She was telling him when he interrupted. "Ms. Holloway, what I think I should do is come over there and talk to you. She's in your area somewhere, more than likely. When will you be free?"

She told him after five-thirty, and he said he'd be there. She gave him the address and hung up. After that there was nothing any of them could do except wait.

A few minutes before twelve, Carolyn and her children left to have lunch with Teddy. They would be back at one-thirty, Carolyn said tiredly. She looked ready to drop.

"You hungry?" Frank asked.

"No. Later maybe."

He nodded. "Think I'll mosey over to the courthouse, see what's happening. Want a ride, Shelley?"

"Sure. I'm meeting Bill for lunch. He said he'd pick me up at the office."

"No problem," Frank said. He glanced at the rain. "We'll let Alan earn his keep. He can drop you, drop me, and pick me up in an hour or so." He gave Barbara a sharp look. "You won't go out anywhere, will you? Bailey's supposed to come around any minute now."

"I won't leave the house. Promise," she said. He would chat here, chat there, and come back knowing what the damn jury was up to, Barbara suspected. He had a way of getting people to tell him things. She decided to study him more carefully, how he handled the press, how he wormed information out of people, who would later swear they hadn't breathed a word. When they were all gone, the house felt very empty.

A few minutes later, the phone rang. It was Patsy Meares, from the office. "Barbara, I was just on my way out when a young woman showed up asking for you. Vicky Tunney."

"Is she there now?"

"Right here."

"Put her on, Patsy."

Vicky sounded hesitant, as if she already regretted this. "I wondered if maybe we could have lunch, talk a little."

"Look, Vicky, I'm at home. Why don't you come over here. We'll have privacy, more than in a restaurant."

"Actually, I don't want to eat," Vicky said. "Just talk. Are you sure it's okay?"

Barbara reassured her, gave her the address, and hung up. Where? Living room? Too big. Dinette? She shook her head, remembering how Frank had prepared two separate places for the first visit with John. She found a tape recorder in Frank's desk drawer, checked the tape, and put it on a table, with a magazine over it. Then she ran upstairs to get her little tape recorder and put in a tape; she slipped it in her pocket, uncertain where to place it yet.

She hurried back to the study and said, "Testing, testing." Then she played the tape back. Okay. It would be fine on the table. A minute later the doorbell rang and she ran to open the door.

Vicky stood there in a long black SkyView poncho, and at her side was Cy Rowland, wearing another one just like it. He was holding Vicky's arm with one hand; the other hand was hidden under his poncho. They both entered.

"We can go to the study," Barbara said.

Cy shook his head. "Get a coat and hat or something. We're going out."

"Cy, stop it!" Vicky cried. "We came to talk, just talk, remember?"

"That's what we'll do," he said, watching Barbara. "But not here. Get your coat."

"No."

"Ms. Holloway, I have a gun in my pocket, the safety's off, and it's aimed right at Vicky. I'll shoot her, then you, and, just to make it complete, myself if you don't do what I tell you without any argument."

Vicky tried to wrench away from him; he pulled her closer with a jerk. She gasped and her face blanched.

Wordlessly Barbara went to the closet and brought out her own hooded raincoat. She took off her jacket and tossed it onto the table, put on the raincoat, and they walked out together.

FORTY-EIGHT

THEY WALKED TO a white Ford parked in the driveway. "You drive," Cy told Barbara. He kept his grasp of Vicky's arm, kept her pulled tight against him. Barbara opened the door and got in the car. "The seat belt," he said almost gently. She fastened it. "Now both hands on the wheel."

He had Vicky open the back door and get in, then he slipped inside. He told Barbara to start the engine. The key was in the ignition.

"Cy," Vicky said, "let's just sit here and talk. You're so tired. We're all tired. Let's—" She made a gasping sound.

"No talk yet," he said softly. "Later. Not here. Drive. Turn on Sixth. No speeding, nothing fancy. And don't talk. Not yet."

Barbara started the car, backed out, and headed for Sixth. He sounded too remote, too detached, disassociated. He sounded dangerous. She drove carefully. The only sounds were of traffic and the metronomic swish of windshield wipers.

She drove through town, past the garden shop her father liked, past the pet store where she had bought the kitten toys, past a foreign auto repair shop. "Stay right, up Highway 99," he said. Past a lumberyard, over train tracks, heading north past a strip mall, Dairy Queen, gas station, convenience stores. . . . The rain was hard; the road was in bad shape—potholes, standing water. She slowed down.

"Cy," Vicky said quietly, "let her go. Tell her to stop and get out. I'll go away with you. Canada. We can get to Canada before night."

"Shh," he said. "Don't talk."

"Please," she said. "There's time now to stop this. Let her go. Let's go away before something bad happens. I love you, Cy. Please."

Barbara looked at him in the rearview mirror. He was watching her. His expression was bleak, hopeless.

"Shut up, Vicky," he said in a low voice. "I don't want to hurt you, so just shut up. Let me think."

They passed more lumberyards and the airport road, and now the countryside was turning into fields that looked like swamps in the driving rain.

"Slow down," he said after another few minutes of silence. "Turn right at the next intersection."

She didn't know the road, couldn't tell if he did, or if this was simply a random turn. She signaled and turned onto a country road that vanished before them in the rain. The road was narrow and unmarked; there was no other traffic here, no houses visible, no outbuildings, only sodden fields.

"Slow down, way down," he said after a moment.

Barbara tensed, ready to slam on the brake, or the accelerator, something, but he began talking in a low voice to Vicky. "You're the only person who's never tried to hurt me. You know that? The only one. I want you to do something for me, honey."

She was crying. Her voice was muffled and choked. "Cy, I love you. I'll always love you. I'll go away with you, anywhere. God, I wouldn't hurt you. You know that."

"I know, I know," he said softly. "Lois was an accident," he said in a monotone. "I was drinking hot chocolate—you know, my big pottery mug—and she said . . . Never mind. I hit her with the mug. Chocolate was everywhere in the snow. Then I knew they'd see the marks and guess, so I hit her again with a rock. Brian said we had to make it look like the kid did it. No drawn-out investigation, no congressman poking his nose in, just say the kid did it, a nutcase out of control. Everyone knew about the accident, that she was on the spot when it happened. Brian was sure it would work to blame it on him. We got her down on the kid's sled and left it on the trail near her, but someone else must have found it."

A truck appeared in the rearview mirror, not going much faster than they were. Barbara pulled over as far as she could, and no one spoke until the truck passed, and continued at no more than twenty-five miles an hour. Barbara was doing fifteen. The rain and mist had veiled the truck before Cy spoke again.

"But the congressman poked his nose in anyway," he said, as if there had been no pause. "And then Brian was the nutcase. He raved about a car bomb, a letter bomb, a sharpshooter, knocking him off a cliff. . . . But they couldn't do anything that might bring in the FBI, a real investigation. It had to be personal, no politics. Then Brian found out the kid would be on the coast with his mother." He stopped talking. They crept forward through the driving rain.

"You knew about it?" Vicky whispered.

He didn't answer.

Barbara slowed even more. "Let us out here, Cy," she said. "You keep the car—"

"Listen, Vicky," he said. "Tell the cops what I said." His voice was low and intense, compelling. "Tell them everything you heard Saturday, Friday night. Will you do that for me?"

"What are you going to do?" Her words were nearly inaudible.

"Just tell them everything. And be sure to say that if I can't have SkyView, Brian can't have Gold Mountain. Remember that. It's important. Tell everybody that!"

"Let us get out!" she cried. "Please, just let us go and you run away!"

"Stop the car," he said to Barbara. "You're getting out here, Vicky. You'll get a little wet, but you don't mind that, do you? It's been good, honey. It's been good."

Barbara stopped the car. He reached past Vicky and opened her door. She didn't move. "No!" she cried. "Cy, please—"

"Out with you, honey," he said, and pushed her out the door. She staggered, slipped in the mud on the soft shoulder of the road, caught her balance, and twisted around to reach for the door handle; he had the door closed already. "Drive," he said.

Barbara pulled away, watching Vicky in the rearview mirror. Vicky was running back toward Highway 99. She drove faster; then she caught a glimpse of Cy's face, saw a new, expectant expression. That was what he was anticipating; he wanted her to drive faster and faster. Then what would he do, hit her in the head, cause an accident that would kill them both? She eased her foot off the accelerator. He leaned back, keeping his gaze on her in the mirror.

"Will you tell me the rest of it now?" she asked.

"What for? What difference does it make?"

"None, probably. Just curious. How did you manage Praeger?"

She thought he wouldn't answer; his remote gaze remained fixed on her face. Then he said, "He called me. He ordered me to stock that cabin, told me where it was, everything. He gave me a shopping list, ordered me to fill it and have everything ready when he got there. He wanted a place to hole up awhile.

He knew no one would be up that road until spring, and he had an obedient errand boy. I took the truck out there and looked the place over, and then I went back to the McKenzie Highway and waited for him. He told me to get in his car, we'd see if he had enough supplies for a week or so. We drove up the road to the cabin and got out. Then I ordered him. For two years he'd been ordering me around, keeping me broke, holding a club over my head. But I had a gun; I was giving the orders."

His voice was low, toneless. His gaze never wavered from her face; every time she glanced at the mirror, she saw his eyes. He looked calm, peaceful. No, she thought, he had the fixed expression of someone already dead. He had made certain his message to his brother would be delivered; now he had nothing more to do except die. He had accepted death already.

"His jacket and gloves were in the car," he said. "He'd had the heater on full blast; it was like an oven. I took his matches, and I began to back out. Not fast. He came after me. He could almost touch the car, we were so close. He was yelling. He fell down and got up, fell down again, over and over. Then he didn't get up. I waited, but he didn't get up. I went to him, found the cashier's check, and took that, too, and I backed out some more, and waited some more, until the car ran out of gas. A long time. But he didn't get up. He went to sleep in the snow."

Keep him talking, she thought. Maybe he would lose that disconnected look, realize what he was doing, order her out. . . . "Did he know about Lois Hedrick?" she asked. She was driving ten miles an hour; he didn't seem to notice or care.

"He saw her go up the chairlift. He wanted to talk some more to her and he waited. Then he watched. He was out the night Brian and I moved her. He waited and watched. He was crazy. He'd cock his head a funny way and get a strange look, and if you said anything, he'd say, 'Wait a minute. Let me hear this.' Crazy," he said again.

They had driven into orchard country; pale floating globes of trees in bloom emerged from the screen of rain; each seemed to have an interior pink light that tinted the white blossoms, made them glow. Spectral trees appearing, vanishing, appearing. . . .

Ahead, she could see an intersection with an occasional car heading north or south.

"Turn right," he said when they drew nearer the crossroad. River Road, she realized. They were heading back toward town. Traffic picked up; a school bus was half a dozen car lengths ahead of them, stopping, starting. There was a screech of brakes on a side street; he jerked to look, and swiftly she undid the seat belt catch, then caught the strap under her arm so it wouldn't recoil. He had become more alert; he leaned forward again, watching the traffic.

Then he said sharply, "Pull over!"

Flashing lights of a police car were coming toward them; cars moved to the side of the road and stopped. As the police car sped by, he turned to watch it. She unlocked her door.

The bus had stopped again, a dozen children were crossing the street, oblivious to the rain.

"Stay in the left lane, straight up River Road to Fifth. We're going back to your neighborhood, Alton Baker Park."

Startled, she met his gaze again; he was remote once more, distant, no longer watching the traffic, keeping his gaze on her.

It was mixed residential and commercial now; it would be like this the rest of the way, with no place to jump out. She would be hit by oncoming traffic. She followed his directions.

"Why did Brian kill poor old Mrs. McDonald?"

"She saw something. Anyway, he would make it look like the kid had done all of them. No risk. Brilliant Brian." He was animated with bitterness for no more than a second, then he said, "No more talk. Just drive." He sounded very tired.

Past the bakery outlet, past the intersection where Martin's restaurant was only a block away and might as well have been in a distant country, past the county jail, where rhododendrons and azaleas were in glorious bloom in a cruel travesty of a park. She turned at Yuppie Heaven and drove past the turn to Frank's house, then entered the riverside park, where she knew every stone, every tree, every zig and zag of the trail.

"Park," he said dully. There was one parked car in sight. She passed it, not slowing more. "Pull in and park," he said with an edge in his voice. They were getting near the end of the parking section, just a widening of the road, actually.

She stamped on the accelerator and turned the wheel hard. There were logs and boulders to keep cars off the grass; here at the end, shrubs marked the boundary of the parking strip. The front right wheel hit a rock and the whole car shuddered, the rear end slid on the wet pavement, and then the left wheel hit; the car tilted a second, settled. With the first shudder, she had her door open and the seat belt off; she threw herself out the door and rolled into the shrubbery. She hit hard; her leg grazed a rock and she felt as if her wrist had broken; she scrambled in mud to get deeper into the shrubs.

For a second the car was still trying to move, the engine running, the wheels digging in, then it sputtered and stopped.

She crouched low, edging away from the car, toward the greenery along the trail . . . more trees, more cover. . . .

There was a shot, and she flung herself flat, pressed her face hard on the muddy ground, holding her breath. Silence returned, more profound after the explosive gunshot. She heard a man's shout, a second one, followed by a woman's piercing screams. She closed her eyes for a moment, then raised her face to the rain, drew in a breath, another.

FORTY-NINE

SHE WAS ON the couch in the living room, her wrist bandaged, an ice pack in place on it. She was floating dreamily. Whatever they had given her was magical; it let her float around and forget the many abrasions, the headache, the throbbing in her wrist—not broken, but sprained. Cy had become distant, someone she had known once, who had shot himself in the head. Carolyn had helped her shower, toweled her hair, helped her dress, tucked a blanket over her on the couch, and she wanted to do more, but Barbara couldn't think of anything else to ask Carolyn to do. Shelley brought a pillow and changed the ice pack, and she wanted to hover.

Frank had told the police there would be no statements until she was examined at the hospital, then no statement until she came out of the influence of the painkiller and tranquilizer. They would be back at six.

Bailey was furious with her, with Frank, with Alan, with the world. She thought it was funny that he was so angry, while she was so peaceful. Then Frank and Shelley left with the Wendovers, and Bailey sat in a chair opposite her and glowered. She drifted until Frank came back with Shelley. When he opened the door to enter the house, she could hear a clamor of voices, and she knew, to her regret, that she was coming down.

She had told him most of it, but in a disconnected, disjointed way; now she sat up, hearing a soft grunt of pain when she moved her arm. Shelley was there instantly to see if the ice pack needed renewing.

"It's okay," Barbara said. "What's happening in court?"

"Hung," Frank said. "Started out seven to five, guilty; now it's ten to two, not. Sproul—the fat lady—and the young one—McClaren, the twenty-three-year-old—are holdouts. Ariel's been reading them the riot act, yelling for them to get off their butts and get to work. They are forming a strange dislike for him, I hear." He started for the other room. "You want something? No alcohol yet, not until that junk's out of your system."

"Very strong black coffee," she said. What she really wanted was another shot of whatever they had given her at the hospital. Her wrist was throbbing with every heartbeat.

"What are they saying about today?" she asked Bailey.

He was holding a drink as if someone had threatened to take it away from him. "Nothing. The cops are investigating a shooting in the park. Period."

The doorbell rang, and he went to look out the window, then to open the door on the chain. He called, "It's Sheriff Tourese."

Frank was in the hallway with a tray by then. "Let him in.

The more the merrier." He put the tray down in the living room and went back out to to meet the sheriff.

Barbara could hear them talking in low voices.

Then Sheriff Tourese entered the living room; he surveyed Barbara soberly. "How're you doing?"

"Not bad," she said.

Shelley brought the coffee over and would have spoon-fed her if Barbara had permitted it. Barbara waved her away. "Thanks."

Frank asked if he wanted anything, and the sheriff said coffee would be good. Bailey brought him a cup and poured for him.

"I just can't believe Vicky would set you up like that," the sheriff said heavily.

"She didn't," Barbara said. "She went to the office to talk to me; she was alone then. He must have been waiting for her. I don't think he had a plan in his head, except eventually to kill himself. All the rest was just happenstance; things happened with no one in charge."

"I called her right after I talked to you," he said. "Found her at her folks' place down in Pleasant Hill, where I thought she might be. I asked if she knew where he was, and I asked her to give me a call if he showed up. She hung up on me."

"He was probably standing right next to her," Barbara said.

The police arrived then: Detective Noh from the district attorney's office, and city police officers—a lieutenant in civilian clothes, and two others in uniform. Barbara answered questions and made her statement. One of the uniformed officers keyed it into the computer and printed it out on the spot. She read it, handed it to Frank to read, and then signed it.

"Have you told Brian or Arthur Rowland?" she asked then.

"We sent someone to tell them. It's hard news to break on the telephone," the lieutenant said.

"How is Vicky Tunney? You're not holding her, are you?"

The lieutenant and Detective Noh exchanged glances, and the lieutenant said. "Don't worry about her. She'll be all right. I guess we're through here. If anything else comes up, we'll be in touch."

"Lieutenant," Barbara said scathingly, "I just told you that Cy

Rowland accused his brother, Brian, of murdering Knecht and
Mary Sue McDonald. Why not go ask him a few questions and
leave Vicky Tunney alone?"

"We'll be asking questions," the lieutenant said. He started
for the door. "Thank you, Ms. Holloway."

Sheriff Tourese followed them out.

"Those assholes!" Barbara cried. "Vicky's grieving, in
shock, and they're holding her! She's probably the only innocent in this whole goddamn mess!"

Bailey grinned and said to Frank, "I think the dope's worn
off. She sure sounds back to normal."

"What I'm going to do is call Martin and ask him to rustle up
some dinner. Bailey, you up to collecting it when it's ready?"

"Yep. Make it a lot."

Frank grunted and walked out. In a few minutes the doorbell
rang again; the sheriff had returned. "Forgot my hat," he said.
"They'll turn her loose," he told Barbara. "They'll check her
statement against yours first. Her story is that Cy came around
late Sunday night and stayed. Didn't talk, didn't sleep, didn't
eat, just sat staring off into space. She said he'd been like a
maniac up at SkyView from Friday night until they all took off
on Sunday. He was yelling that he had killed for them and they
still sold him out, things like that. But when he showed up at her
parents' place, he didn't say a word, and scared her out of her
wits. She said it was as if he wanted to say good-bye but
couldn't bring himself to leave. Then I called, and she decided
she had to talk to someone, and thought of you. Cy still didn't
say anything, but went out and got in the car with her. When
they got to your office, he stayed in the car in the parking lot
and she went up to see you alone. At the house here, he showed
her the gun and said he'd come in, too."

"I believe that," Barbara said. "She certainly didn't know
what he was up to. I don't think he knew what he was up to."

"Well, I'll be on my way. You know, when you came over to
the office, I had a feeling that you might find a way through the
tangle. I had a feeling. Take care of yourself, Ms. Holloway. Be
seeing you."

                    *   *   *

The next time the doorbell rang, it was Martin, who had brought the food himself. He stood in the living room, eyeing Barbara with grave disapproval. "Maybe you should come back to my place, where no one beats you up."

"Soon," she said. "Very soon. Things happening over there?"

"Not really, but when they don't find you around, they begin asking me for advice. What do I know about the law? Do I look like Miss Abby? We miss you, Barbara."

As soon as he left, Frank said he didn't give a goddamn what anyone else did, he intended to eat. They went to the dinette and ate a Colombian chicken dish with three kinds of potatoes, fresh green beans, avocados, a vegetable salad enough for a dozen people, hot rolls. . . . Finally Barbara was allowed a glass of wine.

Bailey said he would take Shelley home and see that she got inside with her door locked and then he'd come back. "You two plan to stay put, keep the drapes closed, the doors locked?" he asked darkly.

"You must be kidding," Barbara said. "I have a dancing date, bud."

He left with Shelley. Frank and Barbara were still at the dinette table. "You gave me a scare," he said.

"You found my tape?"

"Yes. There was an APB within minutes, but—"

"But. I know. I keep thinking I should say how sorry I am."

"Right."

"I really am sorry," she said then, and added, "but it wasn't my fault."

He laughed. "Ah, Bobby. What I aim to do is clean up this stuff and then watch the news, see how much they release."

"Ariel won't sweat out the jury any longer, will he?" she said, not really asking. "He'll accept a hung jury, a mistrial. Heflin won't rearrest Ted, not now, with everything falling apart. It will be over." She moved her coffee cup toward him as he cleared the table. "Then Ariel will tell me what punishment will fit my crime. He might hang me."

"Might," Frank said equably. "You ready for more ice?"

He refilled the ice pack and they went to the living room,

where Bailey joined them in a few minutes, and together they watched the news. The account was brief: Cyrus Rowland had shot and killed himself that afternoon; the police were investigating. Brian Rowland had issued a statement in which he said his brother had suffered from a bipolar disorder for many years, that he had become severely depressed over the pending sale of the ski resort SkyView. Then the reporter said that Barbara Holloway, the notorious defense attorney, had been injured in an accident, had been treated at Sacred Heart Hospital and released. Ms. Holloway had not appeared in court that afternoon.

"My God, more insanity," Barbara exclaimed. "Now it's Cy Rowland's turn."

"Well, wasn't he nuts today?" Bailey asked.

"Yes," she said after a moment. "But he wasn't when he killed Lois Hedrick and Owen Praeger."

There is no such thing as insanity, she thought as she twisted and turned, trying to find a comfortable position in bed. Her wrist hurt, the scrape on her leg burned, her head ached, and she was as depressed as she could remember ever being. And if people knew she snuggled with a rock, she thought, wouldn't they decide that she was a bit nuts herself?

She began to think about connections. If Lois hadn't known Knecht from her school days, would she have thought to get in touch with him? If Brian hadn't known about Teddy's accident, that Lois had been there, would he have thought of framing Teddy? If Teddy hadn't been obsessed with rocks, they wouldn't have gone to the mine, and she and John—but even that, she thought with wonder, even that was connected. If she hadn't fallen in love with him, and been so frightened by insanity, would she have pursued John's medical records? Even her mad neighbor from the distant past was connected. In her mind's eye, a web was forming, each interstice necessary, all connected. . . .

She drifted into an uneasy sleep finally, but it seemed that almost instantly she was awake again, this time holding her breath, listening. Her door was open a crack; she had closed it. A faint light sifted into the room. And someone else was in it.

She felt for the rock and, grasping it hard, opened her mouth to scream.

Someone said softly, "Shh. It's just me."

She bolted up, bringing a stab of pain to her wrist. "John!"

"I'm here. Shh. I'm sorry I woke you up. I tried not to."

He rose from a chair near her bed and sat beside her—a dark figure against the light from the hall, his face invisible.

"What are you doing here?"

"Watching over you," he said. "It seems to me that someone has to."

"How did you get in here?"

"I saw the news and drove over from the coast. Bailey saw me pull into the driveway and came out with a gun. I thought he was going to shoot me. He consulted with a famous lawyer and they let me in. I promised not to disturb you. But look how that worked out."

She reached out and touched his face, as if to test whether she was dreaming, and he caught her up in his arms. "God, I love you," he said. "I love you, love you." He kissed her fiercely, then abruptly drew back. "What the hell!" She had dropped the rock.

"It's all I had from you," she whispered.

He put the rock on the nightstand, left to close the door, and came back, pulling off his clothes. Pale light was coming through the drapes.

"It's six o'clock," she said. "How long have you been here?"

"Midnight."

"You've been in that chair since midnight?"

"Shh. Move over." He lay down and drew her to him. "God, I've wanted to be with you. I love your body, the way your hair smells." He kissed her throat, her breasts; his hands roamed over her body even as her hands were roaming his. "Ah," he said when she opened her legs to his fingers.

"That happens every time I see you," she whispered.

He kissed her mouth, and she took him into herself.

"Why did you leave?" she asked when they lay side by side, exhausted, his arm over her, her leg over him.

"I thought I'd lost your case for you, thought I still couldn't be trusted, even when another man's life was up for grabs. I had to get away and think."

"Why did you come back?"

"When they said you had an accident, nothing else mattered—I had to be with you."

"Will you stay with me?"

"Yes."

She closed her eyes, and he stroked her cheek. "You have to sleep," she said. "I have to get up and shower and appear in court."

"Now?"

"In a little bit," she said, turning to him again.

When she went downstairs, Frank was at the table, reading the paper. He hardly glanced at her. "How's the wrist?"

"Okay." It was hurting like hell. She went to him and put her arms around him. "Thanks, Dad. I must have done something really great in a past life to get you in this one."

He grunted. "Eat, and we're off," he said gruffly.

In court at nine they were kept waiting, milling about in the corridor outside Courtroom A. A cordon of police held spectators and media people back. Carolyn was biting her lip nervously, and both Reid and Gail kept eyeing Barbara as if they were under orders not to ask anything and the orders were killing them.

"The judge is talking to the jury," Frank told Carolyn. "Won't be long. You doing okay?"

"I think so."

He patted her shoulder.

They were called in at nine-thirty. Judge Ariel asked the foreman if they had reached a verdict, and was told no. He asked if they would be able to reach a decision, and was told no. He announced that he was dismissing them. He thanked them all and declared a mistrial. He told Ted he was free to go, and he made a curt little nod in the direction first of Grace Heflin, then

Barbara, and he thanked them. He stalked out as angrily as he had stalked in weeks earlier. It was over.

Ted sat as if stunned. "You're free," Barbara said to him. He looked at her in disbelief. Then he leaped up and turned to Carolyn and grabbed her and held her. They were both crying. Gail and Reid were hugging each other; they crowded in to hug Ted and Carolyn, and now the jurors were coming around. Mrs. Sproul walked out without a glance at Ted; she looked indignant. The young woman looked at Barbara with a disdainful expression and shrugged. Several jurors hung around, obviously intending to speak to Ted.

Barbara saw Grace Heflin approaching. Heflin held out her hand and they shook. "That was a good job," Heflin said.

"Thanks. You did a good job, too."

In a low voice, Heflin said, "We're taking the golf bag to test it for blood traces. If we find any, we'll go the DNA route. Just thought you'd want to know." She rejoined Marcus Truly at their table and began to gather her things.

The police lieutenant from the night before came to Barbara then. She couldn't remember his name. "Ms. Holloway," he said, "we'd appreciate it if you wouldn't repeat anything Cyrus Rowland said about his brother until we're through with our investigation. Brian Rowland has no idea how much his brother talked to you and Ms. Tunney. She agreed not to talk yet. We released her, of course."

She nodded. "All right. Fair enough."

"Thanks," he said, and walked out through the spectators, who seemed in no hurry to leave the courtroom.

Frank put his arm around her shoulders, and Shelley was beaming at everyone like a little girl with the one and only Christmas present she had ever dreamed of.

"We still have the press conference, a few things to attend to," Frank said. Barbara grimaced.

Ted and Carolyn and their children had drawn apart finally, and Ted was shaking hands with a juror while another one waited.

Then she heard Teddy's voice calling out, "Hey, Dad!" She spun around and saw John and Teddy making their way through the crowd. Teddy ran to his father and threw his arms around him. Ted was crying as he held his very tall eight-year-old child.

John was limping a little. That's what came of sitting up all night in a chair, she thought, and went to him, took his hand. "We'll have to go rest someplace where it's quiet and peaceful and all that happens from day to day is that the sun comes up, the sun goes down," she said. He gave her hand a squeeze. Then, with him on one side and her father on the other, Shelley and the whole Wendover family coming after them, they started the walk through the courtroom and into the waiting crowd.

If you enjoyed *For the Defense*, don't miss
any of the legal thrillers of

KATE WILHELM

"One of the masters of psychological fiction in America."
—*San Francisco Chronicle*

DEATH QUALIFIED

A *New York Times* Notable Book

Oregon lawyer Barbara Holloway is "death qualified"—able to defend clients who face the
death penalty. And now she has been asked to
defend Nell Kendricks, accused of murdering
her estranged husband. But after seven years
of separation, would Nell kill him? Ultimately,
in a small-town courtroom, Barbara must find
the truth. . . .

THE BEST DEFENSE

Barbara Holloway enjoys her peaceful small-town Oregon life—until the sister of a murderer comes to her with a case she cannot refuse. Barbara unearths a conspiracy to allow a killer to go free, and when she is targeted by a huge smear campaign, she realizes that even the best defense may not be enough.

JUSTICE FOR SOME

Judge Sarah Drexler hopes to have a happy reunion with her son and daughter at her father's California home, but instead she is plunged into a morass of secrets and tragedy. Her father dies unexpectedly, a private detective is killed, and one of her own children is a suspect. Suddenly she is trapped between her love for her family and her loyalty to the law.

A FLUSH OF SHADOWS

"Suspenseful gems . . . Nothing is as it first seems in these stories. They unfold at a spellbinding pace."
—*The Seattle Times*

From the suburban Northeast to a beautiful hidden valley in the Rockies, from a luxury resort in Florida to a small-town backyard, Kate Wilhelm takes us on a chilling expedition through realms of psychological unease. Readers with a taste for the mysterious, the unusual, and the truth will find this collection of five short novels sublime.

by KATE WILHELM

Published by Fawcett Books.
Available at your local bookstore.

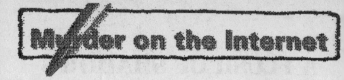